STONY POINT

We gratefully acknowledge the support of the Canada Council for the Arts and the Ontario Arts Council for our publishing program. We also acknowledge the financial support of the Department of Canadian Heritage through the Canada Book Fund.

We are also grateful for the support received from an Anonymous Fund at The Calgary Foundation.

Cover design and illustration: Val Fullard

Library and Archives Canada Cataloguing in Publication

McKay, S. Nöel, 1962–, author
        Stony point / S. Nöel McKay.

ISBN 978-1-77133-168-5 (pbk.)

I. Title.

PS8625.K397S76 2014   C813'.6   C2014-905023-2

MIX
Paper from
responsible sources
FSC
www.fsc.org   FSC® C004071

Printed and bound in Canada

Inanna Publications and Education Inc.
210 Founders College, York University
4700 Keele Street, Toronto, Ontario, Canada M3J 1P3
Telephone: (416) 736-5356 Fax: (416) 736-5765
Email: inanna.publications@inanna.ca Website: www.inanna.ca

STONY POINT

a novel by

S. Noël McKay

inanna poetry & fiction series

INANNA PUBLICATIONS AND EDUCATION INC.
TORONTO, CANADA

For my mother

Chapter 1

—m—

Tuesday, May 26, 1903

ON ITS WAY WEST, the Canadian Pacific Railway train stopped in Frank, Alberta. Lucille Reilly stepped down from the coach car onto the wooden platform of the tiny station. She looked around in the bright afternoon sunshine. Turtle Mountain loomed above with a broad scar running down the centre of its face where the portion of its summit had slid down. A blanket of limestone rubble covered the valley. More mountains towered in the distance along the winding valley of the Crowsnest Pass. *How am I going to find Stanley in all this wilderness?* Lucille asked herself as her eyes appraised the rugged landscape.

She straightened her shoulders and lifted her head, refusing to be discouraged. A robust woman of medium height with a wide bosom and broad hips, she wore a straw skimmer hat with a white band and a bow on the right side of the crown. Her skirt and bodice were in the style of a tennis costume: the cream bodice had buttons running up the left side and its bishop's sleeves were baggy but not large. The skirt had a black belt with a large silver buckle at the waist. Lucille carried a parasol in her right hand that was too frilly for her outfit but served as a concealed weapon she never went anywhere without. As she waited, she glanced at a little watch that hung from a silver chain around her neck. In less than thirty minutes, she would arrive in Stony Point, another town in the Crowsnest Pass west of Frank. Her brother-in-law had disappeared from

1

Stony Point nearly three weeks ago. It was Lucille's mission to find him.

With enough anguish in her own life, Lucille did not need to gawk at that of others. For this reason, she stayed away from the wreckage of the landslide. But even though almost four weeks had passed, one could still marvel at the extent of the disaster. Eighty million tons of rock had crushed the eastern edge of Frank and spread out over the valley for more than a square mile. Presently, in the town, workmen were pushing barrows or carrying shovels and picks up and down either side of Dominion Avenue. At the station, returning evacuees stepped off the train with bundles in their arms, and to the left of Lucille a ragged boy was trying to sell a fist-sized rock to one of the train passengers. "Some of the big rocks still got blood on them from rolling over folks," the boy enthused. Lucille shifted restlessly from foot to foot. Absolutely nothing was fascinating about the number of people the slide had killed or left destitute.

"Lady, you want to hold Frankie Slide? Cost you a nickel, but she's lucky."

Two girls stood in front of Lucille. The bigger one wore a brown dress of rough homespun and a white ribbon in her hair. The smaller one wore a grey dress, black stockings, and scuffed, mismatched shoes. Between them they pushed a baby carriage, an ancient wicker contraption with a dent in its front end. A baby lay in the pram against some cushions. The infant, who could not be more than a year old, wore a white cap and skirts. She looked from side to side with growing irritation on her little face.

"Her house got flattened when the slide came down," the bigger girl continued. "They found Frankie here sitting on a hay bale outside and not a scratch on her."

"Is that right," Lucille said. The baby, no doubt, was one of several Frankie Slides in town, but maybe she was the real, true one. Lucille could certainly use some luck. She gave the girl a nickel and knelt down to say hello. Frankie Slide whimpered and drew away at first, but Lucille smiled brightly and talked to her, and soon she coaxed a smile out of the baby. She remembered her sister's two children home in Winnipeg and missed them sharply.

"How about I give you another nickel," she said to the girls, "and you can take Frankie home. I think she's getting tired." Lucille thought some more. "And I'll give you a quarter if you fetch me a newspaper." The two girls gasped together in disbelief at their good fortune. They hurried away, pushing the baby carriage in front of them at breakneck speed.

Lucille scolded herself for handing out her coins so freely. But the girls were poor, and with the coal mine in Frank still closed, money in their house must be tight. She looked up again at Turtle Mountain. The Blackfoot and K'tunaxa tribes called it the "Mountain That Moves," and never camped around it; the white men had merely laughed at the superstitious Indians until the slide. Now, many feared that the rest of Turtle Mountain would come crashing down at any time. Lucille believed the danger was exaggerated. The broad base of the mountain and its concave summit looked as solid as a boulder, for the moment.

The two girls returned. They thrust a copy of the *Frank Sentinel* into Lucille's hands. She paid them just as the conductor in his blue uniform blew his whistle. "All aboard," the man called out, "for points west: Blairmore, Stony Point, town of Crowsnest...." Lucille climbed back aboard the coach. She sat down on the wooden seat, and, in a few minutes, the train lurched forward. Soon, the pistons were pumping and the engine was chugging as the train left Frank behind.

The landscape of the Pass rolled by. In the background, the jagged summits of the mountains sat under the blue sky, and white snow streaks ran down the crevices at their tops. Below the mountains were hills covered with forests of stubby green pine trees. The Oldman River wound its way through the valley, first on one side of the train tracks, then on the other. To Lucille, the river looked like a skinny creek, but then, she was used to the Red and the Assiniboine in Winnipeg. The mountains, however, were certainly impressive.

She turned away from the window and glanced around the crowded coach. Immigrants on their way to their homesteads filled the seats. In front of Lucille sat two broad-shouldered men who wore *sorochka* and bushy black beards. They spoke to each other in Ukrainian. Next to her, an elderly Italian woman fanned herself and her squally grandchild on her lap with a paper fan. All of the immigrants fingered their leaflets that praised Canada as "The Granary of the World" in a variety of languages, and had pictures of farmers with wheat crops towering over their heads like church steeples. The leaflets said nothing of snow, cold, drought, isolation, or grasshoppers. Lucille sighed to herself and shook her head.

She laid the *Frank Sentinel* in her lap for a moment and looked out the window at the mountains rolling past. She had only enough money to stay for two weeks. If she could not find Stanley after that, the money her sister had given her would be gone, with nothing to show for it, and God knew Lottie had little to spare now. Her lawyer had offered to pay for a private detective, but she had refused to take his money; Mr. Parr was already representing Lottie for free in her dispute with the life insurance company over Stanley's policy. Lucille did have eight dollars of her own savings. Her only chance of increasing that sum was gambling with it. It was a crazy idea, and, in her imagination, she could just hear practical Lottie groaning. But she would not go back to Winnipeg a failure, and already she was certain she would need more than two weeks to find Stanley.

Presently, she opened the *Frank Sentinel*. Inside the paper was an advertisement for the Empire Hotel in Stony Point, which boasted that it was the best two-dollar-a-day house in the North-West Territory, with steam heat and electric lighting.

With a grim expression, she tapped the advertisement with her thumb. Stanley had stayed at that hotel while he had been in Stony Point. With no other place to start, her assignment for today would be to investigate the place. Someone there must have seen her brother-in-law. The paper also carried an ad for "The Pruitt House," a boarding house on First Street North in Stony Point. It cost four dollars a week with meals included. Lucille would stay there if the house allowed a single woman. If it did not, she would camp out at the train station or pitch a tent somewhere. She was not going to leave that town without finding out what had happened to Stanley.

Lucille looked up. The train was slowing. Eagerly, she peered out the window. Down the tracks, another train station came into view, the same size as the one in Frank. The name "Stony Point" was painted in big white letters on the sloping roof. Two minutes later the train stopped, and the conductor strode through the coach calling out, "Stony Point." Lucille took a deep breath. She rolled up her newspaper and clutched her canvas bag in her hand. Her mission was just beginning.

Chapter 2

—〰—

LUCILLE'S LUGGAGE CONSISTED of her canvas bag, a couple of valises, a hatbox, and her portable typewriter in its case. Fully loaded with her bags, she walked out onto King Edward Avenue, the main street in Stony Point. The town looked much like Frank. Wooden buildings with false fronts and large windows on the ground floors lined either side of the wide dirt street. She walked past the General Store. It was a whitewashed, two-storey building, and through the windows one could see rugs for sale hanging from wires bolted into the ceiling. The Post Office sat across the street from the General Store. A man carrying a mailbag over his shoulder walked up the steps, unlocked the door, and went inside. The wooden sidewalks were otherwise deserted. Lucille turned the corner onto First Street. If she could get a room at that boarding house, she would stow her bags there, rest up a little, and then visit the Empire Hotel.

She steadied her bags in her arms as she walked. Here, instead of a sidewalk, a narrow gravel pathway ran alongside the wagon wheel ruts in the middle of the road. To Lucille's left, a house stood on blocks. The roof of this house had been badly repaired; a large patch of wooden board stood out in the sunshine. A crate in front of the door served as steps. She would not stay in that hovel. Next to it, however, sat a tidy bungalow painted grey, with a shingled roof and some flowerpots sitting on the railing of the small veranda. A tin sign to the left of the door said, "Pruitt House." Some chickens in the backyard cackled at Lucille's approach. She opened the gate of the white picket fence and walked up the stone pathway to the door.

She used the iron knocker. A voice sounded from inside, then came a child's heavy running footsteps. The door opened and a woman with a white kerchief around her head in the Galician style nodded at Lucille. She was the same height and had thin arms and hands red with work. Her dark blue dress was clean but worn. Next to the woman, a girl of around ten hopped about. She also wore a Galician kerchief and looked at Lucille with eyes that were exactly like her mother's. Lucille said, "Good day to you, ma'am, and young lady. I saw your ad in the paper and I was wondering if I could rent a room here."

The woman stared at Lucille. Although her skin was pocked and rough, her face was kind. She also could not understand a word Lucille said.

The little girl beside the woman spun around and raced back into the house. "Miss Kate!" the girl called. "A lady's at the door."

The Galician woman, meanwhile, opened the door wide and gestured for Lucille to step into the front parlour. The window blinds were raised, filling the room with sunshine. The house had a beamed ceiling and a brick fireplace at the far wall. A clock sat in the centre of the mantelpiece, with some photographs in frames to the left of it, and a commemorative plate with "Queen Victoria Diamond Jubilee" in ornate gold letters to the right. A sturdy rocking chair occupied the corner, and the pillow that rested on its seat had a picture of the Queen embroidered on it. Next to the rocker was a small table on which the family Bible sat underneath Eaton's catalogue. Not a speck of dust could one see anywhere.

Lucille turned around as another woman entered the parlour. She was a small but hardy-looking young woman who could not be more than eighteen. Her dress was black mourning and her blonde hair was tied with black ribbons. She had a round face with pink cheeks and a tiny bud of a mouth. Under the waist of her dress, her abdomen was as round as a globe with an advanced pregnancy. Instantly, Lucille assumed the woman was a widow. She thought with a shudder how terrible that must be for this poor young woman. She smiled, curtseyed, and offered the pregnant woman her hand.

"Good day ma'am, my name's Lucille Reilly. I was wondering if I could rent a room."

The woman looked at Lucille with her mouth open in astonishment. Meanwhile, the Galician woman thrust her head out the front door and with bewilderment on her face looked from right to left at the empty veranda. Where was this strange woman's husband? She then directed her gaze toward the woman and shrugged when she met her eyes. Meanwhile, surprise, and then what looked like relief appeared on the young woman's face as she turned to once again face Lucille. She pumped Lucille's hand.

"Why gosh yes ma'am, you can stay here. I'm Kate Pruitt. You can call me Kate. I've a room for you in the back. It's small, but if there's anything you need you just have to shout." She took three steps toward a hallway. Lucille bent down to pick up her bags again, but the Galician woman said something to her daughter in rapid Ukrainian. The girl curtseyed to Lucille and picked up one of the valises. She had a dark complexion and a pixie nose. A wisp of black hair poked out from underneath her kerchief. Lucille smiled brightly at her. "And what is your name, young miss?"

"Lanka," the child answered.

"This is Mrs. Ruzicka and her little girl," Kate said as she led Lucille down the hallway. "Her menfolk are in Slav Town making them a cabin. They're going to settle here. They were going to settle in Frank, but the slide happened a week after they got there. Mrs. Ruzicka says she'll be darned if her family's living anywhere near that mountain." Kate stopped in front of the room, and Lucille stepped inside.

It was small but clean. Against the wall, to the right, stood an iron-framed bed, tidily made, with a grey blanket and a white pillow. Next to the bed was the washstand. Lucille set her bags on the floor and walked forward. The basin and jug on the washstand were of spotless white china. A covered soap dish sat next to the basin. A beaten rug lay on the wooden floor, which was clear of dust. Lucille nodded to herself. The room was certainly good enough. She took her bag from Lanka with thanks. She then opened her purse and paid Kate the rent for a week. Kate put the money in her apron and invited her to have tea with herself and Mrs. Ruzicka.

"Mrs. Ruzicka's fixing supper tonight," she said with enthusiasm. "She cooks like an angel and the bread she bakes is straight from heaven." She then left to allow Lucille time to unpack.

Lucille first opened her valise and took out her corsets. She rolled them inside the top drawer of a three-drawer hardwood bureau. As she did, she looked at herself in the bevel-plate mirror above it. She saw a thirty-year-old woman with a slightly crooked nose looking back at her, but after all her travel she did not look too tired. She rolled up her cotton underskirts and laid them in the drawer with her corsets. As she always did whenever she unpacked from a journey, Lucille thought of the day when she would follow this process in reverse and head home. *By that time, I better know what happened to Stanley*, she thought grimly as she rolled up her bodices and put them in the bottom drawer of the bureau.

Now that the bureau was filled with her clothes, Lucille took out her copy of *Ten Days in a Mad-house*, by Nellie Bly. Maybe she had been fanciful to bring it along, but newspaper reporters like Nellie Bly and Kit Coleman were her inspiration, and she never went anywhere without the book. She placed it on the little shelf above the bed. Then, she set her portable Underwood typewriter on top of the bureau. Idly, she wondered if she still had a job. Like Kit Coleman when she went to Cuba to cover the Spanish-American war, Lucille had not asked the editor of the *Red River Herald* if she could go to Stony Point; she had simply boarded the westbound train in Winnipeg. In this way, she had not given Mr. MacDougall a chance to tell her a frontier town was no place for a lady. With a shrug of her shoulders, she decided to send him a weekly dispatch; he could either print them or go chase himself. She chuckled to herself. Audacity was fun.

The last item she unpacked was a family portrait. The man in the photograph wore a derby hat, a dark suit, and a stiff white collar. He had twinkling eyes and a broad, genuine smile as he stood in front of a house with his arm around a woman. Stanley Birch was not a handsome man, but his good humour radiated from the photograph. The woman in the picture beside him wore an afternoon gown and a white hat. Sister Lottie was a taller, more slender version of Lucille. She held a baby in long skirts in her arms and in front of her, a two-year-old boy in a sailor suit gazed at the camera and sucked his thumb. Lucille paused for a while with the photograph in her hand. She then tucked it under her arm and walked out into the kitchen of the boarding house.

There she found Kate at the stove. The young woman in her black dress rested her hand behind her back to balance the weight of the baby in her womb. The kettle came to a boil. Kate took it off the stove and poured the steaming water into a large teapot. Mrs. Ruzicka, meanwhile, stood at the end of the kitchen table mixing dough in a large ceramic bowl. Lanka had gone outside to play with some other children.

"I've some pastries ma'am," Kate said as she set the tea tray on the table near Lucille. "Would you like some?" She turned around and waddled back to the pantry.

"There now Kate, you needn't be running around like that," Lucille said. "I'll be just fine with no pastries."

"Oh, it's no trouble. I've a craving for sweets. Mrs. Ruzicka made these and I can't get enough of them." She returned to the table with a big round cookie tin. She stuffed a pastry into her mouth before giving one to Mrs. Ruzicka and one to Lucille. It was a succulent pastry, a little pocket of crust with a blueberry filling.

"My, what are these?" Lucille asked.

"I don't know, but they're good. Mrs. Ruzicka calls them *varenyky*."

Lucille ate her pastry, dusted her hands, and picked up the photograph. "Kate," she said, "I was wondering if you could help me." She showed the young woman the photograph. With her little finger she indicated the man next to the woman in the white hat. "That's my brother-in-law, Stanley Birch. He's a reporter for the *Red River Herald* in Winnipeg. His paper sent him to Frank to cover the Slide. While he was in Frank, he got to know a man from the coal miners' union. Stanley came with him here to Stony Point to research a story on the miners, for a follow-up to his story on Frank. One day, he sent my sister a telegram. He said his story was almost finished and he expected to be home by Thursday. That was just over three weeks ago. We haven't heard anything from him since. Tell me, do you remember seeing this man in town?"

Kate shook her head. "Sorry ma'am, but I've never seen him." She looked down at her expanded pregnant abdomen. "I don't get out much lately. But I did hear a newspaperman from Winnipeg was in town. Matthew Brown, the union man, he's gone too."

Lucille spread her hands flat on the table and rocked backwards. Her mouth fell open as she stared at Kate. "There are two men missing?"

"Yes ma'am."

Lucille shuddered. She clasped her hands to Kate in appeal. "Does this Matthew Brown have a wife? Someone I can talk to?"

"He does, but he sent her and their kids to stay with her folks in High River when he got fired from the mine for talking union. He didn't want them in danger. A smart move that turned out to be."

Lucille sank with disappointment.

Kate picked up the picture again. "These people sure make a pleasant family. The little boy in front's just a dear."

Lucille straightened up and beamed with pride. "That's Edward, Lottie's eldest. The baby is Abner. That picture was taken when they bought their house on Selkirk Avenue. Edward's four now, and Abner's two." Lucille fell silent and lowered her head. She found herself choking down tears. "Stanley just dotes on those boys. He adores Lottie. He always wires her twice a day whenever he's away on a story. The only reason he wouldn't contact her is if he were…"

Kate patted her hand as she gave Lucille her picture back. "There now, it shouldn't be too hard to find out what happened. This is just a small town after all."

"I hope you're right. Lottie … she…." Lucille's voice trailed off as she searched in her mind for the right word to describe Lottie. Her sister, who had always been so forceful and sure of herself, now spent her afternoons in a kitchen chair staring into space with vacant eyes, her sewing forgotten on the table in front of her. Lottie was convinced her husband was dead. But there was no body or any explanation for what had happened.

"Lottie's stuck," Lucille concluded. "She can hardly get up out of a chair and the boys keep asking her when Daddy's coming home. She can't go on without knowing what happened to Stanley. And on top of everything else, that rotten life insurance company won't pay her a dime until we have a body." Lucille gritted her teeth. Even the thought of the insurance company could start her off on a twenty-minute rant.

"But hasn't anyone done anything?" Kate asked. "That paper he works for, what about them?"

"They sent a wire to the North-West Mounted Police here. The police said yes, he'd been in town. He'd been staying in the Empire Hotel. The management there gave them Stanley's bag when he didn't show up to check out. They said they didn't know anything more, but they would be 'making enquiries'." Lucille took a breath. "We've been hearing 'making enquiries' for two weeks now. Nothing's happened. Lottie and I have gotten such a runaround over this that I believe somebody's trying to cover something up."

"Talk to those Mounties again," Kate said. "They'll get off their butts once they see the man's kinfolk are out looking for him. But watch out who you talk to, and what you say. Henry Best..." as she said this name, Kate hesitated and Lucille looked curiously at her. "Henry Best don't stand for no man talking union in his mine," she continued. "He fires every one, and sees to it they get blackballed all over the Crowsnest too. The boys need their jobs. They lost a lot of money after the Slide happened and the mine was closed for so long."

"Well, I'll be going to that Empire Hotel tonight after supper. Maybe someone there will talk to me."

Kate agreed that this was a good idea. Lucille's talk with the young woman had done much to lift her spirits. She now had a base of operations here at the boarding house and a new friend in Kate who knew the town and its people. Now she could start her investigation.

Chapter 3

—ᨑ—

LUCILLE LEFT THE BOARDING HOUSE after supper. The meal had been delicious although the food was strange. Mrs. Ruzicka had made dozens of little pastry pockets that she had filled with a mixture of potato and cheese. The Galicians called these *pyrogy*. Mrs. Ruzicka piled them on Lucille's plate along with sausages that her husband had picked up at the town butcher's. Mr. Ruzicka was a small man in his forties. Like his wife, he had aged prematurely from a lifetime of hard labour; he had a curly shock of grey hair, bandy legs, and a raspy voice. Also like his wife, he spoke no English, but he had a quick smile and a generous way about him.

"I'm going to be awful sorry to see these people go," Kate had said to Lucille as they drank tea together on the veranda after supper. "They're good, sober, hard-working folks."

The Ruzickas' two sons were living in Slav Town. Although they had been happy in Kate's house, Lanka and her parents would join them in a few days. Like all Galicians, they valued family togetherness highly. Lucille had agreed with the sentiment. To start getting her sister's family back together, she finished her tea, said good-bye to Kate, and stepped off the veranda with her parasol in her hand. Kate had called after her. "Good luck, Mrs. Reilly. But remember, watch your back."

Lucille had turned, waved, and continued on her way. Now, on King Edward Avenue, she passed a wooden Indian in front of the tobacco shop. Next to that, an array of women's hats in the window of a clothing store caught her eye. One had a shapely curved brim and an abundance of flower trimmings. Lucille bit her lip and resolutely turned away; her budget had no room for hats. She strode onward past the red-and-blue stripes of a barber's pole. A rough wooden bench stood under the front window for all the loafers that a barbershop seemed to draw like iron filings to a magnet. Across the road, opposite the tobacco shop, was the Union Bank, the only brick structure in the town. Next to the bank sat the log building that was the North-West Mounted Police station. Across from the barbershop, west of the police station, lay the broad expanse of a park. At the rear of the field, a wire backstop rose up behind the home plate of a baseball diamond; to the side of it were two sections of bleacher seats freshly painted green. Lucille walked on.

At last, she came to a small tea room shuttered up for the evening. The Empire Hotel, a large whitewashed building with a row of eight windows behind a balcony on the upper storey, sat across the street. A sign over the front door on the ground level said, "Lobby." From an open door on the east end of the building came men's lively voices and the racket from the hotel bar. Lucille lifted her skirts and crossed the dirt road, keeping her eyes peeled for horse droppings. Soon, she paused in front of the hotel. The bell on the door jingled as she opened it and went inside.

The lobby was more spacious than she had expected. A red telephone booth waited with its glass door open in the corner to her left, and a carpeted staircase to the right led to the upper floor. The front desk had a ledger on it. Behind the desk, a row of pigeonholes on the wall held the hotel room keys or mail for the guests. Lucille approached the desk and rang the metal bell near the ledger. No one appeared. At that moment, shouts, the tinkle of breaking glass, and drunken laughter came from behind the side door. From the sounds of things, the proprietor must have gone back to the bar to break up a fight.

Suddenly, the sound of a door opening and closing came from upstairs. Footsteps approached as a man descended the staircase. Lucille backed away from the desk to look at him. He was tall with broad shoulders and he wore a brown tailored suit with a spotless white collar. He stopped at the bottom of the stairs and when his eyes fell upon Lucille, they lit up and the man smiled. He had a striking face, even teeth, a square chin, and light brown hair. Without thinking, Lucille stroked her hair under her skimmer hat and smiled back at him; the man was so attractive it was impossible not to respond.

His blue eyes twinkled as he said, "Well, what to my wondering eyes — how do you do, ma'am?" He approached Lucille with his right hand out. She blushed and curtseyed while he took her hand; he had a firm grip that hinted at his strength. Already she could see herself riding in a buggy with him.

"I'm Henry Best, the chairman of Dominion Coal." As he spoke, he lifted his head and jingled the coins in his trouser pocket. "I was just coming downstairs to ask Wright to fetch us a deck of cards," he continued. "I'd like to ask you to join us. May I have your name?"

Lucille paused and calculated. She forgot how handsome the chairman was and remembered that Stanley had been investigating this man's coal mine when he disappeared.

"Do you play poker?" she asked. He gaped at her. "My name's Lucille Reilly and I used to play some in Winnipeg." Indeed, because of poker, her name had become a curse word in the newsroom of the *Red River Herald*. She jingled the coins in her purse. Best's mouth opened and closed once before he could speak again.

"Well, ma'am, my friends and I would certainly be happy to oblige you. In fact, I think poker would be just the thing." He jerked his head in the direction of the staircase. "We're upstairs in the dining room."

Lucille took his arm and he led her up the stairs. She could feel the solidity of his arm muscles through the fabric of his coat.

Again, she shivered; undoubtedly, the chairman of Dominion Coal was one handsome man whose forceful demeanour only added to his appeal. She glanced again at his neatly pomaded hair. *He looks too good,* she thought suddenly. When they reached the top of the stairs, the door to the dining room opened and another man stepped out. At the sight of Lucille, he drew back in surprise.

"By gosh, Henry," he said. "We told you to find a pretty girl, and you came through." lHe bowed. "How do you do, ma'am?" This man looked enough like Mr. Best to be his brother, only his facial features were narrower and his hair darker. He also wore an expensive tailored suit and his face was clean-shaven.

The chairman stepped forward to introduce him to Lucille. "Ralph, this is Miss..."

"Missus," Lucille interrupted.

"Mrs. Lucille Reilly. This is Ralph Best, my cousin. Mrs. Reilly plays poker."

"Why, you don't say!" Ralph swept Lucille into the dining room with inviting waves of his arm. Before he continued on to the outhouse, he slapped his cousin on the back and winked. "Good job, Henry. You can sure find a way to liven up an evening."

Lucille preceded Best into the dining room. The chairman introduced her to his friends who were sitting around a gleaming oak table. Will Butler, a heavy-set man with round cheeks, stood up and blushed pink when Lucille smiled at him, while Charles McIvor glanced from her to Best with envy in his eyes. He had a skinny build and a long black moustache. Both men glowed with the abundance of food and drink; Henry Best was one of the boys and unstinting in his hospitality. The chairman now sat down across the table from Lucille and lit a cigarette that he took from a silver case. Charles McIvor looked at the woman with a grin.

"Did you see the slide in Frank, ma'am? Wasn't that scary? I'll tell you, that gol-darned CPR's making out like bandits again. All that slide did was give them eighty million tons of quarried limestone, for not even a song. If you want to buy any, they want market price for it. The CPR can stick its market price." His snapping eyes and sleek moustache warned of a temper about to boil over, but then his voice became calmer. "Us lads here are all in the cement business up in Calgary." With a flourish, he handed her a business card that had the name "Western Cement" printed across it in heavy block letters.

"Why, that is an outrage," Lucille said. "I'm sure if God dropped eighty million tons of cement in your backyard, you'd give it away for free."

The men around the table fell silent and exchanged uneasy glances. Lucille's gaze fell on Best across the table from her. In one swipe, her joke had erased all the good humour from the man's face; now, to her surprise, his blue eyes frosted over and his mouth stiffened. On the table, his large hand rolled up into a fist. She could smell the hostility from him. *Now he's not so good-looking.*

"Hey, here's the evening show," he said with mockery. "The woman's going to tell us all she knows about business." He looked around at his friends with a grin. "That'll take about three seconds."

At that moment, the door opened. Ralph Best walked in and resumed his seat at the table to Lucille's right. The owner of the hotel followed him. Aside from being a little red in the face, Arthur Wright looked none the worse for breaking up the fight in the bar. He was of medium height with a heavy-set frame, a thick shock of white hair, and round spectacles. He looked askance at Lucille for a moment but took the order. In a few minutes, he returned with the drinks and a deck of cards in his apron. Henry then placed several quarter-dollar coins on the man's tray; the cash made Wright's eyes glitter. He bowed to the gentlemen before he slipped out the door.

After the host left, Ralph Best drew the high card. While the man dealt, Lucille rested her head on her fist and gazed idly out the window through which the evening sunshine was coming in at a sharp angle. Henry Best was still beaming antagonism at her with his snapping eyes and tight mouth. Clearly, he disliked sassy women. Her own hostility toward the chairman kindled up in response. *I'll give him "business."* Best, meanwhile, folded the hand of cards he had been dealt. He reached up and undid the button on his crisp white shirt collar. He had a tanned, muscular neck that many women would find attractive. He slipped the freed collar into the pocket of his coat and leaned forward.

"Mrs. Reilly, is it? Where's Mr. Reilly?"

Lucille gave him a bright smile. "I beat his skull in with a lead pipe. Then I left his body in a ditch back in Winnipeg." Immediately, silence fell. The four men inhaled deep breaths. Best paled and his chin swung open. Ralph suddenly clapped his hands together and exclaimed.

"She had me going there for a second! By God Henry, this one's a corker."

The men rocked back and forth, roaring with laughter. They slapped their thighs, and all except for Henry, gave Lucille appreciative glances. But the chairman's eyes narrowed. He opened his mouth only to clamp it shut again. Finally, he stubbed his cigarette out in the tin ashtray and picked up the deck of cards.

The game went on for a few hours. Against the growing darkness, one of the men switched on the electric light above the dining-room table. Lucille folded most of her hands at first while she observed the men around her. She first watched Charles McIvor on her left. This man teased the others and winked at her constantly. He also bluffed on every hand. She took a pot from him with a pair of tens and from then on McIvor stopped winking at her. Ralph Best, by contrast, paid attention to his cards and his sharp eyes watched the other players. His eyes also tended to sparkle when he had a strong hand. They were twinkling merrily at this moment, so Lucille folded two pairs. All of her powers of observation would not make her hand beat a superior one.

As Henry raised his cousin's bet, she looked at her remaining stack of money. She had lost some on this hand, but had nearly twelve dollars left, acceptable since she had started with eight. Meanwhile, after more bets, Henry and Ralph turned over their cards. Ralph's three kings lost to his cousin's straight. In some temper, he slapped his hand down on the table and cursed.

"Damn it Henry, if you aren't the luckiest rascal in the Territory." The men cleared their throats and jerked their eyes toward the woman present. Ralph shrank and his face flushed pink. He bowed his head to Lucille. "I do beg your pardon, ma'am."

"Don't be embarrassed Ralph," Henry said. "She's a tart. I'm sure she's heard worse."

"I've never seen any worse, that's for sure." Lucille lifted her hand to her mouth in theatrical chagrin. "Oh I'm sorry. Did I speak out of turn?" Henry jerked his chin at her small pile of bills and coins.

"What are you going to buy yourself with all that money? A new gown?"

"No," Lucille answered. "I'll use it to stay here in town while I look for my brother-in-law. His name's Stanley Birch. He's a reporter for the *Red River Herald* back in Winnipeg. He was curious about the eighteen men who were killed in the explosion in your coal mine last July. Stanley went missing from here three weeks ago. Did you ever meet him?"

"I believe I did. Yes, he came to interview me one day." Henry looked around the table with his mouth curled in derision. "The fellow didn't understand that explosions in coal mines go with the business. If he wanted to cry over dead miners, he should have gone to Coal Creek." He chuckled. "He's gone missing, you say? Maybe he started following a pretty butterfly on the way home and got lost." The other men laughed with him. All were businessmen who understood how the world turned. Henry looked around. "C'mon lads, this game's for schoolboys. Let's play for some real cash. And, since she's got no money, Miss Apple Tart here can stake her other purse — the one she's got up her skirts."

The men gasped. Ralph glanced at Lucille and frowned at Henry but voiced no objection. At that moment, Lucille startled everybody with a bray of laughter. Henry scowled, but Ralph said, "C'mon children, this is just a friendly game. Henry, have a drink and relax."

"Bull! What's so friendly about a game when she won't be friendly with us?"

Lucille snorted and tossed her head. "You want friendly? I want to see you put your money where your mouth is. I'll stake what I've got. Only, if I win, I get to jab you in the family jewels with the tip of this." She thumped the pointed end of her parasol down on the wooden floor.

Ralph clapped his hands. "All right, funny joke. Henry was just kidding about that." He nudged his cousin forcefully with his elbow. "I do beg your pardon, ma'am," he said as he turned to Lucille. "My cousin can be a boor when he's been drinking. Can't you, Henry?"

"He'd be just as much a boor if he were sober as a judge," Lucille said.

"C'mon folks, a few more hands and we'll call it a night." Charles McIvor shuffled the cards with some impatience. He had lost heavily, but maybe he could win some money back and salvage the evening, something that would not happen if Henry and the crazy woman kept butting heads. The focus of everyone's attention returned to the game. Henry glanced downwards at the table as five cards slid his way. Lucille looked at her cards.

Will Butler bet two dollars on his hand, which Henry covered, as did Lucille after a slight hesitation. Ralph and McIvor folded, the latter with a disgusted throw of his hand. After the remaining players drew their cards, Butler laid a bet of five dollars on the table. Henry raised the bet to twenty. Ralph exclaimed at the sum, McIvor whistled, and Butler groaned. Henry turned to Lucille. "What about you, Miss Apple Tart? You haven't got enough to cover this bet, unless you're willing to stake your other purse as I said before."

She cocked her head at him with insolence. "Does this mean you're staking your family jewels? That's the only way I'll make that bet." She thumped the tip of her parasol again.

Henry snapped his fingers and pointed at her. "Keep talking like that and I'll make my foot go up your arse."

She only laughed. "A thousand. I bet a thousand dollars. If you won't stake your jewels, I'll let you slink out of it by betting money. A thousand dollars."

Each man around the table sucked in air. With shock, they reeled backwards on their seats, clapped their hands to their heads, and stared at Lucille. The amount was breathtaking — more than a year's income for a skilled worker.

Henry sneered. "Your whole body isn't worth ten dollars, you stupid tart!"

"Didn't I just hear you say I could bet my 'other purse'? So, I'll bet what I have against your family jewels or a thousand dollars that my hand's better than yours." She looked at the men around her and back to Henry. "Why, what's this?" she asked. "Are you afraid?"

Henry sat frozen. He glanced first to one side, then the other. Ralph puffed smoke from his cigar and looked at his cousin with his eyes narrowed in speculation. Will Butler and Charles McIvor were also watching him closely. The men would talk behind his back if he shrank from the woman's challenge. He took a drink from his snifter of brandy, reached for his coat, and pulled his wallet from its breast pocket.

"When you pay this bet, I'll have it outside, in the middle of the street, in front of the whole damned town," he said as he signed his name and placed his cheque in the centre of the table.

Lucille jerked her chin at him. "Show us your cards."

Henry picked up his hand and turned it over. "Full house."
She glanced at the queens and threes. "Oh, that's a lovely
hand," she said. "But it's not as good as this." She turned
over her cards.

McIvor, Butler, and Ralph lifted their arms and exclaimed
in a roar at Henry's spectacular turn of bad luck. Four sixes
made up Lucille's hand.

Henry cried out with fury. "You bitch!"

"It's been a pleasure meeting you, Mr. Best. You're such a
gentleman." She smiled at him sweetly and put his cheque in
her purse. She then swept up the other bills and coins in the pot.
All the time, Henry watched her with his fists clenched on the
table and scarlet rage burning on his face. He looked around.
All of his friends were laughing, especially Ralph whom he had
burned earlier with his straight. If he made any more fuss, this
incident would be the biggest laugh of the North-West Territory instead of just the Empire Hotel dining room. He forced
himself to relax and sip his brandy. Then, as he spoke, he put
as much contempt as he could into his voice, like he had only
lost a dime. "Stupid damned women can't play poker for cow
patties." His friends laughed harder at the remark.

In the meantime, Lucille scurried out of the dining room. To
the right, a tin sign marked "Exit" pointed down a staircase.
She flew down the stairs. She would not put it past Chairman
Best to come after her and wrest his money back, but she was
damned if he would have it. One hand of cards had given her
enough money to stay in town for however long it would take
to find Stanley. Frankie Slide had been lucky indeed.

Downstairs, behind the bar, Arthur Wright was filling a
mug with beer from the tap of a large keg. He frowned as he
looked up at the ceiling. He was sure he had heard an angry
shout coming from upstairs in the dining room. But then he
heard much laughter too and he relaxed. The gentlemen were
only having a joke with that floozy. Now that the fight was
over, the miners who were his customers down here in the bar

sat with their arms around each other's necks, singing a song. With many guffaws and roars of drunken laughter they sang about, "The Late Colliery Explosion at Patricroft, Wigan," along with Luther Hartley, who sat in the corner of the bar pressing together his squeezebox:

Oh, what a dreadful spectacle for to behold the dead
When all their lifeless bodies upon the bank was laid,
To recognize their features, it scarcely could be done,
The uncle from the cousin, or the father from the son.

They were so mutilated, alas! it is well known,
How some of these poor colliers were all to pieces blown,
The head from off the shoulders, was severed I declare,
While bodies, legs and arms, they were scattered here and
there.

These boys turn into children when they get liquor into them, Wright thought with disgust. They would spit and brag, hold farting contests, and bait the notoriously bad-tempered Abe Carter the way little boys might tease a vicious but safely chained dog. It was just such tomfoolery that had started the fight earlier, when the barman threw out both Carter and his opponent, Sly McNab. Wright had since heard the two were down on their asses together in the dirt of the alley, wallowing like hogs.

Suddenly, Luther Hartley's squeezebox fell silent with a wheeze, and the words to the mining song died on the lips of even the lustiest singers. An apprehension of more trouble made Wright spin around. He jumped backwards. A woman had invaded the bar!

The urgency that had driven Lucille had made her careless. She had taken a wrong turn out of the dining room and now, instead of the lobby, she found herself in the forbidden area of the bar. She froze in confusion at the unfamiliar surroundings.

In front of her, a man stood with a mug of beer in his hand and open-mouthed astonishment on his weathered face. He wore a cap, a grey shirt, and a shabby waistcoat. Behind him, the men at the bar all leaned backwards to get a glimpse of Lucille through the drifting tobacco smoke.

Suddenly, there was a snap from a pair of fingers. Lucille turned around to see Arthur Wright. He pointed to the door.

"You! Out! Now! Or I'll call the Mountie!"

From the back of the bar a wag spoke up. "What makes you think Brock can handle her?" The men roared with laughter, and many of the coal miners among them coughed heavily.

Lucille paused for a moment. It annoyed her terribly that men could enjoy a place of their own and have its sanctity enforced by law, but women had no such places. Regardless, it would do her investigation no good if the town Mountie were to kick her out of Stony Point. She secured her purse with Henry Best's cheque in it under her arm and hurried out the swinging doors.

Chapter 4

Wednesday, May 27, 1903

THE NEXT MORNING, as soon as it opened, Lucille strolled through the front door of the Union Bank. First, she filled out a deposit slip. Then, she approached the barred wicket and took Henry Best's cheque out of her purse. The skinny, bald-headed banker who wore a gun at his hip peered at the cheque through the lens of his monocle. He choked in astonishment and examined the cheque again. "Please excuse me a minute, ma'am," he said, and stepped through a door out of sight. Lucille had expected this reaction. She waited.

Outside a long whistle came from a locomotive engine and the wooden floor under her feet vibrated as yet another coal train rumbled past Stony Point. The office door behind the banker's desk presently opened again and the man reappeared. He shrugged his shoulders, threw up his hands, and shook his head as he muttered about "poor Mr. Best" and "damned clever women." Nonetheless, he unlocked and opened the door to the big safe in the wall and counted out one thousand dollars. He slid the stack of cash under the wicket to Lucille and wished her a good day.

With her business at the bank complete, she went to the CPR telegraph office at the train station. Here, Lucille wired seven hundred dollars to Lottie in Winnipeg. This money would pay her sister's mortgage and expenses until well into next year. She then walked back up the wooden sidewalk to Stony Point's North-West Mounted Police station, a one-storey log building with a flagpole set in a small brick square in front of it. The flag, with the Union Jack in the upper corner, billowed out in the wind. Lucille lifted her skirts and climbed up the wooden steps to the door. She knocked and a man's voice invited her inside.

The policeman, seated behind a desk to Lucille's left, had brown hair and a clean-shaven face. He wore the red serge tunic of the Mounted Police and the brown leather strap of his Sam Browne belt diagonally crossed his chest. The policeman lit up at Lucille's appearance and rose from his chair. He was a tall man, with a large nose, baggy eyes, and the build of a rail fence. When he smiled, wrinkles creased his forehead and the corners of his eyes. A yellow stripe ran down the outer seam of his dark blue riding pants. At Lucille's approach, the man introduced himself as Corporal Brock of the North-West Mounted Police. He was at her service.

"Good morning, Corporal," Lucille greeted him. "I was wondering if you could help me. I've come here from Winnipeg to find my brother-in-law."

These words instantly erased all the goodwill from the corporal's face. He leaned forward and scowled at Lucille. "You're not that woman who was in the Empire Hotel bar last night, are you?" he demanded.

"Yes, I am. That's where Stanley Birch, my sister's husband, was staying."

Corporal Brock shook his finger. "Look ma'am, I don't know how things are done in Winnipeg, but the law here in the Territory prohibits women in bars. They're no place for a lady and you ought to know that. If I hear you've been in a bar again, I'll have to arrest you as a woman of the town. Now what would your family think of that?" His brusque manner and harsh words angered Lucille.

"Fine, I'll just stand outside and shout through the door. I'll tell everybody how the Mounted Police have known for a couple of weeks now that two men have gone missing and they've done nothing to find them. I'll tell them how these men have wives and children who don't know what happened to them."

The corporal raised his hands as he retreated under the onslaught. "Now then, hold on a minute. That's not fair. We have these disappearances under investigation. I assure you we take them seriously. We've questioned some people." He paused. Lucille's eyes narrowed and her lips pressed together in a scowl.

With a great sigh of misery, the corporal reached into his desk and pulled out a notebook to which he referred. "We found out that on the evening of the day he disappeared, May the fourth, Mr. Birch had supper in Mrs. Perkins's tea room with Matthew Brown, a former coal miner. They left the tea room together afterwards and no one has seen either man since."

Lucille waited for a moment until it became obvious that the corporal had finished speaking. "That's all?" she asked.

"Yes. If you ask me, your brother-in-law was careless about the friends he kept. I say Brown's a former miner, because Mr. Best fired him when he found out he'd been stirring up trouble with a lot of anarchist troublemaking down at the mine. He's quite the unsavoury character, known to associate with radicals and foreigners. Because of that, I wouldn't put anything past him. Brown could have knocked your brother-in-law over the head, stolen his money, and lit out for the States. That American union he was working for is probably hiding him somewhere."

Lucille sat for a moment blinking her eyes. Finally, she said, "You really believe that?"

"Yes ma'am, I do."

"Well, I've known Stanley Birch for years, and he never had an amount of money on him worth stealing. And I wonder why Matthew Brown — this 'agitator' — would rob and kill a reporter? Someone who could get him favourable publicity?"

The corporal shrugged. "You never know what people like that are capable of. Maybe they had a fight and Brown knocked your brother-in-law down and killed him accidentally. He's scared to face the music, so he runs off. Don't worry your head now, ma'am. If this Brown character is still alive, we'll find him."

"Did you try talking to Mr. Brown's wife? I understand she's with her family in High River. Did you talk to her? What did she say?"

"Yes, we've talked to her. She says she hasn't heard from her husband, nor seen him either. See, now that's the kind of character you're dealing with here. Someone who leaves his wife and children without a word."

For a moment, Lucille thought of Matthew Brown's wife; no doubt the poor woman was in the same state as Lottie, a grieving widow without a body to grieve over.

"Or," she said, "the reason Mr. Brown can't talk to his wife is because he's pushing clouds." She leaned forward in the chair. "Someone told you to sit on your hands. Who was it?"

The corporal groaned and waved his hand at her as if Lucille were a bothersome fly. "Look ma'am, you don't know what you're talking about. Everybody knows these godless agitators have loose morals. Now, our investigation is proceeding and if you'll just stay out of the way, it'll proceed a whole lot faster." He closed the notebook and put it back in the desk — a sign that the interview was at an end.

Lucille stood up. "I've stayed out of the way, and your investigation's gone nowhere." Brock met her gaze with sullen defiance. She shrugged. "Well, I'll bid you a good day then and I'll be sure to let your boss, Commissioner A. Bowen Perry in Regina, know how helpful you've been. I just need to get Mr. Birch's bag if you'd be so kind."

The mention of his boss subdued the corporal. He took a ring of keys that hung from the post behind his desk and led Lucille to the door of a storeroom that was in a corner of the station to the right of the tiny jail cell. Stanley's English travelling bag sat on one of the wooden shelves, the leather bag with the capped corners — the one Lottie had ordered for her husband from Eaton's catalogue the Christmas before last.

Lucille signed for it and carried it out of the police station. Constable Brock made no move to help and just before she closed the door behind her, he shouted a parting admonition. "And stay out of bars!"

Lucille shook with suppressed fury. With the bag, she made her way back down the wooden steps of the post. *Miners running amok, for heaven's sake*, she thought with disgust. If a ridiculous story like that was the best the North-West Mounted Police could do, their establishment was a sad waste of the public dollar. She reached the bottom of the stairs. *But at least I've got Stanley's bag*, she reminded herself. His notebook was inside it, hidden under a false bottom.

As she walked, she glanced behind her at the tea room opposite the Empire Hotel. The woman who must be Mrs. Perkins was sweeping the step outside the door. Lucille decided she would take Stanley's bag back to the boarding house and also hide there the rest of the money she had won off Henry Best. Then, she would come back and interview Mrs. Perkins. She walked with her parasol in her right hand and the leather bag in the other. The bag was light and she remembered with sad nostalgia how Stanley had horrified Lottie one day, by going off on a story with only his straight razor in his pocket.

Suddenly, Lucille's pace slowed as a thought came to her. It was lucky she had not said anything about the notebook to Corporal Brock. She remembered how quickly he had ended the interview when she had asked him who had ordered him not to investigate the disappearances. She had a sudden conviction she must not give any evidence she uncovered to the Mounted Police. They might accidentally "lose" it. She glanced suspiciously from side to side as she carried the bag, though the only other creature she saw was an ox under a yoke that lifted its tail, made droppings, and bawled. She hurried along to the Pruitt boarding house.

She approached the house from the back alley. It had a

spacious yard. A small chicken coop made out of old barrels stood along the fence at the east side and opposite that was a large shed with padlocked doors. The continuous babble of water from the Oldman River came from behind a curtain of thick bushes and young trees. Kate was hoeing her garden. The young woman wore a black kerchief and her feet were bare. She turned the soil over thoroughly as she padded up and down in the black dirt, humming contentedly. The five speckled hens that were her chickens scratched and pecked at the ground at the foot of the big pine tree nearby. Up on the veranda, Lanka struggled with a rug as big as she was. After much effort, she took the end of it in her two little hands and shook it out over the railing. Both looked up and smiled as Lucille opened the rear gate to the backyard.

"Hello Kate, hello Lanka," she called out as she approached. She stopped in front of Kate and noticed the rifle the young woman was carrying. It was a small caliber weapon that hung like a trooper's from a canvas strap over Kate's shoulder. It had a shiny wooden stock and a polished barrel.

Lanka, with a child's sharp observation, noticed Lucille looking at the weapon. She jumped up to her and spoke with enthusiasm. "Miss Kate saw a fox sneaking around the chicken coop. She says she'll plug him if she sees him again."

One of Kate's hens was already missing a leg to a fox. The hen was her best layer and she could not wring her neck; instead, she had rigged up an artificial limb for the bird out of wire and a twig. Presently, this hen pecked at the ground near Lucille's foot looking none the worse. "She's going to show me how to shoot too," Lanka said.

Kate turned to the girl. "Now, only if your mother says I can. She might not want her little girl trotting around with a rifle. Remember, these aren't toys." Kate and Lanka both looked down at the bag Lucille was carrying.

Lucille shook it and said, "My brother-in-law's notebook is in here." Since the bag had nothing to do with her, Lanka turned around and skipped away two steps. But Kate's mouth fell open as she looked at it.

"Oh, ma'am, take it into the kitchen. After I'm done this hoeing, we can have a look at it. I've been thinking about your poor sister all morning. How horrible it must be to have your husband disappear."

Lucille had to smile. There was compassion on Kate's youthful face, but also the curiosity of a child Lanka's age. "Well then," she said. "I'll make something to drink, and we can all sit down for awhile." She carried the bag through the back door of the house with Lanka following her. Lucille set the bag on the floor near the kitchen table, unpinned her skimmer hat, and hung it up on a hook beside the door. She turned around to Lanka. The little girl danced with enthusiasm when she suggested lemonade. She skipped restlessly around the kitchen as Lucille mixed lemon juice, sugar, and cold water in a jug on the counter.

Suddenly, Lanka stopped. "Mrs. Reilly, where's your husband?"

"My husband is far away and believe me, we're all better off for it."

At that moment the door opened. Kate stepped inside, her round cheeks pink from exertion. She rested her hands on her rounded abdomen and lowered herself into a chair at the table. Lanka pulled at her arm, and she asked the girl to go fetch their sewing baskets. Lanka stomped her foot in a protest. But Kate made her a deal; if she would fetch the baskets, Kate would let her feed the chickens later. Lanka loved the birds; she could even get the hen with the artificial leg to sit on her lap as friendly as a house cat. The girl hurried out of the kitchen.

"Her folks are in Slav Town putting their furniture in their cabin," Kate explained when the girl was gone. "She got to being underfoot so I'm watching her for now." Lucille smiled. As young as she was, Kate had the makings of a competent mother.

Lanka returned with the baskets. While Kate got to work mending a skirt, and Lanka turned to her embroidery hoop, Lucille poured them each a glass of lemonade. She then picked up Stanley's bag and unbuckled the straps. She reached down past the tangle of clothes and found the false bottom. From under it she pulled out a notebook.

"Stanley's notebook, right where Lottie said it would be!" Lucille could not keep herself from exclaiming in triumph. She turned the pages. The sight of Stanley's cramped but legible handwriting seemed to bring him into the Pruitt house kitchen; indeed, she found herself looking over her shoulder as if he was standing there, watching her. Stanley would be wearing his old brown coat that was worn at the elbows and that dented bowler hat in which he had taken so much pride, although Lottie had begged him to get a new one. Lucille grimaced at a sudden, sharp jab of grief. She opened the notebook and sat down.

Stanley's dispatches from Frank took up the first part. Lucille read his account of the men who had escaped early graves. In spite of the rising gas and water level, seventeen miners had dug their way through a coal seam out of the buried Frank mine. Thirteen hours after the slide, the men had crawled out of a hole fifty yards from the mine's entrance, to the astonishment of the crew sent to rescue them. Stanley had also interviewed the town banker, Mr. Farmer. Rumour claimed that the slide had buried a fortune under the ruins of the bank. But Stanley had found the building intact and Farmer sitting in front of the door. When asked about the rumour, the banker only pulled aside the lapel of his jacket to show the hilt of a pistol in his waistcoat. If any man thought he could loot the bank he could come and try, Farmer had declared.

But to Lucille's disappointment, the second part of the notebook appeared to contain only dry facts: production figures for the Dominion Coal mine, the advantages of Crowsnest Pass coal over Lethbridge coal, and how the Western Federation of Miners had tried to organize the miners in the Crowsnest Pass before the United Mine Workers of America took over their role. A hand-drawn illustration of something called a "hoist scale" covered several pages. But she found no clues as to why Stanley had disappeared. She flipped through a few more pages and found the interview with Henry Best. She clenched her teeth. It was amazing how such a handsome man could so easily turn into a crocodile after one was exposed to his ugly side.

"What's the matter?" Kate asked.

"Henry Best. He started off looking like a prince, but he kept getting more ugly every time he opened his mouth." The young woman looked at Lucille with apprehension.

"When did you see Henry Best?" she asked.

"Last night. He was at the hotel with some of his friends." She tittered and Kate's eyes stretched wide in alarm. "I think I put a crimp in his evening."

The young woman turned pale. She had thought Mrs. Reilly had been out too late last night. "What did you do?" she asked, full of suspicion.

"I won a thousand dollars off him in a poker game."

Air burst from Kate in a gust. She cried out and rose halfway from her chair, pregnant belly and all. Lanka looked up from her needle. "You all right, Miss Kate?"

"Yes sweetie, I'm fine. This naughty Mrs. Reilly just likes to joke around, don't you? You didn't say *one thousand dollars?*"

"Yes, I did." Lucille smiled to herself. "I don't think Mr. Best wants to play cards with me anymore."

Kate clapped her hands to her head and groaned. She could not even imagine such a huge amount of money. All in a card game! "Oh, Mrs. Reilly, you've really done it now! A thousand dollars? He must be livid!"

Lucille snorted and shrugged. "Pooh, he can afford to lose it, can't he? And I've already sent most of it to Lottie." Kate raised her voice.

"Mr. Best has a sore spot where his money's concerned. It ain't just money to him, it's..." she paused for a second as she

thought of the right expression, "it's the points in the ball game."
Now Lucille was silent. Kate's words made her remember the
ice in Best's eyes and his big fist clenched on the table. Maybe
she should keep quiet about the money. "Anyway," Kate continued, "there's no undoing it now." With a grim expression
she drank from her cup of lemonade. "So, what happened at
the police station?"

Lucille gave a scornful snort and told her everything. "That
policeman was a blockhead!" she concluded. "He was more
concerned about my going in a bar than about two men who've
disappeared. And that addle-brained story! My word!"

Kate stared at her with open-mouthed confusion. "Matthew
Brown a robber?" She laughed at the idea. "Well, he's far from
an angel, but he's an honest man. Before he got fired he was
the check-weighman up at the mine. He and my brother Seth
played together on the ball team a couple of summers ago when
we all settled here from Lethbridge. That was just before Seth
and Granny left for the sea."

"Oh, you've a brother?"

"Yes, well, he's my half-brother." Kate explained that her
father, Harry Pruitt, had first married a Dewar who had been
the mother of her half-brothers, Sydney and Seth. After his
first wife passed away, Harry Pruitt had then married Kate's
mother, an Aitken. After she died of a fever, Kate's grandmother
had stayed with the Pruitts to raise Harry's children. Sydney
had stayed home to make furniture since the Pruitts had been
woodworkers for many generations. Seth, however, had gone
to sea with Granny. "He always wanted to see the world,
and they've sailed all the way to the Sandwich Islands," Kate
said. "They've been at sea for a couple of years now. They're
working my Uncle Noah's tramp freighter out of Vancouver.
Seth works the boilers and Granny cooks and does laundry. I
expect them back pretty soon now."

Lucille was relieved to hear Kate had some family. It had
distressed her to think the young pregnant woman might be

alone in her condition. When she finished her lemonade, she put her glass in the basin. She put Stanley's bag away in her room; later, before she went to bed, Lucille would look at the notebook more closely. She hid the remaining three hundred dollars in the bottom drawer of her bureau. Finally, she took her purse and parasol and said goodbye to Kate and Lanka as she walked out the door of the boarding house.

Soon Lucille arrived at Mrs. Perkins's tea room. The shop window had gilt lettering that said, "Perkins: tea, coffee, sandwiches." The bell on the front door jingled as she stepped inside. She took a deep, appreciative breath of the smell of coffee and fresh bread. A girl moved back and forth behind the display case at the rear of the shop, mopping up the puddle from the icebox where the cold drinks were kept. A woman in her early forties who had been wiping a table straightened up to face Lucille. She was a slender woman with broad hips and wore a plain blue skirt with a clean white shirtwaist. She had a square face with heavy eyebrows and wore her dark brown hair neatly pinned up. Her face was wary. "Can I help you, ma'am?"

"Yes, I would like to buy a root beer." Lucille took a nickel and the photograph of her sister's family out of her purse. "I was also wondering if you could help me." She placed the nickel on the counter, then showed the woman the photograph. "I was told at the police station that you were the last person to see Stanley Birch and Matthew Brown. Stanley Birch is my sister's husband."

Until that moment, the woman's posture had been stiff with suspicion; at the sight of Stanley in the photograph, her expression changed from suspicion to alarm. She turned pale, glanced at Lucille, and shuddered. She sighed and turned to the girl behind the counter. "Nellie! You mind things here a moment," she said as she took the bottle of root beer from the girl's hand and gave it to Lucille.

"Yes, Mama."

Mrs. Perkins then wiped her hands off on a rag and gestured for Lucille to follow her outside. She went around to the east side of the building. Lucille followed her with some apprehension. *Why is this woman afraid?*

Mrs. Perkins finally stopped with her back to the wooden boards of the wall. She folded her arms and said, "Yes, ma'am, I did know Mr. Birch. He was a real gentleman — my Nellie was quite taken with him. He always had a smile and a kind word for us." She hesitated and then continued. "Anyway, that evening, Mr. Birch and Mr. Brown came in just after six-thirty. They'd been at a meeting with some of the miners in the Oddfellows' Hall. Of course, like always, the meeting went on longer than Mr. Brown thought it would. He was supposed to be in Frank the next morning and he'd missed the train. Mr. Birch said he would walk with him to Frank. He knew it was a bad idea for Mr. Brown to be going there by himself." Mrs. Perkins took a breath. "They left together around seven-thirty and that's the last anyone saw of them." As Mrs. Perkins spoke, Lucille paced up and down with the photograph in one hand and the root beer in the other.

"Didn't the police look for them?"

Mrs. Perkins shook her head. "No ma'am, not the police. It was the coal miners who looked for them. They searched every mine shaft and crevice around town. They didn't find anything. What I'd do if I were you is get in touch with John Rupert. He led the search. He's the organizer for the United Mine Workers of America; he replaced Mr. Brown. He's in Fernie now, but he shows up here in Stony Point every other week or so."

Lucille thanked the woman for her time. Mrs. Perkins went back inside her shop, and Lucille went back to the Pruitt house. As she walked, she drank absently from her bottle of root beer and got lost in thought, picturing men to whom Stanley was a stranger hacking their way through thick bushes in search of him.

That evening, after supper, she went to her room. She set aside the basin and jug from the washstand and sat down in front of the small window. The sky had plenty of daylight left; in it, Lucille finished reading Stanley's notebook. On one page, her brother-in-law wrote down an observation that struck him the most: he had never seen an elderly coal miner. Men who looked to be in their sixties were actually in their forties, as the strain of the job and the inevitable lung disease from the dust cut twenty years off every miner's life. The coal companies refused to compensate the men for the damage to their health or pay miners injured at work. They also required the men to pay for the explosives they used on the job; as a result, the miners bought the cheapest explosives. The interviews Stanley had had with the men made plain their belief that substandard explosives had caused the disaster last July. The Dominion Coal explosion had taken place in a room mined by a pair of experienced contract miners. These men would never have taken the foolish risk of blasting the coal without first cutting the coalface, the exposed area of the coal bed from which the men dug the black gold. The explosion killed those miners, the fire-boss on the shift, and the men working the rooms on either side. A cloud of afterdamp, the lethal gas from the explosion, killed the others. As she read, Lucille marvelled to herself how any man could mine coal for a living. If he did not die from breathing in the dust, the dangerous conditions would finish him.

After reading these observations, she leafed through Stanley's illustrations of the "hoist scale." Lucille wondered to herself why he had spent so much time drawing a piece of mining equipment. She shook her head and turned to Stanley's interview with Henry Best. The chairman of Dominion Coal sounded like a gramophone with a stuck needle. Lucille could picture his smirk as Stanley asked him first about the three dollars a day that the miners earned. Best had answered that his wages were "competitive" with those of the other coal mines in the

West. When Stanley asked him whether Dominion Coal could not provide the miners with safer explosives in view of the lives lost in the explosion in July of 1902, he replied that if it did, Dominion Coal could not remain "competitive" since no other company paid for miners' equipment. Finally, Stanley had asked the chairman how he felt about the presence of the United Mine Workers of America in the Pass. Best said that this "third-party negotiator" was notorious for its non-British subjects among its leadership, just like the Western Federation of Miners. Any labour unrest was due entirely to agitation by these foreigners. With that comment, the chairman had ended the interview. Following the transcription of the interview, Stanley had added a note to himself explaining that the Western Federation of Miners was the first body that tried to organize the workers in the Crowsnest Pass. They decided to concentrate instead on hard-rock miners in the United States, leaving the United Mine Workers of America to organize the coal miners in Canada.

As she read up to the end of Stanley's notes, Lucille found herself glaring out the window. Outside, a squirrel scampered over the grass. She wondered how much Best would care about "remaining competitive" if his position as the wealthy mine owner did not allow him to disregard eighteen workers killed in a disaster caused by cheap explosives. She wished she could punch a hole through the insulated wall of privilege the man enjoyed.

On the last page, Stanley had written that the men were going to take him into the pit the next day, so he could see for himself what a coal miner did to earn a living. The rest of the pages in the notebook were blank. Lucille stared at them for a while. Stanley had always insisted on finishing any project he started. He had always said a job unfinished was a job done badly. *I should go into the coal mine and finish Stanley's work*, she thought. But already she could hear the objections. A coal mine was no place for a lady. A bar was no place for a lady.

The world itself was no place for a lady. Anger boiled up again inside her at the restrictions men placed on her. It was the reason why she enjoyed playing cards, because, for however briefly, four of a kind made her better than the man with the full house. Lucille made a face and closed the notebook with a thump. She did not care what anyone said. She would find some way into the mine.

She then laid her paper on top of the bureau and shook her bottle of ink. "Dear Lottie," she wrote at the top of the page. She told her sister everything she had found out so far: about how Stanley had gone missing in the company of Matthew Brown, the union organizer; about Corporal Brock of the Mounted Police and his ridiculous story; and, about what Mrs. Perkins had told her about the fruitless search for the men by the coal miners. She asked Lottie to go to the library or to the *Red River Herald's* archive room and find her a telephone number or something that she could use to contact the United Mine Workers of America. She told her sister she would send Stanley's bag and notebook to Winnipeg on the train tomorrow, putting them out of the reach of the Mounted Police. She concluded the letter by writing that tomorrow she would hang up the posters around town, the ones with Stanley's picture on them that she had had made up before she left Winnipeg.

"Maybe they'll get someone to talk," she wrote, "but I don't know. Nothing about this is going to be easy. The Mounted Police have done such a horrible job that I'm beginning to wonder if they had something to do with Stanley disappearance. They're no friends of ours, that's for certain."

Lucille folded the letter into an envelope and sealed it. She drew the blind over the window and undressed, untying the laces on her corset. She kept her laces as loose as she could ever since she had read some magazine articles that said tight lacing on a corset squeezed a woman's organs. At the same time, she glanced up at the little shelf on the wall above her bed, where she had put *Ten Days in a Mad-House*. In the book, Nellie

Bly told of how she had disguised herself as a lunatic in order to investigate an insane asylum in New York. Nothing about her mission had been easy either. In the asylum, Mrs. Bly had uncovered horrible conditions; it was freezing cold in winter, the food was rotten, and the staff routinely abused the inmates. Mrs. Bly's investigation had embarrassed the authorities and led to public demand for reforms. Lucille had read this book so many times she could almost recite every word. She carried it with her as an inspiration and good luck charm. Nellie Bly had shown that women could do important things, just like men. As always, Lucille encouraged herself with the thought of her heroine just before she fell asleep.

Chapter 5

—ᚚᚚ—

Thursday, May 28, 1903

LUCILLE AND KATE FOLLOWED LANKA to the Slavic neighbourhood the next morning. There, Mrs. Ruzicka welcomed
them to her new home, a rough wood and tarpaper cabin. Its
roof was half shingles and half sheet metal and its interior was
dark and pitiably small. Nonetheless, Mrs. Ruzicka welcomed
her guests with a small loaf of bread crusted with salt. She then
invited Lucille and Kate inside. Two other Galician women sat
at a worn old table: Mrs. Homeniuk, Mrs. Ruzicka's friend
who had helped her fix up the cabin, and a shy young lady
about Kate's age, Miss Tetyana, who had just married Mrs.
Ruzicka's oldest son, Oleg. Mrs. Homeniuk and Miss Tetyana
clucked like hens at pregnant Kate. The older woman spoke to
her at some length in Ukrainian. Lanka stood behind Lucille
and Kate and translated the woman's speech.

"Mrs. Homeniuk says it's easy to have a baby. All six of hers
just slid out like butter. She says you're a strong girl and you
needn't worry."

Kate glowed. She exclaimed aloud at how delicious the salted
bread was while Lucille smiled and nodded at Mrs. Homeniuk.
Presently, Mrs. Ruzicka brought her a second cup of tea. With
pride, she held out a tray brimming with *varenyky*. Kate's eyes
lit up at the sight of her favourite pastry and Mrs. Ruzicka
pressed another one on both her and Lucille. Lanka, meanwhile, swung like a monkey from the back of Kate's chair. Her
mother snapped at the girl and she bolted upright.

To help keep the restless child out of trouble, Lucille began to talk with her. "Well, Lanka, tell me, are you and your folks happy here?"

"Oh yes," the girl said. "We're much better off here. Mama says in the old country, when a man saw the Count's house, he had to take his hat off." Lucille's mouth twisted. She almost said that it was a shame the Galicians had come here for nothing, for if Henry Best had his way, the men here would have to remove their hats in front of him as well. But she kept her sarcasm to herself. Lanka then said something to her mother and suddenly all of the immigrant women began to fumble in their aprons. Each of them took out a worn, ragged leaflet. Kate took one and covered her mouth to stifle a giggle. On the leaflet was a picture of a farmer on his knees with his arms raised in amazement at a tomato the size of a melon. The writing on the leaflet was in Cyrillic for which Lucille was thankful; at least she could not read the outrageous nonsense it contained.

"Papa says a man can own land here," Lanka continued with enthusiasm. "We're going to save all our money and soon we'll have enough for another homestead." She went on to explain that when they had first arrived in Canada, the family settled on a quarter section north of Regina. Papa Ruzicka had just raised his wheat crop as tall as his hips when a cloud of grasshoppers that darkened the sky ate every speck. Broke and hungry, all the family could do was come to the Crowsnest Pass to earn enough money in the coal mines so they could try all over again.

After visiting briefly with Mrs. Ruzicka, Lucille excused herself and left the cabin. The sun was shining. It was warm enough that she felt comfortable in her shirtwaist and the hat she wore shaded her eyes. A flock of bluebirds had moved into the knot of pine trees at the end of the row of cabins in Slav Town; flashes of blue popped in and out amid the green boughs as the birds darted around. Lucille looked up at the mountains on either side of the town. In the sunlight, their jagged peaks seemed to almost touch the blue sky. As she strolled away in the direction of the train station, she thought of how beautiful it was in Stony Point.

At the station, she took a poster from her canvas bag. She laid it up flat against the notice board next to the telegraph operator's window and drove a nail into its corner with the handle of her parasol. At the top of each poster was a caption that read, "Missing," in large block letters. Underneath the caption was a sketch of Stanley's face taken from the photograph Lucille always carried. His name, height, weight, and occupation were written at the bottom, together with a handwritten note Lucille had added, offering a reward of one hundred dollars for information leading to Stanley Birch's whereabouts. After she finished hanging one at the train station, she walked over to the General Store.

The bell on the door jingled as she stepped inside. Lucille looked around. The General Store had a wide variety of items for sale. As well as the rugs on the overhead wires, metal washtubs and wooden chairs hung on the wall just under the ceiling. The shelves on the three walls contained a dizzying array of boxes of soda crystals, canned foods of every variety, and bottles of patent medicines, many of which contained extracts of opium and cocaine. There were so many shelves that the girl who was stocking them had to stand on a ladder to reach the top level. A slender, pale girl of about sixteen, she glanced down at Lucille as she stepped inside. Across from the girl was a counter with a glass front showing drawers full of goods such as macaroni, baking powder, and coffee beans.

The woman sitting on a stool behind the counter said, "Can I help you, ma'am?" This woman wore a grey bodice and matching cotton skirt. She had to be the mother of the girl on the ladder: like her daughter, her frame was so slender that she looked as if she were made of reeds. Her faded brown hair hung down lifelessly on either side of her face and she peered at Lucille through a pair of round wire spectacles. In her voice and expression, Lucille saw the same wary suspicion that Mrs. Perkins in the tea room had shown to her. She ignored it and showed the woman the poster.

"Good day, ma'am. I'd like to know if I could put this in your window." The woman slid part of the way off her stool. Just like Mrs. Perkins, she turned pale and trembled at the sight of Stanley's picture.

"Are you the woman from Winnipeg?" she demanded. "The one who was playing poker with the men in the Empire Hotel bar?"

Lucille winced. *Small town gossip!* It travelled with a speed that made Mr. Bell's telephone look like two cans tied together with string. Not only did everyone in town know she had been in the bar, the story had grown so that now it had Lucille sitting in the forbidden establishment chewing tobacco with her skirts hiked up, like some kind of Crowsnest Poker Alice.

"I'm sorry to say that you've been misinformed, ma'am. I was in the bar, but not even for a minute. You see, I'm trying to find this man." She shook the poster in her hands. "He was staying at the Empire Hotel when he disappeared."

Anger appeared on the woman's face. She glanced up at her daughter on the ladder; the girl held a can of beans now forgotten in her hand while she listened. Her mother barked at her. "Sairy, you mind your business!" The girl quickly put the can on the shelf as her mother turned back to Lucille.

"No, I can't help you. I could get into trouble. And I don't want women with no husbands who go into bars in this place. To top off everything, you're boarding in the Pruitt house." The tone in which she said the last sentence made the house sound as disreputable as the bar. Lucille gawked at the woman in bewilderment.

"You don't want to stay there," the storekeeper continued. "Kate Pruitt's a bad girl." At that moment, the woman's husband came through the back door. He was a short man with a pale face, thin blonde hair, and an enormous round belly out of proportion to his small frame. At first, he looked as if he were wheeling his big belly in the cart in front of him, but it was actually a dolly loaded with four ninety-eight pound sacks of "All Purpose Cream of the West Vitamin Enriched Flour." As he unloaded them in the corner, he spoke to Lucille. "You don't want to be staying with Kate Pruitt." He repeated his wife's warning. "She was sporting around with Henry Best last fall and look what that got her, hey Polly?"

With astonishment, Lucille's mouth fell open. Polly's colourless eyes lit up; she was happy to have fresh ears for her gossip. Her eyes first checked her daughter to make sure the girl was not listening. Then in a quiet yet vehement voice, she said, "A disgrace is what she is! She's darned lucky she had the brother she did. We'd have run her out of town otherwise. No one respectable will stay at her house. The only reason she had those bohunkies there was because Stony Point got buried in refugees after the Slide. They didn't have anywhere else to go."

Her husband paused, resting his arm on top of his cart. "Syd Pruitt died in the mine explosion last July. He went down to try and save some of the boys, but the afterdamp got him."

Lucille's gaze fell to the counter. She bit her lip while her anger rose. She pictured the cunning with which Henry Best must have stalked Kate as soon as her brother was dead. *That snake!*

"Sally Pruitt, Syd's widow, left to be with her folks right afterwards," the man continued the story. "Kate's been on her own ever since. She actually hasn't done badly for herself. She even managed Mrs. Best."

"Who?" Lucille asked.

"Mr. Best's wife," Polly said with a laugh like the bray of a mule. She looked up at her daughter who had, again, frozen in place with her head cocked. "Sairy, I'll paddle you if you don't move it with that stock!" She lowered her voice back down as she spoke to Lucille. "Don't tell me you've never seen a married man who didn't have a fancy piece lying around somewhere."

Lucille could only blink while she remembered how Best had flirted with her when she first saw him in the hotel lobby. *The shameless cad!*

"You know that rifle Kate carries around?" Polly continued. "It's not for varmints; it's for Ellie Best. Mrs. Best put a dead rabbit in Kate's mailbox last March when her belly started to show. The next day, Kate took a potshot with the rifle at the Best's house. Nobody was in the room that she hit, but the glass from the window sprayed inside, and Mrs. Best knew she might not miss with her next shot. Things simmered down after that."

"But that was only because Mrs. Best found out that her husband was also bouncing the mattress with the nanny." The storekeeper clearly enjoyed a good gossip as much as his wife. "That took the heat off Kate."

"Well," Lucille said, "just so you folks know, I'm offering a one-hundred-dollar reward to anyone who can find my brother-in-law." The man's ears perked up. "If they say they saw the poster in your store, I'll remember you, too," Lucille continued. "Can I hang one up in your window?"

Polly opened her mouth to say no again, but her husband overruled her. After Lucille stepped out the door, Polly turned to her husband with irritation. "Gerald, I don't know about that at all. We might get in trouble if someone sees that poster. And what kind of woman would want to board herself with a harlot?"

"Oh, quit your fussing, woman. We won't make any money if all our customers have to have lily-white morals. Folks are saying that woman took quite a chunk of change out of Best's pocket in the card game. Money's money, I always say. And this isn't a company store, and Henry Best doesn't tell me what to do! If I decide to put French postcards in the window, then that's where they'll go!" Gerald declared with spirit as he wheeled his cart out the back door again.

Outside, Lucille leaned against the corner of the General Store and heaved a great sigh. One would think Kate had gotten herself pregnant, the way all the disgrace came down on the girl's head. Had no one in this town ever made a mistake when they were young? Even she had found Henry Best attractive at first, and if she had been eighteen instead of thirty, he might have duped her too. But should she move out of Kate's house? If she antagonized the townspeople, her investigation would become that much more difficult. It would take weeks to live down her appearance in the bar as it was, and staying in the house of a fallen woman might make it impossible. *Kate's a strong woman. She can look after herself*, Lucille thought as she made her way down the boardwalk. With a laugh, she pictured what it must have looked like when Kate shot out Mrs. Best's window. Doubtlessly, the girl could survive.

But all the same, Lucille was unhappy. It felt wrong to take her money back from Kate. Her lodgings in the Pruitt house were always clean, the food was good; indeed, Kate was always working around the house. Could she reward all her work by leaving? The loss of her rent money would strain the girl's finances. Lucille asked herself if she could do that to a woman who had been a friend to her. With a miserable face, she adjusted her sack full of posters on her shoulder and continued on down the boardwalk.

She continued to hang up posters wherever she could. In nearly every case, the sight of Stanley's face in the picture inspired apprehension and dismay. Mr. Lesniak, the Polish butcher, agreed to hang one in his window. But the barber refused and did everything except chase her out of his shop. She was about to hang one next to the door of the Mounted Police station, but then she changed her mind; she would make up a special poster for that space. Instead, she dropped in on Mrs. Perkins in her tea room.

That woman was happy to hang a poster up in her window. Lucille bought a coffee and chatted with her for a few minutes. Business for Mrs. Perkins was going well. Now that the CPR line through the Crowsnest Pass had been repaired, the coal mines were running like well-oiled machines to make up for lost time. The whistle at Dominion Coal gave one blast every morning at six. Seeing the confusion on Lucille's face, Mrs. Perkins explained that every morning at six o'clock the mine whistle blew: one blast meant work for everybody, two meant work for tipple and haulage workers only, and three meant the mine was closed. A blast from the whistle at any other time than six in the morning meant an explosion. Mrs. Perkins did not have to say what happened in that instance. Lucille imagined how the town must have looked that day last July, with the whistle screaming and the miners' wives running together through town to the shaft entrance.

After she finished her coffee, Lucille left Mrs. Perkins's tea room and paused for a moment on the street as she looked across the way at the Empire Hotel. An ox cart loaded with barrels stopped at the east side of the building. Arthur Wright came out the door and he and the carter rolled a keg of beer off the end of the cart and into the bar. Lucille paused for a moment. She wanted to hang up a poster outside the door to the lobby and the bar of the hotel, but she had not made any friend of Arthur Wright the last time she was there. Hostility was all she could expect, but she must try. She set her mouth and lifted her skirt to cross the dirt road.

This time in the hotel lobby, she found a heavy-set young man behind the front desk. His face was round and spotted, his hair cropped short, and his apron stained. As Lucille approached him, his eyes squinted like a pig's, whether in lust or hostility she could not tell, but she would bet money that the two went together in this oily young man's head. His eyes fell upon her bosom and stayed there as Lucille took one of the posters out of her bag and showed it to him. "Good day," she said, in a clipped tone. "I was wondering if I could hang this up on the wall outside." The young man continued to stare at her bosom as if she had not spoken.

"My face is up here!" Lucille barked. Now malice positively slid off the young man's face.

"I've got to ask my stepfather." He stepped out the door to the left that led into the bar. In the interval, Lucille grasped hold of her resolve. But when Arthur Wright appeared, he met her with an even face and approached her with his hand out. She took it slowly with surprise.

"Good afternoon, Mrs. Reilly. I would like to apologize if I was abrupt with you the other night. I know you are a perfectly respectable woman. It's just that I have a business here and if I lose my license, I will have to close down. You understand, don't you?" He hooked his thumbs inside his apron and paused.

"Yes, I do," Lucille said as she blinked. The contrast between what she had expected and what was actually happening stunned her.

"I've heard you've been asking around town about your brother-in-law," Wright continued. "I'd like to help but I don't know much. I only talked to Mr. Birch once, when I checked him in." Lucille showed him her poster. He glanced at it with mild interest and waved his pink hand. "Sure, I've no problem with you putting it up. And if you ever want any help, all you have to do is come here and talk to me. How long do you plan on staying in town?"

The sudden question startled her. Wright wore a bland expression. Lucille watched him closely as she would a card player whom she suspected of a bluff. "I'm staying here for as long as it takes me to find Mr. Birch."

The hotel man shrugged. "Well, ma'am, you might want to watch yourself. Some people in town might take it bad if you interfere in things that aren't your business."

Lucille froze. Wright's jowly face remained impassive, but the alarm in her head was clanging. "I'll keep that in mind, Mr. Wright. And if this ever gets to be a legal matter, I'll remember who helped me and who didn't. Good day." She stepped outside and hung up two posters, one beside the door to the lobby and the other outside the bar.

As she made her way back to the Pruitt house, she thought over the encounter. Lucille stopped in her tracks as she remembered how Corporal Brock had known she was the woman from Winnipeg when she had interviewed him. When Wright had threatened to kick her out of the bar that night, he had spoken of calling the Mountie in a way that made it clear he expected an immediate response from the police. The half-threat the hotel man had just made to her moments ago, with his raised eyebrows and mild tone, was actually coming from Corporal Brock. Lucille's mouth twisted in anger. She looked over her shoulder at the log building of the North-West Mounted Police station and decided she would give Corporal Brock something to threaten her about himself.

At the boarding house, she climbed up the steps, opened the back door, and found Kate kneeling at the foot of the black stove. At the sound of the door opening, Kate turned around. Lucille groaned in dismay at how tears had run streaks through the coating of stove ash on her round face. At the appearance of Lucille, Kate gulped and wiped her eyes impatiently on her forearm. Lucille hurried to her, knelt down, and ran her handkerchief over the girl's tear-stained face in a motherly way.

"There now Kate, what's wrong?" she asked. Kate took a deep breath and wiped her eyes again. She would not meet Lucille's eyes.

"Men are dogs," she declared at last.

"Well, I won't argue with that."

In spite of her tears, Kate giggled. Lucille rose up and unpinned her hat from her blonde hair. "I heard in town about you and Henry Best," she continued.

Kate looked at the floor and wondered how to explain that she had been unable to resist the appeal of wealthy, handsome Henry Best who had approached her when she was grief-stricken over Sydney. But Mrs. Reilly had an understanding face that said an explanation was unnecessary. Instead, her shoulders only rose and fell in resignation.

"I guess you'll be wanting to leave the bad girl's house, then." She sniffed and pulled her own handkerchief out from her apron, blowing her nose into it. Lucille sighed. She helped Kate up to her feet and sat her down in a chair at the kitchen table. She then took the ash pan from underneath the stove and poured its contents into a barrel. With that done, she looked in the icebox for something cold they could drink.

"Well Kate," she said at last, "I'm no good at picking men either, and I was older than you when I messed up." A distant look came into Lucille's eyes. "But I've no husband anymore, so I'm in disgrace too. Of course I'll stay."

The young woman stared back with surprise. A bright smile appeared on her face and her tears instantly receded. Kate knew she could count on Mrs. Reilly. As Lucille took the jug of yesterday's lemonade out of the icebox, an inspiration struck Kate with such force that she straightened up and rested her hand on her round abdomen. *Wouldn't it be grand if Mrs. Reilly were to marry Seth*, she thought. But then she grimaced. She wondered what had happened to Mr. Reilly. As Lucille set two glasses on the table, Kate looked at her closely. "So where is your husband?"

A grim expression had settled over Lucille's features. Kate marvelled at the bitterness in her eyes and felt sad for a moment that such blue eyes could be so injured. Seth could fix that straightaway. Meanwhile, Lucille thought that since she knew Kate's story, it was only fair that she share hers. "My husband's in his grave, from too much whiskey. About a year before he died, Irving came home from the bar one night. He started picking at me because he always got quarrelsome when he was drunk. He wanted to know why his supper wasn't ready and he said I'd best pick up my ass and fetch him something to eat. I said, 'My ass isn't the only thing that needs picking up around here.' Then he beat the daylights out of me. I don't remember it — I don't remember anything from the time I sassed him until I woke up in the hospital." She paused and stared at the table. "After I got out, Stanley talked with a lawyer friend of his and got me a separation. He moved me in with himself and Lottie. He even found me a job at his paper." She paused and stirred her lemonade. "Anyway, after he beat me up, Irving's family pulled some strings. Instead of jail, they got him checked into a sanitarium. His sister swore to me he was dry when he got out. But with Irving you could always bet your last nickel he'd fall off the wagon sooner or later. He ended up drowning with his face in a puddle behind one of the bars on Main Street."

Kate rested her chin on her fist. To know her boarder was a widow made her want to skip around the kitchen table with relief, but she forced herself to stay in her chair and keep the grin off her face. "Why, that man was as much use to you as a whistle on a plough," she said. "But now you can marry my brother Seth. He needs a good wife, and you and him would fit together like a hand in a glove."

Lucille stared at Kate with her mouth open in disbelief at how the girl had decided, sometime during her confession, to marry her off. She could not choose whether to laugh or box Kate's ears.

"Young lady, I'd sooner tie a rope around my neck and be hitched to a bucking bronco than get married again. One husband was enough for me."

"But Seth don't drink. He was going to be a prizefighter and he wanted to stay in shape. I know he likes to fight, but Granny says boys will be boys and there's naught you can do about that." She lifted her chin proudly. "I'm not even worried about him being ashamed of me when he gets home. I'm his little Katie and I always will be." She lowered her head and spoke in a whisper. "All the girls in Lethbridge said he was nice-looking too."

In exasperation, Lucille raised her hands. "Look Kate, I'm

not getting married again. I'm sure your brother's very nice, but even if a Russian prince made me an offer, I'd turn him down. I'm not getting married again and that's final."

"All right, all right." Kate rolled her eyes up innocently. "Not another word, I promise." But at the same time, the girl wagered imaginary money on the proposition that Mrs. Reilly would change her tune after she met Seth.

Now that Kate had promised not to utter another word about marriage, Lucille regained her good humour. She went and fetched her typewriter from her room. It was time to compose her dispatch for the *Red River Herald*.

While Kate tidied up and prepared supper, she stole glances at her boarder from time to time. It seemed Mrs. Reilly was forever reading or writing. The clatter of keystrokes from her typewriter sounded like the racket from a loom. It was good that she had this serious side to her; Seth disliked giggly, empty-headed women.

In her dispatch, Lucille related all the details concerning Stanley's disappearance that she had discovered so far. To spark the readers' curiosity, she concluded her piece by saying that the disappearance of *Red River Herald* reporter Stanley Birch was a mystery worthy of Sherlock Holmes, and that she would remain in Stony Point until she solved it. She pulled the sheet of paper out of the typewriter and read over her two-page dispatch. Her only ally in her mission was publicity. But what if Mr. MacDougall refused to print this dispatch? The only message she had received from her editor had been an angry telegram telling her to "Stop this nonsense right now and come home." Lucille would coerce him. First, she would send MacDougall the dispatch; then, in the letter she would write to her sister tonight, she would ask Lottie to send the man his own editorials from earlier editions of the *Red River Herald* that declared his paper the "champion of the common man." Was Stanley not a common man too?

Chapter 6

—m—

Monday, June 1, 1903

HENRY BEST FINISHED HIS BREAKFAST and sat back in his chair to light a cigarette. As he always insisted, his cup of coffee was near at hand. Outside, the sun shone brightly. Henry's gaze rested for a moment on the green leaves of the paper fern in a skinny red vase under the window. Beyond that, the Bests' china cabinet — tall, made of oak, and terrifically expensive — occupied the far corner of the dining room. Its doors were fastened shut with a chain so that the children would not destroy the china inside. While he smoked, the voice of Henry's wife buzzed in his ear like a mosquito's. He blinked suddenly and turned to her. "What's that again?"

Ellie Best paused and repeated what she had just said. "The bill came yesterday from my couturier's in Paris. It's for seven hundred dollars."

Henry clapped his hand to his head. "Seven hundred dollars! Damned dressmakers — why the hell am I mining coal?" he exclaimed. He grumbled to himself while smoke streamed from his nose. He could no longer afford Ellie's eye-popping bills, not since he had lost those thousand dollars in the card game, a loss that still hurt like a nagging toothache. Yesterday evening, Henry had gone through his accounts; when he had finished he had buried his face in his hands and groaned. Because of the lost money and Ellie's spending, he knew he would be forced to give up his ambition to be the first man in the Crowsnest Pass to own an automobile. The bear hunting trip he made to

55

Kananaskis every October now looked doubtful too. Henry set his teeth together in growing anger. If he could not have his automobile or his hunting trip, he was damned if Ellie was going to have her dresses and her jewellery.

Ellie, for her part, drew back and looked at her husband with surprise. Their bargain had always been understood: she did not mention his affairs, and he did not object to her spending. So why was he being so difficult suddenly? "But darling! Do you want me to walk around looking like a miner's wife?" She shuddered at the idea.

"Goddamn it, I'm not paying any more of these bills! Half of the dresses you've got now are still in their wrapping." Henry's mother-in-law, Mrs. Nesbit, sitting at the far end of the dining table, clucked her disapproval at the language he used in front of his daughters. Henry turned to the older woman and snapped two words: "My house!"

Mrs. Nesbit pressed her wrinkled lips together and lowered her head. She was slender with long hands; in that respect, Ellie looked just like her. Also, the two women shared a tight, thin mouth, only Mrs. Nesbit's wrinkles had ploughed deeply into the delicate skin around the corners. She wore a dark blue dress with white lace around the stiff collar of her bodice. Her grey hair was pinned up in a tight bun on top of her head.

"Darling, please!" Ellie pushed a shred of fried egg around her plate with her toast. She kept her corset so tightly laced she could hardly breathe, let alone eat. "Mother's here to help us."

Henry made a face. The fact of the matter was that after his wife had discovered his little slip-up with Pearl Brewer, she had punched the girl several times in the face as she dismissed her. Now, it had become impossible to find another nanny. The only person who would help her with the girls was her mother, and now even Mrs. Nesbit had had her fill. The old woman was leaving for her home in Seattle in two days.

In view of his mother-in-law's imminent departure, Henry could have predicted Ellie's next question. "Why don't Phyllis and Robert take the girls for a little while?" To Ellie, "a little while" would mean until their daughters were eighteen. Henry grimaced while he pictured Phyllis, his sister, dancing for joy when he thrust those little hellions on her. He would have to pay her for taking the girls, yet another expense. Displeasure clouded his face. Ellie was forever tearing out her hair over her daughters and their antics, unlike Henry, who found the children easy to manage. If Eleanor or Mildred made faces or talked back, he cuffed them immediately. The girls knew he would stand no hogwash from them; indeed, when their father snapped his fingers, they obeyed. He often spotted envy in his wife's eyes at how, for him, the girls stayed quietly in their places.

Henry now glanced to his right at his daughters in their nightgowns and slippers. Both girls rested on top of multiple pillows that boosted them up to the table. Eleanor had just turned five. People often remarked upon how much the girl took after her father: she had his sandy brown hair, blue eyes in the exact same shape but smaller, and square chin. Presently, Eleanor was clowning around with her fork; she wobbled the implement back and forth on her fingertip. Three-year-old Mildred of course copied her sister's actions. She still had the round cheeks and large eyes of a baby, but she also had Ellie's dark brown hair and thin mouth. As always, the small girl clutched her rag dolly under her arm. If anyone tried to take the doll, Mildred would scream loud enough to shatter the windows of the house. The sight of Eleanor playing with her fork irritated Henry. He snapped his fingers at the girls. "You two — upstairs! Now! Mrs. Nesbit, take them to the nursery."

Eleanor and Mildred slid off the chairs. Mrs. Nesbit's mouth stiffened to hear Henry address her as he would a servant but, nonetheless, she clapped her hands at the children and took each one by the arm, leading them out of the dining room. As they walked out, Eleanor began to whine. When they were gone, Henry picked up his cup of coffee and drained it. Ellie put her fork down on her plate next to the cold fried egg.

"I'm going to write to Phyllis and Robert this afternoon," she said.

Henry slapped his hand down on the table. The dishes rang and Ellie jumped. "You're not writing anyone. The girls are staying right where they are." His daughters were not good for much, but they did keep their mother occupied and Henry already had enough expenses. "And I don't want to see any more damned dressmaker's bills, or jewellery bills, or any more of that rubbish. You have to start living within your means, Mrs. Best." Ellie's eyes fluttered as she struggled for a deep breath in her corset. Her shoulders rose and fell under her grey bodice. Two patches of red shone on her cheeks as she swallowed. Henry stood up. "Don't bother waiting up for me. I'll be at the office until after midnight." He strode out of the dining room. Soon, the front door opened, then closed, marking his departure.

Alone at the table, Ellie sat for a moment. What business was urgent enough to keep Henry at the office all day and all night? *He'll be at his mistress's until after midnight he means*, she thought. *For sure that's where the money's going.* At that instant, from upstairs, Mildred screamed. Her little feet thundered on the floor above Ellie's head. She continued to scream at an ear-splitting pitch, drowning out the voice of Mrs. Nesbit as she remonstrated her. Ellie rested her forehead in her hands and tried once again to take a deep breath. The screams above doubled in volume as her mother gave Mildred three quick swats on her rear. It was not even nine o'clock and already Ellie felt a headache coming on. Henry had only to walk out the door and screaming children were no longer his concern. Of course, he found managing the girls a breeze; he was so seldom in the house when they were about. She resented that as much as she resented his infidelities.

"Ellie, get up here," her mother called from upstairs. Mildred's screams had subsided to deep sobs. "I need some help. My hip's sore from falling yesterday." She paused. "Ellie!"n Ellie groaned and stood up. "And make sure you bring my medicine. It's on the mantelpiece in the parlour." She retrieved the bottle and the spoon before she went upstairs.

In their nursery, Eleanor and Mildred had everything they could want. An elaborate dollhouse sat on a table in the corner. It had a shingled roof and miniature rooms with carpets and little pieces of oak furniture; indeed, the dollhouse was furnished better than the real house. A rocking horse with a red velvet saddle stood underneath the window. Its rein hung from its muzzle and straw stuffing protruded from its belly from when Eleanor had thrown it to the floor and stomped on it in a fit of rage. The girls' dolls crowded the shelves of a tall bookcase in the corner by the window. Each doll had a porcelain head and a velvet dress that made Ellie's Parisian wardrobe look shabby. The doll Henry had given Eleanor for her fifth birthday was missing from the collection; the girl had smashed it over Mildred's head three days ago in the heat of one of their squabbles. Everything in the room, the wallpaper, the coverlets on the little twin beds, and the clothes cabinet opposite the shelf of dolls, was done up in pink and white. With all of these beautiful things, Ellie was mystified as to why the girls spent a good part of every day screaming and crying.

Mildred was standing in her underwear with her fist screwed into one eye. Gulping sobs bubbled from her. Now that Ellie was here, Mrs. Nesbit left the girl and turned to Eleanor who had ducked down out of sight behind the dollhouse. Her grandmother took Eleanor's arm to get her into her brace. Immediately, Eleanor pulled away and began to scream as loud as Mildred. Ellie muttered incoherently under her breath. It was another lovely start to another wonderful day.

She jerked Mildred toward her and fitted the girl into the posture brace. These had been Mrs. Nesbit's idea. No one would marry the girls if they slouched; they must learn to carry themselves with womanly grace. In this instance, Ellie had agreed heartily with her mother. Mildred now wiped her eyes and cried miserably while Ellie, with anger burning on her smooth cheeks, tightened the buckles on the metal brace with impatient tugs. When she was done, she pulled Mildred back around and shook her finger in the three-year-old girl's red face. "Now, I don't want to hear another peep out of you, girl. Do you understand?"

Mildred howled again as she plucked resentfully at the brace. Although the three-year-old child was unable to express it, for the ninth time that morning she wondered what she had done to deserve all this scorn; clearly, being a girl was a grievous and unforgivable crime. Meanwhile, Ellie turned away from Mildred and confronted Eleanor, yelling, "That goes for you too," over her screams. Mrs. Nesbit glanced at her daughter and shook her head.

Finally, Ellie and her mother got Eleanor into her brace as well and both girls dressed and calmed down. Mildred rested on a little stool with her dolly and hiccuped. She kept a wary eye on her sister next to her who sat with her needle in her hand and her sampler in her lap; Eleanor was apt to jab Mildred with the needle whenever she wanted some excitement. For the moment, Eleanor fidgeted in her brace with her lower lip swollen in resentment. Mrs. Nesbit sat down on the edge of Eleanor's bed. She folded her arms and fixed her angry gaze on her daughter. "Honestly Ellie, what on earth is wrong with these girls? They're just a pair of wild Indians!"

"Gee Mother, I didn't know that." Ellie rolled her eyes and sank down onto another small nursery chair. Her strangling corset compressed her ribs and forced her to keep her legs straight out in front of her. Her gaze rested on her right foot in its green slipper. The current fashion was for delicate, tapering feet, but Ellie had ugly feet with that little toe that stuck out. She would have had the surgery to cut off the offending toe, like some women did, but she was frightened of the anesthetic. Ellie scowled at the rest of her body with the same dissatisfaction: the round bosom, wide hips, and knocking knees — hers was a weak, defective woman's body that was no good for anything. *How I hate it*, she thought as she clenched her teeth. She wished she could take a saw and cut the whole thing off — somehow.

While she sat, Mrs. Nesbit began to fidget as restlessly as Eleanor. She shifted over to where Ellie had placed her bottle of laudanum on the little washstand between the girls' beds. She pulled the cork out of the bottle and, with relish, smelled the opium and liquor inside. "Now Ellie, if you don't get some control over these girls, the Lord knows how they'll end up. Who's going to marry them if they're still running around like savages when they're grown? They nearly killed me yesterday." She paused as she poured herself a spoonful of the laudanum. Yesterday afternoon, Eleanor and Mildred had waited until their grandmother had fallen asleep on the parlour sofa. Then they had tied a loop of twine around the old woman's ankles and yelled, "Fire!" Mrs. Nesbit had fallen heavily on her hip while the girls ran away, laughing merrily. As usual, Eleanor had been the instigator, and Mildred her eager accomplice. After the prank, Mrs. Nesbit had declared the Best house an insane asylum and she was leaving. She would take the train out of Stony Point and then Ellie would be on her own with the girls. The grandmother put the spoon of laudanum in her mouth and tilted back her head. Her fidgets soon eased and a sleepy-eyed glow of contentment began to replace her irritation.

After a while, she continued. "Now I understand Henry can be … difficult, Lord knows. But it's a man's world, Ellie. You can't do anything about it. You should try being pleasant. If only you would just brighten your outlook, then you'll see it's not so bad." She put her spoon to the mouth of the bottle and poured herself another dose. Her head shook in a delightful rush when the spoonful hit her stomach.

Ellie looked at her mother with irritation. She bared her teeth, then said, "Am I supposed to sit idly by while every whore in town steals my husband?" Even at the thought, her cheeks grew pale as she crushed the fabric of her skirt in her fists. A young, pink-cheeked hussy, and the homeliest sow in the Crowsnest whom she had hired to mind the girls, had been just as weak and defective as she. *Who are they to take what's mine? Do they think they're better than me?* At this thought, rage bubbled inside Ellie like coffee in a pot. Her scowl distorted her forehead.

Mrs. Nesbit waved her hand, unsteadily, in dismissal. "Oh fiddlesticks girl, you're the wife. You're the one he comes home to every night." Ellie bit her tongue. Many nights Henry never came home, but pointing that out to her mother would be a waste of breath. "Really Ellie, why make a fuss over nothing?" Mrs. Nesbit continued. "Just turn a blind eye. A proper lady takes no notice of those things."

The set of Ellie's face was grim. *That sneaking slut of a nanny! And that whore, Kate Pruitt!* She would have taken care of the little hussy by now, if only these damned girls were not tying her down to the house.

"I'm not sitting down for anything. Any dirty whore who shakes her tail at Henry's going to pay! I'll scratch her eyes out. Filthy sluts!" While her mother groaned, Ellie worked herself into a fury. She rose from the chair and paced up and down the nursery. Sparks of anger snapped from her brown eyes as she muttered to herself.

Eleanor and Mildred watched and listened, but Mrs. Nesbit took a deep breath. "Oh, Ellie! Look at everything you have! There isn't another woman in town with such a beautiful house or fine clothes. Do you ever go hungry? No! If I were you, I'd be counting my blessings. At least Henry doesn't get drunk and beat you." Mrs. Nesbit now shook her head with irritation at Ellie's sour face. Her daughter would be so attractive if only she would smile. Ellie had to quit worrying about what Henry did as pouting would fix nothing, and how could she expect her husband to come home eagerly to a shrew? Instead, she must concentrate on her children. The girls must learn to mind her, particularly Eleanor who, without proper discipline, was becoming more sulky and rebellious by the day.

Ellie listened to her mother with one ear, until she sat up from the impact of an idea. "Mother, why don't you take the girls with you when you leave? I'll get Henry to pay for a nanny."

For a moment, Mrs. Nesbit stared at her daughter with her mouth open. "I will not! They'll be the death of me. And how's sending them away going to teach them to mind you?"

Ellie's voice rose in frustration. "But they're driving me insane! Every time I turn my back they're up to something. All day long. I can't stand it anymore!" With difficulty she restrained herself from tearing her hair. "Oh, why couldn't they have been boys? Boys get to do things! The only thing girls get to do is get married. Hooray!" Ellie declared with a sneer. As their mother ranted, Eleanor and Mildred glanced at each other from under lowered brows.

Mrs. Nesbit turned sarcastic. "Well gosh, Ellie. Maybe you should have ignored Henry and that floozy, just like I said. You'd still have a nanny."

Ellie screamed with exasperation and stormed from the nursery. She could either listen to her mother's rebukes or her daughters' shrieks and she was sick to death of both. She hurried into Henry's office, a large anteroom in front of her husband's bedroom. Behind his desk hung an ornately framed print of a fox-hunt; this picture, Ellie knew, concealed a wall safe behind it. Across from the desk, a stuffed black bear's head overlooked the office from the panelled wall. The desk was empty save for her husband's leather cigarette case and the candlestick telephone. Henry loved gadgets and so the Bests had a second telephone down in the parlour. Ellie turned her head away from the trophy bear's raging eyes and sharp

teeth and snatched a cigarette from the case. She then ran
down the stairs, banging the door behind her as she escaped
the prison that was the Best house. Outside, on the veranda,
in the sunshine and fresh air, Ellie sat down on the concrete
bench beside the door. She stuck the cigarette between her lips,
looking furtively from side to side. Then, she took a box of
matches out of her purse. Henry and her mother both would
turn blue if they saw her smoking like a man. But just like her
husband, she too could walk out the door.

Later on that day, Kate was planting in her garden. First,
she pounded a number of stakes into the ground around the
perimeter and attached a wire fence to them. It was a struggle
to grow anything at this altitude and she hated nothing worse
than seeing vermin eat up her hard work. She made her way
up the dirt rows, poking a hole into the soft black soil and
dropping in a cabbage or a cucumber seed. Her baby weighed
heavily in her womb. Kate adjusted the rifle hanging from her
shoulder and put both hands behind her back, stretching. The
day was breezy and warm. The hens clucked and pecked in
the grass and dirt beyond the hip-high fence. Abruptly, she
heard the gate to the backyard open and close. Mrs. Reilly
was just returning from the CPR telegraph office.

"Kate," she called. "I've got a telegram from your granny."
The young woman beamed with pleasure. "Oh, ma'am, can
you read it for me? I've got my hands full."
Lucille sat down on the steps leading up to the veranda
and read the telegram to Kate. The old woman was happy
to inform her granddaughter that she and Seth were well and
her brother sent his love. Uncle Noah's tramp freighter was
picking up a load of oranges and grapefruit in Los Angeles, a
busy little port town." Kate's grandmother expected to arrive
home in just over a week, depending on how thick the fogs
were around San Francisco. When she finished, Lucille looked
up. To her surprise Kate looked more apprehensive than happy.

She thought for a moment, and then said, "You haven't told your grandmother about the baby."

Kate's lower lip swelled out like a child's. She shrugged. "I reckon she'll find out soon enough."

Lucille kept silent, merely handing Kate the telegram, which the girl tucked behind her apron. It was a Pruitt family matter and none of Lucille's business.

"Here Kate, why don't I help you with that." She ran inside, put on an apron, and, in a few minutes, started planting seed potatoes in the dirt at the other side of the garden from Kate.

As they worked, Lucille told the young woman all about the work she had done the other day, hanging up Stanley's "Missing" posters. "A lot of people were scared of them. But not that Mrs. Perkins in the tea room. She said Stanley was always kind to her and her daughter, and that she wanted to do something for him." Lucille bent over again to plant a parsnip seed. "Arthur Wright let me hang one outside the door to the Empire Hotel. He didn't look concerned at all. He asked me to come talk to him if I ever needed help." She made a sour face and looked from side to side before she continued. "If I breathe a word to him, it'll go straight to Corporal Brock. He and Wright are hand in glove."

"Some of the boys from the mine won't drink in Wright's place," Kate said confidentially. "Matthew Brown was drinking there one night and talking about the union. He got fired the next day. It might not have been Wright who told Henry; there were a lot of fellows in the bar that night. It could have been a lot of people." She paused as she tucked a seed into its dirt bed. "Did you meet Wright's stepson? Howard?"

"The one with his eyes on my bosom? The spotty boy?" Lucille smiled.

"That's the one. He give you any trouble?"

"Other than not being able to find my face? No."

"Watch out for him," Kate said. "One day a few weeks ago I came out of the General Store and Howard was waiting for me. He said a lot of stuff I won't repeat, cause I'm still a lady, no matter what anyone says. He shut up fast when I flashed my knife." She took a step forward to plant another seed.

"Well, he sounds a right coward," Lucille said. "I'm sure he's not much to worry about."

"Howard will have something to worry about when Seth comes home. Seth feels awful strong about his house and his womenfolk."

Outside the garden, the dominant hen gave an angry squawk. She ruffled her feathers and charged the squirrel that was darting about at the foot of the tree where Kate hung her clothesline. Suddenly, Kate cried out with surprise. Lucille spun around and saw the girl standing in a puddle of water that was soaking into the ground. Confusion lay on her face. "What ... what did I do? I didn't have to go to the outhouse."

Lucille's stomach dropped down to her feet in dismay. She hurried to the girl. "Oh Kate, your baby's coming. Here, I'll get you inside."

Kate's rosy face began to fill with anxiety. She blinked and her lips trembled. With care, and saying many things that she hoped the young woman would find encouraging, Lucille led her up the veranda stairs and through the back door of the house. By that time, tears were streaming down Kate's face; no doubt she had been dreading this moment ever since she first realized she was pregnant. Inside her room, Lucille helped her undress and laid her down on her bed. She was shaking with worry herself. Her only experience with childbirth had come second-hand, from Lottie. "I'll go fetch the midwife," she said. "Who is she?"

Kate looked up at her from under the coverlet. Her eyes were wide with fear. "It's Charity MacLean, the doctor's wife. But..." A sudden contraction cut off her breath. Her face went from pink to red as she gasped and groaned.

"I'll bring her. Just hold tight and don't worry. Lottie had both her boys as easy as sneezing."

Lucille rushed out of the boarding house. With her skirts hiked up in her hands, she ran down the trail and around the corner. Doctor MacLean lived in an apartment above the Post Office. She ran up the wooden steps at the side of the building. Urgently, she knocked on the glass window of the door. It opened on a tall, homely woman in her late forties whose abdomen stuck out under her dress like the bow of a ship. The strange woman eyed her with hostility. Lucille clasped her hands together in appeal. "Good day, ma'am. I was told you're the midwife. Kate Pruitt's gone into labour."

The woman only shrugged. She looked Lucille up and down once then pressed her thick lips together. "The little slut made her bed. She can lie in it." The door slammed in Lucille's face.

Surprised, Lucille hesitated for a moment with her mouth open, then anger boiled up inside her. She raised her fist to batter the door again but immediately lowered it. What good would it do Kate to have a woman like that attending her child's birth? Instead, Lucille drew in a breath and shouted as she descended the stairs. "Gad! I must be living in an uncommon righteous town, with everyone so darned ready to cast the first stone!" At the foot of the stairs, she paused. She bit the knuckle of her finger and looked around. Where else would she go? She remembered poor terrified Kate and groaned. If only Lottie had a telephone, she could call her sister for advice and hang the expense. But suddenly a possibility sprang up to her mind: Mrs. Ruzicka. The Galician woman always had been kind and was also a mother herself. Lucille spun around. She could think of no one else. Hiking up her skirts again, she ran off towards the Slavic neighbourhood. Even if Mrs. Ruzicka were too busy, maybe the immigrant women had a midwife of their own who could help.

Lucille found her in front of her rough cabin. Over her kerchief, the Galician woman wore a broad straw hat against the sun. She was sitting on a stool at a metal tub, scrubbing clothes against a washboard. A few feet behind her on her own stool,

Miss Tetyana wrung out a heavy, wet shirt. Nearby, Lanka was rinsing the laundry in another tub of water, twisting and pushing a dolly stick taller than she was. Lucille trotted up to them. She clasped her hands together, ready to get down on her knees to the woman, so great was her agitation. "Good day, ladies. Lanka please, tell your mother I'm so sorry to ask her, but I don't know what else to do. Kate's having her baby and she's terrified. And that mean old stick who's supposed to be the midwife just slammed her door in my face. Can your mother help? Or is there another midwife around somewhere?"

As Lucille spoke, Mrs. Ruzicka looked at her with the same pleasant expression that was always on her work-worn face. She turned to Lanka who was skipping around with joy at all the excitement. Her daughter translated what Lucille had said into Ukrainian. Suddenly, Miss Tetyana straightened up and Mrs. Ruzicka clapped and exclaimed happily. As the woman spoke, Lanka took hold of Lucille's hand. "Mama says don't worry. It'll be a while yet before the baby comes. Get Miss Kate comfortable, and we'll be over as soon as we're done with the wash. Miss Tetyana will look after the house."

Gratitude flooded over Lucille, and she shook Lanka's hand. "Thank you, thank you so much. We'll never forget this."

She hurried all the way through town back to the boarding house. Kate looked somewhat better. Her body was more relaxed as she lay under the sheet, and she managed a wobbly smile as she wiped tears from her face with a handkerchief. She looked resigned as Lucille bent down over her. "There now Kate, I found Mrs. Ruzicka. She's doing her washing, so she can't come right away, but she and Lanka will be here later."

The young woman started to cry again, wiping her eyes with the handkerchief. "Oh, thank you ma'am. But I was a bit anxious about the garden getting planted. It's too late in the season to leave it anymore."

Lucille patted her arm. "Don't worry about it; I can finish it. We were just about done anyways."

"Thank you, ma'am, you've been awfully kind. And if anything happens…" Kate suddenly cried out sharply.

Lucille gently laid her finger over Kate's soft bud of a mouth. "Not another word. You'll have a lovely baby here soon, and everything will be fine."

She left the door open and told Kate to shout if she needed anything. She then went outside to the garden to finish the planting. In the yard, the hens had gathered together in a clucking knot, as if discussing among themselves the sudden excitement of the humans. They cocked their slender heads and scratched at the ground with their sharp claws. Lucille watched them as she worked with the basket of seeds over her arm. The lucky birds only had to lay eggs to reproduce.

Once she had planted the garden, she went back inside to check on Kate. The girl was lying on her back with her blonde head on the white pillow and her knees up. Her hands were resting against the top of her round abdomen and she panted rapidly against the pain of another contraction. To Lucille, her face looked a bit too red. "I'll get some witch hazel," she called out to the girl as she left to find the medicine cabinet. The bottle was between a small flask of elixir and a tin of baking soda that served as tooth powder. Lucille returned. She poured some of the sharp-smelling witch hazel on a clean rag and gave it to Kate.

"You want a sandwich?" Lucille asked. "Anything to drink?" Kate shook her head.

She thought for a moment, unwilling to leave the woman in labour alone. "I know," she exclaimed with a jerk of her hands. She hurried back to the kitchen and grabbed her canvas bag from the table. In addition to letters, at the Post Office she had received a copy of Rudyard Kipling's book, *Kim*. She sat down in a wooden chair next to Kate's bed and read aloud, carrying them both out of the little bedroom and into distant India. Even though her contractions were painful, Kate's anxiety eased as she listened. The shadows in the room grew long; finally, just before seven o'clock, there was a knock at the back door.

"That's Mrs. Ruzicka," Lucille said. She put the book down on the washstand and hurried to the door. She welcomed Mrs. Ruzicka and Lanka. The Galician woman carried a bundle of clean rags under her arm along with her knitting.

Lanka chattered with excitement. "I can't wait until the baby gets here."

Lucille led them into the bedroom where her landlady was struggling through another contraction. Mrs. Ruzicka laid her hand on Kate's abdomen and concentrated a moment. She spoke and Lanka translated. "The baby's turned the way it's supposed to be. It shouldn't be long now." But it ended up being another three hours.

Lucille busied herself and served the guests sandwiches and tea. As the evening went on, Mrs. Ruzicka sat in the rocking chair knitting, while Lanka worked with her needle and embroidery hoop. When she was not making tea, Lucille continued to read aloud from *Kim*. Later, when her voice grew tired, she stood up out of her chair and brought some more tea and cookies.

"Are you still going to read? I like the story," Lanka said.

"I'm glad you're enjoying it, Lanka, but I've gone on long enough. Why don't you tell us a story?"

Lanka paused with her needle in her hand. Mrs. Ruzicka said something to her. The girl rose up out of her chair and approached her mother. It amused Lucille how Mrs. Ruzicka constantly fussed over her daughter like she did now, lifting the girl's hands and checking her fingernails for dirt, adjusting and tightening her Galician kerchief, all the while chattering to her in rapid Ukrainian. Lanka turned to Lucille and smiled broadly. "Mama says a woman shouldn't be without a husband. She says you should get married right away."

Lucille stifled a laugh. "Well, tell Mama I appreciate her concern. Now, how about you tell us all a story, Lanka. I'd like to hear one. So would Miss Kate." All this time, Kate had been lying on her side with her arm over the mound of her abdomen. Lanka looked at her.

"Sure honey, tell us a story," Kate urged.

Lanka turned to her mother and said something to which Mrs. Ruzicka smiled and nodded as she rocked in the chair with her knitting needles clicking. Lanka, her hands clasped in front of her as if she were reciting in school, began.

"There once was an old red mitten that got lost outside in the woods one cold night…" She went on to tell of how a mouse found the mitten and curled up inside the shelter it gave, out of the biting cold. Then a frog came along and asked the mouse if he too could take shelter in the mitten. The mouse welcomed the frog inside, and the woollen mitten stretched out over the snow to accommodate them both. Throughout the night, six more animals came: a badger, a calf, a sheep, a wolf, a pig, even a bear. Still the mitten stretched out around the menagerie and gave shelter to all. Lucille smiled as she pictured eight animals all curled up inside one mitten.

Suddenly Kate, who had been wearing a brave face, rolled over onto her back and cried out. Lanka fell silent, and Mrs. Ruzicka put aside her knitting and laid her hand on the girl's forehead. She lifted the bed sheet and smiled, saying something.

"The baby's coming now," Lanka said.

Lucille scurried out of the room to boil some water. As the kettle heated on the stove, she found a clean basin and filled it halfway up with cold water from the barrel. From the bedroom, Kate's shrieks of pain made her cringe. Mrs. Ruzicka's voice spoke soothingly and Lanka translated, telling Kate to push or breathe. Kate's cries rose in a crescendo. Then Mrs. Ruzicka exclaimed with triumph.

"A boy!" Lanka crowed. "A fine boy!"

Lucille filled the basin with the hot water and hurried back into the bedroom with that and Kate's knife. Mrs. Ruzicka had laid the newborn onto the new mother's stomach with the cord still attached. Kate wept, both with relief that the ordeal was over and with excitement at her first look at her newborn son. After she cut the cord with the knife, Mrs. Ruzicka set the basin of warm water on top of the bureau. As she bathed the infant, he wailed just enough to show he was healthy. He lay in Mrs. Ruzicka's hands with his eyes squeezed shut from the effort of birth, his tiny hands in fists. When Mrs. Ruzicka was done, Lucille took the basin outside to dump its contents. Lanka passed her mother an armful of the clean rags, all of which had been cut into triangles. Mrs. Ruzicka turned the newborn this way and that, wrapping him up in the swaddling like a tiny cloth package.

Lanka paused in front of Kate, who had just expelled the afterbirth, and announced, "Mama's got to introduce the baby to the house." Lucille and Kate watched curiously as Mrs. Ruzicka, with the infant in her arms, chattered to him as she showed him the floor, the ceiling, and the bureau. She walked out of the bedroom, still chattering, and Lucille followed her and Lanka. Mrs. Ruzicka first went into the kitchen, where she showed the newborn the stove, the table, and the icebox. She then carried him to the parlour. After again introducing the baby to the ceiling and the floor, Mrs. Ruzicka set the tightly swaddled infant over her shoulder. She spat into the corner of the parlour to the right of the fireplace. Lucille exclaimed with surprise. "What's she doing?"

Lanka looked at her with all seriousness. "Mama's the *maty bozha*. The godmother. She has to protect the baby from the Evil Eye," she answered as she crossed herself, while her mother spat in all four corners of the room. At last, with the ritual complete, Mrs. Ruzicka handed Lucille the bundle and prepared to leave. The newborn slept contentedly in his tight swaddling. Only a short time ago, Lucille remembered, her nephews Edward and Abner had been newborns. She thought about how brief a time the baby would be this size. Then she asked Lanka to wait. She walked back into Kate's bedroom and handed her son to her. Kate already had the glow of a new mother. She smiled with pleasure at her baby in his tidy package and took him to her breast.

"I'm just going to take the lamp and see Lanka and her mother home," Lucille said. "I'll be back in a few minutes." Kate nodded as she stroked the baby's hair; it was so fine and new that it had no colour yet. Lucille left her to get acquainted with her son.

Kate was still sitting in bed embracing the baby when she returned. Outside, the Oldman River babbled and crickets sang. Kate rocked him as she hummed to herself. "His name's Albert," she said to Lucille with pride. "Albert Sydney. My very own baby. I was going to name him Agnes if he'd been a girl, for my Granny."

"Well, hello then, Albert Sydney, and welcome to the world," Lucille said from where she was kneeling at the bottom drawer of the bureau. She had opened it and placed some pillows inside to improvise a cradle. By this time, she was exhausted. She made sure Kate had everything she needed and then retired to bed. She was too tired to start a letter to Lottie; instead, she pulled off her clothes as idle thoughts ran through her sleepy brain.

Chapter 7

—w—

Tuesday, June 9, 1903

ONE AFTERNOON OVER A WEEK LATER, Lucille walked to the Post Officewhere she picked up several letters and a telegram. After she put them into her canvas bag and stepped outside into the bright sunshine, she nearly bumped into the muzzle of a tall black horse. The animal carried Corporal Brock of the Mounted Police on its back. In spite of the hot weather, the Mountie wore his scarlet tunic with its collar buttoned up and his brown felt hat. Beads of sweat stood out on his wrinkled forehead. His face was red and he blew hot air through his big nose with a blast. The horse also champed on its bit, as if it were as angry with the woman as its rider. Lucille paused with the tip of her parasol resting on the ground.

"Well, I see the Mounted Police finally got mounted," she said.

From his saddlebag Corporal Brock took the posters that she had hung up outside the door of the station. He had crumpled them up and now threw them at Lucille. They bounced over the wooden sidewalk and rolled away in the wind. "That wasn't funny, Mrs. Reilly." Lucille looked up at the policeman and blinked innocently with her long lashes. The other day, when she had hung up the "Missing" poster next to the door of the police station, she had nailed another poster opposite the first. This one she addressed to the "People of Stony Point" at the top. It detailed the runaround she and her sister had received from the authorities, and it advised the townspeople that if one of their relatives went missing,

74

the last place they should go to for help was the North-West Mounted Police.

"It wasn't meant to be funny," Lucille answered. "Oh, by the way, did Commissioner Perry say he enjoyed my letter? And have you found my brother-in-law yet?"

Corporal Brock's big nose flared and anger boiled up in his baggy eyes. Lucille attempted to walk around the horse, but the Mountie jerked its reins and it stepped back in front of her. Lucille raised her parasol.

"By God, you don't need Arthur Wright to slip me your threats now, do you?" she shouted. "If you want to threaten me, Corporal, from now on you do it yourself. I won't listen if it's coming from your human gramophone."

"I don't know what you're talking about," Brock shouted back.

"That's a lie!" She waved her parasol, and Brock's horse retreated. It reared up slightly and Lucille hurried around it out of the corporal's reach. Brock called out after her. "I'll be running you out of town one of these days, woman, do you hear me?"

Lucille turned around and brandished her parasol at the corporal as she crossed the dirt road. It was a windy, sunny day. She adjusted the strap of her canvas bag over her shoulder and held on to her hat in a gust. It was often windy in the Crowsnest and an abundance of crows lived here; presently, one landed on top of the false front above the General Store and squawked. Judging from Brock's reaction, her letter to A. Bowen Perry had made the furious commissioner burn up the telephone lines between Regina and the Stony Point station. Lucille had noticed Corporal Brock cantering around town more often on his black horse. All of this sudden activity was only a show, she believed, but at least she had goaded him into movement.

She walked down the dirt trail back to the Pruitt house. Her letter to the commissioner of the NWMP had brought the most results so far. She picked up her pace. *I should write more people*, she thought. In her mind, she put together a list: the Territorial representative, Premier Haultain, and the editors of every major newspaper in the West. She would hound them relentlessly. She would make all of these men fear the sight of her handwriting and after she had done that, she would start in on their wives.

In addition to the letters, although no one had yet come forward to claim the reward, the "Missing" posters had brought Lucille an unexpected benefit. The ones on either side of the door to the NWMP station and the resulting embarrassment to the police had amused the townspeople. As frontier settlers, they admired audacity and they enjoyed few things more than a spirited fight. This past week Lucille had seen sympathy on the faces of the people she had met, and no one brought up her appearance in the Empire Hotel bar anymore. Although no one said anything, all the kind faces she had seen made her certain the people were rooting for her.

Lucille returned home to the boarding house to find Kate sitting at the kitchen table nursing Albert. Since the birth of her child, she had shed the mourning clothes she had been wearing for Sydney. Today, she wore a white organdy dress and a bodice with a grey frill around the chest. Her plain slip-on shoes and a grey ribbon in her hair completed her outfit. While Albert nursed, Kate hummed to herself and rocked the baby, looking at everything with an otherworldly, new mother smile. But then she frowned as a fat wasp buzzed around insolently under the beams of the ceiling. Insects had invaded the house. They flew in her face while the horseflies bit baby Albert and made him cry. Every summer, the horde of flies were a terrible nuisance.

Kate watched as her boarder laid the mail down on the table and unpinned her straw hat. Lucille tore open Lottie's package. It contained skirts, barrow-coats, and head shawls that Abner had outgrown long ago. It also contained a thick envelope with a round lump inside it. Kate wrapped one of the shawls around Albert's head as Lucille opened the envelope. A trickle of sand-dry cookie crumbs leaked out of it. Kate squeaked with amusement as Lucille read the accompanying letter aloud: "Dear Lu: The boys and I were making cookies and they wanted Aunt Lu to have one. Enjoy." After the two women laughed together, she continued to read: "I went to Mr. MacDougall's office with the clippings, like you said." At first, MacDougall had welcomed the wife of his missing reporter; he had sat Lottie down in a chair in his office and had his secretary bring her a cup of tea. Lucille's dispatch had been sitting on his desk. The editor had tried to evade the question of whether or not he would print it; finally, when Lottie had pressed him, he told her he would not. Lucille's report had presented the union organizer in much too favourable a light, and he had not wanted his advertisers thinking that the *Red River Herald* supported "troublemakers." He had added that printing Lucille's dispatch would condone the woman's rebellious behaviour. MacDougall had then concluded by saying that if Lucille would come home, and cover Madame Dupont in Saint Boniface with her newborn triplets, he would be happy to print her dispatches. If she would not, she could consider herself fired.

Kate gasped as she placed Albert over her shoulder and patted the infant's back. Lucille turned to the second page of Lottie's letter: "We had a few words," her sister wrote. At this point, Lottie had showed MacDougall the clippings from his own editorials. Clearly, his assertion that the *Red River Herald* was a champion of the common man had been a lie, just like his promise that readers could rely on the *Herald* for unbiased coverage; at the same time, the paper never criticized the Tory party and forever carped at the Laurier Liberals. Mac-Dougall had only laughed at Lottie before he bid her a good day. Women, he had declared, understood nothing about the newspaper business. "He knows who's buttering his bread," Lottie wrote in a blunt conclusion.

"Oh gee, ma'am," Kate said. "I'm sorry you lost your job."

Lucille sat a moment as bitterness steeped inside her. Mac-Dougall had acted like Stanley's friend. The editor and his wife had been guests in the Birch house and, at a dinner of Manitoban newspapermen, MacDougall had introduced Stanley proudly as the *Red River Herald's* ace reporter. But the influence of the advertisers' money had blown all of that away like smoke. MacDougall did indeed know what buttered his bread, and it was neither friendship nor sincerity. At last she sighed and spoke.

"If MacDougall's fired me, I'll just have more time to write letters." Lucille shrugged. So, the paper for which Stanley had worked the past six years had abandoned him. She would have to make her own publicity by writing letter after letter after letter.

She put Lottie's letter aside and picked up the telegram from the miners' union. It said that John Rupert would be in Stony Point next Sunday for the baseball game between the local team and the boys from a neighbouring coal-mining town, Natal in British Columbia. At that time, Mr. Rupert would be happy to meet with Lucille and answer any questions she had. Lucille snorted to herself as she tucked the telegram into her bodice. From the police, she had had nothing but evasions and delays. From Stanley's paper, she had just received her own dismissal. But from the union, she had received concern and offers of help. Nothing would keep her from attending that baseball game on Sunday.

For the present, she sent her typewriter back to the offices of the *Red River Herald* in Winnipeg. With it, she included a note for MacDougall that told him where a man who deserted his friends could stick the typewriter and his job. Lucille knew she would not get a reply but she hoped the editor would feel some shame when he read it. Now, she concentrated on her letters. She no longer needed the typewriter; in her experience, handwritten letters had much more impact. Her first was to

Lottie. In it, she conveyed Kate's gratitude for the baby clothes and also asked her sister to find the addresses of all the officials to whom Lucille could write. In the few days before the baseball game, she was proud of how many letters she had finished.

On Sunday, Lucille sat at the kitchen table writing to Frank Oliver who owned and edited the *Edmonton Bulletin*. As both a politician and a newspaperman, Oliver would make a powerful ally if she could persuade him to support her. Therefore, she wanted to take special care with this message, but the words would not come together, and Lucille was getting angry with herself. She yawned and rubbed her forehead. She had slept poorly the night before, plagued by a nightmare that featured a vision of Irving's fist hurtling toward her eye. It had disturbed her so much that she had spent the rest of the night tossing on her bed. She shook her head in irritation. She had to finish this letter and meet Mr. Rupert at the baseball field later this afternoon. She clenched her teeth with determination and kept writing.

Later, she and Kate had a late lunch of pork and beans. Afterwards, when she returned from the outhouse, Lucille stopped in amazement at the sight of Kate and Albert. Kate wore a light green bodice with a matching skirt and a straw hat with a green feather sticking up out of it. She carried Albert in a shawl. The baby wore a little lace cap. His eyes were squeezed closed and his tiny hands were clasped over his mouth. The young woman looked so attractive and the contented baby in her arms enhanced the effect. This baseball game would be the occasion of Kate's first appearance in town since her son's birth. Her smart outfit was a challenge to anyone who might drop a remark about Albert. Lucille instantly forgot her aggravating letter and exclaimed with pleasure, "Why, Kate, you and Albert make me look right dowdy." Kate beamed and jiggled the baby in her arms.

The two stepped out the door of the house and turned toward the baseball field. The sun was shining, the temperature was warm, and a stiff breeze blew away the mosquitoes. They walked together past the shack next door to the Pruitt house, where they saw that the "For Rent" sign had come down off its door. Some new neighbours would be moving in shortly.

Everyone in town was walking to the baseball field. A boy in short pants and a cloth cap raced past Lucille on the trail. On King Edward Avenue, the postmaster and the telegraph operator in their blue uniforms tipped their hats to the women. Kate whispered to Lucille from the side of her mouth that it was supposed to be a secret, but Mr. Ned Williams, the telegraph operator, was courting Mrs. Perkins and for that reason the woman always knew things no one else did. His rival was Mr. Harvey, the banker. At that moment, Lucille spotted that man with his arms pumping at his sides making haste toward the tea room. He wore a brushed derby hat and a pressed coat to go along with the pistol on his hip. She could only laugh. So much for keeping secrets in this town.

The wide field of green grass that lay between the Mounted Police station and the Empire Hotel was used for more than baseball games. At the east end of the park was a brick firepit the size of a wagon wheel and some picnic tables for cookouts. Behind this area, a large wooden gazebo with a weather vane on top of its roof stood in front of a row of pine trees. The baseball field itself lay east of the gazebo. Kate told Lucille that Henry Best had paid for most of what she saw: the picnic tables, the gazebo, the backstop behind home plate, and the timber for the bleachers. The rumour currently running through town was that next year, Mr. Best was going to build a church on the vacant ground next to the Oddfellows' Hall, which would make Stony Point the first town in the Crowsnest Pass with its own church.

"Really?" Kate nodded.

"He's got his heart all set on politics," she said. "He says as soon as the Territory becomes a province, he'll be the first premier." The girl clutched her baby in her shawl before she sat down on a spot three rows behind the line from home plate to first base. She told her boarder all about the speech Henry had made last Dominion Day only nineteen days before the mine explosion. For the occasion, he had worn a snappy grey coat with matching trousers. The collar around his neck had been crisp and white. He had climbed up to the bed of a wagon and addressed the gathering of men in front of him, lauding the many freedoms they enjoyed as citizens of Canada.

"A lot of the fellows walked away saying he looked like a winner," Kate continued. "And he had all the supervisors from the mine and other important men around, and they were all nodding and clapping. And believe it or not, I saw a few women giving him a second look."

Lucille set her cheek on her fist and chewed the inside of it while she pictured the scene. *Politics are such utter hogwash.* Meanwhile, the townspeople filed into the bleachers. Chatter filled the air and peanut shells cracked as they waited for the ball game to start. On her part, Lucille contemplated what Kate had just told her about Best's political ambitions. Clearly, he was not concerned that having a young woman walking around town with his bastard would hurt his chances at public office. Indeed, to some men, fathering a bastard proved one's manhood. They would wink, chuckle, and clap the perpetrator on the back. Lucille remembered how, back in Winnipeg, the *Red River Herald* had endorsed the campaign of a man running for mayor who had fathered a baby with his housemaid. MacDougall had only sneered and waved his hand when she had pointed that out. "That's irrelevant," he had said. Lucille now sighed to herself. Women might feel differently about the issue, but they could not vote.

Soon, the people clapped and whistled as the Stony Point team jogged onto the field in their blue uniforms. The men limbered up; the young miners, a few boys who worked at the sawmill, and the blacksmith's burly eldest son stretched and ran in place on the grass. A few minutes later, the men from Natal in their white uniforms walked onto the field. The spectators hissed. The home team won the coin toss and elected to bat first. The blacksmith's son stepped into the batter's box, spat on his hands, and sliced the air with the bat a couple of times before taking his position next to the plate. He glowered at the skinny Natal man on the pitcher's mound. The pitcher wound up, threw, and the foul ball flew backwards. The wire mesh of the backstop rang as the ball bounced off it.

"Wait 'til Seth comes home," Kate said when the man struck out. "He can hit. He can make the ball sail all the way to Blairmore." Albert whimpered and she tucked him under her shawl.

Lucille would bet money that in a month no one would remember the baby had come out of the wrong side of the blanket. Right now, even among the women, only Polly Wilson and Charity MacLean were whispering. Certainly, the men in town did not care. A woman as delicate and pretty as Kate would have many suitors, for women were scarce on the frontier. As she looked them over, Lucille counted roughly three men in the bleachers for every woman. But it would likely be a while before Kate married. She had told Lucille she would not marry a miner; after Sydney died, she had promised herself she would never again stand outside the shaft of a coal mine waiting for word of a loved one. Also, Kate would never take a man who could not accept Albert. Lucille was confident that soon Kate's disgrace would fade into the past. She would marry a good man some day, although it would take time.

In the middle of the third inning, her landlady nudged her with her elbow and pointed. Two men had just appeared at the other end of the bleachers. One was a tall, heavy-set man with broad shoulders and a bushy black moustache. He wore an old derby hat and a shirt without a collar. A hound dog with short legs and long ears followed closely at this man's heels. The other man was also tall but with a slender build; he wore black trousers, a black cloth cap, and wire spectacles.

"That's John Rupert," Kate said. "The tall skinny fellow, next to the man with the dog."

Lucille craned her neck. Rupert nudged the arm of a miner sitting on the bleacher. The man, with some of his friends, followed the union organizers behind the seats.

Lucille waited until the inning ended and then stood up. She looked from left to right, then walked around behind the bleachers. Here, about forty miners were listening to Rupert up on a soapbox with reservation on their whiskery faces, while they passed around a jug and spat tobacco.

"Look lads, we ruin our health and risk our lives every day we're down in the pit," the organizer said. "We can wait from now until the second coming for Dominion Coal to pay a decent wage. They're only going to laugh if we don't join the union. If we stick together, then the company will have to treat us fair. We're being robbed now."

The men shuffled their feet and grunted agreement.

"C'mon, boys!" Rupert urged. "Sign your union card." No one stepped forward. "The lads in Fernie are going to form a local any day now," the organizer continued. "We've got to stand with them. Remember how they helped us carry bodies out of the mine last July? After all you boys went to Coal Creek to help them when their mine exploded? Miners stick together!"

The men looked at each other and lowered their eyes as Rupert appealed to the sense of brotherhood that every coal miner shared. "The company can't make profits without us," he raised his voice. "If we go on strike, what's Henry Worst going to do — dig the coal himself?"

Some chuckled at the nickname they had given the chairman of Dominion Coal. However, just as many groaned and waved their hands.

"Look Rupert, is the union going to pay my bill at the store?" A man in front of the gathering demanded. "Are they going to feed my wife and kids? You know what'll happen? If we walk, the company'll just bring in some Chinks to dig the coal. And then two, or three, or eight weeks later — however long we're out — we'll go back to work and everything'll be exactly the same. Some of us will go back to work. All of the lads who joined the union'll get fired and blackballed. The boys in Fernie got nothing when they walked out with the WFM last summer." The man talked louder while others groaned in disagreement. "And the fellows over in Michel got nothing last fall. Unions don't change a damned thing!"

"Christ, Mack!" Rupert exclaimed. "Can you pay your bill at the store now? On what you make?" The union supporters stuck their thumbs in their waistcoats and laughed heartily in agreement with this point. "The boys in Coal Creek got half-an-hour off for lunch." The anti-union miners jeered, but Rupert raised his voice over theirs. "That time, they got half-an-hour. Next time, we'll aim for an eight-hour day and compensation if your ass gets blown off. They won't give us everything we want all in one shot, no. But we've got to start somewhere. Old Henry Worst up on the hill buys gewgaws for his missus that cost more money than you'll ever make your whole life. His saddle horse eats better than you do!" The miners groaned again and began to argue among themselves.

"Union be damned!" A heavy-set fellow spat on the ground. "I do whatever the hell I want."

"We can't go on like this," a pale man said with a cough. "I'm sick from breathing in the dust. I've worked all my life and I'm going to end up in the poorhouse!"

"But I've got a family to feed!" Another man protested.

"Going up to the company and saying 'pretty please' won't get us jack," somebody else declared with impatience. "I want the WFM back. Those boys were the stuff."

"I knew a fellow in Frank who got his legs crushed when the trip broke loose and rolled over him," another miner said. "There he was, crippled, no money, no sweet Fanny Adams from the company. God knows whatever became of the poor devil."

Lucille listened to all of the arguments. The miners truly were in a horrible position. They spent ten hours a day in the pit with the shadow of death hanging over them at all times. After all his work, the most a man could expect was to earn just enough to pay his rent and feed himself. If he had a family, it was impossible to stay out of debt. Maybe a union could make a difference, but the movement needed more support. Henry Best would laugh if only a portion of the miners went on strike. He would fire all the men who walked out, the union would lose, and the defeated miners would be worse off than before.

Lucille was mulling over this problem when footsteps approached her. She turned to see Rupert tip his cap as he stepped forward. Meanwhile, the big man's hound dog nosed the hem of her skirt in a friendly way. "Mrs. Reilly, is it?"

Lucille curtseyed and nodded as she shook his hand and that of his partner, Harold Kowalski.

The organizer jerked his chin over his shoulder to indicate the miners who stood in a knot arguing. "Those boys are going to talk until the sky folds up. I've got to give them time but they'll come around. Meanwhile, we can talk."

Lucille and the two men strolled around behind the backstop of the ball diamond. By this time the players were back on the field and the home team was losing by three to nothing. The crowd in the bleachers was grumbling. The three left the noise of the game behind them as they drifted to the picnic tables a hundred feet away.

Rupert sat down at one of the tables. He reached inside his coat pocket and took out his tobacco pouch, sticking a pinch under his cheek while Kowalski wandered around over the grass with the dog following him closely. Rupert had a resilient, sunny expression and he smiled often. But he could not tell Lucille much. He, Kowalski, and a dozen men from Stony Point had searched for Matthew Brown and her brother-in-law, the newspaperman, for a week after their disappearance. The town blacksmith in Blairmore had said he had seen Brownie and Mr. Birch walk through that settlement on the evening when they had vanished, so the searchers knew the men had made it that far. The team had covered the few miles between Blairmore and Frank. They had lowered volunteers down into old mine shafts with ropes, chopped aside heavy brush, and climbed up hillsides. The searchers had been unable to find a trace of the missing men, not a button or a footprint. It was unsettling how completely the two had vanished, Rupert said in conclusion, like they had faded into thin air.

With despair, Lucille looked around at the mountain peaks on either side of the Pass and the forested hills below them. What was the point in looking for Stanley's body after the miners had already searched so thoroughly? Absently, she knocked her parasol against her shoe. Maybe she should just pack up and go home to Winnipeg. But then, she pictured the disappointment on Lottie's face and thought how jubilant Corporal Brock would be if she left. She shook her head impatiently. She could not abandon her mission.

"Well," Rupert spat tobacco and brushed his hands on his pants. "I have to go see if those boys have talked themselves blue in the face yet." He stood up. Even though the *Red River Herald* had fired her, Lucille still had her reporter's curiosity. As they walked back together toward the ball field, she interviewed Rupert. The union organizer walked alongside her with his hands in his coat pockets.

"So, Mr. Rupert, do you really think the union will help the miners? Enough to make it worth the money they'll lose if they strike? You must agree, the half-hour off for lunch the boys in Fernie got doesn't sound like all that much."

Rupert shrugged and paused a moment in thought before he answered. "Well ma'am, one day the working class is going to rise up and overthrow the bosses." He spoke with conviction. "Until then, all we can do is join together and fight. We've got the government against us. It's just made up of the same rich," he gulped to avoid speaking a vulgar word, "so-and-sos who own the coal mines and the factories and the railways and by God, they look after themselves. We've got the newspapers and the churches against us because the bosses pay them to be on their side. All the working man has is the union. The union expands," he raised his hands and spread them to illustrate his point, "and takes in every worker. We unite, and then we struggle. We gain an inch here and an inch there, and in five or so years from now we can look back and see we've changed things about six inches worth. It doesn't sound like much, but it's better than it was before. If there's no union, nothing changes."

"A lot of people say that if the miners don't like their jobs, they should just quit and get better ones," Lucille said.

Rupert's laugh was bitter. "Yes ma'am, that sounds easy enough. So let's say all the miners quit and get better jobs — wherever those are supposed to be. Then who's going to dig the coal and keep the trains running?"

She thought about this point. As humble as they were, the coal miners played a crucial role in the settlement of the West. She told Mr. Rupert how the newspaper for which she and Stanley had worked portrayed organized labour as a menace, union men as foreign agitators, and strikes as an affront to the public; miners walking off their jobs drove up the price of coal and deprived people of heat in the freezing winters. None of the papers ever mentioned the dangers of the coal miner's job or how much the coal companies truly owed the men who worked in the pits.

"I have to go down into the mine, Mr. Rupert," Lucille declared, as she dropped the notion of returning to Winnipeg. "Some of the miners were going to take Stanley down into the pit with them, but then he vanished and never got to go. I have to finish the story for him. People have to know how the miners live before they'll sympathize with them. Don't you think so?"

The organizer sighed wearily, scratched his head, and fiddled with his spectacles. They had walked back behind the bleachers. Some of the miners were still arguing, but a few were approaching Rupert to sign union cards.

"Well ma'am, I'll agree with that, but a coal mine's sure no place for a lady." Lucille's face soured with disappointment and she rolled her eyes at hearing this phrase yet one more time. "There're gas pockets," Rupert spoke in a stern voice. "The explosives the boys have to use aren't safe. You know what happened in that mine last July."

"I'd be in no more danger than Stanley would've."

But Rupert grimaced and shook his head. "I'll see what I can do." He tipped his cap to her and he and Kowalski rejoined the miners.

Lucille walked around to the front of the bleachers. On the field, the Natal batter flied out and the inning ended. She climbed back up the sturdy beams to where she had been sitting with Kate. The girl looked up at her return with anticipation on her face. Lucille sat down and told her everything Rupert had said. The young woman's eyes stretched wide with dismay when Lucille told her she had thought of going back to Winnipeg. "Oh Mrs. Lucille, you can't leave already."

"No, you're right, I can't. I'll be darned if I give Corporal Brock that satisfaction. What I will do tomorrow is walk to Blairmore and put up some of my posters. A hundred-dollar reward might jog someone's memory."

Chapter 8

—ɯɯ—

HENRY BEST CLOSED THE DOOR of his house behind him as he left for work the next morning, cutting off the racket of Mildred's screams. He ambled down the stone path to the carriage house. His mood was sunny although grey clouds churned in the sky above the mountain peaks and the temperature was much cooler than yesterday.

The carriage house was a small barn painted red about a hundred yards from the main house. Henry rolled open the sliding door and stepped inside the dimly-lit interior with its pleasant smells of hay and horses. His buggy stood up against the wall to his left and the family surrey to his right; both were covered with tarps. At the other end of the carriage house, his saddle horse thrust his head out of his stall. Henry would ride Sultan to the mine this morning. He enjoyed a good ride, either on a horse or on a woman. The exercise cleared his head and made him ready to tackle another day of running his coal mine. He stepped up to the horse and rubbed the beast's head.

"Sultan, how are you?" The stallion tossed his mane and clamped his teeth on Henry's shoulder in a rough equine greeting. His owner led him out the front door of the carriage house. *A magnificent animal*, he thought as he brought Sultan a pan of oats. While the horse ate, Henry whistled and brushed him. English bred, a fox-hunter, the stallion was tall and had a polished brown coat. His temper was spirited but not intractable;

Henry treated the beast with a firm hand, so to him, Sultan was no more than a large dog. Soon, he had the horse saddled up. He took hold of the reins and mounted. With a noisy snort, Sultan reared; Henry applied pressure with his knees and the horse cantered away down the dirt road to town.

He let Sultan run and soon he was galloping through the west end of Stony Point. He flew past the single miners' hotel on the left and the liquor store on the right. No one was on the street now; the miners were all an hour into their shift and none of the businesses in town were yet open. Henry finally pulled up the horse just outside of town on a dirt road with the rough shacks of the Slavic neighbourhood to the west. Sultan was hardly panting. Indeed, Henry suddenly had to grip the animal hard with his legs and tighten the reins while the stallion pranced around in a circle. Sultan's long ears were pointing straight back at the livery stable a few dozen yards behind them. Someone must have boarded a mare there yesterday.

Henry laughed to himself as he made the horse turn to the mine. Sultan always came unhinged whenever he smelled a mare, just like his master. At that thought, Henry recalled the face Ellie had given him earlier when she thought him distracted by the breakfast. One would think she had bitten into a rotten apple with her mouth twisted up like that. Why did the woman always have to be pouting over his mistresses? He was a man and men chased women; it was nature, the same force that was making Sultan buck and snort now. Ellie's failure to understand this was yet more proof that women had feebler intellects. Indeed, his wife's constant sulking was beginning to irritate him. He remembered how Ellie's bad temper had caused Kate Pruitt to shoot out a window of the house. At the time, it had been damned amusing to have two women fighting over him, but then he had received the bill for new window glass and the one from Ellie's jeweller in Montreal. Presently, he scowled. If his wife had any sense, she would quit her fussing and be thankful her husband was a man instead of a milksop. There would be ice hockey in hell before Henry would let a woman dictate to him.

As he lost the scent of the mare, Sultan's bucking subsided and the horse trotted down the dirt road that lead to the mine. A squirrel chattered in the pine trees some distance to the left. Henry lifted his seat in time with the horse's gait and took a deep, contented breath of fresh air. Sultan had endless stamina and could jog all day. It was his breeding, and that too was nature. The strong mated with the strong and produced strong offspring while the weak died out. Henry contemplated this truth as Sultan tossed his head and walked up a gentle slope. All the authorities in every newspaper and magazine had designated the white race as superior. *It's a proven scientific fact*, Henry thought. *Look at women and their feeble minds. Look at the Indians here in Canada or those Negroes in the Congo*. Lesser races always lost the struggle for existence; eventually, they would vanish like dodo birds and for the same reason: they were unfit to survive. That also was nature and any man who denied it was a sentimental idiot. Charles Darwin had swept aside all that love-thy-neighbour bosh like a card house. The world ran on struggle, red in tooth and claw. Henry rode on, thinking how lucky he was to be living in such a modern, enlightened time.

He would be the first to agree that not all whites were equal. On the one hand, there were men like John D. Rockefeller and J. P. Morgan. The wealth and power of these men inspired in Henry a feeling close to religious awe. They snapped their fingers and presidents jumped; certainly, it was their place to rule. On the other hand, men like the workers in his mine were by nature lazy, sullen, and stupid, *just like the Indians and those Congo Negroes*, Henry thought, and it was their place to work. When they picked up notions above their station, chaos resulted. Anarchists had become so brazen they would murder a president of the United States in broad daylight. God knew what would become of the world if troublemakers kept stirring up fools.

Henry consoled himself with the promise that one day machines would dig the coal. Why not? Nowadays, every time a man turned around, something new appeared. When he and Ellie visited New York City last year, one of his old friends from college took him out driving in his automobile. Even though a man had to squat down and turn a crank to start the contraption, and its engine chugged and popped like gunfire, Henry had, ever since, longed for one of his own.

A few weeks after that, in Calgary, he and cousin Ralph had watched their first moving picture show, which had cost half a dollar to see. Henry had disregarded the cost since the moving pictures were a genuine miracle. The film had shown a street in Chicago, with wagons, omnibuses, and the occasional motorcar zipping up and down; in amazement, he had almost waved at the pedestrians as they hurried by on the screen. But the most exciting development was the latest: wireless telegraphy. Henry was scratching his head over how it worked, but Mr. Marconi had succeeded in transmitting signals across the Atlantic, proving that it did. In no time, it would allow ships at sea to communicate over thousands of miles and vast audiences to hear information simultaneously over a "broadcast." Progress was speeding along these days. Some new invention would soon eliminate the need for a manual labour force; and, when it came, inferior men would die out and the superior class would win the struggle for existence.

As Henry rode, deep in thought, Sultan blew a gust of air from his nostrils and trotted around the bend. The power house and lamp house of Dominion Coal came into view at the end of the road. The mine horse was pulling the trip out of the mouth of the main shaft. Henry's mouth set in determination. This was his mine. If a worker wanted something, he expected the man to come to his office cap in hand, just like Ellie had better smile and look pretty. There was a natural order to things no one could violate.

In the white building that housed his office, he stepped inside and hung his coat and hat on the rack. Outside the front window, the horse's hooves clopped over the railroad ties while it pulled the trip to the tipple, the long building to the left that clung to the hillside on a downward angle, in which the breaker boys picked waste rock out of the coal and the conveyor belt dropped it into waiting CPR coal cars. As usual, he was the first man to arrive that morning. Henry always began the day by pouring coal from the scuttle into the pot-bellied stove to make a pot of coffee. As he ground the beans, Pitboss Sanderson knocked on and opened the door to the anteroom. The man carried a leather folder filled with morning reports in one hand. In the other, he grasped a Haldane Box by the oxygen tube on top of it. The canary inside the box that the men used to detect gas was singing merrily. Sanderson held the folder away from his body since he was black with coal dust from his leather cap down to his brogans. He looked like a ghost or a shadow with a pair of eyes shining in its head.

"Morning, Mr. Best." Henry took the folder from the man. Its brown cover was stained with dusty black fingerprints.

"Morning, Sanderson. The mine's producing?"

"Yes sir, but there's blackdamp in Level One near Slant Two." He held up the Haldane box. "Poor Harry here dropped like a rock when we went in. I've got the brattice crew there now; it shouldn't be a problem."

Henry nodded. Pockets of this gas, a suffocating mixture of carbon dioxide and nitrogen, often built up in the mine. "Good work, man. Carry on."

Sanderson bowed and left.

While the coffee perked, Henry opened the windows at both ends of the anteroom. It was just before eight o'clock. The rumble from the fans, power house, and tipple came through the open windows, but it was still quiet enough to hold a conversation. At that moment, Mr. Sitwell arrived. Henry's secretary was punctual, efficient, and quiet: three qualities his boss appreciated. A skinny man in his forties, he had a shiny bald head and a long black moustache. He said good morning, hung his derby hat on the rack, sat down, and was soon hard at work.

Henry stepped inside his private office and sat down behind the gleaming surface of his desk. Inside the folder, the first report was the clock-in sheet. Five of the miners had been late that morning. Henry understood there had been a ball game in town yesterday, and of course, many of the lazy bastards had gotten drunk afterwards. With his pen in his hand, he ran his finger down the clock-in sheet and docked the pay of each miner who was late. A man was an idiot if he failed to do his own accounting. He spent the rest of the morning in steady activity: finishing paperwork, making phone calls to the CPR about the supply of coal cars, and calling the pitbosses at various locations in the mine.

At one point, he sat back in his office chair and gazed at the large map on the wall across from his desk. A maze of white lines lay over solid blocks that represented the rooms and pillars, areas of coal left to support the overlying strata, of the mine. A red pin sticking out of Level One near Slant Two indicated the presence of gas. A man had to fight to get the coal out of a Crowsnest Pass mine. The face lay at a sharp angle that meant for awkward digging. The rooms and tunnels needed massive amounts of lumber for beams to support the roofs. Pockets of gas were always building up. But the CPR bought the coal as fast as the company could dig it. Currently, the railroad paid Dominion Coal $1.70 per ton, a ridiculous bargain for them since they paid $2.50 for inferior coal from Lethbridge. Henry was always seething over the lower price for his Crowsnest Pass coal that he mined at such an expense.

Nonetheless, he and the shareholders were still growing rich. *The shareholders*, Henry thought with a sudden grimace.

Although his family was well off, the capital necessary to start a mine here in the Pass had been far beyond their means. Explosives to blast out the first shaft, lumber for beams, and manpower to clear away the debris had required a huge sum of money. Therefore, like every businessman, Henry had needed cash from the Old Boys. Finding investors had been easy; he had turned a few men's heads with his accomplishments running his father's mine on Vancouver Island. Most of all, he was one of the boys — not an old one — but growing in that direction.

But shareholders were the nagging wives of the business world. George MacBain of Toronto smoked cheap cigars and filled the air with their reek. He had a blinking, confused manner that set Henry's teeth on edge, but he was as rich as God. Louis Hammond of Montreal, who owned the second-largest share in Dominion Coal, had once takenHenry's office by surprise attack. He had barged in before Sitwell could tackle him and demanded to see the books. That evening, he had made Henry stay until half past nine while he ran over the figures with a magnifying glass. The performance had turned out to be the man's idea of a joke. In turn, Henry's idea of a joke had involved propositioning Hammond's wife when he visited Montreal a few months later; Stella had turned him down but with a twinkling eye. Consequently, Hammond had grown to hate him with an abhorrence as black as the dark side of the moon, but he said nothing since Dominion Coal was earning cash by the wagonload. Last year, the company had mined 158,000 tons, even with the explosion in July that had closed the mine for two weeks. Henry's goal for this year was to mine 170,000 tons. One day he would be premier, but not if he failed his shareholders.

That afternoon, Lucille was walking back from Blairmore. Her big canvas bag, which had been filled with her "Missing" posters, hung empty from her shoulder. Pebbles crunched under the soles of her boots as she picked her way along the bank of the rushing Oldman River that flowed on her right. A mouse, frightened by her approach, shot across the path into the knee-high grass. Large rocks lay under the surface of the running water. Up above, clouds hung over the mountain peaks, but the stiff wind at Lucille's back broke them up and pushed them west, making rain unlikely. As she walked, she kept an eye out for an insect that she could catch and impale on her fishhook. Before she left the boarding house that morning, she had told Kate she would catch a fish for their supper tonight. At that instant, a cricket sprang up out of the grass making a rapid clicking noise. Lucille darted at it and gleefully snatched it up.

Compared to Stony Point, the village of Blairmore was so sleepy it was as if it had fallen into a puddle of molasses. The town had a number of buildings, including three hotels, but at that point, its growth had abruptly stopped. The talkative woman in the General Store had explained to Lucille that if only it were notfor a land dispute, Blairmore would have taken over from Frank after the slide as the busiest town in the Crowsnest. The woman said that an early settler, H. E. Lyon, had opened a store and claimed squatter's rights over part of the town site. Another settler, Felix Montalbetti, had also built a cabin in the town site when the two quit the railroad. After Montalbetti sold his claim to a lawyer who wanted to divide the land into lots and sell it, Lyon had claimed squatter's rights. The dispute had been festering ever since and no one could get clear title to the land. For this reason, Blairmore had no mine, no growth, and few settlers. But since Lucille had no part in the land dispute, the few merchants in town had no objections when she placed her posters in their windows. She now picked her way down the rocky embankment to the Oldman. At the edge of the water, she settled down on a boulder and tied a string to the handle of her parasol. A green sapling hung over the creek a few yards away. A crow settled down on a branch of the tree and squawked at her. It cocked its slender head and stared at her with calculating eyes. Lucille remembered quiet, languid Blairmore again. Perhaps the town should count it as a blessing that it had no mine.

She impaled the cricket on the hook and cast the line. The babble of the water was soothing, and across the river the crow squawked one more time and flew away. Crowsnest Mountain was a pyramid in the distance to the west. Lucille relaxed while she fished. She recalled meeting the town smith in Blairmore who had seen Stanley and Matthew Brown the night they vanished. She had allowed the burly man in his leather apron to examine the workmanship on her parasol; he had stared with impressed eyes at the iron shaft and the springs. In return, he had answered Lucille's questions. He had shaken his head firmly when she asked if Mr. Birch or Mr. Brown had looked troubled or been in a hurry when they had walked through town that evening. To the contrary, they had been joking together.

What happened to them? At that moment, the chugging from a locomotive engine became audible from the west. Lucille turned around and climbed up the big round stones of the riverbank. She raised her head above the edge. The railroad tracks lay on top of a gravel embankment about twenty-five yards away. Just then, a ribbon of white smoke appeared through the curtain of trees. The big black engine huffed along the rails. Both cargo and passenger cars made up the train; each coach had a row of windows on its side and a sign above them saying, "Canadian Pacific Railway." It was to power these trains that so many miners had died. Just as the government had intended, the railroads meant settlement, which resulted in markets for goods manufactured in Toronto and Montreal. At last, a red caboose moved on down the tracks. The racket of the train finally died; the fading *chugs* of the train sounded lonesome.

Lucille drew her line back and forth in the current. Because of Brock's hostility, she was certain the police had had something to do with Stanley's disappearance. But what could Stanley have done in the brief time he had spent in Stony Point to anger the police enough to kill him? Her brother-in-law had not even mentioned the North-West Mounted Police in his notebook. Lucille asked herself if the police were covering up for Henry Best, but that made no sense either. It was true Matthew Brown had been organizing for the union, but if Best killed every man in the Crowsnest who talked union he would have few miners left. She grumbled to herself and looked down at her line. The fish would not even nibble the hook. At that moment, a shadow appeared on the water. She looked up, then froze.

A young black bear rested on the opposite bank of the river. The animal had crept out from the dry bush without making a sound. He sat down on his haunches, tossed his head, and stuck out his tongue, sniffing the air to determine if Lucille had any food. She could only marvel at how much the bear looked like a gigantic dog, with its canine muzzle and long white teeth. Even though the beast was still a juvenile, he had massive shoulders hinting at the strength within them, and his claws were about four inches long. If the bear had come out on her side of the river the animal certainly would have ripped off Lucille's head. She blinked rapidly at this thought as the bear looked down at the rocky embankment. Clearly, he planned to cross the Oldman onto her side. She looked around and picked up a rock.

"Go away, Mr. Bruin. Shoo!" The bear grunted displeasure as the rock bounced off the boulder in front of him, but he did turn his huge frame around and lumber back into the bush. Once the animal was gone, Lucille took deep breaths. Sweat had popped out on the back of her neck and her heart was racing. She scolded herself for daydreaming. Here in the wilderness, danger could appear at any moment.

Back at the boarding house, Kate's concern for her baby was growing. Albert had seemed fine this morning, but his skin had turned a pasty white by afternoon. His nose was running and he cried steadily. His forehead and round cheeks were unnaturally hot; it was this fever that alarmed Kate the most. She found a bottle of rubbing alcohol and a clean rag. She took the baby into her lap and dabbedthe alcohol onto the rag. Albert screamed as she passed the rag over his face, and the sharp pitch to his cries made Kate tremble with anxiety. She looked around the kitchen. Suddenly, the chickens in the yard began to cluck up a racket. Kate clutched Albert to her shoulder and stood up. Heavy footsteps ascended the veranda stairs and an old woman's voice called out, "Katie? Hello?"

Kate looked at Albert in her arms. "Oh gad, it's Granny and Seth," she exclaimed with a mixture of relief and apprehension. She opened the door.

A small old woman stood on the veranda wearing a blue sack dress with a clean lace collar. She had large, bulging eyes and the curve of her chin was just visible in a mass of soft flesh. She leaned on a heavy walking stick and carried a large sailor bag from a canvas strap over her left shoulder. She wore a broad-brimmed straw hat with a red band circling the crown. Instantly, the old woman's bright eyes fell on Albert and then rose back up to Kate. She gawked at the young woman first with astonishment and then with growing anger. "What's been going on here then?" she demanded.

Albert again began to cry. Kate sighed; she could not put this off any longer. "This is Albert, Granny. He's mine. You've got to doctor him up; he's been poorly all afternoon."

Granny's voice rose. "Hoot lassie, and what is it you've been doing?"

Kate made no reply. Instead, she thrust the wailing baby into her grandmother's arms and ran to hug Seth, who was standing on the veranda behind her. Seth seemed to be twice as big as when Kate had last seen him and he also had a full black beard. But he still wore that old derby hat in which she remembered him best. He carried a heavy oblong bag under each arm and his tool chest sat at his feet. Kate wept to see him. Her half-brother put the bags down and wrapped her up in his arms. He leaned back with a happy grunt and lifted Kate from her feet, as if she weighed no more than a bag of sugar.

When he put her down again, Kate spoke breathlessly. "Oh, I'm so thankful to see you both again."

Her grandmother handed her walking stick to Seth and then seized Kate by her ear. With the baby securely under her other arm, the old woman dragged Kate down the hallway and into her room. She thrust Kate inside, gave screaming Albert back to her, and stood with her hands on her broad hips. Her wrinkled cheeks shook with anger and she thrust her fuzzy chin out like a bulldog's. Kate shrank down another size while her ears burned with shame. Her grandmother had that effect. Even though she was smaller than Kate, she was as intimidating as an army.

"Who's the father?" the old woman demanded. Kate's lips shook as she fought this losing battle with her tears. She mumbled something. Instantly, Granny's hand flashed out and smacked the side of her head. "Speak up child, I can't hear you."

"Henry Best. Henry Best's his father. But I don't want nothing from him. Albert's my baby!"

Granny was silent for a moment. She inhaled and released a deep breath. Red patches stood out on her cheeks. "I told you that man was no good, did I not? I told you to stay away from him."

Kate nodded grimly as the tears flowed down her cheeks. Indeed, Granny had warned her, but that had been part of the attraction. "But he always said such nice things, Granny. And he was so different from all the miners, with their dirty hands and always fretting about how they're going to pay their bills."

"Aw, Katie Pruitt!" the old woman groaned with disgust. "Why did you not think about his wife, while he was saying all those nice things with his clean hands?"

Kate pressed her lips together as she hesitated. For a second time, anger filled her bulging eyes. Just as she raised her hand again, her granddaughter answered quickly. "One day just before the mine blew up, Mrs. Best went riding past me in her buggy. She gave me a look that would have soured milk. So I thought that if she was going to be giving me ugly looks, I ought to let her have a reason for them." The young woman fell silent and looked down at the floor.

Granny grasped Kate's chin and pulled her head forward so that she looked in her eyes. "And that did you what sort of good?" the old woman demanded.

Kate wailed. "None! All I did was hurt me!"

Abruptly, her grandmother threw up her hands in disgust and shook her head while she grumbled to herself. In his mother's arms, the baby wailed again. Kate jiggled him up and down and spoke with desperation. "Granny, please doctor Albert. He's been cranky for hours, and his face is burning up. We've got to do something."

The old woman pressed her knobby fingers against the baby's hot forehead.

"It's all these darned flies — they bite him and make him sick," Kate added, her voice trembling with anxiety.

Granny straightened with a sudden thought and held up her finger. "Flies? I've got the answer to them."

Kate watched as she dug inside her sailor's bag. From it, she took a coconut that she twisted open and held against the wall. Kate gasped as eight wiggling legs appeared from inside the coconut. The largest spider she had ever seen climbed onto the wall. It sat there for a moment, stretching its legs as it recovered from its journey. The spider was a colourful creature that, with its legs, had the circumference of a saucer. Kate stared at it with her mouth hanging open. "Gee Granny, what is that thing?"

"This is Dinah. I swapped for her off an Indian woman in Ecuador. Mark my words, girl, with Dinah here, we'll soon have no more flies in this house. Mind, you must never startle her, nor try to pick her up. She's got a wee bit of a nasty bite. Don't you, missy?" Now that she had flexed her slender legs, the spider zipped up the wall to the ceiling; Kate blinked amazement at how fast she moved.

"There now, you go have a wee look round your new house." Granny turned back to Kate and spoke in a normal tone of voice. "We'll doctor up the bairn, and then Seth and I want to visit Syd's grave. We'll say no more; what's done is done, and I'm sure you're wiser now."

Kate hastily wiped her tears and went to fetch her shawl. When Granny declared the last word was said on a topic, that was the last word.

Lucille arrived back in Stony Point later that afternoon. As she trudged up the boardwalk on her tired legs past the General Store, she longed for a cold drink and a wash. Her bag was still empty, and she was afraid Kate would be disappointed when she told her the fish weren't biting. She was about to turn onto the trail leading to the Pruitt house, when a crash and men's shouts came to her ears from up the street. Her curiosity gave her a jolt of fresh energy. She hurried past the barbershop and stopped across from the Empire Hotel.

Here, a number of men had gathered outside the door to the bar. Through the doorway, one man carried another by his collar and the seat of his pants; he tossed him out into the alley like Lucille would throw a pail of slops. The loafers in the street cheered, clapped their hands, and doubled over laughing. Lucille drew back and blinked. It was as if that young bear she had seen by the river had come back disguised as a human: the man in the doorway had a bushy black beard, straight brown hair, and shoulders as broad and muscular as the bear's. A third man with blood streaming from his nose appeared in the doorway behind him. He tried to jump on the bearded man, but his opponent reached back with his massive hand and grasped this man's shoulder. He lifted him off the floor with one arm and threw him out the door after the other man, who lay on his hands and knees in the dirt struggling to rise. Lucille cried out in dismay and turned to look at the Mounted Police station. Of course, Corporal Brock was nowhere to be seen.

The bearded man now lumbered toward the first man he had tossed out the door. One could tell the man on the ground was drunk because of his unfocused gaze and the way his head rocked back and forth on his shoulders. He squawked with fear and covered his eyes when the bearded man seized his collar, dragged him to his feet, and bellowed above the shouts and laughter from the idlers.

"You got anything else to say about my sister?"

Lucille now exclaimed with surprise. This bear must be Kate's half-brother, Seth! The drunkard cowered in his grasp. The big man grunted disgust and threw the man down on a pile of horse droppings. He then straightened his derby hat on his shaggy head and marched down the opposite boardwalk with his sailor's boots stomping. A few of the loafers followed in his wake, pilotfish to a shark. Determined not to miss the fun, they trailed after the bearded man as he headed toward Luigi's, the other bar in Stony Point. Lucille watched the man leave with her mouth hanging open. *And Kate thinks I'm going to marry that big lout*, she marvelled to herself in shock.

She found another surprise at the boarding house. She stepped through the back door into a kitchen filled with the delicious smell of roasting ham. Kate sat at the table with Albert in her arms and her gaze fixed on the ceiling. Lucille unpinned her hat and looked up too. At the sight of a large spider, she gasped and stepped backwards. The spider clung upside down from one of the ceiling beams. The creature's elongated front legs moved deftly as it stitched a thread into a web the size of a dinner plate. Already, the spider had made several kills; these were attached to the side of the beam in tidy white packages.

"My goodness," Lucille exclaimed. "What is that thing?"

Kate beamed as she turned to her. "Isn't she cunning? That's Granny's spider. She brought her here all the way from Ecuador."

Lucille now noticed the old woman who had opened the door of the stove to baste the ham. "Well, thank heaven she brought us something to eat too. Those fish wouldn't bite for peanuts." She had been looking forward to meeting Kate's sailor grandmother and approached the woman with her hand out. "How do you do, ma'am?"

The sailor met her gaze. There was an aggressive tilt to her bristly chin and her eyes were bright. She spoke with a Scots accent. "Good day to you, Missus. Katie has told me all about you. You're our boarder, are you not?"

"Yes ma'am."

"Sit down, and have some tea after your long walk. Did you see our laddie in town?" Her back was bent with age, but she was very broad in her hips. This solid build conveyed the strength in her character.

"Yes I did," Lucille answered. "He was throwing somebody out the door of the Empire Hotel bar."

Granny heard this news with a shrug. "Aye, that's our laddie. He'll be needing something for his hands then." She took a large glass jar down from the rack above the stove. With a small pair of tongs, she picked some silver strands from the jar and spread these over a clean cloth.

Kate clutched Albert to her and spoke up. "That spider thread works miracles. Albert here was sick earlier; he had a fever and he kept howling. Granny made a poultice for him, and now look." She held up the baby. Albert's nose was still running, but his fever had gone down and he was sleeping contentedly.

Lucille looked at the baby for a moment. Then she turned to Granny and offerd her condolences for Syd's death.

"Aye well, what can you be doing," Granny shrugged. She brought Lucille a cup of tea and sat down at the table. "He could be proud of the way he went, and there's few enough men who can say the same. Katie tells me you're looking for some kin of yours." Lucille explained to her about Stanley.

"Matthew Brown went missing too, Granny," Kate spoke up

as she patted her son's back. Albert rested with his head on her shoulder. "You remember, Seth's friend from the ball team."

"Yes, he and Stanley were walking to Frank when they vanished." At the sound of an insect's buzz, Lucille looked up again. The buzz was coming from that insolent fat wasp that was always barging into the kitchen, and now flew just below the spider's web. Silently to herself, Lucille rooted for the spider to catch the wasp. For a moment, she feared the insect would escape, but just as the wasp turned toward the kitchen window, the spider darted out from behind a beam. She snatched the wasp out of mid-air in a net she had spun. Lucille and Kate cheered and clapped their hands.

"See, Dinah up there is death to wee beasties," Granny boasted. The spider wrapped her kill and hung it up on the side of the beam with the others. Then she scuttled back behind the beam out of sight. "Like I was telling Katie, you'll be fine with Dinah as long as you don't startle her," the old woman said. "She doesna like strangers in her house either." Kate tried to choke down a snort of amused disbelief.

"Aye, she gets right cranky," the old woman insisted while the girl covered her mouth with her fist to suppress her laughter. Along with Kate, Lucille also was biting her tongue. "Ye two may laugh, but one day you'll see it's true," Granny declared.

The poor old lady, Lucille thought. *She's a little unbalanced in the head. Whoever heard of a pet spider?*

Suddenly, heavy footsteps climbed up the veranda stairs. The back door opened and Seth came inside. Lucille turned around. The young man wore a white cotton shirt spattered with a few drops of blood and green trousers with suspenders that served to emphasize the bulk of his shoulders. He hung his old derby hat on a hook beside the door. Now, from this close distance, it seemed to Lucille that the house was too small for Seth; they might have to cut a hole in the ceiling to accommodate his shaggy bear head. As he turned around, her eyes met his and she looked away.

Granny reached out and took his right hand. There were deep, bleeding scars on his knuckles. "Hoot laddie, looks like somebody bumped his teeth on your fist." She sat him down at the table, and he wrapped his right hand in the cloth laced with silk.

Kate spoke up. "Did you find Howard?" She turned to Lucille. "Seth went to bust up Howard for saying nasty things to me in the street. He always protects his womenfolk."

"Naw." The young man had a deep voice. He set both his fists on the table and it creaked under their weight. "But I did find a few other galoots."

Lucille could not keep her face from wrinkling up in revulsion.

Seth frowned and raised his voice. "I'll not have idle buggers bandying my sister's name about in bars."

In dismay, Kate patted sleeping Albert's back rapidly. Seth and Mrs. Lucille were supposed to be a match. Quickly, she looked from the woman to her brother and back again. Her eyes shifted as she thought of something to say that might bring them together. "Seth, this here's Mrs. Lucille Reilly, our boarder. She's been ever so kind to me and most helpful with Albert. Mrs. Reilly, this here's Seth."

Lucille hesitated before she took the man's hand. "Good day, Mr. Pruitt."

"Ma'am."

The family ate supper together. Kate watched every gesture and motion of her brother and Lucille. Seth slouched over his plate and fixed his eyes on the ham and potatoes, while Lucille talked about her journey to Blairmore and told Granny about her sister and the children in Winnipeg. To Kate's growing frustration, her brother and Mrs. Lucille ignored each other all evening. It was like trying to light a fire with soaked wood to get them to talk to each other.

Luckily, over supper Granny did most of the talking. Early in the voyage, insects had invaded her galley. Consequently, in the marketplace of a tiny village in Ecuador, Granny had bought Dinah from an Indian woman in a bowler hat. The woman had been reluctant to part with her spider, which she said had come from deep in the Amazon jungle. But in her hut there had been a leaflet touting Canada as the "right land for the right man" and after a lengthy dicker, she had finally allowed Granny to make an immigrant of Dinah. Aboard the boat, the spider had webbed every nook in the galley and in four days the insects had vanished. Overall, it had been a long but prosperous voyage. Granny and Seth had invested a portion of their savings in Uncle Noah's cargo and it had returned almost twenty percent. With that, in addition to their wages, they had both made a comfortable amount of money.

After supper, Seth went outside to the back veranda. He sat down on the wicker chair and took a clay pipe from his pocket. As he filled it, he looked over the backyard that he had not seen in nearly two years. The chickens had retired to their coop. The tree to the right near Syd's tool shed was still there, although it was significantly taller. Inside the house, Seth could hear Lucille and Kate laughing together as they washed the dishes.

Granny stepped outside, sat down beside him on the wicker chair and took her knitting out of her apron. "Ah, it's good to be home," she said at length. She turned to the young man. "You going to bust up Henry Best tomorrow morning?"

Seth smiled to himself as he puffed. Granny was no blood relation of his, but she had been a mother to him since he was eight years old and knew his mind sometimes better than he did. "No man's going to play a trick like that on my sister and walk around laughing about it."

"Well, I'd rather you didn't."

Seth looked at her with surprise. "We Pruitts take things sittin' down now?"

Granny sighed as her needles clicked in her hands. "No. It's right and proper for a laddie to defend his sister, and I'd be thumping ye over your head if you didn't," she said. "But if you hunt down Henry Best, it won't be just a harsh word from the Mountie you'll get. Best's a rich man, so you'll go to prison. They'll put a ball and chain on your leg and have you breaking rocks. You wouldn't survive that, laddie. Then Katie and I will have lost you as well as Syd." She pulled out a length of yarn. "Besides, do you think a man like Henry Best is going to worry long over a fat lip? No, laddie, with a man like that you hit him in his pocketbook. That he'll think about."

Seth remained silent. A puff of smoke issued from his pipe. Every word Granny spoke was the truth. "Then I won't go looking for him. But if I see him around town, I'll have to bust him up. If I don't, I'll have every yahoo in the Crowsnest wanting to have a go at me."

That night, as she crawled into bed, Lucille pictured Seth Pruitt. She was afraid she would have to disappoint Kate, whose eager looks in her direction she had spied all evening. As much as she hated to say so, the young man was a lout. In addition to how eager he was to swing his fists, he ate slouched over with his elbows on the table. He was not even all that good-looking, in contrast to what Kate had led her to expect. He was excessively brawny, and Lucille had spotted him frowning at her with that bearded face that made him look more than ever like a bear. Although his family clearly loved him, Lucille would not marry that man on a bet. With that thought, she fluffed up her pillow, blew out the lamp, and went to sleep.

Chapter 9

Friday, June 19, 1903

ELLIE BEST'S TWO DAUGHTERS WOULD NOT be the death of her, though the girls tried their hardest. Every interaction they had with their mother turned into a battle. One morning, after Henry had left early for the mine, Ellie opened the door to the nursery to find the girls shrieking with laughter as they jumped on their beds, for which she had scolded them a thousand times. She had swatted their rears, and with a screaming child hanging from each arm, dragged them down to the dining room for breakfast. After that, the girls had screamed their refusals to wear their posture braces. Ellie had spanked them again. Before lunch, when she had phoned Henry at the mine just to talk to an adult for one minute, Eleanor had slipped through the door of the nursery with Mildred trotting fast behind her. Ellie had found the girls in the parlour playing catch with a ceramic unicorn figurine. At the sight of her enraged mother bearing down on her, Mildred had dropped it. The figurine shattered on the floor and Ellie had spanked the children again. After that, with her daughters screaming, she had collapsed onto the Louis XIV sofa and rested her forehead on her hands. She could spank Eleanor and Mildred until her arm fell off; their behaviour only grew worse. But she must have a vent for her frustration, or it would keep building until her head popped off.

The children riled her deliberately, Ellie knew. Making their mother furious had become a game for Eleanor and

Mildred, and what happened at lunchtime proved this fact. In the dining room, she sat the girls down at the table. Mildred perched on top of three cushions with her rag dolly under her arm. Eleanor wore a long-waisted pink dress of gingham with a lace trim around her shoulders. Mildred also wore a pink gingham dress and a white hair ribbon. A small bowl of soup sat in front of each girl. From her chair, the one in which Henry sat whenever he ate at home, Ellie pointed her finger at them both. Her eyes were narrow and her mouth was tight. "Now, you two eat and I don't want to hear a peep out of either of you." Eleanor and Mildred picked up their soup spoons. The resentment on their faces mirrored that on their mother's.

As she ate the soup, Ellie gazed out the window into the front yard. Daylight was shining on a lovely summer afternoon. The sky was such a loud blue and the front lawn such a brilliant stretch of green that it hurt one's eyes to look at them. She stared at the tall pine tree growing next to the dirt trail that led to the town. She wondered what Henry was doing. When she had tried to call him earlier, Mr. Sitwell had answered the phone. He had said that Mr. Best was down in the pit at that moment, but he would be sure to let him know his wife had called. Ellie had pictured her husband beside Sitwell while the man spoke, ordering him to lie with crisp, imperative gestures. He had played that game with her often.

She stirred restlessly in her tight corset. *If only I could do something.* One day, in a letter, her mother had scolded her, saying that if she would buckle down and earn Henry's regard he would stop treating her like a pesky child. Right then and there, Ellie had decided to learn about the mining business. She had even dreamed of going to the office with her husband sometimes to help him with his work. She had read his journals, studied his papers, and at evening parties asked questions of his associates. Soon, Ellie forgot about Henry as she became fascinated with the process of bringing coal to market. The figures for Dominion Coal's production, wastage, and net profit had rolled from her tongue with ease.

One afternoon, while the nanny had tended to the girls upstairs, Ellie had sat on the parlour sofa with one of Henry's journals open in her hands. She had paused from reading and stiffened at a sudden, unsettling thought: *If I were a man, I could run my own mine. It's not as hard as Henry pretends it is.*

At that moment, hoof beats had pounded on the gravel outside. The front door had opened and closed. Her husband had arrived home from work. Ellie had jumped up from the sofa in some dismay, afraid Henry would be angry if he saw her with his mining journal. But in the end, he had only laughed, and that had hurt more than any harsh word. He had yanked the book out of her hand in the same way Ellie would yank a pair of scissors out of Mildred's.

"You're a damned woman," he'd said. "Don't meddle with things you can't understand." Thus, the door to the possibility of doing things had slammed in Ellie's face; meanwhile, Henry had whistled to himself as he climbed the stairs to his office. Ellie had written back to her mother saying her husband had no regard for women, period. Mrs. Nesbit had never responded.

A few months later, Ellie had been certain that if she became more aggressive, she could make Henry stay home and perform a marital act on her for a change. If she were lucky, she would get pregnant again and have a son this time, even though Doctor MacLean had recommended she avoid having another child. For some reason, giving birth to Mildred had been a nightmare. She had bled excessively and the chloroform made her vomit. But Ellie was desperate. A son would make up for everything. Instead of girls, she would have a little man of her own who would make his mother proud. But this effort had failed too. When she had gone to his bed and thrust her hands into Henry's pajama pants, her robust husband had shrieked like a nun. Then, with the coverlet yanked up to his chin, he had shaken his finger in Ellie's face and told her proper wives did not behave like that. Now, at the dining-room, Ellie drew a breath and made a face. She was more likely to get pregnant being married to a squirrel.

Mildred's sudden howl brought her back to the dining table with a jolt. Eleanor's bowl of soup lay in shards on the floor. The liquid soaked Mildred's hair, streamed down around her ears, and stained her dress; all the while, the girl screamed and clutched her head with one hand and her doll with the other. Next to her, Eleanor laughed merrily. Then she turned to Ellie. In that moment, everything about the girl — her twinkling eyes, the smirk, even the sassy tilt of her head — was identical to her father. Ellie's hand flashed out and slapped Eleanor so hard she rocked from side to side on her cushions.

"You little fiend! Look what you've done!" The girl now screamed along with her younger sister, but Eleanor's cries had a pinch of amusement in them. Her mother threw her head back and groaned. She would have to wash Mildred, struggle to get her back into the brace, and put a clean dress on her — the same tiresome morning routine all over again. She fell forward with a sob. Henry was out doing things in the man's world. He was able to earn money, respect, and prestige. Ellie, meanwhile, was forced to endure a five-year-old laughing at her.

There was nothing to do but get started. "Mildred, shut up," Ellie shouted as she grasped the arm of her youngest and yanked her down off the chair.

Thankfully, Mildred quieted down to sobs, but she was still raging. She twisted around in Ellie's grasp and shouted the worst insults she could think of at her sister: "Stupid girl! Filthy slut!"

Ellie looked at Eleanor with undisguised hatred. Of course, she had to take the child upstairs with herself and Mildred; God knew what Eleanor would destroy down here on her own. Ellie grabbed her hand, but her eldest yanked it out of her grasp. The dishes rattled as she kicked the bottom of the table with her thrashing feet and screamed at the top of her lungs. Ellie pushed her off the chair. Her daughter continued to scream.

"Oh God, where's diphtheria when you need it?" Ellie did not bother to keep this sentiment to herself. She dragged the girls up the stairs. In the bathroom, she shoved Eleanor into a corner. She twisted the knob on the faucet of the bathtub and as the lukewarm water flowed, she jerked the sodden dress and brace off of Mildred. All the time, her dark eyes snapped with fury. She heard in town that Kate Pruitt had recently given birth to Henry's bastard son. The little slut even wore her best outfit as she walked around with the baby, as contrite and retiring as a brass band. Apparently, a woman had to be a whore to have a baby boy. *We'll just see about that one of these days*, Ellie thought with a sullen face.

While she was washing Mildred, she noticed a bruise on the girl's head where the soup bowl had struck her. She groaned in disgust, stood up, and opened the door of the medicine cabinet above the sink. Inside it, she found one of her mother's bottles of laudanum on the top shelf. Ellie paused and looked up at the green glass bottle with a cork in its top. Her mother must have forgotten it when she was packing to go home to Seattle. At first, Ellie laughed to think of the old woman jittering with the fidgets all the way home — Mrs. Nesbit must have nearly chewed off her foot. Then she turned around to look at her daughters. Eleanor, with tears drying on her cheeks, had squatted down in the corner under the white porcelain sink. She sucked her thumb as she pouted. In the bathtub, Mildred dunked her rag dolly under the water to clean her, her anger forgotten. Ellie reached into the medicine cabinet and took out the tin of salve, but the bottle of laudanum remained in her sight.

While she dabbed grease onto the welt on Mildred's head, a thought raced through her mind. *It'll keep the girls quiet.* She would not give them too much — just enough so they would be manageable. It would be so much easier. Good mothers gave laudanum to children much younger than Eleanor and

Mildred; some doctors even recommended it. It could not do any harm. Why had she not thought of it before? Ellie took a deep breath and helped Mildred out of the bathtub. She draped a white towel around the shoulders of her youngest.

"Eleanor?" she said.

The girl took her thumb out of her mouth to answer. "What?"

"If you'll be a good girl and go fetch a clean dress for Mildred, Mama will give you girls some honey."

Eleanor paused and looked at her mother. With her calm tone of voice and straight shoulders, the woman had the appearance of someone in control of herself. It was a strange thing to see; however, the promise of a reward persuaded the girl. She trotted off to the nursery and came back with a white gingham dress for Mildred. Ellie quickly dressed her youngest, and before she led them out of the bathroom, she put the tin of salve back in the medicine cabinet and took out the bottle of laudanum.

Later that afternoon, Lucille returned to the Pruitt house after picking up the mail. In her grey skirt, long-sleeved shirtwaist, and straw hat, she stepped through the gate of the whitewashed picket fence. Seth followed her in and closed the gate after him. He insisted on accompanying the women everywhere, including when Kate went to the General Store, or when Granny went to the Post Office to order herbs from Eaton's catalogue. Lucille did not object. Although she disliked Seth, she had to confess she did feel safer when she strolled down the wooden sidewalk with the bear. Actually, nowadays, Seth had lost most of his ursine appearance. He had gone to the barbershop the day after he returned from the sea; when he came back with his hair trimmed and the beard gone, the change had astounded Lucille. Seth indeed had striking features: a square chin, prominent cheekbones, and eyes that twinkled often with silent amusement. It also helped that he was the quietest man she had ever met. He could happily go all the way to the Post Office and back without saying a word.

Lucille said hello to Kate, who was weeding the garden, and stepped through the back door of the house. In the parlour, the carpet sweeper rolled back and forth as Granny hummed to herself. Like Kate, the old woman was rarely still, despite her age and the mild arthritis in her feet. When she did sit down, without a meal to prepare, she would take a ball of knitting out of her dark blue apron, and her needles would click while she knitted a sock. Lucille had offered to help her, but Granny had instead ordered her, with a brandish of a frying pan, to sit down at the kitchen table and keep scribbling. She was most impressed with the letters her boarder was writing to important men in faraway places like Regina and Ottawa.

Today, after slipping off her shoes, Lucille set her canvas bag on the table. She took out the letters, her first replies. One came from the office of the territorial representative, the second from a man on Prime Minister Laurier's staff, and the third from Premier Haultain's office. She sat down at the table and eagerly tore open the envelopes. But as she read the letters, her face fell. She began to mutter and clench her fists. Although they had each come from a different man, clearly they were form letters. All expressed appreciation for her concern. They spoke in general terms of the care the politician or party took on behalf of the citizens of the North-West Territory. Finally, each letter ended with a request that she mention the representative to her husband at the next election. By the time she put down the letter from one of Haultain's secretaries, Lucille was fuming. These letters conveyed the same empty promises she had been hearing ever since Stanley had vanished. Suddenly, she pictured the faces of the men to whom she was writing; all wore expressions of bored indifference at the idea of one missing reporter and his bereaved wife and children. *By God, I'll make them care,* she thought, rising from the table with barely suppressed rage.

She went to her room to fetch her paper, pen, and ink; meanwhile, she began to compose answers in her head. She sat down again at the table and made sure the cork was in her ink bottle before she shook it. She then dipped her pen and began. After awhile, Lucille put down her pen and read over her answer to Haultain's staffer. She had listed all the newspapers to which she had written regarding Stanley's disappearance, hoping to embarrass the premier. She sat for a while wondering what else she could say, when she happened to look to her left — Dinah was sitting in a patch of sunlight on her arm just above her elbow.

Lucille stiffened in dismay. Usually one found the spider under the ceiling or high up on a wall. But Dinah presently was doing no harm, and Lucille began to relax as the little creature wound strands of thread around the tips of her rear legs to make a set of brushes. With these brushes she combed the hairs on her abdomen; at the same time, she wrapped silk around the ends of her palps and polished her fangs. Venom dripped from the tiny fangs and burned pinhead-sized holes into the white fabric of Lucille's sleeve. Dinah preened in this way for several minutes with her colourful legs flexing. She moved with a dainty grace that made Lucille smile. Only the Governor General's wife, Lady Minto, would make as much fuss over her toilette.

Lucille watched in fascination. Dinah, in turn, tossed away her brushes and watched her. The spider had three large eyes at the front of her carapace and five more little beads in a crescent under these main eyes; their arrangement made her look as if she were wearing a tiny, bizarre grin. But in spite of her numerous eyes, Dinah still had an arachnid's weak vision; she felt her way with her slender palps like a blind man would with a stick. The sheaths that enveloped her fangs twitched but remained folded. Lucille stayed motionless with the spider on her arm as Granny walked into the kitchen.

"Aye," the old woman exclaimed with satisfaction. "See,

Dinah likes you, and she doesna take to people quickly." She put the carpet sweeper away in the closet. Lucille smiled at yet another fancy the old woman believed about the spider. In any case, Dinah was certainly pretty in her own way. She was deep purple in colour, with patches of orange and yellow at each of the joints in her spindly legs. The black hairs covering her round abdomen stood erect in a sign of good health.

"C'mon Granny. To her I'm just a big land mass like Turtle Mountain."

"Nay, she knows who's a friend," Granny insisted.

Meanwhile, outside, Kate stepped over the fence's wire mesh onto the patchy lawn of the backyard. Albert lay in the sling in front of her. The baby was crying for a changing, and Kate pulled him out of the sling to place him on the ground. Nearby, the doors of the large shed hung open. An array of squares, bevels, and calipers lined the rear wall, along with a number of saws of different sizes. The lathe rested in parts on the ground, and a chest of drawers that held planes, clamps, and other tools rose opposite the lathe. On a stump, Seth honed the blades of the chisels that he had taken out of his own tool chest.

"See," Kate said as she picked up Albert in his clean diaper. She dandled him in front of her. The baby sucked his fingers and stretched out his other tiny hand. "I kept all of Syd's tools for you. You'll not find any rust on them." Her half-brother grunted. He wore faded overalls and the brim of his derby hat shaded his eyes. The tip of the chisel scraped back and forth over his whetstone.

Kate's shoulders rose and fell in irritation. Sometimes, one had to pry words out of the young man with the claw hammer that hung in the shed behind him. "You like Mrs. Reilly?"

The chisel stopped scraping. Seth frowned at his sister, but Kate only patted Albert's back and tilted her chin up as she met his gaze.

"No, I don't," he said. "She looks down her nose at everybody." His eyes narrowed as he continued to sharpen the chisel. "She should have stayed in Winnipeg if the frontier's too rough for her."

Kate drew back and her mouth fell open. She huffed in vexation. Why did a match between her half-brother and their boarder have to be so difficult? "That ain't true," she declared. "She's been as kind to me as I could want. Granny likes her, too. I know she don't like to see fists flying around, but that's because her husband, who was a drunk, beat her up real bad one time. Her husband died of whiskey, thank goodness. She needs a good man now, her being so kind and all. Sometimes at night I can hear her having bad dreams. She keeps saying, 'Irving, don't hit me again'."

Seth jumped up and restrained himself from throwing his whetstone onto the ground. "Get on with you," he growled.

At that moment, Kate turned around. From next door came the bawl of an ox. Seth put the chisel and whetstone away in his tool chest and strode around the side of the house to look at the shack next door. An ox cart stood on the road in front of the hovel. It was piled high with trunks, crates, and furniture. Two women, one middle-aged and one younger, were preparing to unload the cart. The young man walked back to the rear door of the house and climbed the steps to the veranda.

At the kitchen table, Lucille looked up as the door opened. Seth came inside and removed his hat. When he saw the spider on her arm his eyes twinkled in a way she found disturbing. He spoke to Granny. "The new neighbours are moving in next door. We should go say hello."

Granny sat up with enthusiasm. "Aye lad, so we should."

She took her old straw hat down from the hook on the wall next to the door. Lucille also was eager to meet the new neighbours. Her letter was giving her nothing but frustration, so she had Granny gently push Dinah off her sleeve with the tip of a knitting needle. She then put on her hat and followed the old woman and Seth out the back door. Outside, Kate tucked Albert under her arm and followed them.

The two women with the ox cart turned out to be a mother and daughter. Seth reached inside the cart and grasped the end handles of two large trunks. He straightened up as easily as if the trunks were two pillows and carried them on his shoulders into the house. The older woman watched him with astonishment on her homely face. She introduced herself as Mrs. Harriet Baxter from Edmonton. She looked to be in her mid-forties, and was slender with dark curly hair. She had bulging eyes, round cheeks, and prominent front teeth. Mabel, her daughter, was a shy girl who wore a brown homespun dress and scuffed shoes. With Seth's help, they quickly unloaded the ox cart.

Mrs. Baxter invited everyone inside her shack. The shabby exterior of the house was matched by its cramped, dirty interior. Kate swept the floor and Mabel unpacked the family's belongings. Lucille found a tin bucket. She filled it with water and washed the layer of filth off the windows. As she washed them, she looked around with her mouth firmly set. Mrs. Baxter had explained that as an experienced miner, her husband had immediately found a job at Dominion Coal and was working there now. But all the family could afford to live in was this miserable shack. The whole place had only two large rooms. In the front room, a pot-bellied stove stood on bricks in the corner. The window in the other room had cracked glass, and daylight streamed through another crack in the roof; Seth was up there now with a board of scrap wood, a hammer, and nails. The shack had no place to eat or wash. Why did a working man and his family have to live in a hovel? But Mrs. Baxter appeared satisfied with the place. Other miners' families in Stony Point lived in shabbier huts than this; in Edmonton, the Baxters had lived in a tent.

"It'll get better," the woman said after Lucille, Kate, and Mabel sat down with her and Granny for tea at a rough wooden table. "Ralph'll be making good money in the mine. Mabel here's got a job already, too. The pitboss who hired Ralph said the mine chairman's been looking for a nanny for his two little girls.

Why, Mabel jumped on that with both feet." The woman fell silent at the dismay on the faces of her guests. "Why, what's wrong?" she asked.

"If that's Henry Best he's talking about, don't ever send your daughter there, ma'am. Not for any money," Granny said.

"That pitboss knows better. Someone ought to take a buggy whip to him," Lucille said with anger. Surprise and alarm lay over Mrs. Baxter's face.

Kate bounced sleeping Albert in her lap while she explained. "Mr. Best don't keep his hands to himself, ma'am. No girl's safe there. And then there's Mrs. Best. She beat the stuffing out of the last nanny they had when she found out about the girl and her husband. To Mrs. Best, it's always the girl's fault. Don't let Mabel go to that house whatever you do."

"Why that…" Mrs. Baxter choked with indignation. She turned to her daughter and stuck her finger in the girl's face. "Mabel, you stay out of that house!" She continued to sputter. "That's outrageous. Mabel's only sixteen. I bet that darned pitboss was having himself a good laugh! Things like this won't happen after the union comes. We left Edmonton for the Crowsnest because we heard the union was coming here. Have the boys formed a local yet?"

"Well no, ma'am," Granny said. "But we do have a Ladies' Auxiliary and we'll be having a Pie Fest here on Dominion Day…"

Lucille gawked at her with her mouth open. "But Granny, we don't have a local yet."

The old woman turned to her with a little impatience. "Well, when we do, we'll have a Ladies' Auxiliary ready to go with it." She turned back to Mrs. Baxter on whose face amusement had appeared. "The union's coming, no doubt about that. It'll just take a wee bit of time. After the slide in Frank, the mines were shut down for awhile. The boys lost a lot of money and for now they can't afford to go on strike. So, the union's got to push uphill. Plus, one of the organizers went missing, along with Mrs. Reilly's brother-in-law." Granny boasted about all the important men her boarder was writing to about the disappearance.

Lucille had to both smile and grimace at the same time. She explained to Mrs. Baxter about how Stanley was going to go inside the mine before he vanished, and how she wanted to go into the pit herself, both to finish Stanley's work and to see for herself how the miners had to earn their living. But the union was reluctant to allow her inside the mine.

Mrs. Baxter drew back and waved her hands. "Bah, if you wait for men to do anything, nothing happens. I'll tell Ralph to take you down for a shift."

Lucille sat for a moment blinking her eyes. "But I don't want to get your husband in trouble."

Mrs. Baxter only shrugged again. "Well, as long as you stay out of sight, nothing should happen. And I've a mind to put a bee in their bonnets. Mabel..." the woman's voice choked off as anger came over her face again.

Granny, meanwhile, looked at Lucille with concern. Kate's face was also anxious. "You do know what you're getting into, I hope," the old woman said. "That mine's not safe. There's the blackdamp. You can't see it, you can't smell it, but it'll kill you dead if you blunder into a pocket. The coal dust is like gunpowder — one spark and it explodes. I wouldn't take a dog into that mine, Missus, let alone a man."

Coming from Granny, these words made Lucille pause. What would she do if there were an explosion? In her imagination she heard the blast, pictured the billowing smoke and creeping afterdamp, and heard men screaming. But Stanley would have been in the same danger had he gone down in the pit, and Nellie Bly certainly had been in danger in the insane asylum.

"I have to go. Stanley was going to go, but somebody killed him before he could finish his story. I owe it to him."

The next evening, after supper, Mrs. Baxter and her husband

dropped by the Pruitt house. Seth greeted the couple as he walked out the door on his way to practice with the baseball team that would play in Michel the next day. Mrs. Baxter had made some tarts; as she sat down in the parlour with the other women, she related the happy news that Mabel had found a job as a hired girl at the Patterson ranch just east of Frank. While they visited, Ralph Baxter remained quiet. Of a medium height, he had a gaunt build and thin, iron-grey hair around the sides of his bald head. He wore old but clean overalls and a white shirt. His upper lip was partially paralyzed and on his right hand the little finger and part of the finger next to it were missing. It seemed as if the man had left bits and pieces of himself all over the coal mines of the West. At last, he leaned forward in the chair and asked Lucille if she still wanted to go into the mine.

"I want to talk you out of it, ma'am," he said frankly. "There's miles of tunnels and shafts and it's as dark as the inside of a dog. You won't have a lamp and if you get lost, we won't be able to go looking for you. And I expect it'll rile Henry Worst if he finds you nosing around his mine."

Lucille thought a moment before she replied. She told Mr. Baxter about Stanley and how her brother-in-law had never left a story half-finished. "You see, he'll never rest if I don't finish his work for him. It'll mean he lost. I can't let that happen. I owe him and my sister too much. Plus, all of those men I'm writing to seem to think I'm just a silly woman who doesn't know what she's talking about. I have to prove them wrong."

Mr. Baxter raised his hands. "All right, ma'am," he said. "We'll go Monday. But be careful."

Chapter 10

—⁓—

Sunday, June 21, 1903

LUCILLE SPENT THE NEXT DAY PREPARING for her trip into the mine. She studied the regulations and then picked up an old pair of trousers, a shirt, and a coat out of the charity barrel in the Salvation Army wagon that had stopped near the Stony Point schoolhouse the day before. The clothes already were heavy with coal dust. The shoes were a size too big but she could stuff rags in the toes and they would do. All the time, she remembered what Granny had told her of the danger. *If there's an explosion*, Lucille thought grimly, *it'll just mean my number was up. I could die tomorrow no matter where I go.*

Early the next morning, she braided her long hair and tucked it up inside an oversized woollen cap that she pulled down over her head. Then she put on the men's clothes. The trousers bagged around her legs and the hem of the coat hung down almost to her knees. She folded her arms around her breasts, which she had bound with a band of linen. The shirt and trousers reeked of coal and dirt but at the same time, without her corset, Lucille was astonished at how free she felt. In front of her mirror, she took deep breaths and twisted from side to side; a boy who looked like a young hobo looked back at her. When she crept out of her bedroom, it filled her with amazement at how easy it was to walk without constantly worrying about tripping over a skirt. Through the back door of the Pruitt house, she gazed at the feeble morning sunshine. A mist hung over the ground. While she left the boarding house behind her, a notion was taking shape in her mind. In spite of what medical authorities kept insisting, a woman's body was as good as a man's; if only every woman were free of the strangling corsets and impractical skirts, she would see that too. The feeling Lucille had was scary and exhilirating at the same time — it was as if she had been wearing chains all her life but had never known they were there.

A mountain to the east blocked the sun and cast the path to the Baxter's under a shadow. Still enjoying her deep breaths, Lucille walked awkwardly in her oversized, rag-stuffed brogans. Mr. Baxter was just finishing a breakfast of bacon, toast, and coffee that his sleepy-eyed wife had prepared. Lucille said hello to Mrs. Baxter, who clamped her hand over her laughter at her shabby male appearance. Then, she followed Mr. Baxter out of their shack and up the dirt trail that led to town. Around them, birds twittered at the morning while Baxter spat tobacco into the dirt. He adjusted the pick on his shoulder while they walked. He wore a cap of waxed leather with a wick mounted above the bill. His cylindrical lunch box hung at his side from a thin chain, along with the copper flask that held his blasting powder. He clanked as he walked, and puffs of coal dust rose up from his old pair of overalls. As they trudged up the wooden sidewalk on deserted King Edward Avenue, Lucille told him all about her search for her brother-in-law and the number of important men she had written. "All those dratted politicians could not care less about a newspaperman who's gone missing," she grumbled. "Stanley counts as much as Henry Best."

The miner gave a wry smile and spat tobacco again. "Well, I'll sure drink to that ma'am," he said. "Look, there's some of the boys now."

A few dozen miners had gathered outside the three-storey Hillview Hotel where most of the single men in town lived. They sat on top of barrels or on the edge of the wooden porch. Like Baxter, they all wore shabby work clothes and carried picks and shovels. Although the men spat, smoked pipes, and made jokes, unhappiness clouded their weathered faces. This man's eyes held grief, or that one's mouth was compressed with bitterness. The thought of the ten-hour shift ahead oppressed everyone.

As Baxter and Lucille approached the hotel, a heavy-set man with a great round belly boosted himself up on his shovel. It was Baxter's mining partner, Pearson. Baxter explained to the man about Lucille, and Pearson tipped the cloth cap he wore on his shiny bald head. Like Baxter, he carried a tin lunch box from a chain over his shoulder. He wore an old blue kerchief around his neck and a shirt that had been white in the distant past but was now grey with coal dust. Lucille had feared the man would be hostile, but his round-cheeked face broke into a wide grin at the idea of taking her into the mine.

"Oh yeah, the lady from Winnipeg. You're most welcome, ma'am," he said as he, Baxter, and the other men walked along the dirt road to the mine.

Lucille kept quiet as she accompanied them. By this time, the sun had climbed over the jagged mountaintops in the east. It shone with blinding force. On the right lay a small pond that the prolonged dry weather had turned into a marsh. Cattails wilted over the puddles of muddy water, and a swarm of mosquitoes rose up and attacked the miners as they passed. A man swatted at them and grumbled. The scrubby grass along either side of the road was brown and a cloud of dust rose up from the feet of the tramping men as they hiked down the dirt road to the rocky summit of a mountain up ahead. A white streak inside a crevasse proved that here in the Crowsnest, snow could hang on the peaks even near the end of June.

The Dominion Coal crew marched around a bend. The smoke stacks of their employer's power house came into sight. It was a large building of red brick with a metal door at one end and grimy slits for windows. It hummed like a beehive as the turbines powered the fans, the conveyor belt in the tipple, and the hoists for the coal cars. Farther on was the large, rectangular lamp house with a slanted roof covered in black tiles. The miners trudged past the power house and gathered outside the door to the lamp house. They set their picks and shovels down on the ground and talked about guns, hunting trips, and prizefights. Meanwhile, the eyes of every man focused on the whistle on the roof above the door. Promptly, at six in the morning, it sounded one blast, announcing the mine was open with work for all.

"Gosh, we've been working every day since they rebuilt the track through Frank," Pearson said. "Maybe one day I'll make all the money back that I lost when it was closed."

Presently, the door to the lamp house opened. While the men filed inside, Lucille slipped in between them and hid behind a tall, heavy-set man in overalls who carried a timber packer's hammer. She pulled the bill of the cap down over her face and made herself as small as possible. No one noticed her.

Inside the lamp house, each man took a card down from the rack on the wall. He pushed the end of the card into a register, turned a crank, and clocked in. On the opposite wall hung a large map of the underground tunnels. The locations of gas pockets and areas where cave-ins might occur were written on a blackboard beside it. After he clocked in, each miner took a small metal tag with a number on it out of his pocket. He gave the tag to the pitboss behind the counter — a short, pear-shaped man with small hands and a ruff of wiry hair that encircled the pink bald spot on his head. The boss slipped the tag onto a board hanging on the wall behind him, next to a bird cage that held fluttering, chirping canaries. The board had rows of numbers on it that corresponded to each tag. Then the pitboss lit a Wolf Safety lamp and passed it to the miner. The flame flickered inside the chimney of double-meshed metal that housed it. The miners handled their lamps with care as they stepped outside. A man who allowed his lamp to go out had to take it back to the pitboss to have it lit again; the boss would bite off a chunk of his rear and the other miners would laugh.

Back outside the lamp house, the men on the haulage crew thrust their hands in their jacket pockets and walked up a slope toward the towering wooden staircase that led up to the tipple where the mine cars were emptied of their coal. Half a dozen boys of twelve or thirteen years of age followed behind the crew. The breaker boys picked rocks out of the coal as it rolled past them on the conveyer belt. The timber packers shouldered their mallets and ambled away to the stack of lumber in-between the horse stable and the main entrance to the mine. Lucille concealed herself inside the knot of miners approaching the black mouth of the counter entry, through which the men accessed their rooms.

Across from them, on the tracks leading into the main entry, hoof beats clopped as a draft horse pulled a string of coal cars into the mine. The horse wore a leather contraption on its head to protect it from falling debris. The husky brown Belgian pranced in its harness as it pulled the coal cars; of all the workers in the mine, it was the only one who looked happy to be there. Mr. Ruzicka was tending the animal; Lucille recognized his bandy-legged gait and shapeless grey hat.

The miners filed into the shaft. On Lucille's left, a huge exhaust fan roared as it drew stale air out of the mine. She followed the miners and soon found herself in the dark. The lights from the Wolf lamps bobbed along ahead of her, but they cast no more illumination than a candle, and Lucille remembered what Baxter had said about getting lost. It would be easy to become disoriented in the dark tunnels, and the invisible pockets of poison gas made her shudder. Luckily, Baxter began a noisy discussion with Pearson about the future of the North-West Territory. He liked R. B. Bennett's proposal that the Territory should split into two provinces with Calgary as the capital of the one farthest west; Pearson however supported Premier Haultain's idea of one huge province called, "Buffalo." Their voices were easy for Lucille to follow as she made her way with the miners into the pit.

She climbed after them up a ladder made up of rough wood-en boards nailed in a vertical passageway. At the top, another passageway turned for a short distance and took her inside a large room. Baxter raised his lamp. Even in the weak light, one could see the beams that the timber packers had set in place all along the walls and across the ceiling. A curtain of tarred cloth that hung from nails in the beams divided the room in half, with the coal chute to the left and the coalface itself to the right. A breeze brushed past Lucille's cheek. Air from the fans blew gas away from the coalface, around the brattice curtain, and out of the room. She pressed up against one of the beams on the wall, and like the miners, tied a kerchief over the lower half of her face. Already, particles of dust were scraping against the delicate tissues of her nose and throat as she breathed. She wondered how a man could breathe the coal dust every day of his working life. But she would not complain.

Pearson spat on his hands and lifted his heavy stone pick. He drove it with a grunt into the coalface that slanted outwards. Chunks of coal rattled down onto the shale floor of the room. He kept swinging the pick until a rough vertical slot ran down the middle of the face. Then he chopped out a horizontal section at the bottom of the slot to make an undercut. When he was done, the heavy-set man was sweating. He scratched his bald head underneath his cap. Already he looked like a shadow, with only his eyes visible. Pearson was not old, but he wheezed in the dust and wiped his face with the kerchief he wore around his neck.

"We'll get the woman to cut the face if you're tired," Baxter said as he looked up from preparing the explosives. The tiny flame from the wick on his hat glowed. Lucille smiled. The other man groaned theatrically.

"Bah, Missus. I give Baxter all the soft work. Takes a man to swing a pick." He and Baxter stopped badmouthing each other long enough to put their heads together and call for the fireboss. Lucille hid herself between the beams. In the darkness, all she could see of the fireboss were his bulging eyes. The man carried a roll of fuse over his shoulder and a long hand drill. While the boss bored a hole, Baxter and Pearson held the drill steady in the groove Pearson had cut into the angled coalface. Lucille went cold with dread as she realized the men were going to blast the coal. From her reading, she knew the procedure was routine in a coal mine, but while Sparky, the fireboss, placed the charge in the hole and unwound a length of fuse from the bundle over his shoulder, the reality of the danger she faced struck her with the force of a hammer.

Baxter and Pearson retrieved their lamps and tools and stepped out of the room and into the passageway. Lucille followed, chewing her lips in anxiety. She would look like an idiot if she pleaded with the men not to blast the coal, so she bit her tongue, kept silent, and flattened herself against a rough beam. There, she clamped her hands over her ears and repeated three Hail Marys under her breath. Baxter, Pearson, and Sparky made jokes. The fireboss lit the fuse with his lamp and called out: "Fire in the hole!"

"Fire in the hole," the miners answered.

Lucille set her teeth and squeezed her eyes shut as the sparkling fuse burned down the length of the passageway. Five seconds after the tip of it vanished around the corner, a jarring blast shook the mine. Even though Lucille had plugged her ears, they still rang from the noise. Choking dust filled the air and Baxter coughed as he waved his hand in front of his face. Lucille covered her mouth and nose with her arm to no avail as the dust from the explosion filled her lungs. Her jaws ached from clenching her teeth. No doubt the men were as frightened as she at the explosion, but blasting the coal saved ten times the effort that scraping at the face with the pick and shovel would take. The miners coped with the danger with jokes, shrugs of their shoulders, and a stoic fatalism that one had to admire.

With the coal blasted, Sparky picked up his drill and lamp

and hurried away at the call of the men working another room. Once he was gone, the two miners picked up their shovels and dug into the pile of shattered coal.

"This is where we make the money," Baxter said to Lucille with a groan as he tipped a shovel full of raw coal into a basket. The basket was made out of heavy wicker with a handle at each end, so the men could carry it between them to the coal chute. Once the basket was full, Lucille saw that it would take many shovels of coal to fill the miners' quota of a ton per day. Baxter and Pearson groaned in spite of themselves as the day wore on and the basket grew heavier with each load. It was back-breaking work. Lucille helped the miners by feeling around in the dark for stray lumps of coal and putting them in the basket. Her efforts made little difference she knew; occasionally, as she crawled over the rough shale floor, her hands found a lump of coal the size of her fist. But it was much better than standing idle and wondering if she would come out of the mine alive. The miners appreciated her efforts. To keep her entertained, Baxter and Pearson badmouthed each other with enthusiasm. Nonetheless, it was with great relief that Lucille at last heard one of the pitbosses call up the ladder that it was time for their lunch break.

All of the miners left their rooms. Lucille kept the flickers from their lamps in sight as she followed Baxter and Pearson down the ladder and into the tunnel of the counter-entry. The men walked outside into the sunshine and fresh air. Lucille found herself staggering in the blazing daylight, blinking wildly into the stark light of the day. Every man was black with dust. At a pump that stood over the horse's water trough, they washed the dust from their hands. Charlie, the mine horse, splashed water on the men as he drank. The men scratched his head between his ears. Like a dog, the horse followed the men to the benches to the right of the counter-entry. Mr. Ruzicka tied a bag of oats around the animal's nose. Then the man joined his two sons on the bench: strapping Oleg, the young husband of

Miss Tetyana, and Yvan, a lad who worked as a timber packer alongside his brother.

The benches were made of cracked beams unfit for use in the mine. A tin pot of coffee was percolating on a tiny stove. The men opened the tops of their lunch boxes, pulled out sandwiches wrapped in waxed paper, and ate. Lucille sat on the ground at the end of the bench next to Baxter. She had washed her hands but not her face. The coal dust that covered her was a black cloak that she hoped would shield her from the eyes of the pitbosses who seemed to be everywhere. About fifty yards away to her right, a pitboss in blue overalls descended the wooden steps down from the tipple and another — the jowly, balding man who had given out the lamps to the miners that morning — leaned next to the door of the lamp house smoking a pipe. Lucille avoided looking at them and hoped they would not notice her. Instead, she pulled a slice of bread from her pocket and crammed it into her mouth, although it tasted like coal dust.

But a pitboss did see her. About an hour after the lunch break, Sanderson observed to Nelson, the lamp house man, that the new miner, Baxter, had brought his son down into the pit to teach the lad the miner's trade. "I saw the boy sitting next to his old man at lunch break," Sanderson said as he brought a sheaf of reports inside the lamp house.

Behind the counter, Nelson frowned with confusion. It was he who had hired Baxter the other day, and he remembered how the man had said that he had a wife and a daughter. Nelson immediately had thought of using the girl to curry Henry Best's favour, but Baxter had never mentioned a son. After Sanderson left the lamp house, Nelson sat for a moment in thought. He should tell Mr. Best that there might be a union spy in the mine. He put on his hat and hurried out the lamp house door.

Henry was on the telephone to the CPR when Nelson stepped inside his office. The purchasing officer with whom he was speaking, Mr. MacNaught, always beset him with complaints about the price of the coal, the quality of the product, and demands to lower the cost. He expressed all his gripes in a long whine that set Henry's teeth on edge. After five minutes of speaking with the man, he could feel his blood boiling like water in a teakettle. At last, with Nelson in front of him, Henry set the earpiece on the hook of the phone and snapped at the pitboss. "Yes, what is it?"

"Sir, do you remember one of the new miners saying he was bringing his boy down into the pit?" Henry frowned. Nelson explained what Sanderson had just said to him in the lamp house.

As he listened, Henry's anger found a new point on which to focus. "I don't want strangers snooping around in my coal mine, Nelson, do you hear?"

The pitboss shifted from foot to foot and wrung his cap in his hands. "No, sir. Yes, sir."

At that moment, Henry scowled as a thought struck him. "Sanderson said it was a boy. Do you think it could be a woman?"

Nelson shrugged. "Well, I don't know. It was Sanderson who saw the person, whoever it was." The man jumped as the chairman rapped his knuckles on his desk.

"Then Sanderson better get his ass up here on the double. Where is he?"

"He's in Slant Three."

Henry snatched up the telephone again. He reached Sanderson and ordered the man to report to his office. While he waited, he tapped a pencil on his desk. His breath came in short gasps. The day after the card game, he had called a fellow businessman in Winnipeg who told him that the *Red River Herald* did indeed have a woman on their staff — the sister-in-law of the man who had interviewed him. A damned nosy male reporter was bad enough; a woman reporter was an abomination. Henry ground his teeth at Lucille's presumption.

Her insolence, her questions, and the "Missing" posters she had hung up around town had gone past being a mere nuisance. Now she had infiltrated his coal mine. He wanted that woman out of the mine and out of Stony Point. Since she would not leave on her own, he would plant the sole of his boot in her fanny and give her a push.

Sanderson hurried into the office. The man closed the door behind him and looked around with an uneasy grin. His teeth shone white against the black of the coal dust covering his face.

"That miner, the new man Baxter — does he have someone with him in the pit?" Henry asked.

Sanderson's eyes darted from side to side. "Yeah. I saw a boy sitting next to him on the bench at lunch break. I thought he was teaching his lad the trade."

"Baxter doesn't have a boy," Henry snapped. "Could it have been a woman?"

Sanderson glanced at Nelson, then back to Henry. He shrugged and a puff of coal dust rose up from his shoulders. "Yeah, I guess it could have been a woman."

"You guess?" Henry rapped his desk with his knuckles again and addressed both men. "Go down there and find her. Tell the others to look. When you've found her, bring her up here to me."

Nelson nodded and strode out of the office; Sanderson, with the voice of his boss burning his ears, hurried after him. Left alone, Henry sat for a minute, rolling a pencil around between his hands. When his pitbosses brought Miss Apple Tart to him, he was going to give her something over which she and Kate Pruitt could compare experiences, something that would go well with the thousand dollars she had swindled from him in the card game. He would certainly add a fat lip and maybe a black eye for a bonus. After he was through with her, Lucille Reilly would run out of Stony Point so fast her feet would arrive in Winnipeg before the rest of her caught up.

Down in the pit, in Baxter and Pearson's room, Lucille was

back on the shale floor on her hands and knees, feeling around with her hands for lumps of coal. As the miners shovelled, Pearson talked with her about Matthew Brown.

"I remember him real well," the heavy-set miner said as he placed his shovel blade down on the floor for a moment. He rested his elbow on its handle to wipe his sweaty brow with his forearm. "Small guy. So skinny it looked like a good breeze would blow him away. Even his wife was bigger than he was."

"Kate Pruitt told me he was quite the character," Lucille said.

"Yes Missus, that he was. Little terror of a guy. I remember just before Best canned him, he went stomping across the yard out there one day, mad as a hornet. That ugly lump Nelson tried to block Brownie's way into Old Man Worst's office, but he shoved right past him. Oh, he was spitting angry. He was the check-weighman, you see. He said someone had been meddling with his scale while he was off on lunch break. He said he was going to the newspapers about it."

Lucille felt her heart jump. "Check-weighman? I've heard that before. What does it mean?"

"Check-weighman weighs the coal cars before they go into the tipple. If all the coal we dig adds up to a ton, then Best has to pay us our three bucks a day."

"If we're short, then he doesn't," Baxter said.

"That's right." Pearson dug into the coal with his shovel. "A man can also fiddle with the scale to make it add a pound or so to every car. If we mine more than a ton, Best has to pay us a bonus. That's why Brownie got so mad about it. Both management and the boys down here in the pit have to trust the check-weighman. That evening in the Empire Hotel bar, Brownie said he wondered how many men were going to vote for Henry Best for premier if they found out he cheats his miners?"

Lucille laid her hand over her forehead. The pictures of that "hoist scale" Stanley had drawn into his notebook jumped up in her memory.

At that moment, the voice of Pitboss Nelson sounded only a dozen or so yards away. The man was cursing the timber packers who were hauling up a beam by a chain out in the passageway. Nelson had stumbled over them in the darkness and the men, who were only doing their jobs, exclaimed indignantly in Polish and Ukrainian. At the racket, Lucille rose up in alarm. Out in the passageway, Nelson's voice sounded again: "Dumb bohunk sons of bitches." She darted around the brattice curtain to the other side of the room, away from the two miners. She felt around the cold rock wall. Her hands found the sheet metal surface of the coal chute.

Lucille thrust her feet inside it. She balanced herself on her hands as Baxter supported her by holding steady the shoulder of her coat. Pearson, meanwhile, stepped out into the passageway. He called out with great offense: "Hey! What's all this vulgar language? Can't a fellow get any sleep?" Men's laughter came from the neighbouring rooms and then Nelson was cursing Pearson as he struggled to get around the big man into the coal room. "Why, what did I do?" the miner kept saying in a bewildered voice.

Lucille squashed the thumb on her right hand, bashed her head against the roof of the chute, and braced her back and feet against the sides. Inch by inch she slid down the few feet into the coal. At the bottom of the chute, she stood ankle deep in it. Coal crunched under her feet. The chute was narrow enough for her to cling to its sides and land without injury, but it was also steep enough to make climbing back up a challenge. The dust made her eyes water and itch, and she jammed her fist into her mouth to choke down a cough. She could hear Nelson's voice coming from inside Pearson and Baxter's room.

"You boys have an unauthorized person in here," the pitboss said.

"Look around. You see anybody?" Pearson answered.

"There's no one here," Baxter said. "And somebody better watch out when he's out of this pit. I heard some cowardly bastard tried to use a fellow's daughter to kiss up to his boss. If I ever see him near my wife or my lass, he'll find his elbows where his ass ought to be, hey Pearson?" The heavy-set miner spat on the floor.

"I've a baseball bat you can use."

Nelson grumbled as he ignored the men. He walked around the room holding up his Wolf lamp, making sure to shine it into the spaces between the beams that supported the side walls. The pitboss soon approached the mouth of the chute. Lucille clenched her teeth, covered her head with her hands, and kept perfectly still.

"Damned lamp doesn't light up shit," Nelson grumbled as he withdrew his head from the chute.

"Strike a match," Baxter suggested.

"Aye," Pearson said. "We'll sit down and have us a smoke."

In spite of her situation, Lucille had to smile. She had been listening to these two miners perform their vaudeville act all day. With great relief, she heard Nelson order the two men to let him know if they saw anyone unauthorized trespassing in the mine.

"We'll be sure to hop to it," Pearson said. The footsteps of the pitboss retreated as he left the room.

After a moment, Lucille heard Pearson's voice above her. "Missus? Are you all right?"

"I'm fine." Lucille looked up. The feeble candle flicker of light from a Wolf lamp was visible about four feet above her head. Pearson fitted his shovel into the chute and lowered it down, but the handle of the tool was just out of Lucille's reach. She swallowed and forced down the claustrophobia boiling up inside her. Although now on the way up she was struggling against gravity, she was sure she could wedge herself back up the chute. She was just lifting her right leg to begin the climb when the coal gave way. Startled, Lucille lost her grip. As she fell, the miners cried out. The coal sank down the chute like water down a drain. A rumbling filled her ears and the end of a stick scraped the side of her leg. She cried out as she slipped at last through the hole at the bottom of the chute.

When she popped out above the coal car, the sleeve of her old coat became snagged on the rim. With jarring force, Lucille's right arm wrenched upwards, breaking her fall. The sleeve of the coat ripped and she dropped, landing with a crash onto a pile of raw coal. The rest of the coal rained down on top of her. Rocks battered and pounded her, until finally, the coal drop ceased. Lucille allowed herself to relax. She could still breathe, although that was difficult in all the dust. As she sat in the coal car neck deep in black rocks, she tallied up her aching thumb, wrenched shoulder, and how in general she felt as if she had just boxed a couple of rounds with a prizefighter. But at least she had escaped Henry Best's pitbosses.

Suddenly, she heard footsteps approaching. It was Nelson again. After he had searched the rooms, he had come down to ground level and conferred with the other bosses. No one had noticed an intruder. All of the miners claimed they had not seen anybody. It was remarkable how the men could all go blind at the same time. Lucille ducked her head back into the rocks of coal. Nelson's heavy footsteps approached and retreated on her left. As he walked down the length of the trip, the boss held his lamp aloft in the darkness. His rough voice echoed off the timbered walls of the passageway.

"You," he barked to Mr. Ruzicka. He then spoke in a slow, loud voice as if to a child. "Woman in mine-y. You no let her out, hokay?" There was a pause. Nelson grunted. "Damned bohunks are as dumb as Chinks." He grumbled in disgust as he walked away.

After a brief interval, the trip lurched forward with a clang. The horse's hooves clopped as it pulled the string of coal cars out of the mine. Lucille struggled to free herself. She set her hands on top of the rough lumps and swam up out of the coal. Now that she was free, she could use her hands to defend herself if Nelson were still nosing around the mine. If he caught her, he would take her straight to Henry Best.

That snake would throw me down a shaft without a second thought, and that's likely the kindest thing he'll do, she thought to herself as the horse pulled the trip toward the mouth of the tunnel. They passed through the entry. Again, the powerful daylight stunned her. She clenched her eyes shut and took deep breaths of clean air. A few cars ahead of her, Mr. Ruzicka walked on his stick alongside Charlie. Beyond him, just around the bend, the white building that Lucille knew housed Henry Best's office looked over the iron rails. She pulled herself up out of the coal car. Just as she swung her leg over the side, Mr. Ruzicka turned around and winked at her. Lucille waved quickly at him in response before she ran. When she reached the lamp house, she looked back over her shoulder. The horse continued to pull the coal cars toward the tipple. No men were hanging around the lamp house or the gaping mouths of either tunnel; instead, all the supervisors were in the mine looking for her. She must leave now before her luck ran out. She pulled the collar of the dusty coat over her face and hurried away from Dominion Coal. Her feet crunched down on the gravel path as she ran. At the marsh, she staggered to a halt, panting.

For a few minutes, she rested with her hands on her knees. Her throat and nasal passages felt like they were covered in sand and, for a moment, she wished she were back at the mine so she could soak her head in the horse's trough. But she must get home. It was possible, indeed likely, that Henry had sent some goons after her. In spite of her exhaustion and thirst, she hastened forward. She allowed herself to walk only when she reached the entrance to the alley that led to the Pruitt house.

Outside in the backyard, near the tool shed, Seth sat on a stool and leaned over his workbench. He had clamped a cedar board of three feet by four feet onto the bench. He was carving the board with a knife; every few minutes he paused and sharpened the tool on his whetstone. The knife was tiny in his big hand and Seth's tongue poked out with concentration as he scraped it into the wood. The wind that rushed constantly through the Pass made the row of saplings behind the yard sway to the left. Air rushed through their green leaves and carried the shavings away from the carving. While Seth carved, a young man wearing old clothes black with coal dust approached the yard from the dirt path outside the gate. Seth sat up. His full lips stretched open with astonishment as the stranger opened the gate and strode into the yard. Gasping, the intruder hurried to the water barrel, grasped the ladle, and drank with a grunt of relief. Seth dropped the knife and raised his hands. "Mrs. Lucille!"

Lucille did not even glance at him as she glugged water from the ladle. She was black from her head to her feet. Her bright eyes stood out against the ebony background of her face, like any miner's after a shift. Seth rose up from his stool and the motion caught Lucille's attention.

"Good afternoon, Mr. Pruitt," she said at last. While she drank another ladle empty, Seth scratched his head with his mouth hanging open. Lucille then continued on up the steps of the veranda with the big man trailing after her. In the kitchen, Granny and Kate sat at the table. Granny was mixing some potion in a bowl and Kate was bathing Albert. The baby in the tin basin cried out with shock at the feel of the water and shook his tiny fists. Lucille looked at him with envy.

Granny put down her wooden spoon and exclaimed, "Hoot Missus, and thank God you got out of there alive. Are you all right? How was it?"

Lucille smeared the coat of dust on her forehead as she wiped her brow with her forearm. "It was horrible. Those poor men. I wouldn't do that job for a hundred dollars a day." She went on to tell them how a pitboss had spotted her, and how Baxter, Pearson, and Mr. Ruzicka had made sure she left Dominion Coal unharmed. "It was a close shave a few times," she concluded. "But at least now I know what it's like for the miners."

"There's dust all matting up her hair — it's all over her."
Lucille blinked rapidly at the sound of Seth's voice. She turned
around. The young man loomed above her in his woollen shirt
and suspenders. Anguish shone in his eyes and twisted his
mouth. "Who took you inside that mine? I'll bust him up."

"You'll do no such thing, Seth Pruitt! I asked Mr. Baxter from
next door to take me into the pit and he did, even though Best
would have fired him if they'd found me."

Kate, meanwhile, fetched a wooden bucket, a sponge, and one
of Lucille's clean skirts. As she pressed these into the boarder's
hands, Granny said to Seth, "Now laddie, don't you be getting
all excited. Here, if you want to do some good, you'll keep
watch while Missus has a wash in the river."

Lucille took the sponge and bucket in her hands and glanced
at Seth. She was longing for a bath, but she did not want him
anywhere near her while she washed. The frown had vanished
from the young man's face; his eyes now twinkled and his white
teeth showed in a grin. Lucille kept a wary eye on him as she
walked back down the stairs of the veranda.

On her way to the river, she noticed the board clamped
to Seth's workbench. She peered at the carving. A toy train
ran in a relief three inches wide just underneath the top of
the board. The little engine stood out in remarkable detail
with pistons, wheels, even a plume of smoke rising from the
smokestack. Along the tracks, tiny drums, blocks with letters
on them, tin soldiers, and other toys lay scattered. The detail
in the carving was amazing. Lucille could only stand with her
mouth open as she gazed at it. Seth waited beside her with
his chest puffed out.

"My gosh Mr. Pruitt, it's lovely" Lucille said at last.

The young man grunted and shrugged. "Baby Albert should
have a proper cradle."

She looked again at the man's broad shoulders and large
hands with scars on his knuckles. It amazed her how he could
use those hands both to smash in the teeth of a barroom lout

and carve this wonderful relief on a cradle for his sister's baby. With a new eye, she saw his broad forehead, bright eyes, and the feathery brown whiskers on his cheeks. *What a strange young man Kate's brother is*, Lucille thought, as she made her way down the narrow trail through the bushes to the river.

She picked her way with care down the slope of the rocky embankment. Seth sat down on the edge of the riverbank within shouting distance but with his back turned to her. He lit his clay pipe and began to whittle at a block of wood. The Oldman River rushed by Lucille's feet, running swiftly over large rocks. Occasionally a fish jumped. She set the bucket, sponge, and soap down with care on a rock and frowned at her battered state while she eased off the coat with its ripped sleeve. Her abdomen and legs all felt stretched out of shape, as if a blacksmith had pounded them with a hammer, and her right arm was stiff and painful.

As Lucille undressed, she shook out her hair and a cloud of black dust rose up around her head. She drew up a bucket of water and cried out at how cold it was. But it was wet, and the cold eased her aching arms. At one point, she gritted her teeth and dunked her hair in the icy Oldman. When she jerked it back up, a stain of coal dust was dissipating quickly in the flowing water. How could the miners not get sick breathing in that dirt for ten hours a day?

"Mr. Pruitt," she called out while she was in the middle of washing. She wanted to know the young man was staying where she had left him.

"Yes?"

"Kate told me you were a prizefighter."

"I had a couple fights when we were still in Lethbridge."

"What made you quit?"

"I wouldn't take any dives in the ring. Don't never bet money on a prizefight, Missus Reilly. They're all fixed."

Lucille scrubbed the bar of soap through the length of her hair. Although the water in the Oldman could chill beer, the sun was warm. In a bush on the opposite bank, a flock of tiny brown sparrows twittered a chorus.

"So you decided to be a sailor instead?"

"Yes. Only I don't think I'll be going to sea anymore. Granny can't make another voyage because of the arthritis in her feet. It was only fun when Granny was aboard. She'd take her frying pan and clobber anyone from Uncle Noah on down, if they gave her any malarkey." Lucille smiled to herself. The other sailors on the tramp freighter must have been terrified of the old woman. "Granny don't take nothing sitting down," Seth continued with pride. At last, Lucille was as clean as she was going to get. She put on the dress and climbed back up the rocks with the bucket in her hand.

That evening, when she was writing to Lottie, Lucille put her pen down for a moment and squeezed her cramping hand. She had just finished telling her sister about her adventure in the coal mine, and what she had found out about Brown the check-weighman, and the tampering with the hoist scale. Now she should write her about Mr. Pruitt and the cradle he was making for Albert. But she hesitated. She remembered the carving on the side of the cradle. How could she ever have thought of Mr. Pruitt — Seth — as a lout? Even if he were a terror outside the house — he had spent one night in Corporal Brock's jail already for brawling — inside the house, he was a dutiful son to Granny and a loyal brother to Kate. Before she could stomp her foot down on the thought, Lucille wondered what he would be like as a husband.

She took a deep breath as alarm filled her. She rose up from the kitchen table and paced around. She could not fall in love with Seth — it was impossible. She would go home to Winnipeg one of these days and never see him again. To her dismay, at that prospect, her lips trembled and her stomach dropped to the floor. She bit the inside of her cheek and thumped her fist on the table. The last thing she needed was to start mooning over a man who didn't even like her; she needed that even less than another husband. She must avoid Seth as much as she could from now on, or she would not be able to leave Stony Point when the time came. Still, she wrote Lottie that Kate's half-brother had turned out to be a pleasant young man, now that she had gotten to know him a little.

Chapter 11

—m—

Wednesday, June 24, 1903

LATE IN THE AFTERNOON, Seth was drinking root beer in Luigi's bar at the western edge of Stony Point. Today, Granny was holding her first meeting of the UMWA Ladies' Auxiliary in the Pruitt house. Nearly a dozen women, including Mrs. Baxter, Mrs. Ruzicka, and other miners' wives had gathered in the parlour of the house to plan the Pie Fest they were going to hold on Dominion Day next week. Seth was glad then to relax in the company of men. He also liked this bar that had taken over from the Empire Hotel as the miners' choice in Stony Point. The men, who all dropped in after their shift tired and wanting a beer, never pestered him nor mentioned Kate's name.

Seth waited until he was certain all the women would be gone from the house before leaving the bar. He then tipped Luigi a nickel and walked out the door. An abundance of daylight remained this early in the evening. He adjusted his derby on his head and gripped his suspenders in his hands as he walked along the wooden sidewalk. But he froze when he approached the Empire Hotel. Arthur Wright's stepson had just set foot out the door. Fragrant pomade slicked down Howard's hair. He also wore a store-bought jacket and trousers. His woollen cap sat on his head at a rakish angle. Tomorrow was his day off, and he was on his way to the brothel that stood just off the railroad tracks a few miles west of town. Howard had been dodging Seth ever since he had heard Kate Pruitt's prizefighter

144

brother was back from the sea, but it was impossible to elude the man forever in tiny Stony Point.

To onlookers, Seth appeared to suddenly grow by two sizes. His shoulders expanded under their suspenders and he stretched up to his full height. One of the butcher's sons who was walking by drew back in alarm at the look of murder in the big man's eyes. He scrambled out of the way into the broad dirt road.

"Boy!" Seth barked. Howard's head swung around. He paled, his lower jaw dropped, and his eyes shot wide open as he retreated with his hands up. Seth's boots stomped as he charged up the boards. "You got something to say to my sister?"

Howard spun around and ran. Seth bolted after him while a number of idlers on the scene laughed and cheered. The noise they made drew more spectators; faces appeared in windows and a few men stepped out of the Empire Hotel bar to watch the fun.

Seth's pursuit of Howard lasted only a few seconds. As he ran, he thrust his leg out and tripped the hotel boy. Howard cried out, flew forward, and landed with a crash on the boards. The wood scraped the skin off his hands and bit into his knees. Trembling, the human opossum rolled up with his hands clasped behind his head and his knees pressed into his round belly.

"Aw c'mon, Pruitt!" he cried. "I was just jokin' with her." Seth bent down and grasped the back of Howard's collar with his left hand; at the same time, he raised his right fist. "Get up!" he roared.

Howard cried out again as the big man dragged him to his feet. He blubbered and covered his face. The instant he was upright, the hotel boy dropped to his knees again and curled back up on the wooden sidewalk. The spectators pointed and jeered. Seth pushed his hat back and forth on his head; his mouth hung open in amazement at the shameless display of cowardice. He growled with rage and seized Howard's collar again.

"My stepfather! He told Henry Worst about the union man and that reporter from Winnipeg! When they left for Frank!"

Instantly silence fell. The laughter died and the grins evaporated from the faces of the men around them. They gasped and exchanged looks.

Seth lowered his fist. "You lie!"

Howard covered his face again and screamed in desperation. "No! He was watching from one of the rooms. He ran down and used the phone in the front lobby when he saw them leave the tea room. It's true!"

"Then you're telling the Mounties." Howard moaned in protest as Seth grasped him by his ear. He marched the hotel boy down the wooden sidewalk toward the NWMP station. They left the miners behind them. All of the witnesses to what Howard had said joined together in a knot and muttered among themselves.

Soon, Seth and Howard arrived at the station. Seth lifted his right foot and pushed Howard ahead of him. The hotel boy's arms flailed as he staggered up the stairs. Corporal Brock opened the door, wearing his red tunic and dark riding pants.

"What's going on?"

"Howard the coward here's got a story to tell you." Seth jerked his chin in the young man's direction. The hotel boy wrung his hands and wobbled in front of the corporal, his knees rattling in his expensive trousers.

Displeasure wrinkled the Mountie's forehead. "Well, whatever he says is no good if you're beating it out of him."

"Either he talks or I'll bust him up," Seth declared.

Corporal Brock turned back to Howard. "You got something to tell me, mister?"

Howard's fat cheeks shook as he chewed his lips. He glanced at Seth whose narrowed eyes and large, clenched fists turned his bowels to water. "My stepfather..." he stammered.

Brock jerked his head to indicate the interior of the station. "C'mon inside. I've got to take this down."

Seth climbed up one step to follow the two men, but the Mountie pushed him back. "Not you! You go about your business."

Seth took a deep breath. "He lipped off to my sister. What will you be doin' about that?"

"Nothing, until you make a complaint." Seth grumbled and spat on the ground.

At that moment, Arthur Wright appeared. He was still wearing his black trousers, white shirt, and leather apron from the bar. Moisture gleamed on his red cheeks and he puffed for breath like a locomotive. He powered his thickset frame up the boardwalk. A wispy shock of his grey hair stood up in alarm. At the sight of the Mountie, he waved his arm urgently. "Corporal, have you got that fool boy in the station?" he demanded. At Wright's approach, Seth drew back and watched the hotel man with surprise. "That boy's so full of shit that if I needed any I could squeeze his head," the hotel man continued. "And if he thought it would spare him a beating, he'd say he's the man in the moon."

"If Howard's full of shit, what are you so anxious about?" Seth asked.

Wright spun around to face him. "Mind your own business, you damned oaf. And leave my family alone." Seth's arms drifted to his sides. He took one step toward the hotel man.

Corporal Brock jumped down the stairs to ground level. His arm flashed out and blocked Seth. "Pruitt! I'll put you in jail if you start anything!"

"Howard didn't leave my sister alone. He'll be able to scratch his elbow with his foot when I'm done with him."

"That's it! Get your ass home. Now! Or I'll lock you up. Move it!" Corporal Brock shouted.

Seth scowled at the red tunic the Mountie wore. He longed to bust up Arthur Wright, but it would grieve his womenfolk if he went to jail again. Instead, he turned toward home. Before he strode away in the direction of First Street, he looked back over his shoulder. In the distance behind him, Wright cuffed Howard up the back of his head as he marched the boy back up King Edward Avenue toward the hotel. In spite of the man's angry demeanour, Seth was sure Wright must be relieved at how he had taken Howard away from the station before the boy could say anything to Corporal Brock. His own anger receded. Deep in thought, he stepped through the back door into his house.

He found the women busy cleaning up from the meeting and preparing supper. Kate was at the stove with Albert under her left arm and a wooden spoon in her right hand. She spooned juice over the joint of beef sizzling in a tin pan. Lucille, who wore an old blue apron of Kate's, was drying the china cups and saucers. She picked them up with care out of the tin basin in which she had just washed them. Granny was chopping carrots at the kitchen table; as she worked her knife, she said how handy it was to have a secretary in the house to take minutes. She jerked her chin at Lucille. Dinah too was busy. The spider had webbed a corner of the ceiling opposite the back door; presently, her long front legs clawed the air while she reeled in a horsefly she had caught. The exhausted insect struggled feebly until Dinah grasped it and crunched her fangs through its body, injecting it with her venom. She then meticulously wrapped her kill, rotating the insect until it was cocooned.

"Well laddie, all the scary women are gone and you can sit down and relax," Granny said as she turned to Seth.

The young man hung up his hat. "Well, I'd like to relax," he said. "But I found out something in town. It's about Mrs. Reilly's brother-in-law."

Lucille jumped. "Stanley! Has someone found him?"

Seth turned red and shuffled his feet as she looked at him with an excited, hopeful face. Kate turned away and jiggled Albert to hide her triumph. Seth took a bottle of root beer from the icebox and sat down at the end of the kitchen table. As he drank, he told the women everything that had happened. "At first I thought Howard was lying when he said what he did," he concluded. "But Wright was so worked up about it that now I think he was telling the truth."

"That snake." Lucille tore off her apron. She strode to the door and took down her straw hat.

"Where are you going?" Kate asked.

"To the Empire. Wright's going to tell me where Stanley is."

Granny looked up from her carrots and said, "You may as well sit down, Missus. Wright'll be in the bar and you can't go in there." Lucille paused with her hand around the brass knob of the door. Wright would not hesitate to call the Mountie this time. She could already hear Corporal Brock's laughter as he forced her onto the next train out of Stony Point. She hung her hat back up on the hook and sat down.

"He can't stay in that bar forever. I'm going to go down there and he'll tell me what he did," she declared.

Seth spoke up. "I'd rather it was me doing that, Mrs. Reilly."

She looked at him with appreciation. "That's kind of you Mr. Pruitt, but Stanley was my brother-in-law."

"Matthew Brown was my friend."

Lucille fell silent. She pressed her lips together in thought. "Well then, we'll both go to the hotel," she said at last.

The next day, just before noon, she took Seth's arm and walked with him up First Street toward the Empire. She wore her blue skirt and bodice with the wide frill around the shoulders. With her parasol securely in her right hand, she strolled with Seth up the dirt road. He wore his derby hat, a black waistcoat over the top of his union suit, and dark green trousers. Lucille looked at him walking the gravel trail next to her. *I wouldn't call this avoiding him*, she thought with a wry face. Last night, she had been wondering why Howard had said what he had to Seth, until it struck her that the townspeople had seen her out walking with the ex-prizefighter so often — he always accompanied the women when they went out — they must have figured he was her beau. Lucille had groaned, but all she could do against the might of small-town gossip was ignore it. But now she realized it could also work in her favour.

"I'll bet Wright's in some hot water now," she said to the young man as they walked. "It sounds like a lot of men heard what Howard said." She smiled to herself as she pictured the hotel man's awkward situation. Every man who had been outside the Empire yesterday had told another man about the incident; that man told another, and like a flame creeping from one blade of grass to the next, the word had spread all over Stony Point. Wright was likely finished in the town. At the very least, none of the miners would drink in the bar anymore, and Wright would be lucky if the men did not find other ways to retaliate against him.

Lucille raised her feet over the damp ground. It had finally rained in the Crowsnest, pouring until noon, and giving the town relief from dust and the menace of fire. Although the leaves were still soaked, the sun was gleaming and white clouds that had brought the shower split up against the mountain peaks. "Mr. Pruitt, I agree with you that Howard deserved a walloping," Lucille said as they passed the door of the barbershop. "But you're going to get hurt fighting one of these days. I'm sure Granny and Kate want to keep you safe and sound with them."

Seth laughed. "But Mrs. Reilly, you're fighting too. Just not with your fists."

"But that's different. I'm fighting for principles."

"So am I." Lucille's mouth fell open, but she was unable to argue. At the grin Seth gave her, a spear jabbed into her stomach. She turned away.

A few minutes later, as they were just about to cross King Edward Avenue, a horse pulling a buggy trotted down the other side of the street. A woman sat in the buggy behind the driver. She wore a dark blue bodice with a high neck collar and white lace that was tucked and gathered on the front. Lucille gasped with admiration at her hat; it was covered in blue silk with the brim turned up on the left side and trimmed with a looped ribbon and white ostrich feathers. The woman turned to look at her and Seth as she sped by in the buggy. She had a spotless complexion with feathery eyebrows, dark brown hair, and a delicate mouth. But at the same time, she had a proud tilt to her head and hostility smouldered in her eyes. The extent to which it had distorted the woman's face was frightening. As her buggy passed, her eyes fixed on Seth. For an instant, surprise replaced her pride. Her head turned completely around like an owl's as the buggy rattled on down the street. "That's Mrs. Best," Seth observed.

It must be — no other woman in town could afford to dress that well. As she crossed the dirt road, Lucille found herself gazing after the buggy. Whenever she had thought of Henry's wife, and why he was so unfaithful, she had pictured a plain old stick. But the reality dashed that vision. If not for the anger on her face, Mrs. Best would have been a strikingly lovely woman. She needed only a few more years with Henry before all that beauty evaporated and she turned into a wolverine. Lucille rolled her eyes and thanked her stars that Henry Best was not her husband.

She and Seth walked into the lobby of the Empire Hotel. Today Hazel Wright, the hotel man's wife, stood behind the front desk. A thickset woman of medium height, she wore a plain grey skirt and bodice with sleeves that ended at her elbows. She was marking down figures from yesterday's receipts in a ledger that lay open on the desk in front of her. Her forearms were freckled and patchy and a scatter of pimples stood out on her face; she had passed this bad complexion down to Howard. On hearing the door open, Mrs. Wright looked up. Her grey eyebrows met in a suspicious line.

"What can I do for you, ma'am?" she called out.

"I'd like to talk to your husband," Lucille said. "It's about my missing brother-in-law."

"And what do you think my husband could know about that?"

"If he knows as much as I think he does, I'll see him hang. Now, word's going around town that your husband watched from the upper floor of this hotel until Mr. Birch and Mr. Brown left the tea room on the evening they disappeared. Then Wright came down here and got on the phone to Henry Best. I need to know if this is true."

"It isn't!" Mrs. Wright barked.

"That's isn't what your boy said," Lucille answered.

Mrs. Wright hesitated only for a moment. Her voice hardened and her eyes narrowed. "Well, it isn't true. He only said that because this oaf was bullying him." She turned to Seth. "And what were you doing, beating on my poor boy?"

The young man wore a mild face and his hands rested halfway in the pockets of his old waistcoat. "He lipped off to my sister."

"That's a lie too. I raised my boy right. And even if he did, what does the little hussy expect?"

"I ask you to watch how you talk about my sister, ma'am." Seth's voice glistened with frost. The hairs stood up on the back of Lucille's neck at the sound.

Mrs. Wright drew back with a huff. "What, now you beat up women too?"

"No, I'll be beating your husband. Bad."

The woman sucked in a deep breath. Her cheeks puffed out so that she looked like a frog. "My husband doesn't know anything about any brother-in-law. That's all he has to say. So I'll have to ask you to leave. Now." She pointed at the door behind them.

Lucille looked around in mock bewilderment. "This is odd. I don't see Mr. Wright anywhere, but that's supposed to be him talking. You must have a big skirt for him to hide behind, Mrs. Wright. I'll bid you a good day."

Lucille took hold of Seth's arm and pulled him out the door.

They would get no more out of Hazel Wright. She took a deep breath. She had as much faith in Corporal Brock as she had in flying pigs, but she had to try. She and Seth made their way to the NWMP station. As soon as they stepped through the door, Corporal Brock, at his desk, dropped his pen and groaned.

"Good day to you too, Corporal," Lucille said with a curtsey. "It's been so thoughtful of you to keep me informed of the progress you've made looking for Stanley Birch. Would I like to sit down? Why, thank you." She smoothed down her skirt as she seated herself on the wooden chair in front of the Mountie's desk.

Seth grinned at the corporal with all the insolence he could summon. "She's a pistol, eh?"

Corporal Brock rubbed his head with weariness. "Let's make it quick, Mrs. Reilly. I'm busy," he grumbled.

"That's ever such a good idea. Mr. Pruitt here tells me Howard told him about what his stepfather did when Stanley and Mr. Brown left the tea room on the evening they vanished." Lucille then repeated Howard's statement to the policeman. "Now, what are you going to do about it?"

Corporal Brock leaned over his desk. "Nothing! Once I got your sweetheart here away from Howard, the boy went back to the hotel with his stepfather. He didn't say anything about Wright making a phone call. You can write that to Commissioner Perry, but there's nothing he can do about it, either. If Howard doesn't make a statement, I've no evidence to question anyone." Lucille drew a deep breath and gritted her teeth. She wanted so much to contradict the Mountie, but what he said was true. She stood up.

"And don't bother looking for Howard," Brock continued. "He and his stepfather had a big fight last night. Howard left town."

"His stepfather was angry with him for blabbing. Did that ever occur to you?"

Corporal Brock only lifted his hands. "What families choose to fight about is no business of the Mounted Police."

Outside, Seth and Lucille walked slowly down the wooden steps to the boardwalk. Lucille's whole frame sagged. *Will I ever find Stanley?* Even if they had God for a policeman here in Stony Point, He could do nothing without a sworn statement. She looked behind her at the distant hotel. If only she were a man, she could go down herself and beat the truth out of Arthur Wright. But certainly, the hotel man would just keep denying everything. Lucille found herself blinking back tears. It seemed sometimes as if her brother-in-law's ghost hovered around her waiting patiently, marooned in this world until she could find his body and lay it to rest.

Seth reached over and lifted her chin up. "There now Missus, you can't get down. Look at all the posters you put up." He pointed at the window of the General Store, which to her surprise still had the "Missing" poster in its front window. "See, you've kept him on everyone's mind. Somebody'll talk." It was kind of Seth to say so. She forgot all her resolutions and squeezed his arm as they headed back to the boarding house.

Meanwhile, Ellie Best arrived back at her mansion. This time, the reason for all the anger sparking from her eyes was the letter she had picked up at the Post Office today. It was from her jeweller in Montreal. Last week, Ellie had found out about her husband's new mistress in Fernie. She was a married woman whose husband, a CPR executive, was never home — a most convenient arrangement for Henry. The day she had found out about the woman, Ellie had telephoned her jeweller and ordered a new necklace and emerald earrings from his catalogue. But today, instead of the jewellery, she had received this letter. In it, M. Bouton expressed his regrets, but since her last two bills remained unpaid, he must cut off Madame Best's credit until the matter could be straightened out. He concluded the letter by saying that he was certain the delay of his payment was merely an oversight, and he looked forward to serving Madame in the future.

Ellie's eyes had popped out of her head with indignation when she read this letter. How dare Henry not pay her jeweller! It was true the bills she had outstanding with M. Bouton's shop totalled nearly twelve hundred dollars, but if her husband did not like the amount, he could go console himself with his whore. As she entered the house, Ellie unpinned her hat, tossed it aside onto the velvet bench that stood against the wall, and slapped the letter down on the oak table in the foyer. Henry had better pay her account. How would it look to the shareholders if word went around that he couldn't? Suddenly, Ellie smiled to herself. Her husband would be eating at home this evening for a change. She would drop that hint about the shareholders, and he would pay the bill immediately.

With her temper restored, she sat down on the velvet bench and pulled off her shoes. The foyer carpet at her feet was clean and straight, and the table was free of crusts of bread, broken toys, and other little girl clutter. In the parlour, the hardwood floor gleamed under the Persian rug, and the ceramic figurines lined the top of the mantelpiece in the orderly ranks of soldiers. She took a deep breath as she put on her silk slippers. The Best house was now a model of serenity and cleanliness. Ellie sat for a moment and looked around with satisfaction. It was so wonderful to have her house to herself again.

She left the offensive letter behind her on the table and walked upstairs where she opened the door of the nursery. Eleanor was lying on her back on the white coverlet under the pink canopy of her bed. On the second bed, to the left of her sister, Mildred was lying on her side with her rag doll squeezed under her arm and her thumb in her mouth. The girls were now perfect little angels. Every morning after breakfast, Ellie gave them each a shot of laudanum mixed into a spoonful of honey. She would then take Eleanor and Mildred up to the nursery to play with their toys. Within twenty minutes, the eyelids on both girls would droop, their speech would slur, and like a couple of gramophones they would slowly wind down and soon end up asleep with their faces on the floor. Once they were sleeping, Ellie had only to lay them on their beds and then she was free of them. Now, she closed the door on the sleeping girls and went to her own bedroom.

There, she walked past the oak bureau to her *ensuite* where she sat down at her dressing table. The table had a swivel mirror in an elaborate oak frame under which sat Ellie's jewellery box. On its lid of inlaid enamel was a smooth picture of a buxom woman whose white wig rose skyward like a pre-Revolutionary French noblewoman. Ellie looked at herself in the mirror. An elegant, formidable woman with a high forehead, straight nose, and small mouth looked back at her. She spent a few minutes peering closely at her face, looking for blemishes or signs of age. Satisfied, she picked up her hairbrush, the long-handled one with the porcelain back, and brushed her waist-length hair vigorously. In a moment, her strokes slowed down while the image of the young man she had seen in town today came to her again. Ellie remembered the dark brown hair under his hat, his eyes, and his square chin. His shoulders were broad enough for him to carry a sack of flour over each one. She smiled to herself and giggled. She wanted to hang the young man up on the wall, like Henry did with his trophy bear heads, just so she could look at him. *Who was he?* She could not remember ever seeing him in town before. She made a mental note to herself to find out.

Ellie took her time as she trimmed her fingernails with the manicure set in the drawer underneath the dressing table. Then she experimented with several different hairstyles. She also took her pearl necklace and diamond earrings out of the jewellery box and put them on. She tilted her head this way and that and smiled in the mirror. With her ivory comb, she picked out a rich brown tress and pinned it; meanwhile, she wondered, *Who was that woman with that dreamy beast?*

She pictured the blonde-haired, blue-eyed woman in her plain bodice and skirt. Her cheap straw hat obviously came from Eaton's catalogue. In spite of her peaceful house, Ellie set her teeth as her temper began to boil again. *Why does she get to have a man like that?* With a snort, she recalled the woman's generous figure. *The slattern can't even tie her corset properly,* she thought while she took as deep a breath as her tight lacing allowed.

She consoled herself with the certainty that she could have any man she wanted. The instant the handsome young man saw her, he would drop that plough mule in a pile of ox droppings and come running; Ellie had only to smile and wink her eye. At first, even Henry had been helpless against her beautiful eyes and dazzling smile. In those days, he had called on her nearly every afternoon. It had thrilled Ellie to see how she had tamed the rakish but handsome young Mr. Best, even though her family had no money. After the couple had become engaged, she had watched with glee while envy soured the face of every woman of her acquaintance. But her smile vanished quickly as she recalled the brief time that Henry had stayed tame. Who had won, in the end? Was the laugh now on her?

That evening, her husband ate supper at home for the first time in over a week. Ellie sat in the chair to his left and his daughters to his right. While they ate, the odd silence coming from the two girls made Henry look at them with bewilderment. Eleanor supported her head on her fist while she picked at the pork roast and vegetables on her plate with sluggish indifference. The girl's colour was a sickly white. Mildred also had a bad colour. She clutched her dolly to her chest with her left arm and swayed on top of the cushions that boosted her up to the table. She yawned and her eyelids drooped. Henry frowned. He remembered that the last time he had dined at home, about a week and a half ago, the girls had been unnaturally listless as well. He turned to his wife.

"What's wrong with these girls, Ellie? They look like a couple of drunks in a bar."

She glanced at her daughters and shrugged. "Maybe they're just coming down with something."

Henry's frown darkened. Although his wife spoke in a neutral tone, the smirk playing about the corners of her lips angered him. She was playing some kind of game, he could bet on it. "Well, do something with them," he commanded. "They look bad."

"Yes darling, I'll be sure to dose them up with something before I put them to bed tonight." Ellie's knife and fork tinkled on her china plate as she put them down. "Also, I was going to mention, I got a letter today from M. Bouton in Montreal. He says the last two bills he sent us haven't been paid. I'm sure it was just a little mistake. You're so busy at the mine and everything. You can just write him a little cheque for twelve hundred dollars and I'll mail it off. We don't want anyone thinking we can't pay our bills. The wives of those shareholders are a lot of spiteful old crows, and they'll natter their heads off over it if they find out."

Henry dropped his napkin on the table. "Ellie, we've already discussed this. I told you I'm not paying any more jeweller or dressmaker's bills. We have to cut back. Bouffon, or whatever the hell that pantywaist's name is, will just have to wait for his money. I don't have that kind of cash right now."

Ellie stifled a sneer. She laid her hand over Henry's in appeal. "But darling! Please? We must have enough money for such a little thing. You work so hard at the mine, and you're so smart and ambitious."

Henry shook her hand off impatiently. He enjoyed the sweet words but not the whine that came with them. "Twelve hundred dollars is a damned far cry from being a little thing, Ellie," he said. "Now I don't want to hear another word." He turned back to his plate.

Ellie lowered her eyes and fingered her napkin as a surge

of anger welled up in her. She picked up her knife and fork, laid them down again immediately, and squeezed the cloth in her fist. Henry was refusing to hold up his end of their arrangement: that is, he got to have his affairs as long as she got to spend his money. She would bet her diamond necklace that her husband's mistress still received baubles, which meant that yet another woman was stealing what was rightfully hers. Henry, meanwhile, chewed his food with his square jaws working; he sipped at his glass of wine and smacked his lips as he enjoyed his roast. Finally, his wife spoke without thinking. "We don't have the money because you lost a thousand dollars in a card game to yet another *whore*!" She shouted the last word.

The noise snapped Eleanor and Mildred out of their torpor with a hard jerk. The girls froze at the rage on their mother's face. Mama's eyes were blazing and her white teeth were showing in a snarl. No one dared look at Father like that. In growing alarm, the children glanced between their parents. They could do nothing but shrink down and stay motionless like baby rabbits terrified of the hungry dog sniffing around them. Henry only shrugged and grinned. "Sometimes, Ellie, the cards don't fall the way we want. It's just too *bad*!" he shouted his last word back.

Ellie's face glowed red. But her husband would only laugh if she showed more anger. Instead, she swallowed down her fury and shrugged. She took a breath and put on an expression of indifference. "Well, darling, while you're enjoying yourself with that slut in Fernie, I might just look around for something I can amuse myself with." The handsome face of the burly young man rose up again in her vision. She raised her arm to hide her grin with the lacy cuff of her sleeve. "The girls can get so tiresome."

The silverware rang and Eleanor and Mildred jumped. Henry's hand flashed out as quickly as a prizefighter's and seized Ellie's cheek. He pinched, and she exclaimed in surprise and indignation. Henry pulled her head forward and forced her to look at him. His eyes were ice as he jiggled his wife's head in his grasp. "Woman, you ever say anything like that again, I'll get the buggy whip and you won't be able to sit down for a month. And if you ever make a laughing stock out of me in this town, I'll nail your hide up on the carriage house door. Do you understand?"

Frozen with fear like her daughters, Ellie sat still with her cheek in Henry's grasp.

Her husband tilted her head up and down to make her nod obediently. "Yes Henry," he spoke in a falsetto, "I understand. I'll watch my damned mouth from now on." Abruptly, he released her and turned back to his plate. He finished eating his roast with an untroubled mind. It was a husband's right, indeed his duty, to chastise his wife, especially if she spoke with disrespect to him as a man.

For a long while, Ellie sat motionless. Her cheek still hurt from Henry's pinch, and she felt the great red mark standing out on her white flesh. *At least I know where I stand now*, she thought. In this house, she was nothing but a glorified house-keeper and a nanny for the children. Henry would always be able to go wherever he pleased and do whatever he wanted. What happened next confirmed her impression.

Mildred looked from her father to her mother and began to howl. With a scarlet face, the girl rubbed her eye with her little fist and sucked in her breath for another long wail of despair. Eleanor climbed down off her chair cushions and embraced her sister. "Don't worry Mildred," she said. "I'll look after you."

Henry groaned. He laid down his knife with a ring of metal. Mildred's howls grated on his ears — screeches from a monkey would sound like a robin's song by comparison. "Jesus Christ, Ellie, you want something to do? Get that little bugger upstairs. By God, what's a man got to do to get any peace in his own house?" He threw down the napkin, pushed back his chair, and strode upstairs to his office, grumbling about the damned shareholders who insisted their chairman be a family man.

Chapter 12

Wednesday, July 1, 1903

"C'MON LADS," LUCILLE HELD UP A PIE in front of the two miners. "This wonderful blueberry was baked especially for Pie Fest by Mrs. Harriet Baxter. Won't you give two bits for such a lovely pie?"

The miners squeezed their hats in their hands, grinned, and made jokes. It was Dominion Day and the Stony Point UMWA Ladies' Auxiliary Pie Fest was taking place inside a tent that the women had pitched on the grass opposite the ball diamond. The men came inside the tent and gazed like bears at the array of pies, cookies, and tarts, for it was late in the afternoon and all were starving for the picnic supper. Lucille sold the pie to the miners, then waited for a moment, shooing flies away from the treats with her whisk, when her next customer came up. He was a skinny boy in worn overalls whom she recognized from her day at the mine; he was one of the breaker boys. She sold him half a dozen tarts. As he rushed away, she cautioned him not to eat all the tarts at once and spoil his supper, but the boy hurried out of the tent a tart already stuffed in his mouth. Lucille looked around noting that the wooden boxes and tin plates on the table behind her were empty. She now had sold nearly all of her quota.

It was easy to sell pies with Granny around. The old woman sat on a stool beside the exit of the tent. If a man tried to walk past her with empty hands, she would tap his shins with the knob of her walking stick and scold him until he bought something. In addition to collaring the local men, she herded inside the men on the Frank baseball team and held them hostage until they bought pies too. Later, after the women had sold all of the treats Granny, Mrs. Baxter, and several other miners' wives sat down at a table and counted the coins and bills. They put all of the proceeds in a strongbox that they gave to Mrs. Perkins to keep in her safe. From the satisfaction on the women's faces, Lucille knew the Stony Point UMWA Ladies' Auxiliary Pie Fest had been a success.

After she and Kate helped the other women clear up inside the tent, they took tin plates outside and strolled over to the firepit. Around them, the festivities continued. To the left, a group of grey-bearded men stood around the horseshoe pit and argued over who had the closest toss to a ringer. Children ran around everywhere. Lanka Ruzicka threw a firecracker into the dirt track between first and second base on the ball field; at the bang, she and her friends held their sides laughing. The girl was not a bit tired after all the hopping around she had done in the flour sack when participating in the children's races earlier that afternoon. The men of the baseball team, with Seth among them, limbered up and tossed balls around in the out-field. There would be a game after supper between the Stony Point and Frank teams. As Lucille and Kate waited in the food line, the Galician women in their kerchiefs chattered over their big pan of cabbage rolls and Mr. Lesniak grilled sausages over the crackling firepit. Lucille thought that Dominion Day had never been this much fun in Winnipeg.

"I saw Mrs. Best across the street a little while ago, while I was going to the outhouse," Kate said, as Mr. Lesniak laid sausages on the tin plates that she carried, one for herself and one for Granny. Albert slept contentedly in the sling she carried over her neck and shoulder. Lucille carried the extra plate for Seth. "She was sitting in front of the barbershop," Kate continued as she took a cabbage roll. "Looks like her husband's spending the holiday with his fancy piece. She's all by herself, 'cept for her girls." Kate then leaned forward and spoke to Mrs. Ruzicka who stood among the Galician women. "Now I expect you to drop by later and give Albert a kiss, Mrs. Ruzicka. He wants his *maty bozha*."

After loading the plates, they made their way back to the tent. Granny pulled herself up to her feet on her stick, and the three women, with their full plates, walked together to a spot not far from the gazebo where the barbershop quartet was singing, "My Wild Irish Rose." After setting down her loaded plates, Kate spread an old blanket on the ground, and sat down so that Albert rested in her lap. Seth soon joined them there and the four ate their picnic supper.

Lucille remembered how she had come to meet Ellie Best. Their encounter had taken place last Saturday, during her protest outside the door to the Empire Hotel bar. She had worn a sandwich board with one of the "Missing" posters she had hung up around town earlier pasted on it. On her hat she had worn the words, "Where is Stanley Birch?" stencilled to a square of cloth on the crown. The men going in and out of the bar had laughed at her, but Hazel Wright had not seen anything funny about the demonstration.

The woman had walked up to Lucille from around the corner of the hotel, the flesh on her chin and cheeks quivering with anger. She had cocked the shotgun she carried and pointed it at Lucille in her sandwich board. "Woman, I thought I told you, my husband doesn't know anything about your brother-in-law," she had said. "Now, you get away from this hotel and don't come back."

Lucille had gripped the sides of the board, planted her feet, and faced the grey-haired woman. "I'm not leaving until I talk to your husband. And I dare you to shoot that gun!" She had shouted so that all of the men in the bar, Arthur Wright included, could hear.

Mrs. Wright had paused. At length, she had put up her shot-gun, then walked back around the corner of the hotel to the front door. Of course, the woman had gone to phone Corporal Brock. The policeman had been one of the few people in Stony Point who would still talk to her.

Ever since Howard had blabbed on the sidewalk to avoid a beating from Seth, a black cloak of ostracism had settled down over the Wrights. The miners, their wives, and their children had started crossing the dirt road to the opposite side of the street when they walked past the Empire, as if the very boards of the hotel could give one typhus. The only men who would drink in the bar now were Dominion Coal supervisors and the hotel guests. So far, however, Arthur and Mrs. Wright were still walking around town with their heads high. Lucille wondered how long they could keep it up.

She had been waiting for Corporal Brock to arrive when the rattle of an approaching buggy came to her, marking the arrival of Ellie Best. Lucille had first noticed the woman's hat. It had been different from the one she had worn the other day; this one had a wide brim and was covered in silk with an abundance of ostrich feathers over the crown. Mrs. Best had also worn a lilac afternoon dress that matched her hat perfectly. The dress had elbow-length pleated sleeves and a stiff collar that cut into the woman's chin. She had on white kid gloves and carried a parasol, only Lucille had been able to tell that Ellie couldn't use hers as a weapon. Nonetheless, with a snarl on her red face, Mrs. Best had charged up to Lucille, who thumped the tip of her own parasol on the wooden sidewalk. The noise it made had stopped her enemy in mid-stride. But anger had still snapped from the woman's eyes like sparks from a brush fire. "You filthy whore! You stay away from my husband!"

In her astonishment, Lucille had only blinked. Mrs. Best's admonition had been laughable, as if she had forbidden Lucille to pet a rabid dog. "I wouldn't touch your husband with a stick," she had replied.

Ellie had fallen silent. Surprise had appeared on her face and she licked her lips for a moment, at a loss. But she had puffed up again immediately. "You lie! You lying whore! You were playing poker with him right in there," and with her parasol she had indicated the bar with its twin batwing doors. "You slept with him afterwards, didn't you? Admit it!"

"No, it's your husband who's the whore. He's a fool, too; he believes he's entitled to win every time, so he bet too much money. I wired most of that money I won off him to my sister. She's the wife of this man," Lucille had jerked the board in front of her up and down, "who's missing. She has two boys she has to raise by herself now. And I'm beginning to wonder if your husband had something to do with that."

Ellie had only brandished her parasol. Lucille, with a stern face, had taken her own in both hands just in case Ellie had the idea to charge — she would, in turn, drive the metal tip straight into the woman's knee. She had already learned from Kate that if she didn't knock Mrs. Best down immediately, she would never have any peace from the woman.

"Why good afternoon, Mrs. Best." Corporal Brock had strolled up to the two women, tipping his Stetson hat and nodding to Ellie who had spun away from Lucille, smiling brilliantly at the Mountie and twirling her parasol with girlish charm. Lucille had looked from the policeman to the woman and back again. All it had taken to turn Ellie Best into smiles and sunshine was the presence of a man. "I must say, you're looking very fine today," Corporal Brock had continued. "Has this woman been giving you any trouble?"

Ellie, with a toss of her head, had turned back to Lucille. The feathers on her hat had jerked back and forth. "Well, Corporal Brock, it's a fine thing when the town hussy can walk up and down in front of a bar as free as she pleases."

"And it's a danger to the public when lunatics are running around on the loose," Lucille had retorted. "You'd best put this woman in a straitjacket, Corporal. She's going to hurt someone one of these days."

Ellie had jerked up her fists and screamed again. "Shut up, you whore!"

The Mountie had snapped his fingers at Lucille and said, "You! I've had a complaint from Mrs. Wright that you're trespassing. Get along or I'll lock you up. Move it." Ellie had brayed with laughter

Then it had been Lucille's turn to toss her head. "Oh dear. Since I'm not the rich man's wife, I don't get the compliments or the smiles." She had turned to Ellie. "I'm so glad to have met you, Mrs. Best. How wonderful it must be to have such a devoted husband."

Ellie had jumped as if Lucille had stabbed her. As she passed by, the woman had leapt at her like a striking rattlesnake, screaming epithets; even Corporal Brock had looked surprised as he reached out to restrain her. The policeman had soothed Ellie as if she were a high-strung but valuable mare. Lucille had made a face. She had wagered to herself that the Mountie would have treated a coal miner's wife much differently.

Now, Lucille sat on the ground cleaning her plate. The grilled sausages, cabbage roll, and beans had filled her up, and she rested for a moment in a glow of satisfaction. The sun was shining and overhead the jagged mountain peaks held back the rain clouds. Over in the gazebo, the barbershop quartet was singing, "Daisy Bell (Bicycle Built for Two)." Seth swirled sand on his plate to wash it and went to join the baseball team. Soon, Mrs. Ruzicka appeared. Kate took Albert out of his sling and held him out. The baby gurgled in his swaddling while the woman took him in her arms. Mrs. Ruzicka then dandled the infant on her hip. Generally, Albert was the most placid of babies. Granny observed that her Noah had been the same; just like Kate's boy, hours could go by without a peep from him. With a sudden conviction, Lucille shivered and turned to Kate. "If Ellie Best's around, don't ever let Albert out of your sight. It's a feeling I have."

"Shoot," Kate exclaimed. "You can count on that."

Just then, Granny planted her stick on the ground and pulled herself slowly upright. As she rose, she gritted her teeth against the pain in her arthritic feet. Once she was standing, she adjusted her battered old straw hat. Slowly, she began to make her way to the ball field. The other women followed her, including Mrs. Ruzicka with Albert.

Meanwhile, Ellie Best walked east up King Edward Avenue. It had amused her to sit on the bench in front of the closed barbershop, smoke a cigarette that she had stolen out of the case on Henry's desk, and watch the lower order at their games. It was almost as good as a menagerie: the miner's wives in their plain, homemade dresses and Eaton's catalogue hats; the wild antics of children galloping around like horses; and the bandy-legged, ugly men drinking and spitting. But Ellie had stopped laughing when she recalled Henry's words to her over supper the other day. He had treated her as a servant. At the memory, a cloud had dimmed the sunshine and the sight of the townspeople irritated Ellie instead of amusing her. She had stood up, shaken out her pale blue dress, and started walking. Now, the afternoon was flying by and she could smell the enticing aroma of the grilled sausages even at this distance. She would go back to the house and eat a proper supper. Even the food those clodhoppers ate was common.

On First Street, Ellie turned to her left. The gravel under her feet crunched as she drifted forward a few steps. She scowled when she recognized the grey boards and the small front veranda of the Pruitt house. She was always telling herself she was going to get even with Kate Pruitt, but she had not done anything since last March. The little whore, and that plough mule with the lippy mouth who got to have the dreamy beast Seth Pruitt for a beau, must be laughing at her. Ellie had found out everything regarding the young man and the woman from Winnipeg from Mr. Carter, the groundskeeper and handyman who worked for the Bests and who would tell her anything she wanted to know in exchange for a smile and a cup of tea. Ellie hated that Winnipeg woman as much as she hated Kate. As she approached the Pruitt house, she glanced from side to side like a burglar to make sure no one was around. It was long past time for her to show those whores what was what.

She paused at the white fence. *What should I do,* she asked herself. The chickens in the yard cackled alarm at her approach. She could wring the necks of all the birds and dump their carcasses on the veranda. But that would take too long, and the racket the birds would make would draw attention. Plus, the idea of touching Kate's flea-ridden chickens revolted Ellie. Also, if she killed the birds, she could expect to lose a few more windows in her house to Kate and her rifle. Henry would explode if he had to pay for another window. *What else could I do?* A smile appeared on Ellie's face. *Fire.* Neither Kate nor the plough mule would be laughing after their house burned down. Ellie danced a step with glee, but then hesitated. Everyone in town knew she hated the girl, and if only the Pruitt house burned down, it would arouse suspicion. Kate would certainly shoot out *every* window in the Best's house then.

With a scowl, Ellie looked around. The bushes behind the house and the miserable shack next door to it were brown from the prolonged dry weather. She lifted her skirts and hurried past the house and the knot of bushes. Soon, she was picking her way along the edge of the riverbank. The bushes rose on her left and the Oldman flowed past on her right. Ellie thought briefly of the other townspeople and what they were supposed to do if the fire spread out of control. *Who cares if the clod-hoppers lose everything,* she thought with scorn. They were poor and had nothing to lose anyway. It was their own fault they were poor, too — if they weren't so lazy, they wouldn't be poor. Henry said so.

Ellie stopped when she reached the wall of bushes about thirty yards directly behind the house. First, she looked around carefully. She was alone. She grinned to herself as she took the box of matches from her purse and struck one on the heel of her shoe. The first match went out before she could light anything, but she managed to put the second under a withered knot of dry grass. A wisp of smoke wavered up and a tongue of flame appeared. As the fire began to crackle, Ellie clapped her hands and backed away from the spreading flames. Birds whistled terror and flew out of the bush. Smoke rose up in a billowing white curtain. Ellie sent up a prayer that the fire would consume the Pruitt house first. She laughed aloud, lifted her skirts, and ran to the small log bridge that spanned the river. She then hurried up the dirt trail to the Best house, which was less than a mile up the side of the hill. As she ran, her blood raced and her heart thumped. A bit of mischief was just the thing to shake off the boredom and anger that had been choking Ellie all day.

At the ball field, the score was tied at one between the Stony Point and Frank teams. Granny, Kate, and Lucille sat on the ground level of the bleachers behind the line that stretched from home plate to first base. The Ruzickas sat on their right and Mrs. Baxter on their left. The Frank team was batting. The man on first base, a tall fellow with a big moustache, tried to steal second but Seth, who played catcher, had been watching. The ball sailed from his hand, over the pitcher who had dropped to his belly on the mound, and into the glove of the man on second base. He tagged the runner easily. As the spectators applauded, a wag in the second row of the bleachers cupped his hands around his mouth and shouted, "Hey, Mister! Why don't you try ... sliding?" Groans and laughter rippled through the crowd. Lucille rolled her eyes and made a face. Even before the Frank boys had come to town, the joke about them sliding from base to base had grown stale.

Granny looked around and *humphed*. "Hah, and I wonder if that galoot would find it so funny if a mountain had rolled over his house. I wish my stick were long enough to reach his head."

Another man from Frank stepped up to the plate. He had swung his bat twice, when up at the top of the bleachers, Sairy Wilson from the General Store rose up from where she had been sitting next to Sly McNab. With horror on her pale face, she pointed to the north. "Smoke! Over there! It's a fire!"

A moan of dismay issued from over a hundred mouths. At the noise, Lucille's hair stood on end. Lanka turned to her parents and translated what Sairy had said. Mr. Ruzicka cried out and jumped up. His arms swung at his sides as he made haste on his bent legs across the field. Every man in Stony Point was now running towards First Street. Seth was at the head of the group, with Ralph Baxter, Ned Williams the telegraph operator, and the Frank baseball team close behind him.

Mrs. Baxter grasped Kate's arm. "Oh, no! Those are our houses," she exclaimed. She lifted her skirts and raced away.

Lucille stretched out her neck and clapped her hands to her head. A column of white smoke had risen up into the blue sky above the roof of the tobacco shop. She thought of the remainder of the money she had won from Henry Best that she kept in the bureau of her room. She would lose it all, not to mention all of her clothes and other belongings. But it was not only the Pruitt house that was in danger. The wooden buildings and tarpaper shacks of the town were all tinder. A fire could destroy Stony Point.

Like Mrs. Baxter, Lucille lifted her skirts and ran over the grass of the field. She soon arrived at the house. She stopped in horror to see the bushes that stood just beyond the white fence all ablaze; smoke filled the air and the dry wood snapped and popped as the fire consumed it. The chickens in the yard flapped their wings and scrambled about squawking with terror. The men had formed a line between the fire and the house. Seth threw dirt onto the fire with a shovel. His eyes were red from the smoke and sweat trickled down his face. Ralph Baxter next to him used a rake to sweep the dirt, but there were not enough tools for all the men. Many were kicking dirt onto the fire with their hands and feet.

Lucille ran into the yard. In spite of the men's efforts, the fire was spreading. Harriet Baxter, in her own yard, desperately stamped out the smaller blazes that the flying sparks from the main fire were igniting in the grass; these small fires were coming steadily closer to her own shack. Lucille moaned with terror and darted into the house. Without thinking, she grabbed one of her skirts from her room and dashed with it back out the door. She soaked the skirt in the water barrel and hurried with it to the line of men. With the blaze roaring in front of her, she gritted her teeth. She swatted the flaming bushes with the wet skirt and kicked dirt on the fire. Heat like that from an oven warmed her face and her eyes teared up from the smoke. The blaze had spread so far that now it would require an extraordinary effort from the people to save the town.

The next two hours for Lucille were a blur of roaring flames, smoke, and flying sparks. Gerald Wilson and Mr. Evans from the hardware store brought shovels from their stock of tools and passed them out. With dozens of men shovelling, they gradually drove the flames backwards toward the river. Luckily, with the Oldman so close, the line of people passing wooden buckets from hand to hand also began to defeat the flames. Lucille dropped the tattered mass of fabric that had once been her skirt and joined the line. She found herself in between Mrs. Homeniuk from the Slavic neighbourhood and, of all people, Hazel Wright. Every hand was needed to put out the fire. At last, some of the men stepped back, leaned on their shovels, and wiped their brows. The blaze was mostly extinguished. Seth and a few other men were chopping the bushes down with axes to put out the smouldering remnants, but now everyone could take a breath.

Lucille staggered on her shaking legs as she fell back. Even though her hands were empty, she still felt as though she was carrying buckets of water along the line. Deep grooves left by the rough rope handles were visible in her palms. She collapsed onto the steps leading up to the back veranda of the Pruitt house. Wisps of smoke were still rising up from the scorched, barren ground behind the house. All of the vegetation had burned, leaving only a few charred young trees here and there. Lucille now had a view of the pine trees on the opposite bank of the Oldman River, and in the distance beyond, the forested hillside on which the Best house stood. She shuddered. Without the wall of bushes behind it, the Pruitt house seemed vulnerable. She blinked and rubbed her irritated eyes, then drew her hand back with surprise as she realized that her eyebrows were scorched. She looked up to see Seth approaching. He had removed his baseball shirt in the heat and his arms were bare. His muscles stood out in them and smoke had left patches of grime on his cheeks. He carried a bucket of water. He set the bucket down, took the dipper, and held it out to Lucille. As she took it in her hand, Seth produced a cloth from somewhere and gently wiped a smear of soot from her cheek. The look in his eyes made her jump. Having Seth give her water made him seem too much like a husband. At that moment, a distressed clucking drew her attention. Below her, near the steps, one of the chickens was still flapping around. It was the hen with the one leg; the poor bird had been so terrified that as she had scrambled around, her artificial leg had fallen off. Reluctantly Lucille pulled away from Seth then hurried down the steps of the veranda, picked up the struggling hen, and took her under her arm.

At that moment Kate appeared. Albert was fretting in the smoky air and she bounced the baby in her arms as she spoke. "My, that was close," she exclaimed. "For a while there I was just terrified for the house." Her gaze rested on the wide strip of charred ground where the bushes had stood. She frowned to herself. "Gad, it's a shame we lost those bushes, though. I don't like the house being all exposed like this. It's like we've got no curtains on the windows."

"That's what I was thinking," Lucille agreed. All around her, the townspeople were packing up the buckets and shovels, or talking about restarting the baseball game as if the fire had been only a distraction. For her part, Granny was busy wrapping a bandage around the arm of a baseball player from Frank who had stepped too close to the blaze. Now that she had time to think, Lucille began to wonder. The hen under her arm clucked again as she turned to Kate. "What could have started that? Fires don't just start by themselves." Seth also frowned to himself as he too began to speculate.

Kate looked at Lucille, then gazed downwards with bewilderment on her pink face. "Maybe it was a hobo who left his campfire burning," she said.

"But what would a hobo be doing so far from the railroad tracks?"

Kate's mouth fell open. She remembered seeing Mrs. Best hanging around the barbershop earlier today. Her gaze fell upon the Best house, now visible in the distance.

Shortly after Ellie left the house to skulk around Stony Point, Eleanor and Mildred woke up from their laudanum-laced sleep. Their mother had given them a smaller dose as Henry had started noticing something, and had then promptly forgotten about them. When Eleanor woke up, she prodded Mildred until she woke up too. The groggy three-year-old rubbed her eyes and yawned. Eleanor then dragged her sister over the rug. At the door, she made a footstool out of her and climbed up on her back, then twisted the knob. The door to the nursery swung open.

Because Ellie had never allowed them in there, the girls first went to their mother's bedroom, where they came upon the jewellery box on the dressing table that Eleanor promptly opened. With an exclamation of wonder, Mildred grasped a ruby broach, only to have her sister tear it out of her hand. A fight ensued over which of the girls got to wear the pretty jewellery. Glittering stones, a diamond necklace, and an ivory cameo broach flew between them. As they wrestled over it, they broke the string on their mother's pearl necklace, and pearls sprayed everywhere. Eleanor had enjoyed the tussle immensely. After exploring the *ensuite* a little further, Eleanor tore open the mattress of Ellie's bed with her mother's nail scissors that she had found in the drawer of her dressing table. A feather fight with Mildred followed; shrieking and giggling, the girls pelted each other with handfuls of feathers they pulled out of the mattress. When they had finally grown bored, they rested a moment in a snowbank of feathers on the bedroom floor.

Downstairs, they continued to destroy everything they could get their hands on. In the dining room, Eleanor grasped the chain that held together the doors to the oak china cabinet. She pulled it as hard as she could, even bracing her foot on the door, but the chain held fast. The girl looked at the cabinet with her lips pressed together in determination. Her face lit up suddenly, and she trotted to the parlour, hurrying back with the fireplace poker in her hand. With it, she levered off the handles on the cabinet doors, which swung open to reveal the Best family's most expensive china. Eleanor skipped around with triumph, removing plates and hurling them to the floor. If they didn't shatter into enough pieces, she smashed them again with the iron poker. Unsatisfied, she had moved on to the crystal wine carafe and a blue flower vase. Still unsatisfied, she had then given her sister a full jar of honey. Delighted, Mildred sat down on her bottom on the floor near the staircase. Like a monkey, she dipped her hand into the honey and licked off her fingers, one by one. In the process of emptying the jar, she covered herself, the hardwood floor, the carpet, and anything else she could reach with the sticky goo.

As her sister gorged on honey, Eleanor wandered into the parlour, carrying the poker on her shoulder the way a miner would carry his pick. She continued to destroy things: the figurines on the mantelpiece, the gramophone records, even a heavy leaden vase. She twisted the horn off the phonograph and kicked it against the wall. All the time, she fingered the outline of her posture brace under her dress and seethed with rage at her mother, her father, and everyone else in this harsh world that had no place in it for a girl.

Time passed. Mildred hummed contentedly to herself as she raised her dripping fingers to her mouth. Suddenly, she lifted her head at the sound of her mother's footsteps coming up the veranda stairs outside. The front door opened and Mama stumbled in: red-faced, gasping for air, but laughing too. At the sight of her youngest, her mirth died immediately. Mildred looked like a demon child on the floor, with one hand clasped to a quart-sized mason jar of half-eaten honey and eyes staring at her through ropes of hair glued to her face. The three-year old's dolly was stuck to the pinafore of her dress as though it had crashed into Mildred head first. From the parlour came Eleanor's voice shouting with glee.

Cold with dread, Elllie stepped through the doorway. She could not see the floor for the debris. Ceramic fairies and shepherdess figurines lay everywhere in shards. On the wall facing her, shreds of paper hung down like the skin of a flayed man where Eleanor had ripped it off. Sticky footprints of honey stood out on the floor. While obliterating the parlour, Eleanor had walked back and forth into the hallway to check on Mildred like a responsible older sister. At that moment, Ellie's groan made Eleanor stop beating a pillow with the fireplace poker. With feathers sinking to the floor around her, she turned to see her mother, then dropped the poker with a clang. Meanwhile, a red fury was building up inside Ellie with the power of a locomotive.

"Eleanor, why?" she asked finally.

Her daughter bit her finger and glanced at the floor. "Because," she answered with a shrug. Then, like she always did when she knew she was in genuine trouble, Eleanor started to clown. She pulled the corners of her lips out in a funny face and capered about on the Persian rug that was now sticky with honey. Her mother stepped forward and grabbed her hard by the shoulders.

Later, after she locked the girls back in their nursery, Ellie rushed to the desk in Henry's office. She scribbled out a letter that would go with the telegram she would send her mother tomorrow morning. Ellie was sending her daughters to Mrs. Nesbit on the train. Mother could keep them, turn them over to sister Doris, or give them away to an orphan's home. Ellie didn't care. Rage was still blurring her eyesight. She paused and took deep breaths. She recalled her mother's earlier refusal, but clenched her teeth in desperation. Mrs. Nesbit must take the girls. Ellie concluded her letter with a plea: "I'll get Henry to pay anything. I'll kill them if I don't get some time away." She then folded the letter into an envelope.

Chapter 13

—w—

ONE AFTERNOON, ALMOST THREE WEEKS AFTER Dominion Day, Henry Best was riding Sultan from Fernie to Stony Point. The horse jogged down the wagon trail. To the left, a steep gravel embankment led up to the railroad tracks. To the right, a line of mountains tinted blue rose in the distance. After a heavy rainfall a week after Dominion Day, the Crowsnest Pass entered another prolonged dry spell. Today, on the wagon trail, a team of oxen had raised a curtain of dust while pulling a load of beer barrels in a heavy cart. The vegetation in the ditch and beyond it to the forest of pine trees had wilted in the dry heat. Henry felt the sweat under his hatband and wished it would rain again. He had heard all about the Dominion Day fire. When he had examined the patch of scorched ground near the Oldman through his binoculars, he had shaken his head and shuddered at how close Stony Point had come to burning down.

In Fernie, Henry had attended a meeting along with every mining company executive in the West. The UMWA had just formed a local in Coal Creek. At the gathering, the executives had hammered together an agreement to put aside their differences and join forces against the encroaching union. Henry made a speech in favour of a law proposed by Senator Lougheed that would mean jail for any advocate of a strike action who had lived in Canada less than a year. The boys applauded with nods of enthusiasm and at the support, Henry glowed inside at the certainty he would one day be premier. Afterwards, when he said that anarchists had also been stirring up his coal miners, one of the fellows gave him the phone number of a contractor that would provide Dominion Coal with strikebreakers. Another gave him the card of his friend in the Pinkerton Agency. It had, therefore, been a most productive meeting. The only drawback had been the husband of his mistress being home for a change. Henry had shrugged good-natured resignation. Instead of a visit with Sally, he went with some of the boys to a local brothel. His success in Fernie was almost enough to make up for today's annoyance. Dominion Coal was closed.

He slowed Sultan down to a walk as he entered the west end of Stony Point. The horse blew air, tossed his head, and pranced in front of the Hillview Hotel that loomed above to his left. Bed sheets instead of curtains covered the windows and a bearded man hung his head out a window on the upper floor. Down on the porch, a one-legged man sat on a barrel next to the door and played a harmonica for a line of men on a bench. The man on the end was throwing his penknife at the boards between his feet, his whiskery face sagging with boredom. Henry had called Sitwell this morning. His secretary had told him that the mine was closed because a coal train had derailed just east of Frank. Since the CPR could not find its ass with both hands, the Lord knew how long the clean up and repair would take. Henry had damned his best customer for the thousandth time. If he asked for a higher price for his coal, the CPR executives would howl as if they had caught him picking their pockets; at the same time, this was the kind of job they did keeping open the track through the Crowsnest.

Sultan walked past the corral of the livery stable where three men in overalls and cloth caps leaned against the rail. One of these men spat tobacco as he looked at Henry with narrowed eyes. Henry, in turn, spat on the ground. *What's with all the damned sour faces,* he wondered, until he remembered that today was the anniversary of the explosion at Dominion Coal. In a rush, Henry recalled the shock wave that had knocked over the telephone on his desk. *They hold me responsible for that?* he thought with indignation. He looked around and spat again at the idea of slinking away from a rabble of miners. *Those bastards in Coal Creek can form a local, but I'm damned if I'll stand for one in my mine*, he thought with a grimace. Nor would he allow the idle men in the street to intimidate him. Instead of retreat inside his house, he would go to the barbershop and have a shave. His chest swelled with pride as he rode. *These damned miners don't call me Henry Worst for nothing*, he thought.

He stopped Sultan in front of the barbershop and dismounted. As soon as Henry set foot on the wooden sidewalk, some distance behind him the door to the General Store jingled as it opened. A tall young man appeared. He wore a derby hat and a white sleeveless shirt, and carried on each of his shoulders a ninety-eight pound sack of flour. It was Seth Pruitt. The man stopped when he saw Sultan tied to the hitching post. His eyes met Henry's. Henry smiled pleasantly and took his middle finger in his hand, jerking it a few times in an obscene gesture that conveyed the pleasure he had taken in seducing the big man's sister. Instantly, Pruitt spun around and rushed back into the General Store. Henry laughed. So much for big bad Seth Pruitt — how in the hell did someone who ran like a rabbit from an enemy ever get to be a prizefighter? All these big men were cowards at heart.

When he stepped inside the barbershop, the idlers on the bench near the door instantly fell silent. A heavy-set man with bushy whiskers chewed the stub of a cigar in his mouth. Next to him, a skinny man in a woollen cap put down the newspaper he had been reading. Henry nodded to the barber, a small man in a white coat.

"What can I do for you, Mr. Best?" the man asked in a Polish accent.

"Shave and a trim would be perfect."

"Yes sir." The barber clipped the sheet around Henry's neck

and picked up the shaving mug. Henry relaxed while the man brushed his cheeks and chin with hot foam. It was a long ride from Fernie to Stony Point, and it was good to sit and remember what a diversion Kate Pruitt had been. He still thought her the prettiest girl in town. How odd it was that she had such an ape for a brother. He had heard she had given birth to a boy a few weeks ago. Henry had no interest in the baby, other than to grin and clap himself on the back at the proof of his virility. Soon, the barber put aside the mug and pulled out the strop from the chair. He passed the razor back and forth over it briskly.

With a jingle from the shop door, the rhythmic beat of the razor stopped abruptly. Henry opened his eyes. Seth filled the doorway. When the young man had put the bags of flour back in the General Store, the observant Gerald Wilson had seen his scowl. Immediately, he had hurried up and, like a newspaperman, questioned Seth about with whom he was going to have a donnybrook now. It had been the storekeeper who had delayed the young man. Now, Seth fixed his gaze on Henry in the chair. His sleeveless shirt revealed massive shoulders and his big hands were clenched. The idlers held their breaths as he approached Henry who was choking down his laughter. Pruitt was a throwback of evolution; his big shoulders and scowl gave him the appearance of a gorilla. When he was close enough, the young man feinted with his left hand and then swatted Henry across the face with his right. The barber and the loafers cried out with surprise as droplets of shaving foam flew everywhere. In the chair, Henry sat for an instant, stunned and blinking. The blow could have dropped a mule.

"If you've got something to say about that, Best, I'll be waiting for you at the ball field," Seth said.

With a growl of rage, Henry leapt up out of the barber's chair. "You've got a deal, boy!"

Seth walked outside. Henry paused only to tear the sheet from around his neck and wipe the remains of the lather from his face. He too then strode out the door. The loafers, meanwhile, were already running up the wooden sidewalk toward the Hillview Hotel. There, they breathlessly related to the men on the porch what they had witnessed in the barbershop. The hotel emptied in ten seconds. Dozens of men ran to the ball field, with the one-legged harmonica player hopping along behind them as fast as he could.

Word of the fight spread through town faster than the Dominion Day fire. Gerald Wilson put on his bowler hat as he hurried toward the field, while Polly, in the doorway of the General Store, yelled and shook her fist at her husband. The postmaster was in such a rush, he forgot to hang a "Closed" sign on his door before he scrambled out of it. A breaker boy raced to Luigi's bar and shouted through the door that Seth Pruitt and Henry Worst were going to settle their differences on the ball field. Mugs of beer hit the tables, chairs spun, and playing cards fluttered to the floor. The men poured out of the bar and hurried to the field, each afraid the fight would end before he got there.

Near the baseball diamond Seth stopped, turned around, and passed his hat to Ralph Baxter. Henry gave his hat and coat to Sparky, the fireboss. The men chattered anticipation and stepped backwards so that they formed a large ring around the combatants. On one side of it, Seth flexed his big arms and jabbed out his fists. Henry glanced around at the yammering spectators; every man in Stony Point was here. Aside from a furious husband years ago, he had never fought a man in earnest, and the husband had been too drunk to pose a genuine danger. He had sparred a few times in college, but that was all he had for experience. Seth, meanwhile, raised his right fist and protected his head with his left, a prizefighter's stance. Henry squared his shoulders. No matter his lack of experience, this ape had slapped him in front of witnesses. The chairman of Dominion Coal raised his fists, clenched his teeth, and focused his gaze on his opponent.

The crowd roared as he shot forward and swung his right fist at the throwback's head. Seth ducked, nimbly evading the blow. Henry jumped backwards out of his reach. He and Seth circled each other with their fists rotating. Bellowing, the men in the crowd swung their fists along with the fighters. Seth moved in. Once, twice, his right fist darted at Henry's eye; Henry eluded the first swing, but the second caught him on his cheekbone and he staggered. The audience howled. Henry clinched with his opponent and then took the opportunity to drive his right fist twice into Seth's kidneys with all his strength. His opponent shook him off, but not until after Henry landed another blow into his stomach. Now there was some caution in Seth's eyes. Henry stepped backwards. He feinted with his right hand and swung his left at Seth's head. Seth ducked to evade the blow and sprang up again. His right fist smashed into Henry's nose and everyone could hear the bone crunch. With blood streaming down his chin, Henry scrambled backwards, fighting to stay on his feet in spite of his blurred vision. The shouts and whistles from the spectators rose in a crescendo.

At that moment, the fight ended. Corporal Brock had slipped through the crowd of men with his club under his arm. While Seth pressed forward, the Mountie came up behind him, lifted his club, and brought it down with a sharp crack over the back of the man's skull. Seth crumpled down to the grass. Instantly, the audience went quiet. Henry, who still had his fists up in spite of his broken nose, gaped in astonishment. Corporal Brock looked around with his club in his hand. Many of the faces surrounding him were red with liquor and all were looking at the policeman with growing fury.

A tall man stepped forward. "See that, boys!" Rupert pointed at Seth who had pulled himself up to his hands and knees on the grass. "Rich man gets the police to help him win a fight. Working man gets a club over the head!"

The men burst forth with an ear-splitting roar of indignation.

Brock waited no longer; he drew his pistol from the leather holster on his Sam Browne belt and and threatened to fire it in the air. "All of you! Break it up and go home!"

With their eyes on Brock's pistol and red serge jacket, the mob retreated several steps, but still the men grumbled and all their voices together sounded ominous. Henry took his coat and hat back from Sparky. The angry faces were looking his way as well as toward the Mountie. His first instinct was to give them his middle finger, but dozens of men stood against him and Corporal Brock. They jeered as Henry clasped a handkerchief over his streaming nose and ran from the baseball field.

Meanwhile, Brock hauled Seth to his feet. "You're under arrest, Pruitt. Charges are assault and battery. Let's get to the station."

Seth held his ringing head and staggered about as Corporal Brock grasped his arm and led his prisoner off the baseball field. A dozen men followed, yowling and shouting, with some throwing rocks at the Mountie. Brock released Seth and turned furiously on the men. "You." He pointed at one with his club. "All of you. You're under arrest too for assaulting an officer."

The men only jeered louder. Ralph Baxter and another man locked arms with Seth and marched with him over the grass of the field. A dozen other men followed. Although he wore his sternest expression and brandished his club at the rowdier fellows, Brock began to think it would have been better to have let the men have their fight.Now, he had an angry, drunk mob on his hands. It was the start of a riot.

At the Pruitt house that afternoon, Granny, Lucille, and Kate sat around the kitchen table, each busy with her own task. Granny was cutting up scraps of fabric and fitting the pieces together, the beginning of a little quilt she was sewing for Albert. Kate was rolling bread dough in the ceramic bowl. To make it, she had used the last scoops of flour in the barrel, which they had depleted faster than usual because of the Pie Fest. Granny had sent Seth down to the General Store to pick up a couple of bags.

Lucille was gazing at a letter from her sister that lay in front of her. Lottie was pleased with what she had found out during her day in the coal mine, but she begged Lucille to avoid these unnecessary risks. She did not want to know how Lucille had obtained that fortune she had sent her a few weeks ago, and she did not want her to run around in dangerous coal mines. These days, the boys eyed their mother with doubt when Lottie assured them Aunt Lu would return home soon. Lucille decided to write to Edward and Abner and promise them she would come home the minute she found out what had become of their father.

Her gaze fell on the baby on the floor near Kate's feet. He was tucked into the cradle his Uncle Seth had made for him. In addition to the beautiful carvings on its sides, it also had a bonnet overhang that protected Albert's eyes from the sun. The baby had just woken up. Suddenly, in a flash of movement, Dinah appeared on top of the bonnet. She scuttled to the edge and looked down; Albert shook his tiny arms excitedly and gurgled at the spider. Dinah drew a thread out from her spinnerets and began to web the front of the cradle bonnet where Albert's exhalations attracted insects. The baby sucked on his fingers and gazed at the creature while Dinah knitted together her web. Like Albert, Lucille enjoyed watching the graceful motion of the spider's eight legs.

"That Indian woman had a ton of things to say about Albert," Kate was saying as she worked. Granny and Lucille listened while she told them all about the fortune teller she and Mabel Baxter had visited yesterday. The two young women had stepped inside the teepee of an old Peigan woman. First, the fortune teller had told Mabel that she would marry one of the hands at the Patterson ranch. The girl's giggles and blushes had advertised that she indeed had her eye on a cowboy. Kate had then allowed the Indian woman to take Albert into her lap. Her wrinkled eyes had shot open as soon as she touched the baby. She had told Kate that Albert's life would be one adventure after another. He would be a rich man, and one day his travels would take him across an ocean, where he would find true love and become a war hero. Lucille bit her tongue. Every fortune teller who had ever peered into a crystal ball told a mother her son would be rich.

But Kate wrinkled up her mouth. "I don't want Albert going to no war," she declared with a shudder. "Some nasty Boer or the like might shoot him."

Granny spoke up. "It'll be his duty to serve his King if the time comes, Katie."

"Well, that better not happen 'til he's a man. And Lord knows I'll still be fretting."

Suddenly, a racket of cheers and shouts from a crowd of excited men came from the direction of the baseball field. As the noise grew, the hens in the yard began to cackle. Granny looked at Lucille and Kate with apprehension. "Why isn't Seth home yet?" she asked. "He needn't go across the ocean to buy some flour."

Lucille hurried to the door and picked her hat and parasol from the rack. "I'll find him."

Outside on the path, her feet crunched over the dry gravel. The distant shouting grew louder as whistles and drunken laughter added to the melee. At last, she reached the wooden sidewalk. She leaned with her back against the corner of the tobacco shop catching her breath.

Now, she looked down King Edward Avenue and gasped with astonishment at Henry Best, who stood at a hitching post in front of the barber's where he was untying the reins of a handsome saddle horse. He mounted it, and as he rode past Lucille, she could see him holding a handkerchief to his nose, from which blood was streaming. His left eye also had a shiner. Then she turned and looked across the road. She gave a sharp cry of alarm.

Corporal Brock, Seth, and some other men were marching to the NWMP station. While they strode together, the men shook their fists and sang a mining song. "Godfrey Daniels!" Lucille exclaimed. She raised her skirts and scrambled after them. Soon, she came alongside the men. The parade indeed looked like a triumphal procession; Seth was stumbling ahead with Ralph Baxter and another man supporting him. His pale face and unsteady gait showed that he had been injured. The sight was chilling enough, but then a roar of angry voices came from up the street. Lucille whirled around.

A much larger and more enraged crowd of men had gathered in front of the Empire Hotel. A woman's voice that she recognized as Hazel Wright's shrieked defiance at the growing mob. In horror, Lucille's eyes popped open. Most of the boys at the hotel were drunk. They staggered about in the dirt road and brandished rocks and empty liquor bottles. She spun back around and arrived at the Mounted Police station at the rear of the crowd of furious men. She was shaking with fear for Seth and fury at Corporal Brock.

The policeman pushed Seth and the men with him through the door, driving the unruly cattle inside with the end of his club and his booted foot. Then he turned around and arrested a few other men whom he picked at random out of the mob. The remaining men drew back with curses, shaking fists, and sarcastic jokes. The instant Corporal Brock retreated with his prisoners inside the station, a shovel full of horse droppings spattered over the door. The men hoorayed. But as angry as they were, no one touched the pole from which the flag hung. Lucille wove her way through the crowd to the steps outside the door to the station.

"Seth!" she cried. She raced up the steps and burst inside. Brock had just locked the jail door on the men he had arrested. The prisoners gave a noisy cheer at Lucille's appearance. They looked like a basket of fish in the cramped cell. Ralph Baxter and the other man she had seen marching with Seth stood next to each other with their hands grasping the iron bars. Eight or nine more men shuffled around behind them. One man at the rear told a joke and they all laughed.

The corporal scowled at Lucille. "Out!" He pointed at the door as he shouted.

The prisoners hissed and booed like disgruntled theatre patrons. Lucille stepped up to the Mountie. "Where's Seth? What have you done to him?"

"He's under arrest. Assault and battery."

More howls came from the cell. "Then where's Old Man Worst?" Baxter demanded. "He was fighting too."

"How come you just smacked Pruitt over the head?" The short, slightly built man next to him asked. "A man can't even watch a good fight in this town."

"That damned Mountie ought to arrest himself for assault and battery," another man behind them declared. "It ain't fair, what he did." All of the men grumbled agreement.

"Out!" Brock shouted at Lucille for the second time.

"I want to see Seth! If I don't, I'll be writing Commissioner Perry and my sister's lawyer. And if you want to do some good, you'd better get your butt to the Empire Hotel. A mob's breaking the door down."

The prisoners roared approval. At that moment, as if to prove what Lucille had said was true, glass shattered and a shotgun blast cut the air from down the avenue. Corporal Brock groaned, squeezed the brim of his hat in his fists, and ran out the door. Lucille waved her hands with exasperation at his retreating back. She hurried to the door of the cell.

Baxter greeted her with an embarrassed smile. "Gee Mrs. Reilly, guess the pot boiled over."

"Mr. Baxter, are you all right? What happened?"

Baxter shrugged. The small man next to him explained in one sentence about Seth and Henry Best, the fight, and the unjust meddling from the policeman. "It was only Pruitt who got the club over his head when Worst was fighting too and that's why us boys are so mad," he said in conclusion.

"Honestly, all this over a fist fight? Is Seth back there?" Lucille tried to crane her neck over the heads of the men. Her voice shook with anxiety. "How is he?"

"Aw, he's never been better. Hey Pruitt, your girl's here." Baxter laughed.

As much as they could in the crowded cell, the men moved aside. Seth sat on the wooden bunk. His colour was returning, but still he held his head in both hands. On top of that, the only medical attention he was getting came from a drunk who was slapping him on his back and pressing a flask of moonshine into his hand. Lucille had to get him out of there. The set of keys hung from a ring on a hook behind the corporal's desk. She hurried there, picked them up, and sorted through them. The men gaped at her as she approached the cell door.

"Now, don't be getting yourself in trouble over the likes of us," Baxter's heavy-browed gaze fixed itself on the keys.

"Just let me out," the scrawny man next to him said. "I'll go get help for the rest of you." He turned around and laughed while the other men groaned and roared.

"Ah, Tyson, you bugger!" said a voice from the back of the cell.

"Everybody out," Lucille commanded as she unlocked the door and pulled it open. She didn't care what the corporal would do. When she was twelve, a neighbourhood boy, Harry Shoemaker, had struck his head on the ground after falling off a horse. After lying unconscious for a less than a minute, the boy had picked himself up, dusted off his trousers, and laughed off the whole thing. Two hours later, he dropped face first onto his mother's kitchen table, as dead as a rock. She was not leaving Seth in here injured and in danger in the middle of that vaudeville act. *Brock can go chase himself.* The iron bar door creaked as it swung open. The men grinned, laughed, and filed out, eager to join the action at the Empire Hotel.

"Gee Mrs. Reilly, it's a shame how we all rushed by you and you couldn't keep us in here," Baxter said as he walked past. "Old Man Worst must have gone to Blairmore to look for the other end of his nose," the skinny man said with a chuckle to the man behind him.

"Glad to see you again, Mrs. Reilly." Pearson, who had been at the rear of the crowd, tipped his cap to Lucille.

"You too?" she asked.

"See, it's all on account of my wasted youth." He winked at her and then followed his friends out the door.

Lucille stepped inside the cell. Seth rested with his back against the log wall. Droplets of blood covered the front of his cotton union suit and bruises stood out on the knuckles of his hands. He looked up at her and sucked in a deep breath, wincing from the pain in his ribs. She hurried to his side and sat down. She pressed her lips together — she didn't have even a bandage. Lucille glanced at Seth's pale face and gritted her teeth as she remembered Harry with his face in a plate of his mother's beans.

"It's all right, Lucille. Don't fret." He grasped her skirt and, as he did, the hair on her neck stood up and vibrated. She could feel the strength in his arm even through her skirt and a warm shudder crawled down her back. "How come my little firefighter got her skirt all dusty?"

"I ran all the way from the house." Seth squeezed his eyes shut from the pain in his ribs as he turned to her. His hand, which was still injured from the fight, stroked a tress of her hair that had come loose from the pins.

She jumped up and ran out of the cell. "I'll find you something." The ring of keys jingled in her hand as she found the one for the storeroom. The station must have a box of ointment and some bandages somewhere. She forced herself to concentrate, although all she could think about was Seth's bruised hand stroking her hair and his fist crushing the blue fabric of her skirt. At last, she unlocked the door to the storeroom and pulled the chain to the electric light on the wall. On her left were rows of wooden shelves that held labelled metal boxes of evidence, coils of rope, and other tools. She was sorting through this gear when the front door of the station opened and closed.

"Seth!" It was Granny and Kate. Lucille hastened out of the storeroom. Granny wore her old grey shawl and straw hat. Kate carried Albert in her arms and a large canvas bag over her shoulder. Judging from her bright eyes and trembling mouth, the girl was close to tears. Lucille hugged her and took the wooden chair from in front of Brock's desk inside the cell. Granny sat down on it and clucked her tongue over Seth's pale face and the bloodstains on his shirt. "Hoot laddie, look where you are."

"I saw Best in town."

"Aye," she said with resignation. Her shoulders rose and fell. She took her jar of Dinah's silk from the canvas bag. "I'd reckoned you would, sooner or later."

While the old woman doctored Seth, Kate began to pace around with Albert in her arms. "This whole town's just gone right spinny," she exclaimed. "There's a big crowd of men in front of the Empire. They're saying Arthur Wright got Matthew Brown killed and they're going to string him up from a telephone pole. You've got to hand it to Mrs. Wright, though. She's in the doorway with her shotgun and she's holding her ground."

"Only man in that house," Seth remarked with a snort. Granny, meanwhile, dabbed a rag soaked in whiskey and spider silk on his knuckles. He was holding a towel with more of the silk on it to the back of his head where Brock's club had made a lump the size of an egg. Lucille shivered as the hullaballoo from the riot came to her ears from down the street.

"Well if they do string him up, it's murder," she said. "I've no great love for Arthur Wright, but his wife did her bit to put out the fire, whatever faults she has otherwise."

At that moment, footsteps approached the front door and Corporal Brock opened it. John Rupert followed him inside. The phone on the desk was ringing. Brock picked up the receiver and instantly jerked it away from his ear. Even in the cell, Lucille could hear Wright squawking for the Mountie to "Get your ass back here and get those bastards away from my hotel."

Brock strove to calm the man while Rupert approached the cell door. Lucille greeted the union organizer. "We've got us a bit of a muddle here, don't we," he said with a weary roll of his eyes.

In the meantime, Brock hung up on Arthur Wright. He leaned over the desk for a few seconds taking deep breaths. When he raised his head he gaped at the empty cell.

At that moment, Rupert said, "Look Corporal, the boys say they'll lay off Wright if you let Pruitt go and drop all the charges against everybody."

"No!" Brock roared. "They broke the law. I could throw a stick in this town and charge anyone it hit with assault and battery, public drunkenness, and vandalism. People better respect the law!"

At these words, Lucille lost her temper. She strode out of the cell, blew past Rupert who jumped out of her way, and stopped in front of the Mountie. Brock retreated a step and kept his hand on his pistol as she railed at him.

"Yes, Corporal Brock of the Mounted Police, people better respect the law, but not if they're rich. You're forever squawking about the law. What about what's right and wrong? Seth gave Henry Best what he had coming, and if you'd only left it alone, we wouldn't be in this mess now."

While she was speaking, a peculiar expression appeared on Brock's patchy face. When she fell silent, he jerked his chin at the cell. "Where are all those men I had locked up?" he asked.

Lucille glanced over her shoulder. "I let them out. Seth…"

"You let them out. I figured so. That's a felony — aiding

and abetting." To her growing alarm, the Mountie cackled and rubbed his hands together. "I'm putting you on the next train out of town." The drawers of his wooden desk groaned as he opened them one by one. Out of the last drawer, Brock took a form and a pen. "I'm done with you and your questions and your meddling. If I see you here again, I'll make up another reason to run you out. So you best go home now and pack your bag."

In defiance, Lucille clenched her fists; the corporal would have to strap her to a horse to remove her from Stony Point. "You can't do that. My sister's lawyer will gut you."

Brock only shook the form so that it rattled and laughed again. "Bring him here and let him try. I'll get a judge to sign this and you'll never be allowed back."

Seth's deep voice came from the cell. "You'll not be putting her on any train. I'll marry her."

Silence fell. Lucille gasped and clapped her hand to her mouth. Granny gawked at Seth with a rag in her hand and her chin hanging down. Only Kate made a sound. "Yay!" the girl cheered. She squeezed Albert and hopped around in a circle, pink with excitement.

The corporal, however, only brayed with amusement. "Suits me, boy. Then I'll run you both out of town."

At that moment, another gunshot came from the hotel. The angry voices of the men surrounding it rose into a thunder. Above the roar, one could hear a man encouraging the rest to burn the place down. Instantly, all the amusement vanished from Corporal Brock's face. Cold dread likewise soaked Lucille at the thought of the Empire Hotel in flames. In contrast to the Dominion Day blaze, which had burned the bushes on the edge of the Oldman River, the large, centrally located hotel would set the whole town on fire.

Clearly, the same thought had occurred to Rupert who said, "Corporal, you've got a bigger problem here than Mrs. Reilly." He pointed down the street. "If you don't drop the charges against Pruitt and the other fellows, your hotel man's going to be swinging at the end of a rope. From the sound of things, we might have another fire, and God knows if we'll be able to put this one out. What's your boss going to say when he finds out all hell broke loose here on your watch?"

Brock muttered disgust, but at the same time leaned over the desk with his fists clenched on top of it as he reconsidered. At last, the Mountie threw up his arms. "All right, damn the charges!" Another crash came from down the street.

Rupert looked over his shoulder and turned to the Mountie with an urgent face. "We'd best get over there then and let the boys know, before they tear the place down." United in their purpose for a change, the policeman and the union organizer hurried to the door. When Brock opened it, the hubbub of breaking glass, shouts, and crazy drunken laughter from the riot filled the station. Both he and Rupert scrambled outside. Their footsteps made haste to the hotel.

Lucille and the Pruitts found themselves alone. Granny completed her doctoring by wrapping Seth's head in a white bandage. He stood up and looked at Lucille. In spite of his injuries, the young man's eyes twinkled and his white teeth showed in a smile. Granny hummed to herself as she packed up her jars and strips of cloth in her bag. Kate was still beaming at the marriage proposal. Only Lucille was unhappy; she looked at the floor and wrung her hands as she tried to think of something to say. "Look Seth," she said finally, "you don't have to go through with any wedding. See, Brock's forgotten about me already. It was kind of you to try and help, and I'll understand if you want to call it off…"

But he looked her up and down with some indignation. "No. I said I'd marry you, and I will."

Next to him, Kate jiggled Albert in her arms and nodded firmly. "Seth takes giving his word real serious," she declared.

Granny stood up. She leaned for a moment on her walking stick. "Look Missus Lucille, I've seen you mooning for our laddie behind his back for a few weeks now."

Seth exclaimed with surprise and gawked at the old woman. Kate giggled, while Lucille's mouth popped open and outrage spread over her face in red flames. "I have not!"

"I've got eyes, woman. You and our boy suit each other. Why not make yourselves happy?"

Seth placed his hand on Lucille's shoulder. "I *want* to marry you," he said.

"Oh, all right then," Lucille gulped. "We'll go through with it."

"Yay!" Kate cheered again.

The family filed out of the police station. Granny made her slow way down the front steps on her walking stick. She insisted to Seth that he stay away from the house for a few days; it would be bad luck for him to see the bride before the wedding. Kate agreed with enthusiasm. She and the old woman chattered together with excitement as they made plans; all the while, Lucille's cheeks glowed pink and her feet hardly touched the ground. She smoothed out the creases in her skirt as she followed the two women. She felt as if horses were tearing her apart in several directions. She tingled with excitement, but shivered with terror. She thought of the sadness she had felt at the prospect of leaving Seth, and groaned to herself at the idea of sailing off into the unknown with him. But she had given her word.

Meanwhile, Rupert and the corporal had run over to the hotel, and the soles of Brock's knee-high riding boots thundered up the wooden sidewalk. The situation at the Empire had become a standoff. The mob had smashed a few windows and ripped off the door, but Hazel Wright held the lobby with her shotgun in her hands and grim resolution on her face. She had already blasted out a patch of the wall next to the door when a drunk had tried to force his way inside. As he approached the hotel, Rupert waved his arms to catch the men's attention. The shouting died down. "Boys, it's all over. Brock's dropping the charges."

A few drunks slurred abuse at him and the Mountie, but now that their demands were met, the momentum of the riot died. The men put their hands in their jacket pockets and drifted away in the direction of Luigi's bar or the single men's hotel. Rupert followed one, a bony, moustached man in overalls. "There'll be a union meeting at seven-thirty in the Oddfellows' Hall," he said, once they were out of Corporal Brock's hearing. "Spread the word."

Chapter 14

—〜—

INSIDE THE ODDFELLOWS' HALL that evening, John Rupert and two other union men sat down behind a wooden table. On the wall behind them, a portrait of His Majesty King Edward VII hung in an elaborate wooden frame. At seven-thirty, the miners began to arrive. The men stepped inside the hall, folded their cloth caps, and tucked them in the pockets of their coats. The men who had not yet signed union cards lined up in front of Rupert and marked down their names, while the rest sat down on the rows of wooden benches and talked among themselves. They grumbled, still angry about the unfair end to the fight between Pruitt and Henry Worst, and the faces of many were dark with resentment.

Half an hour later, Rupert looked around the hall. In front of him, rows of men sat side by side in their worn jackets and scuffed shoes. He grasped the wooden gavel in his hand and stood up. "Boys, now that everybody's here who's coming, let's take a roll call." All but three of the workers at Dominion Coal were present. It was enough for a quorum.

"Let's take the vote," the organizer continued. "All of those in favour of forming Local 2322 of the United Mine Workers of America here in Stony Point, raise your hands." Every hand rose.

"Motion carried."

For a few minutes the men clapped, laughed, and joked among themselves. When the cheering died down, Rupert spoke again. "Now that that's settled, we need some suggestions for the demands we're going to make."

Hubbub filled the hall as the men talked. In the second row of seats, Baxter raised his hand. Rupert pointed to him.

"The chair recognizes Brother Baxter."

The gaunt man rose up and spoke. "I say, first thing we need is a dues checkoff."

The men nodded to each other in agreement. Removing their dues from their paycheques would be a legal acknowledgement on its part that the union represented the workers.

"All in favour?" Rupert asked.

The hands rose again.

Until late that evening, the miners talked; they stood up in their rough overalls and patched trousers and made suggestions. A few demanded beer and peanuts, but eventually the men voted to demand: a union dues checkoff; a five percent increase in wages; and, in honour of the men killed in the explosion a year ago, a clause requiring the company to provide safe explosives to the miners. The final thing to which the men agreed was a deadline of midnight on the coming Friday for the executives of Dominion Coal to meet with the bargaining committee. If the company refused to talk, the committee would meet over Saturday and decide whether to take a strike vote; Monday appeared probable. At last, late that evening, Rupert closed the meeting. It had been a hard struggle these last few months, but the work had paid off in what was now a solid union membership.

A few days later, Seth and Lucille made their way through town in the back of a wagon that Mr. Ruzicka drove. Lucille wore her grey skirt, bodice, and skimmer hat. She clutched the bouquet Kate had picked for her: a lovely arrangement of blue asters and hyssops. When Kate pressed it into her hands, Lucille had choked down her tears at how lucky she was to have such a friend. The harness on the horses jingled and the wagon lurched down the middle of King Edward Avenue to the schoolhouse where the wedding would take place. Seth sat in the wagon next to Lucille. He had put on his best suit, one of dark blue wool, with a blue waistcoat. His derby hat almost covered the white bandage on his head. His cheeks and the end of his square chin were still a little red from the barber's razor. Lucille with her jangling nerves could hardly look at him, although she held his hand as the wagon rocked and creaked its way to the schoolhouse. Seth had wrapped himself up like a present, just for her.

It had rained early this morning, but now, in the sunshine, the townspeople lined both sides of the dirt road. Women fluttered handkerchiefs and men tipped their hats and whistled; in the rough lumber wagon, Lucille felt like Lady Minto. On every face she saw good wishes, along with anticipation for the dance tonight in honour of the newlyweds.

Soon, the wagon stopped in front of the Oddfellows' Hall that stood across from the schoolhouse, a small building painted red with a sloping roof. Lucille and Seth jumped down. He turned around to help Granny. The old woman wore a flowery print dress. Lucille's maid of honour, Kate, wore her green organdy dress with her Dunbar hat. The Ruzickas and other friends followed them to the schoolhouse.

As she walked with Kate up the cement path, Lucille looked around. The man who would marry her to Seth, the Reverend F. G. Richard, had come to town from Blairmore. Rumour had it that the Anglican minister was marrying another couple today here in Stony Point. But no one had heard of another engagement, and Lucille and Kate were wiggling with curiosity to learn the identity of the mysterious other couple. But whoever they were, these people were not at the schoolhouse. When Seth opened the door, they found only the minister inside waiting with his Bible in his hand.

The wedding went ahead. As Seth took his oath, Granny sat behind him on a wooden bench. She rocked Albert from side to side; placid as ever, the baby slept through the ceremony. Beside the groom, Lucille clutched her bouquet in both hands. Her knees were shaking. She kept her vision fixed on Seth's brown eyes as she forced herself to say, "I do" in a strong voice. At her side, Kate beamed sunshine on the proceedings. Soon, the minister pronounced them man and wife. Applause filled the schoolroom as she pecked her new husband's cheek.

She did not find out who the unknown newlyweds were until later, at the start of the dance, when she stood with her new husband near the gazebo. The wonderful aroma of potatoes roasting in the firepit filled her nostrils. From behind, disjointed chords sounded as the Stony Point band tuned up their instruments: Luther Hartley with his squeezebox, a banjo player, two men with fiddles, and a young man who played the spoons and washboard. A line of friends gave the newlyweds their congratulations. The men clapped Seth on his back and offered him shots of liquor, which he politely refused. Mrs. Ruzicka was vexed that she had not had time to bake a *korovay*, a traditional Ukrainian wedding bread, but, Lanka translated as her mother spoke, she was glad to see Lucille had at last found herself a husband. Mrs. Perkins then walked up with her arm in that of the telegraph operator, her successful suitor. Lucille and Kate exclaimed with joy when she told them that she and Ned would take the plunge themselves one day soon. They then asked her who was the other woman who had gotten married today.

"Oh, I shouldn't repeat gossip," Mrs. Perkins declared, before she glanced from side to side, lowered her head, and cupped her hand around her mouth. Lucille and Kate both leaned forward to hear better. "Ned saw Gerald and Polly Wilson with Sairy at the railroad station. They had her in front of the minister as soon as he stepped off the train. They married her off to Sly McNab."

Lucille drew back in bewilderment. She remembered Sly

McNab, and the perpetually amused smirk on his face, from her day at the mine. Maybe Sairy was plain, but she could do better than that for a husband here on the frontier. Mrs. Perkins lowered her voice and looked around again before she continued. "Gerald had a shotgun under his arm and Sairy was all in tears."

Lucille's mouth popped open as she gasped, and Kate clamped her hand over her own. "Well my gosh," Lucille exclaimed. Her first impulse was to laugh, but she choked down her mirth when Kate spoke up.

"Poor Sairy. Sly McNab's the biggest no-count in the Crowsnest. God help the girl." Lucille had to agree. But she hoped that from now on Polly Wilson would not be so quick to judge others.

At that moment, the band in the gazebo played a chord, then began a lively reel. Seth, Lucille, and a few other couples paired up and danced on the patch of dirt in front of the gazebo. As she looked up into Seth's even features and soft brown hair, Lucille drew her husband close to her. The onlookers whistled and clapped.

The party was still going strong late that night, after the sun finally set. All the townspeople knew this wedding would be the last party in Stony Point before the miners went on strike, so everyone was determined to have as much fun as they could. John Rupert, who had come with his girl Frances, spoke to the miners who scowled when he told them that Dominion Coal had refused to bargain.

At last, just before midnight, Granny grew tired of boasting what a handsome couple her Seth and his Missus made. She rose up on her stick, and Kate supported the old woman's arm to help her back to the house. Albert was growing fussy, and Kate told Lucille that she would bed down herself after she put the baby in his cradle. "You two don't have to worry about me or Granny," the girl said with a fiendish grin. "We sleep like logs."

After they left, Lucille puzzled over the odd statement, until she gasped. For the last few weeks, late at night, she had been wondering what it would be like to be Seth's wife in every sense of the word. Now that she was soon to find out, she didn't know what she felt: excitement, dismay, fear, or anticipation.

She danced one more reel with her new husband, but Seth was now tugging on the sleeve of her bodice. They said their goodnights to the winking men and smiling women, and made their way back to the house in the dark. Seth took his wife's hand; his woodworking tools had left many calluses, but his skin was dry and soft. Lucille breathed deeply of the fresh air and looked up. A band of stars hung in the night sky above her, and she gasped at how lovely it all was. Back at the Pruitt house, however, she began to shiver and rub her hands together. Seth lit a lamp, set the glass hood down over the flickering wick, and led her down the hall. This morning, with shrieks of happy laughter, Kate had moved herself and Albert out of this big bedroom so that the newlyweds could have it.

Lucille was trembling and angry with herself for trembling. She turned around and kept her back to Seth, facing the bureau on which her husband had placed the lamp. She listened to the bumps and shuffling noises that Seth made as he undressed. She was just about to turn around and tell him that she was dreadfully sorry, that this marriage was a mistake, and that she could not go through with it, when she spotted Dinah sitting on the swivel mirror above the bureau. The spider rested on top of her mirror image and brushed her hair. Her long legs flexed as she ran them over her bulbous abdomen. As she preened, Lucille smiled at the pride the little creature took in her eight colourful legs, coarse black hairs, and deadly fangs. According to Dinah, the best thing in the world to be was female.

"You going to stand there all night and watch that ugly spider?"

Lucille turned around. Seth lay in the bed with another lamp burning beside him. It lit up his broad, tanned chest in a flickering light. The white bandage around his head made him look like a buccaneer. He moved his foot under the blanket so that it lifted in an invitation, although the motion stressed his bruised ribs and made him wince.

"She's not an ugly spider. I think she's pretty. She's here to keep me safe." Lucille wrung her hands as she crept over and sat down on the edge of the bed. Her back was pole stiff. Seth's big hands reached out and grasped her shoulders. They began to roll and knead like the paws of a friendly cat. Heat from her husband's body flowed around Lucille and all of her tension drained away. When she turned her head, she glimpsed his naked hip and muscular thigh halfway under the white sheet. She gulped and began to unbutton her bodice. Seth lowered his hands and pulled at her skirt.

"Seth, don't. That's my last good skirt."

"That's why I'm trying to tear it."

In spite of everything, Lucille covered her mouth as laughter spewed from it.

"The spider keeps you safe from what?" he asked.

She pressed her lips together as she hesitated. Seth began to pull the pins out of her hair. Her blonde locks fell loose and tumbled down over her bare shoulders. He ran his fingers through the tresses and pressed them against her scalp, where they began to knead. Lucille reached back and grasped his hand. "Keep me safe from you," she said.

"I'd never hurt you."

"No," she said, with conviction. She turned around and set her hands on the bed to climb into Seth's arms. "No, you wouldn't."

Although the mine was open again, Henry Best arrived at the plant Monday morning in a foul mood. He banged the door as he walked into the office, making Sitwell jump. He scowled as he poured himself a cup of coffee and went into his office without a word. At his desk, he quickly went over the morning reports. The dressing Doctor MacLean had put on his broken nose required him to breathe through his mouth; it was a damned nuisance, in addition to the throbbing pain.

Henry gingerly touched the tip of the splint with one finger. Ellie had shrieked with laughter at him when he got home from the fight, until he told her that if she thought his broken nose so funny, he would give her one of her own just like it. *The damned woman can't even manage her own children*, he thought with disgust. His mother-in-law had sent Ellie a furious telegram after Eleanor and Mildred arrived at their grandmother's house, which said she was going to send the children straight back. Ellie had then telephoned her mother and told her she would kill the girls if she had to look after them for one more minute. His wife's bared teeth, clenched fists, and crazy rolling eyes had actually frightened Henry, as had the sight of all the bruises on his oldest, Eleanor. To avoid a scandal, he had told his mother-in-law to send the girls to Ellie's sister Doris for now. Henry would pay the woman generously for her trouble and they would take the girls back when Ellie had calmed down.

With the arrangement made, Henry had turned to his wife and issued a decree. It had been her fault that the girls had run roughshod through the house. If she had been home watching them like a proper mother, it would not have happened. He had therefore refused to allow anyone to clean up the mess, or replace anything the girls had destroyed until Ellie bucked up, took back the children, and learned how to manage them. His wife had answered that with a sulk. Now, as a result of the wreckage in the house, they had to eat off tin plates just like a miner's family. The doors of the oak cabinet were still hanging open and the shambles of broken china remained on the kitchen floor. With resolution on his face, Henry would put on his slippers and tiptoe gingerly over the glass shards and smashed phonograph records in the parlour. Ellie, meanwhile, seethed over her broken jewellery and the blanket of feathers from her mattress that had formed a pile on the floor of her bedroom. The conflict simmered as Henry and his wife both refused to budge from their positions. Now, Ellie made no attempt to hide her scowls, but her husband only disregarded them.

What did anger him was the certainty that he would have lost the fight with Pruitt if Corporal Brock had not interfered. Every man who had witnessed it knew that, and it was the sight of Henry's weakness that had encouraged the miners to form a local. What was brewing was more than just a labour dispute; it was a challenge to Henry's manhood. No one would respect him again unless he crushed the union. Consequently, last week, when Sitwell had first brought him a message that the UMWA bargaining committee wished to speak to him, Henry had slapped his hand on his desk and stood up. He had walked into the outer office, picked up the candlestick phone off Sitwell's desk, and shouted into the mouthpiece, "You can shove your committee up your ass, you anarchist bastard! That's all the bargaining you're getting from me." The man at the other end of the line had tittered at his nasally, congested voice, which had made Henry slam the earpiece on its cradle with force. He had walked back into his office, huffing and puffing. After that, the union had tried to reach him by telegram, but he had told Sitwell he would fire him if he brought him any more "anarchist rubbish."

The thought of the insolent miners made Henry clench his fists and grit his teeth, while his smashed nose throbbed like a second heart. He thought of the improvements he had made to the town park and the church he was going to build. Just like Ellie, with all her jewellery and a dress collection so large it spilled out of her closet, the buggers would gripe no matter what he did for them. *I give them jobs*, he thought with a bitter twist of his mouth. Of course, the lazy bastards didn't want jobs — they wanted to tell Henry how to run his coal mine. If no one made a stand, soon they would demand an eight-hour day, workers' compensation, and Henry serving them their lunch on silver plates.

He picked up his telephone. The operator put him through to the labour contractor's number, the one that the man at the Fernie meeting had given to him. After he arranged for a crew of Chinese strikebreakers to come to Dominion Coal, Henry hung up the phone and laughed to himself. As lazy and insolent as the miners were, the sight of a lot of Chinese coolies digging the coal would be all it would take to break a strike. The race ploy always worked.

At the end of their shift on Monday, when the miners emerged from the tunnel, the pitbosses stopped them before they left. With the dust-covered men assembled in front of him like so many black shadows, PitbossNelson read a statement from Henry Best. First, it said that the wages and working conditions at Dominion Coal were the same as every other mine in the Crowsnest Pass. Secondly, any man who joined a "third-party negotiator" violated company policy and became subject to dismissal. The statement concluded by saying that Dominion Coal would prosecute "to the fullest extent of the law" any man who interfered with the operation of the mine. The men listened to the address with resentful faces and spits on the ground. At last, the pitboss folded up the statement and dismissed the miners.

The men walked back to town with their picks and shovels on their shoulders. They would go home, wash up, and then gather at the Oddfellows' Hall for the strike vote. Above them, clouds churned in the sky and a wind blew. Their feet tramped down the dirt road. If they walked, one man predicted, instead of that idiot Nelson reading them stories, they would have Mounties reading them the riot act. All the powers of the nation were arrayed against them: the bosses, the police, the newspapers, and the politicians. The weight of them all was as heavy as Turtle Mountain.

"I'm just going to lose money for nothing," a man grumbled. Baxter, Pearson, and the other men turned around.

"Keep talking like that and you'll lose a lot more," another man warned.

"That's just what Old Man Worst wants you to say," Baxter said. "At least let the fight get started before you throw in the towel."

That afternoon at the Pruitt house, Lucille was helping Kate wash Albert's diapers. They stood outside in the backyard pinning the wet diapers to the clothesline. The chickens strutted around their feet clucking contentedly. Kate talked to Albert as she picked the wet rags out of the metal washtub and hung them up. Lucille, meanwhile, was thinking to herself. *Seth isn't normal.* Her insides felt like someone had churned a dolly stick in them but they didn't hurt; instead, they emitted a warm vibration that glowed all the way through. But Seth certainly was not normal. Irving could not have done the things Seth did with her any more than he could have won the Kentucky Derby.

At one point, Kate saw Lucille mooning with her chin resting on her fingers and her vacant gaze stuck on the garden fence. She giggled. "Look, you and Seth keep going like that, you'll have one of these," she boosted Albert up in her arms, "by this time next year, I bet."

Lucille clapped her hand to her head. She had never pictured herself with a child of her own before. But what Kate said was certainly true. She began to smile. A baby of her and Seth's would be special, just like its father. Kate pinned up the last rag on the line and then picked up the empty metal tub. "You're lucky. Henry Best rogered like a squirrel."

"Kate!" Lucille looked at her with shock.

"Well, it's true." Albert, at that moment, gave a hungry cry. Kate and Lucille climbed the steps to the veranda and stepped through the back door of the house. Kate sat down at the table and as Albert wailed in his sling she unbuttoned her bodice.

Lucille stoked the oven to start cooking supper.

"You know, I think Henry hates women," Kate said with a sudden insight while her son nursed. "He dropped me like a hot potato, soon as I got to be a nuisance. He dropped that nanny after he got bored with her, just like he drops every other girl he flirts around with. He sets you up to knock you down. Say, have you heard? The word in town says he's going to fire all the miners now that they've formed a local. He'll have them all blackballed too."

Lucille glanced at her and made a face. "I certainly wouldn't put it past him."

"But at least I've got Albert," Kate said. "And soon, Albert's going to have a little cousin."

Lucille shivered. The prospect of childbirth — with all its danger — was much more concrete to her now.

"Aw, don't be worried," Kate said. "It's nothing to have a baby."

Lucille laughed. "That's not what you said at the time."

Kate laughed too but waved her hand. "Oh pooh. The toothache was worse than that."

Suddenly, footsteps ascended the veranda stairs outside the back door. Granny, who had been visiting Mrs. Baxter, came in first. She removed her shawl, hung it up, and placed the hat up on the hook over the shawl. Seth took off his derby and hung it on the hook next to Granny's hat. Lucille clenched her fists; she had to restrain herself from locking her arms around her new husband's neck and dragging him off to bed, especially when he turned and smiled at her. He had much more control than she did. He walked up and kissed her on her cheek.

"Lucille," he said, as he took an envelope out of his pocket and laid it on the table in front of her. She thought it was from her sister and picked it up. There was strange handwriting on it and a Vancouver postmark.

"That's from Noah," said Granny, as she sat down at the kitchen table. "You can read it to us after supper."

Lucille remembered Granny's son, the sea captain who owned the freighter on which the old woman and Seth had worked on all the way to South America. After the family ate supper, Lucille opened the envelope and read it aloud. Noah and his wife were both well, but he had decided to let his partner take the freighter on a new voyage to Australia. Now that he was staying ashore, he was anxious to have the family together again. In Vancouver, plenty of newcomers wanted furniture that Seth could build, and many young men were around for Kate to marry. When she finished reading, Lucille folded the letter.

Kate rocked Albert in her lap. "I'd like to harvest the garden before we go to Vancouver," she said. "Can you garden there? It rains all the time, I've heard."

"Well, it don't rain *all* the time," Granny said. "And it be good for the spider. Dinah likes the damp."

"I could make more money in a city," Seth said.

Lucille sat for a moment in thought. She was willing to move to Vancouver, only she would feel more enthusiasm if she could bring Lottie and the boys with her. It would be good for Lottie to move out of the house in Winnipeg, with all its sad memories, and start anew in another city. Also, Edward and Abner would make good big brothers for Albert, and her own child when it came. She would write Lottie and present the idea to her.

"Well, we should think on it some," Granny declared. "Right now, we've some fellows to boot in the rear." She stood up and lumbered toward the door. "I bumped into Mr. Baxter when he got home. They're holding the strike vote this evening, and he tells me some of the lads want to back down. That won't do. Best will have a good laugh at those miners, even with his nose bashed in."

Seth, quiet as always, smiled to himself. Lucille could not help rubbing his back, and he reached under the table and squeezed her thigh.

"So, I'm going to go down there and tell them what's what," Granny declared, as she opened the door.

Seth stood up. "The hall's too far away for you to walk to, Granny. I'll wheel you down in the barrow."

At the west end of Stony Point, the Oddfellows' Hall was shaking with the voices of the miners gathered inside it. Rupert and the executives of the UMWA bargaining committee sat at the head table. Although the men had sneered while Nelson read the company's statement, Dominion Coal's threat of mass dismissals and jail for any man who went on strike had done its work. What had been a solid membership now was split into two factions. The majority who favoured a strike shouted and shook their fists at the minority who did not. As the men argued, Rupert banged his gavel and tried to keep order. The organizer estimated that a quarter to a third of the miners would vote against a strike.

Presently, a lean miner with a sharp chin and patchy complexion stood up to speak. He shook a bill from the General Store in his hands. "Look! I've paid everything I can afford, but I still owe the store ten dollars. How am I going to get by on two dollars a week strike pay? And if Old Man Worst gets me blackballed, what the hell am I supposed to do then? Be a farmhand?"

Several men rose up and all began to shout. At the disorder, Rupert sighed and rubbed his head. It always worked like this; the company made a few threats and the membership split like dry wood.

He looked up as the door opened. The elderly woman he knew as Mrs. Aitken of the UMWA's Ladies' Auxiliary lumbered in on her walking stick. Rupert remembered her from the time the town Mountie had put her grandson in jail. She wore her old straw hat and a brown dress with a lace collar. As she passed, the miners shrank from meeting her eyes, except for the miner with the bill from the store in his hand. He spun around to face her with indignation. "Get out of here, you damned old woman! Union meeting's no place for a..."

Her hands moved so fast Rupert did not see them. Wood cracked against bone. The miner staggered backwards with his eyes rolling and his hand clamped over his mouth, while the old woman thrust out her chin. "What kind of man are you? If I were your wife I'd be ashamed!" She turned to the miners. The men who were standing shrank and sat down, pulling their caps down over their heads as if they were going to crawl up inside them. Rupert and the union men could only watch with their mouths hanging open as Granny spoke to the assembly. "Look lads, this old woman's ready to fight." She brandished her stick and the men cowered further down. "Are you?" The men looked at each other and a few began to mutter. Granny inhaled a deep breath then bellowed again, *"Well, are you?"* Her roar made the frame around the picture of King Edward VII rattle against the wall.

As the meeting came to a close, Rupert and the union men laughed among themselves. After the old lady had roared at them, the miners against the strike had clasped their hands in their laps and bitten their tongues. The miners in favour had cheered and laughed. Rupert pounced on the opportunity. Immediately, he had the ushers pass out the ballots. Local 2322 ended up voting for a strike by ninety-seven percent. At the end of the evening, while the men put on their caps and walked out the door, still laughing about Granny, Rupert thought to himself that with a few hundred more old women like Mrs. Aitken, the revolt of the workers would come so much quicker.

Chapter 15

—〰—

Tuesday, July 28, 1903

THE FOLLOWING DAY, Lucille and Seth went to the Post Office with her letters to Lottie and Uncle Noah. The afternoon train had just pulled into the station. A dozen large men stepped off with carpet bags in their hands. All wore derby hats, bushy moustaches, and swaggered as they walked. The goons lit cigars and marched down the wooden sidewalk from the station. All these men with their impudent faces raised Seth's hackles. He placed Lucille behind him inside the recessed doorway of the Post Office. As they passed, a few of the men spat on the dirt road next to the boardwalk, but Seth's massive shoulders, heavy fists, and the warning in his eyes kept them from saying anything.

"Pinkertons from the States," he observed as the men walked away. "Best is getting ready for the strike."

"I wonder if the businessmen and the politicians will ever protect us all against the menace of international goonism," Lucille said bitterly.

Seth laughed. "Naw, they won't ever do that."

At the front of the train, behind the locomotive, the doors of a freight car slid open with a bang. About twenty Chinese men in black pajamas, conical straw hats, and their hair in long braids jumped off the train; as they disembarked, their contractors shouted and cracked reed whips at their feet. Once they were all off the train, the Chinese stood in a ragged line holding their belongings in canvas bags. They wore expressions of guarded misery. With the strikebreakers assembled, the contractors marched them down the middle of King Edward Avenue. From behind Seth, Lucille watched the parade with a wry face. Best always had some ploy or another going; the sight of the Chinese entering town clearly was supposed to cow the union.

Seth turned his head to watch them go. "Poor little buggers," he said. "I bet the only experience they've had digging coal is driving spikes on the railroad."

As they made their way back to the house, Lucille gazed up King Edward Avenue. The goons had assembled in front of the Empire Hotel. Rather than wait for another riot, Arthur Wright had packed his bag and sneaked out of town in the middle of the night. His wife remained behind to look after their hotel. She opened the door and accepted a handful of cash from the chief goon. As the goons filed inside, the Chinese men marched past on their way to a tent city on the outskirts of town. Best must be paying some money to board the Pinkertons at the hotel and to feed and guard the Chinese. The Dominion Coal shareholders would not be pleased with the expense.

Lucille suddenly froze with an inspiration. She squeezed Seth's arm. "What is it?" he asked.

"Look at all those goons at the hotel. Now's the time for me to change my tactics. I'll write the shareholders. They won't be happy to see all the money Best is spending. I'll write their wives and tell them Best won't pay the men a fair wage so the miners' wives and children are going hungry."

Seth grinned to himself as he walked along with Lucille's hand in the crook of his elbow. Just before they turned the corner onto First Street, he stopped. Instead of walking toward the house, he turned her around. "Where are we going?" she asked.

"To the clothes shop. We're getting that hat you've had your eye on."

Lucille smiled and groaned. "Oh Seth, maybe it's not the time..."

"Bah, sure it's time. Things have come to a fine pass in this town if a man can't buy his wife a pretty hat. Then you can wear it to bed tonight."

Lucille yanked on his arm, clapped her hand over her mouth, and turned red.

At the house, they found Kate in the backyard, shaking a basin full of kitchen scraps over the garden for mulch. Granny was sweeping the veranda with a straw broom. Seth and Lucille greeted them and went inside with Lucille carrying the new hatbox. Granny chuckled to herself at the antics of the young people.

Kate was beaming. "I told Lucille we're going to have a cousin for Albert here pretty soon," she said to Granny as she climbed back up the stairs.

"Yes child, for certain we will."

That evening, Granny invited the Baxters over for supper. The Pruitts had bought a large roast beef from the Polish butcher, and with the miners set to walk out tomorrow, it might be a long time before their neighbours could afford to eat meat again. But Mrs. Baxter insisted she and her husband would manage. She sat at the table with a cup of tea as the other women worked around her.

"Ralph and I won't starve," she insisted. "We've got Mabel over at the ranch sending us money; it won't be a lot, but it'll pay the rent. We'll be much better off than a lot of people are going to be."

As the women visited in the kitchen, Baxter stayed outside with Seth near the tool shed. Seth smoked his pipe as he worked the pedal of the lathe; shavings peeled off the stick of wood that was going to be a leg in a rocking chair. Baxter spat tobacco as he sat on a tree stump nearby and whittled his picket, like every miner in Stony Point was doing this evening. "Well, it was a damned funny scene at work today," he said. The miners had worked their rooms as always and kept quiet about the impending strike since the ears of finks were everywhere. When the backs of the pitbosses were turned, they undermined beams and jammed the coal chutes with rocks. The last few men who left the mine that day pried out some rails from the trip track and dropped them down an unused shaft. The pitbosses had acted funny, too. Sanderson denied that there would be any strike and walked around the pit with a grin, pretending everyone was happy. Meanwhile, Nelson with his usual charm had grumbled all day about "lazy anarchist bastards." Baxter whittled his stick and laughed with Seth about how much Nelson was going to enjoy digging coal in the sabotaged mine.

Over supper, Seth and Lucille talked about the arrival of the Pinkertons from the United States and the Chinese strikebreakers. "All of those goons looked like convicts," Lucille said. "They were all wearing these fine clothes but you could almost see the stripes on underneath. I wouldn't be surprised if prison's where Henry Worst found them." She shuddered.

Baxter put his fork down with resignation on his face. "Well, Mrs. Pruitt, that's what those men do — bust heads. Some men lay bricks, some run printing presses, I mine coal, and those boys bust heads. They're even proud of it, the same way your husband would be proud of a chair he made." Granny *humphed* from her end of the table.

Meanwhile, Mrs. Baxter found herself watching the Pruitts' dish cabinet with fascination. She could have sworn she had seen a beetle crawling up the side of the cabinet until something purple darted out, snatched the insect, and vanished with it, all in half a second. While the woman blinked away what she thought was a hallucination, Granny said, "And who'll be doctoring you lads after those goons bust your heads?"

Baxter shrugged. "Well, I reckon we'll be doing that ourselves, ma'am. Lord knows we won't be able to afford Doc MacLean after we walk out."

"No, you'll not be doing it yourselves. It'll be hard enough to keep a man from crossing the line; it'll be harder if the lads have to get their heads kicked in every day with no one to tend them. I'll do it myself. I'm no doctor, mind you, but the sailors on my boy Noah's freighter had no complaints."

Seth spoke up with enthusiasm. "Yeah, Granny can fix anything. A fellow on another boat got scalded real bad when their boiler sprang a leak. Granny patched him up and he was good as new."

Baxter looked doubtful. "Are you sure, Mrs. Aitken? The mine's a long way for you to walk and I know your feet aren't good."

But Mrs. Baxter was keen. "Why, us in the Auxiliary can carry her to the mine." She spoke to the table. "We'll pitch a tent and tend to the boys in there."

Granny agreed. "Seth can hire the mule from the livery stable, and I'll ride to the mine on that. A mule's good enough for me."

Early the next morning, Granny packed up a leather case with yarrow, spider webbing, a large bottle of cheap whiskey, and bandages that Lucille and Kate had rolled. She rode to the mine on the back of a mule, with Seth walking beside her carrying her case. On the way, they met Mrs. Baxter, Mrs. Ruzicka, and other women of the Ladies' Auxiliary. They were pushing a handcart loaded with a dismantled tent and pots of tea and coffee for their husbands. At the end of the dirt road, Seth and the women found a wire fence stretching around the perimeter of the mine. The sun was hot already, but in spite of the heat and dust the miners were pacing back and forth in front of the gateway in the fence with their pickets on their shoulders.

The miners' wives erected the tent just off the side of the road in front of a knot of pine trees. It was six in the morning. Just as usual, the whistle above the lamp house sounded one blast and, as if on cue, the police, goons, and strikebreakers appeared in the distance. They raised a cloud of dust as they approached. Corporal Brock and two other Mounted Policemen rode at the head of the group. They wore their Stetson hats and red serge tunics and looked with scorn at the men on the picket line. Behind the police, the Pinkertons marched as one body. Each of these men had his sleeves rolled up and carried a wooden club, which he smacked in his palm as he approached the line. All of the goons wore grins of anticipation. Behind the thugs came the Chinese men, who trudged up the road in the dust and the droppings left by the policemen's horses.

Granny watched them approach from the entrance to the tent. "Those wee buggers, they're a sight worse off than we are," she observed to the women beside her.

"Good morning ladies," said a cheery voice. Granny turned to see Mr. Rupert and a small, slightly built Chinese man next to him. Mr. Rupert introduced this man as Mr. Joe, whom the UMWA had sent to talk to the Chinese strikebreakers. The young man wore his black hair cut short in the western style and a woollen jacket and cap. Meanwhile, Corporal Brock and the policemen stopped their horses about ten yards away from the picket line.

As the men jeered and waved their sticks, Brock reached back into his saddlebag and pulled out a declaration. He puffed up as he read it. "By the authority vested in me, in the name of the King, you are hereby called upon to disperse." A chorus of hoots, catcalls, and raspberries came from the picket line. Corporal Brock glared at the miners and continued. "If you do not clear this road, we will use force."

Baxter, in front of the pickets, cupped his hands around his mouth and shouted, "Look boys, it's the Referee!" The men roared. They had given Corporal Brock this name after he had broken up the fight between Henry Best and Seth Pruitt.

Another man said, "Corporal, if I had a face that ugly I'd shave my ass and walk backwards."

The men laughed again. Corporal Brock did not bother reading the rest of the statement. With anger on his wrinkled face, he folded up the paper and turned his horse around. He jerked his head to the Pinkertons. The burly men with their clubs advanced on the picket line. The first man raised his club and swiped it at Baxter's head. Baxter dodged the blow and turned back to the picketers. "Everybody down!" he yelled. The miners sat down in front of the gate. As the goons waded in among them, they held their sticks over their heads to protect themselves from the clubs. The Pinkertons lifted the miners by their collars and tried to drag them to the side of the road, but the miners, in turn, let themselves go limp, knowing that if they raised a hand at any of the goons, the police would arrest them. At the same time, a Pinkerton cracked his club off the head of a fifteen-year-old breaker boy two yards away from one of the Mounties who sat on his horse and watched. The goons cursed as they struggled with the dead weight of the men. Suddenly, one of the Pinkertons cried out and jumped away, holding his crotch. The strikers laughed and shouted encouragement to each other.

As he watched the battle, Seth paced about restlessly and knocked his fists together. His scowl grew blacker by the minute as the goons beat the unarmed miners. A few yards in front of him, a Pinkerton with the shoulders of an ox raised his club over Pearson's head and struck the miner. The blow rang out and Pearson collapsed. Seth ran towards the fallen man.

"Pruitt!" Brock trotted towards Seth on his horse. "Mind your own business and back off."

But now the women advanced. They pelted Brock and the other policemen with stones. A horse reared up and whinnied under the onslaught, dumping his rider to the ground. Seth kicked a Pinkerton hard in his pants and the man staggered out of his way. Pearson sat in the dirt. A bloody lump stood out on the side of the dazed man's head. Seth pulled the heavy-set miner to his feet and helped him over to the tent. Granny took the man inside and sat him down on a stool to treat his wound. He was one of four injured miners here.

Meanwhile, behind all the chaos at the line, Mr. Joe walked back to where the Chinese waited for the goons to pull the picketers out of their way. With an eye on the scowling contractors, the young Chinese man addressed the coolies. The leader of the strikebreakers answered him, and their dialogue continued above the noise of the riot. Mr. Joe pleaded with the Chinese to stay out of the mine. The other man asked him what else they were supposed to do. Each of the labourers owed the contractors money for paying his Head Tax and they must work to pay the debt. They continued talking. All of a sudden, anger appeared on the faces of the Chinese and they began to grumble among themselves. Mr. Joe had pointed out that they were being robbed: while a white man received three dollars a day for his work in the mine, the Chinese men would make only one dollar.

After a few more minutes of struggle, Corporal Brock decided to push the Chinese through the gate in spite of the picket line. He gestured to the contractors but the first Chinese man — with whom Mr. Joe had been talking — turned around to his mates. He clapped his hands and began to sing. The other Chinese men laughed and joined in. Corporal Brock impatiently waved the strikebreakers forward but all of them sank down onto the road. The miners on the picket line lowered their sticks and the cries of "Chink" and "slant-eyed son of a bitch" died on their lips. Now, the strikebreakers were on strike too.

Later that day, back at the Pruitt house, Lucille sat at the kitchen table staring at a newspaper in her hand. The editor of this paper had printed her letter about Stanley's disappearance. He had also printed his reply underneath it:

My dear madam,

You will find more scruples in a ditch full of rattlesnakes, than in the businessmen and politicians of this Territory. To expect ethical behaviour from these men is laughable in the extreme.

However, I wish you luck, and remain your friend.
Robert Chambers Edwards, The High River Eye-Opener

Lucille rested her head on her fist and sat for awhile in contemplation. Of all the replies she had received, this note was the only one that had not repeated the twaddle that "all was for the best in this best of all possible worlds." She should frame it. Instead, she set the paper aside and picked up an envelope that had come from the Minister of Labour's office in Ottawa. She tore open this reply from a deputy minister, a Mr. William Lyon Mackenzie King. In contrast to *Eye-Opener* Bob, Mr. King assured Lucille that the authorities took the disappearance of Stanley Birch very seriously. He added that unions, with their radical outlook and foreign leadership, only aggravated the labour strife in Canada's coal industry. After she read the end of the letter, Lucille sat a moment with her teeth clenched. *Drat this imbecile.* With any luck, Mr. King would have only a short career in politics. She took a deep breath before picking up her pen and composing her reply.

After an hour, she stretched her back and clicked open her small watch on its chain. Kate had gone down to the picket line a while ago to see what was happening and had left Albert with her. At that moment, the baby woke up and cried for a changing. Lucille put him in a clean diaper and balanced him on her hip. At first, he whimpered for Kate, but in time, he got used to Lucille and began to smile as she dandled and sang to him. He was gaining weight fast; certainly, by the time he was grown he would have his father's tall, solid frame. Lucille walked with the baby in her arms from the parlour back to the kitchen. On an impulse, she stepped out the back door onto the veranda. The sun was shining, and as she gazed at the scorched area behind the house, she thought she could see green shoots peeping up through the blackened ground.

The chickens in the yard raised their heads and clucked as footsteps approached. Kate appeared with her face pink from running and dust covering the hem of her skirt. A plain straw hat protected her fair complexion from the sun. In Lucille's arms, Albert exclaimed with joy. Kate took him and the two women stepped back inside the house. The girl was shaking with news.

"How's everything down there?" Lucille asked. "Are Granny and Seth all right?"

"Oh, they're fine," Kate said. "But the funniest thing happened. The Chinamen Henry brought in have all gone on strike too. They're all sitting down in the middle of the road and they won't move. So it looks like the miners are winning, so far — if you can call getting bashed in the head winning. Those darned thugs Henry brought in are carrying on. Granny's got a tent full of miners with cuts and bruises. But no one's crossed the line."

Lucille raised her fist in triumph. There were no scabs in Stony Point. With renewed enthusiasm she sat down over her letter.

Early one afternoon, two days later, Ellie Best stepped out her front door and walked to the carriage house. Grey clouds churned in the sky and a chilly, irritated wind pushed the trees around. Ellie found she had to wear her shawl to keep warm. She strode across the gravel driveway with her husband's binoculars inside a leather case that she toted over her shoulder. Since the coal miners had begun their strike, Henry had been leaving the house for the mine every day well before dawn and seldom came home before midnight. His broken nose, the union, and the strike had put him in a permanent bad temper, and he replied to everything Ellie said with rolling eyes and sarcasm. Thank God the foul-tempered bastard was gone all day.

When she rolled open the heavy red door, Sultan thrust his head out the window of his stall and snorted hostility. His long ears pricked forward. The horse then laid his ears and tossed his head at Ellie, who scowled back at him. *How I hate that ugly beast!* Like he always did when she scrambled past his stall, Sultan reached his muzzle out as far as he could. His big white teeth snapped viciously at Ellie's skirt as she slipped past just out of his reach. The other day, she had soaked some grain in rat poison and brought a pan of it to him. It would pay back her husband for all Henry's abuses if she poisoned his beloved horse. But to her astonishment, Sultan had some supernatural animal intelligence. Instead of eating the grain, the devilish horse had whinnied, reared, and lashed at Ellie with a front hoof that was the size of a pie plate. The pan with the grain had gone flying. As she climbed the wooden stairs, she could only tell herself that she would get that damned horse one day.

Up in the hayloft she pushed a bale of hay over to the door. She unhitched the latch and sat down on the bale. In the wind, a sheet of newspaper tumbled over the shaven expanse of the lawn. Ellie clutched her shawl around her in the blustery weather. She looked at the Pruitt house in the distance across the river. At first, she had been disappointed when the fire she had set had burned only the brush behind the house, but Ellie had recovered her spirits quickly when she had discovered that up here in the loft she now had a clear view of the Pruitts' backyard.

Now Ellie watched through Henry's binoculars while the speckled hens wandered about. The birds scratched up the dirt and pecked at grasshoppers and bugs. Then, the back door of the house opened. Ellie leaned forward as Kate Pruitt stepped out, carrying her baby in the sling in front of her. Ellie's face went white and she clenched her fist in her lap. Kate also had her rifle over her shoulder. The girl stepped over the chicken wire fence into the garden, knelt down, and began to pull weeds. Ellie's gaze focused on the bundle in front of Kate.

We'll see how far up on your high horse you'll be without that baby boy, she thought as she ground her teeth. If Kate had not had the rifle, Ellie would have jumped on the bicycle she had ordered from Eaton's catalogue and been down at the Pruitt house in two minutes. She would have taken the razor she had nicked from Henry's bathroom and sliced up Kate's youthful, pretty face with it. Then, she would have seen to the baby. Ellie clenched her fist and sweat broke out on her neck.

She had thought she had a chance the other day, when she had been unable to spot Kate through the windows of the house, and had wondered if maybe the slut was outside and the baby was alone. She had been just about to run for the bicycle, but then that mouthy blonde whore stepped outside onto the back veranda with the boy in her arms. Ellie had sunk down again in disappointment. She had forgotten Seth Pruitt's wife, and instinct told her the cow with her parasol was as dangerous to her as Kate with her rifle. But Ellie knew she would get a chance. All she needed was patience.

Chapter 16

—ᴍ—

Tuesday, August 18, 1903

A FEW WEEKS LATER, Lucille and Kate were washing laundry in the backyard of the house. Lucille sat at a large metal washtub. She had tied her hair back with a kerchief and wore a white apron. She chattered with Kate as she rubbed a skirt against the washboard. The girl stood nearby stirring the wet clothes with the dolly stick as they boiled in another tub. All of the white linens were hanging from lines strung up all over the yard. Lucille wrung out a skirt, and water trickled down her arms. She carried it over and placed it into the boiling tub. As she sat down again on the stool she wiped her forehead. She and Kate were almost finished washing these dark clothes. All they had to do now was take down the dry whites and hang the wet laundry in their place. They had been washing since early that morning; now, Lucille's arms ached and her hands were raw from the soda crystals in the wash water.

Nearby, Seth sat on the wooden stool at his workbench. A large headboard lay clamped to the bench, which he was making for the MacDiarmids, the family who owned the Stony Point sawmill. While Lucille worked, her gaze often fell on Seth. He leaned over the headboard now with his massive shoulders, a hammer in his huge fist. A series of *bams* signalled that a sturdy leg was being pounded into the matching groove in the headboard. Lucille's pride swelled, and she had to put down the heavy wet skirt in the tub of water for a moment. She could not remember ever having felt this way about Irving, even before he had started drinking.

Seth now lifted his hat and wiped sweat from his forehead. The chickens cackled and the women looked up. Nellie Perkins was hurrying toward the backyard. The girl wore a grey apron over her dark blue dress; she was hatless and her hair streamed out behind her. Kate gave Lucille the dolly stick and went to talk with her. Breathlessly, Nellie reported that the Mounties had arrested Granny Aitken. Nellie and her mother had just watched them go past their shop. Granny had been sitting on the Mountie's horse, and the small procession had been headed to the NWMP station.

Kate went pale with concern. "She looked all right?" she asked Nellie.

The girl nodded. "Oh yeah, she was yelling her head off about how she had a right to be anywhere she wanted. She kept trying to clobber the Mountie with her stick. She looked fine to me."

Kate smiled with relief. But Lucille set her hands on her hips and took deep breaths to contain her rising anger. In the weeks since the strike had begun, every miner on the picket line had spent at least one day in the jail. Corporal Brock brought in a new set of men every evening to replace the old. In every case, the charge had been the same: disorderly conduct. It had been the Pinkertons who broke the heads, but only union miners had gone to jail. Lucille had written to the politicians about this injustice until her hand felt ready to fall off. So far, she had received no answer. It was a comfort to know Granny was in good spirits for the present. But could she hold out in the stifling interior of the cell in the North-West Mounted Police station?

As soon as they hung up the dark clothes, Lucille and Kate filled a pot with tea. Together, they walked to the station. Seth followed with a bucket of water in each hand. In spite of the discomfort and stench in the jail, a party was taking place with jokes, laughter, and songs. The miners in the cell were treating

Granny like Queen Alexandra. Against the heat, they took off their waistcoats and fanned the old woman, who sat on the foldaway bed between Pearson and a grizzled miner with a large silver moustache. The other miners lined the floor along the log wall and sang a union song. They greeted the arrival of the Pruitts and the water with raised hats and a noisy cheer. Granny peered at them through the bars of the cell door. "Oh," she exclaimed. "Here's me children."

"Granny, what did you do?" Kate asked, while Lucille gave a tin cup to a skinny man with an Adam's apple like a buzzard's; eagerly, he drank from the bucket. Granny's face fell abruptly as did those of the miners. Lucille worried; she had expected only defiance from the old woman.

"Three of the lads crossed the line this morning," Granny said at last. The women groaned. "I took me stick and I was trying to herd those poor wee lost lambs back to where they should be, but then the police arrested me. So here I am." Lucille rubbed her head while Kate poured Granny the tea. The strikers had managed to go so long with no man crossing the line. It had been too good to last.

"I understand they're hungry," the grizzled miner on the bed exclaimed as the old woman drank her tea. "But, well, I beg you ladies' pardons, but damn it, we're all hungry."

"Bah," Granny said. "If they're hungry, they can whittle themselves a fishing pole. The river's jumping with fish. And they can get themselves a bucket and go pick blueberries. They're growing all over the place. There's no need for anyone to be going hungry. The Auxiliary still has money from the Pie Fest. They can use some to buy a can of beans." Granny clapped her hands. "Everyone needs a wee bit of a rest. We'll have a picnic on Saturday. Everyone can have some fun, and those bloody scabs can watch and see what they're missing."

On the same day, Henry Best met with the shareholders of Dominion Coal on an upper floor of the Alberta Hotel in Calgary. A circle of men sat around a polished wooden table while the chairman addressed them. By this time, the doctor had removed the dressing from Henry's nose. Louis Hammond from Montreal, the bastard, had laughed at its new angle and asked him if he had run into a wall, but the other men made no comments. Instead, they listened to Henry's progress report. Of course, the chairman said, production at the mine was less than five percent of normal, but the shortfall was only temporary. If the company folded and let the union win, the miners would make even more insane demands. It was imperative that the owners stand their ground; if they failed, anarchists and foreign agitators would soon be dictating to every businessman in Canada.

Henry sat down. Hammond occupied the chair to his right. The man had a square head, stiff grey whiskers, and a starched white collar. For some reason, his prickly temper was particularly short this day. He struck the table with his fist and shouted, "What about my money?" The other shareholders grumbled in in agreement. Hammond held up a sheet of paper. "I see here we're paying to board the security team in a hotel. Who the hell are they — the Russian royal family? It's a damnable expense. And, on top of that," Hammond took an angry breath to continue, "some woman in that town wrote to my wife telling her how the miners live. The same damned crazy woman's also been writing to Frederick Haultain. Now he's got his finger in my button hole telling me we've got to settle this strike. This is shabby management," he concluded as he scowled at Henry.

Before the chairman could answer, another man spoke up. "Some woman wrote my wife too," George MacBain of Toronto said with surprise. "She wrote that her brother-in-law's gone missing, along with a union organizer, and no one's tried to find them because of the anti-union sentiment among the authorities." He turned to Henry and pointed his abominable cigar at him. "Have you heard anything about this?"

Henry took a deep breath. "Gentlemen, if you ever met that

woman, you'd agree with me; she needs a buggy whip across her backside. She's nothing but a troublemaker. For weeks now, she's been meddling in affairs she doesn't understand any better than a chipmunk, and stirring up all her friends in the newspaper business with a lot of hysterical nonsense." Henry's eyes filled with amusement as he glanced around the table. "Now, what man here's going to let a woman talk business to him?"

All of the shareholders, even Hammond, fell silent and lowered their eyes. One man grimaced resentment and shuffled his feet, but another looked at Henry with admiration at how quickly he could extricate himself from a corner. "A few more days and the strike will be finished," the chairman continued. "The miners haven't had a paycheque in weeks and all they have to eat is beans. I received a telegram this morning that said three of them crossed the line. Any day now, all of them will put away their pickets and go back to work."

On Saturday afternoon, Granny, Kate, and Lucille bustled about the kitchen getting ready for the picnic. Granny sliced up a joint of roast beef and wrapped the slices in tin foil. Kate came inside the kitchen from the garden. She beamed as she showed Granny and Lucille a bunch of carrots she had just pulled. They were the first vegetables ready out of the ground and the women agreed they looked wonderful. As Lucille helped Granny pack the wicker basket, she happened to reach up to a cupboard door. She drew back in surprise to see Dinah resting on it. As always, in the house, the spider appeared and disappeared; presently, she basked in the sunshine and her legs rotated as she spun a net.

Suddenly, Seth came into the kitchen with an armload of firewood that he had chopped for the communal fire. Concern cast a shadow over his face. "I was just talking to Baxter next door," he said. "Word's going around that the goons are going to show up at the ball field."

Granny thrust out her chin. "Bah! Let them come! If they make trouble, we'll boot them all in the pants, and maybe then they'll leave town. You'd think they'd get it through their heads by now that they aren't welcome." In spite of her brave words, the faces of Lucille, Kate, and Seth were heavy with apprehension. Nonetheless, when they had packed the basket, everyone filed out the back door.

It was a lovely warm day with a brisk wind. Lucille held onto her hat while she carried the wicker picnic basket. Kate carried Albert in his sling. Seth walked along with a bundle of firewood under each arm, and Granny lumbered on her walking stick. At one point, the old woman had to sit down and rest. Lucille pretended she was tired too and sat down on the edge of the wooden sidewalk next to her; at the same time, she exchanged glances with Kate. If only they could do something about Granny's arthritis. At least Dinah's magical silk allowed her to walk a little distance. They must keep the spider for as long as they could.

Just like on Dominion Day, everyone in town was converging on the ball field. Men from the union executive placed tubs of bottled drinks on the picnic tables, along with jugs of stronger stuff for the miners. Seth placed the firewood in a large pile near the firepit along with the contributions everyone else had made. Granny, Kate, and Lucille joined the Ladies' Auxiliary. The women were making a great cauldron of mulligan stew. Everyone added what they could to the pot; one woman brought a large handful of green beans and another an arm-load of potatoes. The women exclaimed with joy when Lucille added in the slices of beef. As the pot simmered, she looked around with satisfaction. Instead of fretting about the strike, the men were tossing horseshoes or standing in a circle passing around a jug of whiskey. The children ran around squealing and laughing over the field.

Later, they all sat down to eat. Kate finished her stew, and when the Stony Point band began a reel up in the gazebo, she took Albert out of his sling and danced the baby in time with the music. His tiny feet bobbed about over the grass and he screeched with enjoyment. Seth sat on the grass nearby smoking his pipe. He was just about to take Lucille's hand to dance, when he turned his head. Abruptly, his hackles rose as he growled. Lucille followed his gaze.

Eight Pinkertons were approaching the picnic area. The band fell silent as the burly men in derby hats strolled up. The thugs walked with their hands in their coat pockets and provoking smirks on their whiskery faces. Seth rose up and hastened towards Granny. The tiny old woman stood in front of the approaching thugs with menace on her face. Kate would have stayed, but she didn't want to expose Albert to the dangers of a riot. Quickly, she put the baby back in his sling and scrambled to her feet. Other women were likewise taking the hands of their children and leading them away from the field. In addition to Albert, Kate took Lanka with her back to the house after speaking with Mrs. Ruzicka.

Meanwhile, the chief Pinkerton watched the women and children leave. He looked around with mockery on his face. One of the men behind him grinned and spat a wad of tobacco juice into the cauldron of stew. At that, one of the miners snarled. He and his mates formed a hostile circle around the thugs. The insolence on the goons' faces only grew thicker. Mr. Rupert approached the Pinkertons. Next to him, Granny leaned on her heavy walking stick and eyed the thugs as the union representative spoke.

"Boys, I've got to ask you to leave," he said. "This is a workers' function."

The chief Pinkerton, who was the tallest and most brawny of the thugs, looked at Rupert. "We'll go wherever the hell we want, you anarchist bastard."

Granny's hands moved fast. Her stick shot up and whipped forward; the hard knob at the end of it struck the goon in the mouth. Seth pointed at the man and laughed. The Pinkerton held his hand over his bleeding lip and blinked with pain and surprise, as the insolence vanished from the faces of the other goons. They now looked around with rising alarm while the circle of angry miners closed in around them.

Lucille scrambled up and placed herself in-between Granny and the outraged goon. "Look at that!" she exclaimed to the miners. "These thugs are nothing but cowards. Who else would try and menace a harmless old woman?" All of the miners present growled. Now the goons were retreating in twos and threes, except for the chief Pinkerton, who was in too much pain.

Granny stepped forward and shouted at him. She had to bend her neck backwards to look at the tall man. "You'll not be using that foul language here! Now the man just asked you and your boys to leave. You can do it civil or," she brandished her heavy stick, "we'll do it like this!"

"Why, you old bitch!" the thug snarled. He raised his fist, but Seth caught his forearm in his hand. He drove his right fist into the goon's ribs. The Pinkerton's breath whooshed out of him in a gust and he sank to his knees.

Rupert called out to the other miners. "C'mon boys, let's pay back what we owe!"

In the meantime, Kate and Lanka arrived at the Pruitt house. The mother allowed the girl to hold Albert in her lap and then put him in his cradle. Lanka beamed. The baby lay under the bonnet, looked around, and put his tiny thumb in his mouth. Kate sat back and breathed a great sigh of relief. She was just about to unpin her hat, when a boy's voice sounded at the front door.

"Miss Pruitt! There's a fight at the baseball field. One of the goons took a swing at your granny! I think she's hurt." The boy's footsteps hurried away.

Kate paled and rose to her feet. "For goodness sakes." Quickly, she looked from side to side in indecision. "Lanka, stay here and mind the baby." The girl nodded eagerly and Kate raced out the door. As it closed behind her, Lanka looked down at Albert. The baby sucked his fist and looked back at her.

Lanka gave him her little finger and the infant squeezed it in an iron grip. "I helped you get born. You sure are a lot bigger now." Albert grinned toothlessly, gurgled spittle, and kicked his miniature legs. Lanka hummed a song and rocked the cradle as she waited for Miss Kate to return.

Four minutes passed. Suddenly, the front door to the house opened and Lanka looked up. A tall lady with dark hair, a slender figure, and a proud face stood in the doorway. Lanka drew back at the woman's immaculately styled hair under a flowery hat and her white gloves. The stranger's face was red from exertion and the toes of her shoes were covered in dust.

"You, girl," she said. "Go back to the baseball field. Your mother's gotten hurt."

Lanka jumped up in alarm. She wanted to go to her mother, but she had told Miss Kate she would mind the baby. The elegant woman stepped forward, grasped her shoulder in a pinch, and shoved her impatiently to the front door of the house. "I'll watch the baby. Go on, girl!" Lanka, frantic for her mother, cried as she flew out the door.

Once the girl was gone, Ellie Best looked at her husband's son. The baby lay in the cradle with his tongue poking out over his lower lip. He smiled and reached out to her, convinced that since the stranger was a woman like his mother, Lucille, and his grandmother, she must be a friend. Ellie's eyes darted around the parlour. A pillow with Queen Victoria's head embroidered on it rested on the seat of a rocking chair in the corner. It was the perfect size to hold over the baby's face. She glanced back over her shoulder and crept to the rocking chair with excitement starting to bubble inside her. No one would know, and even if someone figured it out, who would ever hang a rich man's wife? Kate Pruitt deserved to lose her child. If Ellie could not have a baby boy, she was damned if an insolent little hussy was having one.

She had just grasped the pillow when at that instant, something colourful with an abundance of legs darted out from under it. The thing clamped itself around her hand. Agony ripped into Ellie's skin — like a hornet's sting but much more intense. She screamed and swatted at the creature that leapt away just in time. The blow to her hand cranked up the intensity of the pain. Only with a supreme effort did Ellie manage to stay on her feet. Through swimming eyes, she saw the large spider that had attacked her shoot up the wall. It vanished behind one of the beams in the ceiling. Ellie's eyes popped out of her head. She dared to look at the injured hand that she now clutched under her arm. Tiny twin puncture wounds lay in the soft flesh between her index finger and thumb; already, the flesh around the holes had turned black. Clasping her right hand in her left, she whimpered in terror as she fled the Pruitt house.

She ran over the small wooden bridge to the trail, past where she had left her bicycle in the ditch. Her only thought was to get back home as fast as she could, so she abandoned the bicycle. Ellie lifted her skirt and tried to hurry, but the road from the Pruitt's to her house sloped uphill; plowing ankle-deep through molasses would have been easier. With every step, her agony and terror increased. Her right hand was on fire. At one point, she lowered it and tried to swing it at her side to add to her momentum but, at the motion, a white sheet of pain blinded her. Ellie tried to scream, but her throat was raw. At last, through her blurry eyes she spotted the dark green pine tree that she could see from the dining-room window of the Best house. She only had to walk a few more dozen yards.

Although it had been so long a prison to her, Ellie wept with relief to see her house. She held her skirts up past her ankles as she scrambled up the driveway with her feet crunching over gravel. Sobbing, she burst through the front door of the Best mansion. She raced upstairs to the bathroom and yanked open the door of the medicine cabinet. Frantically, she searched through the bottles of Milk of Magnesia, Higinbotham's Vegetable Blood Tonic, and Dr. Shoop's Restorative. As she tore through the bottles, she kept her injured hand folded against her chest. It throbbed in time with the thuds from her panicked heart.

The pain was incredible and spreading fast. The spider that had bitten her had injected a ball of fire deep into her flesh under her right index finger. With her eyes bright and her white lips trembling, Ellie found herself pulling on her fingers, as if she could ease the agony by stretching her hand and giving the poison more room. But the venom popped capillaries, rotted flesh, and punctured veins as it spread through her hand and up her arm. The skin between her thumb and forefinger had now turned purple and swelled out to the size of an egg. Suddenly, Ellie felt dizzy. The medicine cabinet swam in her vision. With her head spinning like one of Eleanor's tops, she leaned over, gagged, and sprayed watery vomit into the bathtub. The pain from the slight motion of her hand as she did so forced another stream of vomit from her stomach. Defeated, with her hand burning off, Ellie swiped vomit from the sides of her mouth As she began to comprehend the gravity of her situation she trembled. *Oh God, I'm going to die.* She threw the bottle of blood tonic against the wall and began to sob.

When Kate had arrived back at the baseball field, she had been relieved to find that her grandmother's injury was much exaggerated. The old woman had brandished her walking stick at the backs of the company goons, who were fleeing the field with a number of the younger miners after them. The volume of her defiant shouts had made it clear that she was unharmed. Seth had laughed heartily at the old woman and boasted to the men present that his Granny "didn't take nothing sitting down." Lucille had stood at his side and clasped her head in both hands. It had been impossible to subdue the lawless old woman.

Kate had rushed up to her grandmother and thrown her arms around her neck. "Granny, some boy told me a goon took a swing at you."

"There now, Katie, I'm all right." She had patted Kate on her back as she spoke and jerked her chin in the direction of the fleeing thugs. "They're much more damaged than I am." Kate's knees had wobbled with relief.

Presently, she and Lucille began to pack up the picnic basket. Lucille made a face over the ruined stew in the pot, but she was encouraged at how the miners had run off the goons. No man would cross the picket line now.

All of a sudden, she heard the distressed cry of a small girl. Lanka rushed up to her mother, who was standing nearby, and threw her arms around Mrs. Ruzicka's skirts. "Mama!" The woman looked at her frantic daughter with some surprise and began to soothe her. Kate wondered what had upset Lanka enough to make her leave Albert by himself in the house.

"A lady came," Lanka said, with a tear-streaked face. "She said Mama had gotten hurt in the fight. She said she'd mind the baby."

Kate froze and her face turned white. She could not speak, so Lucille stepped forward.

"Lanka, what did the woman look like?" she asked. "Did she have light coloured hair, like this?" She held up one of her blonde locks. Firmly, Lanka shook her head.

"No, she had dark hair. And nice clothes too."

Lanka jumped as Kate screamed. "Albert!" The young mother then raised her skirts and ran off the field. She flew down the wooden sidewalk while men and women whom she passed spun around to look at her. Lucille ran a few yards behind her. The picture of Albert alone with Ellie Best was making her hair stand on end. At the house, she followed Kate up the back steps and through the door.

"Albert!" the mother cried out again. In the parlour, the baby lay in his cradle. He was a healthy pink colour and he smiled as he held out his hands. Above him, Dinah sat on top of the cradle bonnet, spinning a hunting net. Her spindly legs flexed as she drew a length of thread from her spinnerets. Kate sobbed as she picked up her son. She tore off his skirts and barrow-coats and examined him for an injury. Gradually, as she found him unharmed, her terror subsided. She placed Albert's head over her shoulder and clasped him tightly to her chest, rocking him back and forth.

Meanwhile, giddy with relief, Lucille collapsed into a chair near the door. Her gaze fell on the pillow from the rocking chair that sat on the floor in front of the fireplace. At the sight, her mouth fell open. "Kate look, the pillow. My God, was she going to smother the baby?" In her revulsion her vision swam. She bit her knuckle and concentrated on it so she wouldn't vomit.

"She wasn't up to any good, that's for sure," Kate declared. "That horrid, horrid woman!" Both women sat in shock.

Soon afterwards, Seth and Granny stepped through the front door. Lucille jumped up to throw her arms around Seth. Granny walked over to where Kate sat with Albert in her lap, putting the baby's clothes back on. Kate was laughing as Albert babbled and pulled at her bodice with tiny fists. "He's all right, Granny, nothing's wrong with him."

The old woman peered at the baby. Then she pointed to the top of the cradle. "Dinah scared that woman off. I told you, she doesna like strangers in her house," she said with conviction. Everyone looked at the spider. Kate sat in silence as she rocked Albert in her lap. Lucille froze in astonishment next to Seth. Did Kate owe her baby's life to a spider?

Chapter 17

The idea of losing baby Albert in such a horrible way had left the whole family rattled. Kate sat at the kitchen table where she clutched her son to her breast and trembled as she rocked him. Next to her, Lucille sipped the tea Granny had brewed and tried to comprehend the depravity of a woman who would murder a baby. Next to her, the old woman rubbed her speckled forearms in a silence unusual for her. She then took her knitting from inside her apron and clicked the needles rapidly in her hands, which showed her agitation. At one point, Lucille ran her gaze along the walls and up at the ceiling. Dinah had vanished again somewhere in the house.

At that moment, footsteps climbed the stairs to the back door and someone knocked on it. Seth stood up from the table and opened it. Kate and Lucille looked at each other in surprise to see the homely Charity MacLean, the doctor's wife, standing out on the veranda. She wore a straw hat and clutched a shawl around her shoulders. "What is it?" Lucille asked. She had never overcome her dislike for this woman who had refused to attend to Kate when she was birthing Albert.

The doctor's wife said, "Mrs. Pruitt? My husband's at the Best house. He says Mrs. Best's been asking for you."

Kate whirled around and her mouth fell open.

Lucille peered at Mrs. MacLean in disbelief. "What?"

"He says she's dying. He doesn't expect her to last the night." In astonishment, Lucille now rose up out of her seat. Granny peeped with dismay, her needles clacking ever more sharply. Lucille told Mrs. MacLean she would go to the Best house. She went to put on her shoes and hat.

On Seth's arm, she walked up the dirt road toward the Bests' mansion. In spite of the lovely evening, both she and her husband wore solemn faces. Lucille breathed deeply of the fresh air and gazed at the pine trees on the slope of the hill ahead. Completely perplexed, she wondered why on earth Ellie was asking for her. Certainly it couldn't be to apologize. *Does she know something about Stanley?* Lucille frowned to herself in thought. That made no sense.

Seth glanced at her troubled face and squeezed her arm. "What is it?"

"I can't understand why Mrs. Best would want to see me." She recalled the scene she had had with the woman outside the Empire Hotel, the only time she had had anything to do with her. "She's never been my friend and that's for sure. Do you think she might know something about Stanley?"

Seth patted her hand. "Well," he said, "we'll see what she's got to say. I just wish…" he paused. His shoulders rose and fell. "I just wish things had been different. I mean, I know that woman's no good and she got what she had coming to her for messing with the baby. But I can't ever feel happy about a woman dying." Lucille understood how he felt. Ellie Best's approaching death was nothing to celebrate.

They passed by the closed door of the carriage house and glanced at the smaller door to the hayloft above it. Next to the carriage house, a corral held the saddle horse that presently galloped up, thrust its head over the top of the fence, and bared its teeth. The main house was just as imposing as the unruly horse. The red brick wall loomed high above Lucille's head and purple velvet drapes hung behind spotless windows. At the front of the house, the broad veranda with its white columns and twin oak doors reminded her of a picture of an old plantation home that she had seen once in a magazine. A gravel driveway led up to the steps and a round bush next to the stairs was tidily pruned. Lucille and Seth climbed the steps to the front doors. Electric light fixtures hung in elaborate housings of black iron on either side of the entrance. Seth sat down to wait on the concrete bench while his wife lifted the brass ring of the knocker.

Doctor MacLean opened the door. A short man in his fifties, he had thin grey hair, a wispy moustache, and wore a light brown jacket and trousers. His face was pale, as if he had just suffered a fright.

"Good evening, Doctor," Lucille said to him. "I'm Mrs. Pruitt. I understand Mrs. Best has been asking for me." The physician welcomed her inside.

In the foyer, Lucille paused to look around. Above her, another electric light hung from the panelled ceiling in a shade of white glass with gold filaments on its sides. An oak table with curved legs and clawed feet would have been a handsome piece if not for the gouges on its polished surface. She blinked in disbelief at the area next to the staircase. The floor and walls here shone as if someone had poured a bucket of glue over them, but her nose told her it was honey. The mess clearly had been here for some time; a coating of dust was stuck to the honey and small footprints in it led into the parlour. It was plain to see that the Best children were responsible for the wreckage.

Doctor MacLean thanked her for coming. Clearly rattled, he shook his head and muttered to himself while he led her to the staircase. Before she followed him, Lucille snatched a peek inside the parlour. It featured an elegant fireplace of white marble and a Louis XIV sofa, but it also looked as if someone had turned a mob of vandals loose inside it. Shards of glass and pottery lay everywhere while dust and honey had been ground into what had once been an expensive Persian rug. To the right, a crushed trumpet horn lay on the floor next to the smashed phonograph to which it belonged, and the wall facing Lucille had holes punched into it from which scraps of paper hung. Stiff with astonishment, she followed the doctor up the stairs. Some of the honey stuck to the soles of her shoes. In spite of all the finery, electric lighting, costly furniture, and marble fireplace, something was fundamentally wrong with the Best household.

The oppressive silence in the house strengthened this impression. In addition to the mess downstairs, a cold, sterile air held sway here. Henry and the children were absent. The gleaming surfaces of the hallway tables were bare of toys and the predominant colour on the wallpaper was a dull grey. The sickroom reek of alcohol hung in the air. The doctor led her inside the bedroom closest to the stairs.

The first thing that struck Lucille was the snowbank of mattress feathers covering the floor. Mrs. Best lay in her bed nearby. Lucille turned to the doctor who was tamping out his pipe in a tin ashtray on the windowsill.

"She won't say why, but she's been anxious to see you," he said in a low voice. Lucille stammered a moment.

"Where's her husband? Where are her children?" Disgust appeared on the doctor's wrinkled face. He restrained himself from spitting on the floor.

"Mrs. Best sent her girls away to her mother a few weeks ago." He gestured at the feathers. "You can see they were a handful and because of her husband she couldn't get a nanny. Mr. Best was here a while ago, but he went back to the mine." Lucille gaped. "I had to amputate Mrs. Best's arm and it spooked him to no end. He ran out the door." MacLean made a wry face.

Lucille gawked at the shrunken figure of the woman in the bed. *Had to amputate her arm?* She lowered her eyes and shivered as she imagined what the wretched Ellie Best had suffered. *Mother of God, help us all.*

She found herself wringing her hands as she approached the bed. At the sight of Ellie, she jerked backwards in shock. Mrs. Best lay under a heavy bedspread. She had hollows in her formerly lovely cheeks. Red welts like smallpox sores covered her face and neck. She lay with closed eyes and her breath whistled slightly. A clean bandage covered the stump of her right arm that the doctor had amputated just above her elbow. For a few moments, Lucille could only stare at the woman. *So this is what Dinah's bite can do.*

MacLean, meanwhile, clenched his left fist in his wispy hair as if he would tear it. His pale eyes filled with disbelief. "I can't figure how this happened," he said. "It looks like a rattlesnake bit her, but I haven't seen one this far north in a long while. It must have come off a wagon. Mrs. Best kept saying it was a spider, but the poison must have scrambled her brain. A spider just can't do this much damage."

To keep silent, Lucille bit her tongue. *A spider from the Amazon jungle can.*

"I thought she might have a chance if I cut her arm off," the doctor continued. "Her hand had split open and it was rotting; I've never seen anything like it. I've enough morphine to keep her comfortable, thank God, but I can't save her. The poison's spread too far." He leaned over Ellie's bed and spoke in a soft voice. "Mrs. Best? Mrs. Pruitt's come to see you like you asked." He then slipped out the door.

Ellie's bloodshot eyes opened halfway. She licked her lips and heaved a jerky sigh.

Lucille spoke. "Looks like you shouldn't have meddled with our spider, Mrs. Best." Ellie clenched her eyes shut and sighed again. "What were you doing in our house?"

"I — the baby — I just wanted to hold him."

Lucille bared her teeth. "Oh, with a pillow? The one you were going to hold down over his face?"

Ellie grimaced while Lucille folded her arms over her chest and spun around. She stepped away from the bed and walked up and down the feathery floor, panting with the effort it took to refrain from slapping the dying woman. *I wasted my time coming here*, she fumed. Even on her deathbed, Ellie Best remained a liar.

"I know where your brother-in-law's body is. And that union man's too." She spoke with surprising firmness.

Lucille jerked with shock and clenched her fists. Her excitement rose, but it was still possible Mrs. Best was playing some kind of spiteful joke. She looked at the woman with skepticism. "Go on."

Ellie took a halting breath. She told Lucille how, one evening back in May, Henry had been working in his office here at the house. The evening before that, a strange woman had called. Ellie had believed that Henry had been waiting for another call from this woman, so she had waited in the parlour with her eyes on the second telephone. It had rung some time after seven o'clock. Ellie had jumped on it, ready to scream in the ear of her husband's mistress. But instead, she had heard a man's voice, that of Arthur Wright, who had uttered one line: "They've left town."

Lucille chewed the inside of her cheek. The statement did match with what Howard, Arthur Wright's stepson, had said. "And then what happened?"

Ellie took a deep breath before she spoke again. "I hung up the phone, and I didn't think anything more about it until late that evening." After eleven o'clock that night, two men had come to the house. From the window of her bedroom, Ellie had watched them approach the back door. Her curiosity had been aroused when Henry allowed the rough-looking men inside, in spite of the late hour. So, she had crept out of her bedroom and tiptoed to the door of her husband's office. There, she had heard the metallic clank of the door to the wall safe closing. Henry's voice had become stern as he said to the men, "I wanted that scribbler gone too." A strange man's voice had answered saying, "It's done." Then Henry had said, "And you better not have dropped them down a mine shaft or in a ditch anywhere. That's the first place anyone will look." The same man had responded with, "Of course not." They had buried the "problem" under the rubble from the slide, just north of Frank across Gold creek, about halfway between the CPR tracks and the Grassy Mountain spur track. No one would find them, they had said to Henry. And even if someone did, the men would be accounted for as two unlucky buggers who had blundered into the path of the slide. Ellie took another deep breath and fell silent.

Lucille wiped a tear from her cheek at the vision of Stanley's body lost and forlorn under a layer of crushed rock.

"Henry's gone," Ellie said. Lucille looked down at her as she gasped and continued. "He couldn't even stay after the doctor cut my arm off. He said he had to get back to the office." To Lucille's astonishment, Mrs. Best gave a bitter laugh. "When we were married, his father told me Henry was going to settle down now that he had a wife. And Mother kept saying how lucky I was." Her head rocked from side to side and she muttered in a way that suggested she was falling into a delirium. Lucille turned to leave, but a scream made her jump out of her shoes. "I never got to do anything!" Ellie shrieked again with astounding force for her condition. "I never got to do anything!"

Lucille ran out of the Best house. Ellie's despairing cries echoed in her ears even after she scrambled out the door, and as she walked back down the hillside trail with Seth. She brooded in silence. Even while Mrs. Best lay dying, rage still consumed her like Dinah's venom had eaten her hand. Lucille now shuddered as she pictured what the woman's life had been, shut up in that house with a scoundrel for a husband. *If only that miserable wretch had been able to do something besides get married.* She looked over her shoulder at the trail leading back to the Best house. She thought for a moment of her own marriage to Irving, and how she used to tell herself she had only been unlucky in her choice of a husband. But it dawned on her now that a woman's welfare should not depend on luck or a husband. *We don't need good husbands. We need freedom.* Although this idea was strange and frightening, it came to Lucille like the evening sun burning a hole through a cloud. A bird in a nearby pine tree began to sing.

As they crossed the log bridge over the rushing Oldman River, Lucille put aside these unsettling thoughts and squeezed her husband's arm. During their walk, Seth had kept a patient silence.

"I have to hire a wagon," she said suddenly to him. "Mrs. Best told me Stanley's body's over in Frank. It's buried in the rubble from the slide. I don't know if she was telling the truth, but I have to look." Her husband nodded and patted her hand.

The livery stable was closed Sundays, so on the following Monday, Lucille and her husband rode in a wagon east out of Stony Point. It rattled down the dirt trail while the pair of draft horses snorted and their harnesses jingled. Lucille sat beside Seth on the rough wooden seat. She held on to the back of the bench as the wagon lurched and squeaked. John Rupert rode in the back along with his bodyguard Kowalski and Kowalski's dog, Mose the Nose. That morning, when they had hired the wagon and team from the livery stable, Lucille and Seth had run across the two men outside the Hillview Hotel. Rupert had asked to join them when Lucille told him they were going to find Matthew Brown's body. She had agreed eagerly; the search would go much faster with two more pairs of hands.

As the wagon rolled, the cloudy sky above gave the surrounding mountains a blue tint. A crow followed them, squawking as it flitted from tree branch to tree branch. The Oldman River flowed, a constant hiss in the air. Seth held the reins of the horses and whistled to the animals. At one point, he jerked his head to indicate a crew of men off in the distance who were pushing loaded wheelbarrows back and forth from a set of coking ovens they were building. From the bed of the wagon, Rupert talked about how another capitalist, A.C. Flumerfelt, was going to establish another town here very soon, a town that he had named "Coleman," for his wife's maiden name and his daughter's middle name. Rupert laughed bitterly. Dominion Coal was claiming that they didn't make enough money to give the miners a raise. But if that were the case, why would businessmen such as Flumerfelt be willing to pour so much money into a coke works here? The bosses were making barrels of money.

As they approached Blairmore, Rupert brought up the news that had swept through Stony Point yesterday like a grass fire. Ellie Best had died early Sunday morning. Like everyone else in town, Rupert was bubbling with rumours as to what had happened to Mrs. Henry Worst. People suggested everything from Henry's horse kicking her in the head to the woman taking poison as a possible explanation. He was eager to question Lucille who, thanks to Charity MacLean, everyone now knew had seen Ellie just before her death. But she said only that Mrs. Best had taken ill and had wanted to unburden herself before she died. The Pruitt family had an unspoken agreement that no one would mention a word of what had happened to Ellie in their house so that Corporal Brock would not come searching for Dinah. So, Lucille kept silent and watched the mountains pass by as the wagon rolled along.

A few dozen yards away a train engine blasted steam out of its smokestack as it chugged along the main line track, pulling a long string of coal cars west. The owners of the Frank mine were happy to take advantage of the shutdown at Stony Point. Their miners worked two shifts a day now, Rupert said, just like the mines at Coal Creek, Natal, and Michel. Dominion Coal was losing all of their business to rival mines. He gave a hearty laugh. The mine owners could say they were united against union action, but once again dollars had trumped principles like it always did. The company would have to back down, especially now that the miners had routed the Pinkertons yesterday. "The shareholders are getting the jitters. They'll have to start talking soon," Rupert declared as he chewed tobacco

Soon, the western face of Turtle Mountain came into view up ahead. Rupert jerked his chin at the mountain as they approached. "One day they're going to have to move Frank," he said. "The geologists from Ottawa said that the rest of the mountain could come down at any time."

Lucille gazed at the vast scrape running down the middle of the slope and imagined the tumbling boulders and wall of debris that had come rolling down. It had taken many years, but millions of jolts, taps, and knocks had eventually brought down that mass of rock. The established order of things was no more permanent than the summit of Turtle Mountain.

Soon, they were rolling through Frank itself. With shovels and picks on their shoulders, a number of men in rough overalls and work boots walked to and fro on the wooden sidewalks. More workmen rode by in wagons. Frank was a beehive compared to Stony Point. In addition to the two shifts at the coal mine, dozens of men were working to clear the Grassy Mountain spur track. Much clearing also remained to be done along the main CPR track with plenty of money for the railroad to make selling the limestone that had come down in the slide. As she looked at the busy town, Lucille wondered how much more activity had been taking place here less than a week after the slide, when Stanley and Matthew Brown disappeared? The murderers could have easily hidden the bodies in a wagon and driven straight through Frank without a care. No one would have glanced twice at yet another wagon.

They drove past the Imperial Hotel. Judging from the laughter and happy voices coming from inside the bar, perhaps men were still buying drinks for Sid Choquette and slapping the CPR brakeman on his back. On the night of the slide, with the telegraph line from Frank cut off, Choquette had scrambled over the unstable mass of rock and debris for a mile to flag down the Spokane Flyer before the train could crash into the wall of rubble. God only knew how many lives he had saved.

For his effort, the railroad rewarded the man with twenty-five dollars and a letter of commendation.

Presently, Seth turned to Lucille beside him. "Where are we going, Mrs. Pruitt?"

She stirred. "We take the bridge over Gold Creek. Then turn north."

They crossed the wooden bridge and soon the wagon was rolling up a strip of land between the field of rubble and the creek. When they reached the CPR tracks, everyone stepped down. Seth took the lead horse by its bridle and guided it over the iron rails. After they crossed the tracks, Lucille glanced back over her shoulder where a stone chimney and a shattered roof were visible like an island above the surface of the debris. The Bansemer family, who had lived in that house, had miraculously come through the slide uninjured.

Presently, the wall of rubble at the foot of Turtle Mountain turned sharply to the east. Lucille lifted the front of her dark blue walking skirt and strode forward, feeling her way along with the tip of her parasol. This bend would have concealed the murderers from the view of the men who were clearing the railroad tracks; it was a logical place to bury the bodies. But as she viewed the scene, her morale dropped. All that lay here was an enormous spread of limestone rubble. There was no indication that any of it had ever been disturbed. Seth parked the wagon near a spindly bush and removed the bridles from the horses. "Well," he said at length. He took a shovel out of the bed of the wagon. "Everybody pick a spot and fan out." His boots crunched over the rubble. Seth spat on his hands and began to dig.

Rupert tied some rags around his hands, spat tobacco, and walked over the debris to another spot. Kowalski began to dig at a third spot. His dog Mose walked around near his owner with his nose to the ground and his slender tail permanently wagging. Lucille tended to the horses.

The three men dug through the rubble for over an hour. As

they worked, the dog continued to walk around, sniffing the ground in an expanding circle around Kowalski. Rupert had just set the blade of his shovel down in the ground for a brief rest, when Mose began to scratch at a particular area of rubble in between Kowalski and Seth. The dog's tail was wagging furiously now. He lifted his nose and bayed. The three men and Lucille converged on the area Mose was pointing out. At first, she could see only pebbles where the dog was indicating. But Seth carefully scraped the blade of his shovel over the rubble. Soon a ragged piece of fabric appeared in the dirt.

"That looks like Brownie's cap," Rupert exclaimed.

Lucille hurried back to the wagon and returned with a straw broom. She brushed it over the ground to reveal a bone, still clothed in the tattered shreds of what had been a grey coat. As she revealed more of it with the broom, it became clear that the bone was the round socket of a shoulder joint. Shreds of rotted flesh dropped from the bones. She covered her face and staggered backwards.

"That's Brownie for sure," Rupert exclaimed with both excitement and dismay. Kowalski bent over and rubbed Mose's long ears.

Meanwhile, Seth turned to Lucille. "Your brother-in-law must be pretty close. Maybe you'd like to go back to the wagon."

She trembled. Her face was pale but she shook her head. "No. I came here to find Stanley and that's what I'm going to do."

It took only a few more minutes of digging before the blade of Kowalski's shovel uncovered the battered remains of a derby hat a yard or so away from Brown's body: the same dented hat that Lottie had begged Stanley so many times to replace. In spite of herself, Lucille cried out. Just like Matthew Brown, all that was left of Stanley was a pile of bones with a few shreds of tissue clinging to them. It was only the hat that helped her identify the body of her sister's husband.

Rupert and Kowalski left to alert Frank's Mounties of their find. As Seth carried the tools back down to the wagon, Lucille stood over the remains of her brother-in-law. Her mouth trembled. The wind blew the collar of Stanley's coat back and forth as it lay in the rubble, giving the site a forlorn appearance. Suddenly, she remembered how Lottie had ordered that coat for her husband out of Eaton's catalogue for Christmas two years ago; Stanley had carried on as if his wife had given him His Majesty King Edward VII's coat. Her sorrow welled up at this memory; she gagged and buried her face in her handkerchief. As she wept, Seth's big arms closed around her. He held her close and rocked her as Lucille sputtered.

"Stanley never hurt anyone. He wouldn't even swat a mosquito. Lottie's never going to be able to live with this. Oh, I'm going to kill Henry Best!" She shouted this last sentence loud enough for the men clearing the CPR tracks to hear her. Seth rubbed her back, and eventually she calmed down.

After the NWMP came and collected the bodies from the slope of Turtle Mountain, the group rode back to Stony Point. No one spoke. Rupert sat with his gaze fixed on the wagon bed. As the union representative, it was his duty to inform Gracie Brown that they had found her husband's body and he dreaded the pain he was going to cause the woman. Kowalski wore a frown as he chewed the stub of a cigar. Even Mose was subdued. The dog lay on his belly with his head on his paws. Up on the box, Seth held the reins of the horses with a grim face. Lucille rode beside him with her face in her hands. She had sent Lottie a telegram from Frank, but she must follow that with a more detailed letter, and she had no idea what to say. Should she write her sister that she had found the remains of her husband lying on a mountain slope, buried like a dog's under slide rubble?

At last they arrived back in Stony Point. Seth stopped the horses in front of the livery stable where they found a number of miners waiting for them. Rupert and Kowalski climbed down from the wagon. On the ground, the union organizer spat tobacco and ran his hands through his thin black hair. The miners listened in silence while he told them they had found Matthew Brown's body and that of Mrs. Pruitt's brother-in-law. The NWMP in Frank had taken charge of the two bodies since they had been found inside their jurisdiction. The coroner, a doctor from Pincher Creek, had to examine the remains before the authorities could do anything else. Rupert rubbed his cap back and forth on his head as he spoke. The men must continue their struggle against Dominion Coal in Matthew's memory. He shook hands with Seth and Lucille, and the Pruitts walked back to their house.

Granny and Kate were waiting outside. Lucille hurried to her friends and embraced them. Everyone went inside where the aroma of stew and fresh bread filled the kitchen. Lucille had thought she wouldn't be able to eat anything, but when Granny placed a plate full of stew on the table before her, she found herself digging into her meal with eagerness. As the family ate, she told them how they had picked up Rupert and Kowalski at the livery stable and how Kowalski's hound dog had actually found the bodies.

Granny soaked up her stew with a scrap of bread and spoke with anger. "Well, it's a fine thing when people have to find their own lost kinfolk because the police are too busy beating up miners. It's a disgrace."

"What happened today at the picket line?" Lucille asked suddenly. She had just realized that Granny was home in the middle of the afternoon.

"Oh, there weren't no trouble there today," the old woman said. "The boys are all walking up and down in front of the gate safe as houses. All the Pinkertons have left town. I can't imagine why, when we gave them such a warm reception at the picnic."

For the first time since finding Stanley's body, Lucille smiled. "Bah, those cowards. As soon as everyone stood up to them, they just ran away with their tails between their legs," she said.

The family finished eating. Granny poured some tea and

Lucille held Albert in her lap while Kate took the dishes to the sink. When the young woman took away the bread bowl, Lucille spotted Dinah who had been sitting on the table behind it. The spider stretched her legs and began to preen. Seth had just stood up to go outside and smoke his pipe, when a knock sounded at the back door. Lucille turned in her chair to see Corporal Brock standing outside. She growled, but Seth touched her arm. He strode to the door and opened it.

"Pruitt." Corporal Brock touched the round brim of his Stetson hat. "Could I come in for a moment, please?"

Lucille's heart raced as she grimaced. On the table, Dinah polished her fangs. *Why does she have to show herself now?* If the corporal came inside he was bound to see her.

"No, you can't come in my house," Seth at the door said to the policeman. "You ain't welcome. My wife found her brother-in-law's body today in Frank and she's right upset about it. Why didn't you find the body like you're supposed to?"

Corporal Brock rolled his eyes. "I just want to ask a few questions. You must have heard that Mrs. Best died. I heard that she came to this house on Saturday before she took sick. You know anything about that?"

Lucille stood up with Albert dozing in her arms. She must keep the Mountie out of the house. Quickly, she passed the baby to Granny and walked to the door. She peered at the Mountie over Seth's shoulder.

"Where in the world did you hear that?" she demanded. "We certainly never saw her. Mrs. Best was a darned proud woman. She wouldn't have come to a little place like this." As she spoke, she kept her eyes on the policeman's suspicious face.

Corporal Brock drew back one step as he considered this fact. "I heard that Kate Pruitt came running here all in a lather after the fight on the ball field. Some people said she was scared Mrs. Best was going to hurt her baby."

Lucille scowled. To herself, she cursed all the wagging tongues in this town. "Well, there's nothing wrong with the baby. Really Corporal, you listen to too much gossip. And why didn't you keep those goons away from our picnic? You're always there when it's time to take the scabs through the picket line."

Seth laughed. Corporal Brock shot an angry glance at him before he continued. "This has nothing to do with that. I'm trying to find out what happened to Mrs. Best."

A bitter twist appeared on Lucille's mouth. She rolled her eyes. "Yes, well, we all know how much more important the mine owner's wife is than my sister's husband!" Her speech ended in a shout. "Well, Stanley Birch may not have counted as much as Ellie Best, but he sure did to me and my sister. We'll have some justice if I have to string up Henry Worst myself."

Corporal Brock stepped backwards and looked at her with surprise. "What did Mr. Best have to do with your brother-in-law?"

She took a breath before she answered. "Best had some thugs kill Brown because he didn't want him telling a newspaperman how Dominion Coal had fiddled with the hoist scale in the mine. Stanley's mistake was being the newspaperman."

Even before she finished speaking, the Mountie was groaning and rolling his eyes again. "Honest to God, woman, you can make up a story. Now, about Mrs. Best…"

Lucille snarled. "Yes, about the person who counts. Didn't you ask Dr. MacLean how she died? He's the one who would know — he was there."

"Yes, I did. He said he thinks a rattlesnake bit her."

"Then you best start looking for the rattlesnake. Maybe you'll have better luck finding it than you did Stanley Birch."

Seth laughed again. Under Lucille's barrage of words, Corporal Brock retreated. His shoulders in the red tunic rose and fell as he backed off the veranda.

After the Mountie left, Seth went outside. Lucille sat back down at the kitchen table. No doubt the policeman had his suspicions, but he could prove nothing.

While Lucille had been talking with the corporal, Kate had

taken Granny's straw hat down from the hook and passed it to the old woman; Granny, in turn, had placed the hat over Dinah. Kate now trotted to the door and looked out to make sure Corporal Brock was gone. Then, she removed the hat. In the sunshine, Dinah turned around in some confusion, but regained her bearings by feeling her way with the tips of her palps.

Albert whimpered in Granny's arms. The old woman was still anxious. "That darned policeman. I'll thump him one if he tries to take away me spider."

"No Granny," Lucille soothed her. "Dinah's staying right where she is." After she said that, she sat a moment in thought. Dinah flexed a leg, showing off the orange and yellow patches and the lovely purple colour of her body. Her bright colours warned of the power of her venom. In the blink of an eye, she scurried under the table. Lucille prayed the spider would not kill anyone else.

Chapter 18

Wednesday, August 26, 1903

TWO DAYS LATER, HENRY BEST returned from Seattle where he had gone for Ellie's funeral. As he stepped inside his house, he frowned at how quiet it was. He took his watch from the pocket of his waistcoat; in the silent house, its ticking sounded as loud as a blacksmith's hammer. A week ago, he would have laughed at the idea that he could ever miss Ellie's natter, but now he found he did. He grimaced as he set his bag down on the floor and hung his hat on the rack. He removed his coat with the black armband around the sleeve and hung it on the hook underneath the hat. Even if the house was too quiet, thank God the funeral was over and he was back home.

He sat down on the cushioned bench in the foyer and removed his shoes. His gaze fell on the wreckage in the parlour. Henry made a face. Leave it to Ellie to fail so badly at raising children; his daughters were more like a pair of monkeys than human beings. God knew what the girls would be like when they were grown He glanced again at the debris. Tomorrow, he would order Carter to hire some women to clean the mess in the house while he was out of town. With Ellie gone, he had no more purpose in using the damage to make a point with her, not that the imbecile had ever gotten it. He restrained himself from throwing his shoe against the wall. *Stubborn damned cow!* Was it any surprise she had ended up the way she had?

In spite of his anger, Henry only grumbled under his breath; his father had always said it brought a man bad luck to speak ill of the dead. He already had his behaviour when his wife lay dying on his conscience. Truly that afternoon had been a nightmare. After Doctor MacLean's urgent call to the mine, Henry had rushed home to find his wife with her right arm from the elbow down blackened and swollen to the point that it looked more like a seal's flipper. All that had remained of her hand were little black stumps that had once been her fingers. The smell from the rotten flesh could have wilted a fork. While he had gawked at his wife, Ellie had whimpered in agony and kept babbling some nonsense about a "purple spider." The doctor, meanwhile, had taken a bottle of chloroform, a rubber strap, and a saw from his bag. At that moment, Ellie had opened her bloodshot eyes and caught a glimpse of the shiny bone saw. Instantly, the wretch had begun to scream like the damned.

Doctor MacLean had turned to Henry and raised his voice above the woman's shrieks. "You're going to have to help me. I need you to hold her down."

The colour had drained from Henry's face. He had retreated with his arms raised. "Look, I've got to get back to the office."

The doctor's face had twisted with anger. "Mr. Best!" He had indicated the bottle of chloroform in his hands. "I can't put her all the way under as I might kill her. No, it can't wait. If I don't amputate that arm now, she'll die." His icy gaze and the grim set of his mouth had frozen Henry. The doctor had not needed to say that if he left, MacLean would spread word all over town how Henry Worst had run from his stricken wife.

"For Christ's sake Ellie," the chairman had cried out with disgust. "It's always one damned thing or another with you." He had set his teeth, cursed, and then thrown himself down on the bed next to Ellie's limp body. He had grasped her shoulder and restrained her left arm. Even that slight motion had made her shriek. Henry had clenched his eyes shut and averted his head while the doctor tied the rubber strap around his wife's arm for a tourniquet. MacLean had then taken the saw in his hand. Thanks to the chloroform, Ellie had not struggled. The blade of the saw had squeaked against the bone as MacLean drew it back and forth. The operation had lasted less than five seconds, but to Henry it had seemed like five hours. The instant the doctor had put down the saw, he'd released Ellie and fled from the house with his hair standing on end.

But it seemed the ordeal had been endless. In Seattle, the night before his wife's funeral, he had a nightmare in which Ellie's amputated arm crept up behind him and her blackened flipper hand grabbed his shoulder. The sight of anyone with an illness or injury had always made his flesh crawl, especially someone he knew well. He had not even been able to look at himself in a mirror after Seth Pruitt broke his nose. He shuddered now as he put on his slippers. Henry liked to tell himself that he feared nothing, but he was afraid of whatever had bitten Ellie. What man wouldn't be?

During the preparations for the funeral, Mrs. Nesbit had pulled her head out of her laudanum bottle long enough to make it clear that she held him responsible for Ellie's death. All the time Henry had been there, the old woman had hung over him and grumbled, a black cloud in her mourning dress. Meanwhile, Ellie's sister, that skinny hag Doris, had scowled at him and made a point of whispering with her husband behind Henry's back. He had thought, with a snort, that her attitude was a hell of a thing, considering that she and Ellie had hated each other and had not been speaking at the time of her death. Clearly, Doris was still boiling over how her mother had stuck her with Eleanor and Mildred when she already had a two-year-old boy who screamed if he could not sit in his mother's lap all day. The most awkward moment had come when Doris had pushed the girls toward Henry.

"Girls, say hello to your father," Mrs. Nesbit had called out.

But Eleanor had only twirled a strand of her hair with her finger and stared at the floor with indifference. Mildred had bent her head back and looked at Henry vacantly. "Who?" she had asked.

Doris had muttered disgust while the toddler had sucked her thumb and squeezed her dolly to her chest. Henry's red face had brought peals of laudanum-induced laughter from Mrs. Nesbit. When Doris had complained about the expense of keeping the girls, and had grumbled over irresponsible louts who brought children into the world but failed to raise them, Henry had thrown up his hands. He had agreed to pay an allowance to Ellie's sister and her husband, provide a nanny for Eleanor and Mildred, and to pay for boarding school as soon as the girls were old enough. Money in her hand had, at last, reduced the volume of Doris's nags. The temporary arrangement had now become permanent.

Presently, Henry sat for a moment with a bitter face. Yes, he had been a terrible husband and father. But it was not in his nature to care for a wife, and little girls like his daughters only annoyed him. He gritted his teeth and sighed. In any case, if he wanted to become premier he must get married again. Nobody would vote for a single man. He shook his head and snorted as he grumbled. In bars and bordellos, he had met dozens of men whooping it up and having a grand time, but just like the Dominion Coal shareholders, these same men would always turn around and refuse to vote for anyone who was not a "family man." The hypocrisy was appalling, but what could he do?

After he carried his bag upstairs, he drifted into Ellie's room. He stepped over the pile of mattress feathers still on the floor and opened the doors of her closet. For a moment, he gazed at the array of Parisian gowns hanging inside it. A row of hatboxes lined the shelf above the dresses and many pairs of shoes rested on the floor below, arranged neatly on trees. Henry could almost see Ellie taking down the hatboxes and sitting in front of the mirror in her *ensuite*, trying on this hat or the other. He frowned and hurried out of the bedroom.

A cold shudder ran up his back and again he felt his wife's ghost reaching for him with her rotted hand. He would get rid of Ellie's junk as soon as he could. If Sally, his mistress in Fernie, did not want the gowns he would give the whole mess to the Salvation Army, even though it was a fortune in clothes. For a moment, Henry laughed at the picture of soiled doves and coal miners' wives strutting around the Crowsnest in his late wife's Parisian dresses. He walked down the hallway into his office.

There, he first poured himself a brandy from a bottle in the corner cabinet. Then he sat down behind his oak desk with a grunt of relief. His chair squeaked as Henry leaned back, put up his feet, and gazed at the panels in the ceiling. The evening sunshine was coming in through the window and illuminating the masculine, leather chairs and the trophy bear head on the opposite wall. *Maybe I am a rotten father, but Ellie sure wasn't much of a mother*, he thought as he recalled the wreckage in the downstairs parlour with narrowed, resentful eyes. Still, it was disturbing how one morning his wife had woken up as sound as a bell, only to be dead the next day. Her life had ended in a snap of his fingers.

I should see my boy, that's what I should do, Henry thought. He did not know why the death of his wife had sparked in him a desire to see his son, but it had. He frowned in contemplation as he sipped his brandy, wondering how he could win over Kate Pruitt. Suddenly, the chair squeaked again as he rocked forward from the impact of a brilliant idea. *By God, I'll ask her to marry me!* It was true the girl was awfully young and unrefined, but she was certainly pretty. An attractive girl on a man's arm always made him look a success; the voters would eat it up. As for Kate, what girl in her place would not jump at a chance to be a fine lady? He would only have to hire somebody to polish her manners. Henry sipped his brandy again as he calculated. Marrying Kate was a splendid idea, but first he had to settle the unrest among his shareholders.

The angry shareholders were the reason he was not unpacking his bag. Tomorrow, he would take the train to Calgary to attend another meeting that promised to be stormy. Although Hammond had sent him a telegram expressing his condolences on Ellie's death, Henry knew that behind his back the man was sharpening a long knife. His chief shareholder had never forgotten that Henry had propositioned his wife, and the instant the chairman stopped making money, he had pounced like a cat. In his drive to remove Henry, Hammond was gaining support. The value of the shares of Dominion Coal had sunk like rocks in a pond during the strike, and the bad publicity that damned meddling Miss Apple Tart had generated with her letters was embarrassing the businessmen. Day by day, more of the shareholders were listening to Hammond's pitches. Henry squeezed the snifter of brandy in his hand. He must now pacify the shareholders in addition to crushing the union.

His glance fell on the mail that had piled up on his desk in his absence. Henry picked up the latest issue of the *Frank Sentinel*. Inside the paper was an article saying that two men's bodies had been found under the rubble at the northern edge of town. The bodies were believed to be the remains of Mr. Matthew Brown, an organizer for the UMWA, and Mr. Stanley Birch, a reporter for the *Red River Herald* newspaper in Winnipeg. For a few minutes, Henry sat in his chair staring at the paper. Abruptly, he crumpled it up in his fist. *This is a damned awkward business,* he thought. Of course, the bodies had had to turn up just before the shareholders' meeting; Hammond would jump on this development like a dog on a meat scrap.

Henry scowled to himself as he rocked backwards in his chair. He had expected the affair of Matthew Brown and the newspaperman to remain as buried as the men's bones under the Frank Slide rubble. Now here they were rising up again, most unwelcome ghosts. With his mouth pursed, he rose up, went back to the cabinet, and poured himself more brandy. With the drink in his hand, he paced up and down in front of his desk. He drank from the snifter. Certainly this discovery of the bodies was Miss Apple Tart's doing, but that was irrelevant right now. A man did not lose his head. He rested a moment with his fists rolled up on the surface of the desk and concentrated. *Who owes me?* In his mind Henry ran a finger down a list of powerful men in debt to him. Suddenly, a name popped up; he had given this man's party many hundreds of dollars. He picked up the candlestick telephone. In view of all his donations, Premier Haultain would accept his call instantly. Politicians always listened to rich men with deep pockets.

The next day, at the meeting, Henry launched his offensive. The fourteen men who were his major shareholders sat around the large table and listened while he pointed to the reports for every quarter since Dominion Coal had begun operations. These showed that under his direction, the mine had seen increasing production and rising profits for each quarter; the only exceptions being last July when the explosion shut down the mine, and the last month when the miners went on strike. Henry stressed the need for the executives to stand united in the face of union pressure. He passed around lists of figures that showed how much money any concessions to the union would cost the company. When he finally sat down, the shareholders reacted with a cold silence. All of the faces around the table wore reserved expressions. In spite of himself, nerves churned in Henry's stomach. George MacBain of Toronto lit a cigar and the stench from it wafted over the boardroom.

Hammond lifted his finger, the chair recognized him, and he cleared his throat. "Best, I understand the bodies of a union organizer and a newspaperman turned up in Frank. Haultain telephoned me. He also told me that you had called him and told him to bury everything."

Henry stiffened. He had not anticipated this. The shareholders frowned and tucked their thumbs in their waistcoats.

"This looks bad," Hammond continued. "Aside from the scandal that woman who wrote all those letters brewed up, having their organizer turn up dead has given that union a martyr. Now it looks like we'll never get this strike settled." As he spoke, the man frowned and his bushy eyebrows knitted into a bar across his forehead.

Henry met his gaze. "I had nothing to do with that. Anyone who says I did better be ready to prove it or they'll be talking to my lawyer. I also say that the only way to deal with troublemakers is with a firm hand." He looked around the table at the faces of his shareholders. "You gentlemen invested your money with my company. You've all done well by it."

Hammond spoke again. "That's not the point. The point is, this problem can be fixed. Now, we're all the Old Boys here. Haultain told me that if we elect another chairman, he'd make sure nothing comes of those bodies turning up." Hammond looked around at the assembled shareholders. "Gentlemen, I propose we elect a new chairman, someone with a new approach for how to deal with this strike. I nominate Mr. George MacBain for our new chairman. All in favour?"

Henry froze in shock as ten hands rose up from the fourteen men present.

"Motion carried," Hammond said, with a triumphant stroke of his whiskers. He spoke with a sincerity that the mocking twinkle in his eye belied. "Best, I'd like to thank you for your service on behalf of all of us. I understand you'll be entering the political arena soon. The boys and I wish you the best of luck." The shareholders applauded this sentiment and the secretary entered it in the minutes.

Easy to do that, Henry thought with a bitterness so great it was nauseating. *No one gets a penny for a round of applause.* As soon as he could leave with dignity, he excused himself and walked out of the boardroom.

Whenever he was in Calgary, he always stayed at the home of his cousin Ralph. That evening, the two sat together at

Ralph's dinner table. Henry picked at his food throughout the meal and gulped down glass after glass of wine. After dinner, he switched to brandy, and soon he was swaying, a tree in a gusty wind. Ralph watched his cousin with some concern. Normally, Henry could hold his liquor with any man, but now that he was no longer chairman of Dominion Coal, he looked ten times worse than when he had lost his wife. His face was patchy and his light brown hair was dishevelled from tearing at it. Ralph sipped at his own brandy and tried to cheer up his cousin.

"Look Henry, why don't you come into the cement business with Will and Charlie and me? We're making money so fast we can't even count it. All those foreigners coming into the Territory need places to work and houses to live in. Someone has to build them and they all need cement. Why, construction's going to be where the real money's made for the next twenty years. A man's a fool who doesn't grab his share. The boys and I are going to open another cement works south of town next year and we need a good man to run it. How about it?"

"I'm not the chairman!" Henry shouted. "Those bastards! Do you have any idea how much money I've made for them over the last couple of years? Hundreds of thousands! And as soon as the water got rough, they just dumped me overboard like old baggage. Those milksop bastards! A damned woman writes a few letters and they all tremble in their boots. I never thought I'd see the day!"

Ralph shook his head. "See Henry, never meddle with a smart woman. I knew that woman was too damned quick as soon as I saw her. What she needs is a good hard smack from a husband, that's for sure. Let a woman get above herself and you see what happens." Suddenly, he chuckled. "She was damned amusing though, I must say."

Henry shouted again. "Goddamn the woman! And Goddamn the shareholders! Let them go crawl to that damned union! They've as many balls as a herd of steers!"

While Henry ranted, Ralph rested his head in his hand and rolled his eyes patiently. "Look, you know how it goes. It was nothing personal. They don't give a damn how much money you made them in the last couple of years. They expect you to make them money yesterday, today, and tomorrow. I think you'd be better off with the fellows and me in the cement business. It's just us. We don't have shareholders. A man can make his own decisions."

Henry made an unsteady reach for his brandy snifter; he knocked it over and the liquor spilled on the tablecloth. "Ah, the hell with it all, Ralph. I'll just buy a little ranch and live out there." He belched. "I'll ride around outside all day, just me and Sultan. Hell of a horse, Ralph. You should get yourself a good horse. Hell of a lot better than a woman." Henry's head rocked back and forth as he laughed. His fist struck the table and the silverware jingled. "Hey, did I tell you I've got a boy now?" he asked. "He came out the wrong side of the blanket mind you, but what the hell." At the surprise on Ralph's face, Henry waved his glass and continued. "The Pruitt girl had my son a few months ago. A damned handsome little bit of tail, that Pruitt girl. I want to see my boy, that's what I want. The hell with this business rubbish."

He slouched in his chair with his arms on the table and shed tears as he bemoaned the gutless shareholders of Dominion Coal and how they had used and abandoned him. Ralph waved his hands at his cousin with exasperation and went to bed. Henry, with his face pressed to the dining-room table, snored like a CPR train.

The next morning, Lucille and Granny arrived at the picket line early. She helped the old woman down from the mule and carried her medicine case into the small tent near the wire fence. She then helped the miners' wives haul water from the Oldman to fill the barrel and chop some wood for the fire. With the chores done, Lucille paused outside the tent. A row of miners in their worn shirts and dusty trousers had assembled in the dirt road. The men tipped their hats to her. They spat tobacco and talked among themselves; it had been a few days since anyone had seen a Mountie or a goon at the line, and the men speculated as to what was going on. Lucille looked at the pocket watch around her neck. It was almost six o'clock.

Today, she had accompanied Granny to the picket line because, like Nellie Bly, she had to see as much as she could in order to write authoritatively on the miners and their struggle. The public must know how horrible a job it was to mine coal. They must hear another point of view besides that which they received from newspapers, mere gramophones for the mine owners. Just like Nellie Bly had made herself a witness to the abuse of those labelled "mad," Lucille would make herself a witness to the oppression of the miners. As she waited near the picket line, she thought of possible titles for her book. *Coal Miners of the Crowsnest Pass* was a possibility, or she could add some drama and call it, *Black Gold*. All of a sudden, she looked around in bewilderment. It was twenty minutes after six and still there were no Mounties or scabs.

Suddenly, one of the miners pointed down the road. "Hey, look! Rupert's coming." The union organizer appeared from around the bend in the road, running as fast as he could. When he got close enough to the picket line, he grinned and waved a telegram. The miners lowered their picket sticks and surrounded him. Every man shouted a question.

At first, the organizer huffed air to catch his breath; he bent over while Baxter thumped him on his back. "Say now Rupert, those old bones of yours shouldn't be running," the man said as the miners laughed. They gathered around the union man, eager to hear his news.

"Boys," Rupert said, "you'll never believe this." He handed Baxter the telegram. "The shareholders voted Old Man Worst's ass out. He's not the chairman anymore." Lucille, who had been listening at the edge of the crowd, exclaimed with surprise. The men leaped into the air. Hats flew in the air like a blizzard, and cheers brought the curious women out of the tent. A dozen men asked a dozen different questions all at the same time. Rupert lifted his hands for silence and continued. The shareholders of Dominion Coal had requested a meeting with the bargaining committee of the UMWA. The meeting would take place on Monday. In the meantime, while the negotiators worked out an agreement, the company would call off their goons and scabs. In return, the union would take down the picket line. Some of the miners grumbled, but Rupert pointed out that all the other mines in the Crowsnest working double time had resulted in a shortage of coal cars. The mine would have been closed today in any case.

"But look," he declared. "You got the shareholders to dump Worst. You made the company recognize the union. They see you boys won't be pushed around now."

The men's spirits rose again and they cheered Rupert's words. The union organizer pointed to the tent where Granny and the other women in the Ladies' Auxiliary stood by the door. "Three cheers for the wives, gentlemen. We couldn't have done it without them." The men raised their hats and gave three cheers. The women blushed at the attention and shuffled their feet, except for Granny, who stood with the gaps in her teeth showing in a grin. Rupert finally pointed at Lucille. "And three cheers for Mrs. Pruitt. She stuck it out here until she found Brownie's body."

The men clapped themselves on their backs and headed off to Luigi's. Lucille helped the women take down the tent and pack the supplies. While she was prying a stake from the ground, Rupert took her aside and showed her a second telegram he took from his coat pocket. On it, she read that the coroner had examined the bodies of Matthew Brown and Stanley Birch and was now releasing them.

She looked at the union organizer with confusion. "Is this all?" she asked. "It doesn't say what the coroner found, or if they're going to arrest anyone. Shouldn't it say more than this?"

Rupert could only shrug. "I agree, ma'am, something looks fishy. But truth be told, I wasn't expecting much. Nobody wants to lift the cow's tail and see what's underneath."

Lucille raked her eyes up and down his frame and began to stammer with indignation. "But, but Best had Stanley killed. I know he did — his wife told me herself before she died. They've got to do something."

Rupert pushed his cap back as he scratched his head. He released a deep breath. "Well Mrs. Pruitt, we've one law for the rich and one for the poor. You know how it goes." He tipped his cap and hurried off down the dirt path to join the other miners.

The laughter and hoorays of the men on their way to Luigi's hung in the air after they disappeared around the bend. In a daze, Lucille wandered off to where she had left the mule hobbled. For some reason, the beast was in a fractious mood. She grasped it by its halter. The animal jerked its head backwards. As Lucille pulled on its halter, eventually it sat down on its rear end in the dirt path, chewing on something. It shook its long ears and blinked stupidity, indifference, and complacency. Lucille, for a moment, looked at it with sour humour. "Get going, you miserable beast. You're not sitting in Parliament."

She took the halter in both hands, dug in her heels, and pulled; finally, the mule rose to its feet. She led it up to the tree stump on which Granny was waiting. After she helped the old woman up onto the animal's back, she grasped the halter and led the mule down the dirt road back to town. With her mind still revolving around Stanley's murder and Rupert's telegram, she stared with vacant eyes at the jagged peaks of the mountains in the distance.

"So what did that man say about your brother-in-law?" Granny asked as the mule plodded by the liquor store.

Lucille told her the little the telegram had said. "It sounds like no one's going to do anything. They're just going to give me Stanley's bones to take back to Winnipeg. They expect us to just bury him and forget about it." Her voice rose. "This can't happen. Stanley and Mr. Brown count as much as Mr. Laurier and Frederick Haultain; if they were murdered, would everyone just disregard that?" As she walked, she began to huff and the mule flapped its ears.

Granny took a breath and shook her head. "Now Missus, you're getting upset. It'll do ye no good." The old woman adjusted her straw hat and shrugged her shoulders. But Lucille began to mutter to herself. She dug with the tip of her parasol in the dirt while her face grew angrier by the minute. Granny opened her mouth to speak further, but closed it again. She remembered back to when she was a girl in her village in Scotland, just before she had emigrated with her husband. The landlord's son had raped and beaten a poor crofter's daughter. Nothing happened to him, although everyone in the village had known who had assaulted the girl. Like Lucille at the time, Granny had been boiling over with indignation about what had happened. But in the fifty years she had lived since then, she had never once seen the law come down on a rich man's head.

On the following Monday, Lucille woke up just before dawn. Today, she would claim Stanley's body in Frank. The bed creaked as she sat up, and she noted, with surprise, how dark the room still was. A sliver of light weaker than that from a Wolf Safety lamp was just peeping into the window. A pronounced bite in the air also signalled the end of summer coming down the tracks.

In the kitchen, she found Kate trembling with anxiety. The young woman had picked up Albert to find him listless, runny-nosed, and feverish. Now, the baby was screaming disconsolately. Granny took him into her lap while Kate took the jar of spider webbing out of the case and fixed up a poultice. Lucille stoked up the fire in the stove to make coffee, and then took a wicker basket over her arm and went outside to collect eggs for breakfast. The chickens strutted around her feet. But Frank and what was supposed to happen there hung on her mind. She meant to find out at last if the Mounties intended to investigate Stanley's murder. If she could not get any justice for her brother-in-law, she would make her own.

Just after noon, when Albert settled finally into a peaceful sleep and Lucille knew the baby was going to be all right, she took Seth's arm and set out to walk to Frank. Kate waved goodbye to the couple as she stood outside the house. Then, she went back in and tended to her chores. She emptied the ash pan in the stove, swept the floor, and dusted the parlour. As Kate worked, Granny sat at the kitchen table with her needle and thread mending a shirtwaist. Next to her, Albert lay in a bundle resting on the open door of the oven; on the frontier, nothing revived a sick baby faster. While she sewed, the old woman kept an eye on her grandson. His nose was still running, but his breathing was regular and his colour healthier.

At one o'clock, as the women sat together in the kitchen over cups of tea, someone knocked at the back door. Kate opened it. It was the telegram boy from the train station. He held a note out for her. She fetched her purse and held a dime out for the boy. "What does that letter say?"

"It's from Mr. Best." He unfolded the note. "He says he'll be by your house at three this afternoon. He wants to see his boy."

Kate's mouth fell open. She gave the boy his dime, and he touched his cap and hurried away. The young woman closed the door and turned to Granny. Her delicate pink mouth was set in a determined line. "He's not taking Albert from me. I'll not let him. I'll get my rifle and I'll shoot him in the guts. I don't care if I hang for it. He's not taking Albert!"

While she raved, Granny sighed and rubbed her head. "Katie," she said, "the man has a right to see his boy. It be wrong to keep his son from him."

Kate threw up her hands. "Well, if he wants to see his children he can go fetch his daughters back. Only I guess being girls they ain't good enough for him. What'll he do with Albert if he ever decides a bastard son's not good enough for him either?"

Granny replied with impatience. "Katie, you don't know what he plans on doing yet. And if you don't let him see his son he'll have the law after us. Then you really might lose the bairn. Just let him look at the boy. Then wait and see what happens."

Kate thrust out her lower lip as she paced. Granny was right. She must let Henry see Albert. But she would kill him if he tried to take the baby from her.

Meanwhile, in Frank, Lucille and Seth went first to the NWMP station. There she talked to a Commander Lang, a heavy-set gentleman with thin hair. He said that since the bodies of Matthew Brown and Stanley Birch were hardly more than skeletons, the coroner had had no choice but to list the cause of death for both men as "inconclusive," thereby making it impossible to conduct a murder investigation. Hence, the matter was closed. Lucille jumped out of her chair and demanded to know if the Mounties thought the two men had buried themselves under the slide rubble. Lang only picked his teeth and looked at her with that mixture of amusement and contempt that she was used to seeing on men's faces. Before she could lock her hands around the Mountie's fat neck, Seth caught her around her waist and carried her out the door. Outside, she struggled in his arms for a few moments. Seth clutched her to his broad chest and said he could not have his wife jailed for assaulting a police officer. Gradually, she calmed down. There was nothing she could do but claim Stanley's body. But as she and Seth walked away, Lucille looked over her shoulder at the barn-sized log house that was the Frank police station. *Someone's going to pay*, she promised.

They went next to the undertaker's at the Frank Lumberyard. Stanley's remains had been placed in a plain wooden coffin for which Lucille signed as next of kin. She then paid for the coffin, and Seth and one of the proprietor's sons, William Trelle, pushed it in a handcart to the Frank train station. As they made their way through the town, the men on Dominion Avenue took off their hats. Lucille had kept her composure as she conducted her business at the lumberyard, but Stanley's coffin riding in the cart, and the silence of the working men, made her take her handkerchief out of her purse and wipe her eyes. By the time they reached the small train station, she was biting her tongue down on her tears. Seth comforted her as she wrote out a telegram to Lottie. Stanley's body would ride out of Frank on the next train east. It should arrive in Winnipeg in a few days. The railway clerk rolled the coffin into the freight room to await shipping. Lucille sat down on the bench next to the telegraph operator's window.

Seth placed her head on his shoulder and squeezed her close. "There now. Lucille. You did everything you could."

"He loved his family. He always tried to do the best job he could at whatever he did. And now I'm shipping him back home in a box like a sofa or a piano." She sniffed and wiped her eyes.

Seth patted her back. "Here, we'll go have a cup of tea and a sandwich before we head back."

Lucille sighed and gulped. Right now, refreshments sounded like just the thing. She forced herself to sit up. In the town, a team of bawling oxen was pulling a wagon loaded with barrels up the dirt road. A workman shared a laugh with a pal as they stepped inside the bar of the Imperial Hotel. From nearby, the sound of squeaky baby carriage wheels approached.

"Lady, you want to hold Frankie Slide? Cost you a nickel, but she's lucky." Here again were the two girls with the wicker baby pram. They still wore homemade dresses and white hair ribbons. Frankie Slide, who had grown remarkably since Lucille had first made her acquaintance, rocked back and forth restlessly in the pram and babbled to herself. The woman had to laugh while Seth watched with amusement.

"Look Rose," the smaller girl exclaimed. "It's that rich lady again."

Lucille put her handkerchief away in her purse. "Well girls, I'm not rich, but I sure am lucky, and it's all thanks to Frankie Slide." She paid a nickel and picked up the baby. While she bounced her on her knee she explained to Seth. "See, these girls brought her to me when I first came here. That was the night I took all that money off Henry Best at cards." She squeezed the baby, straightened out her white cap, and set her back in the pram. "Now, you girls better take our Frankie home. I think she's getting tired again." Rose pocketed the nickel, and, in search of another mark, the two girls skipped away with the pram squeaking in front of them. Lucille took Seth's arm and they walked together to the Palm Restaurant and Bakery.

Later that afternoon, Henry rode on Sultan up to the picket fence at the rear of the Pruitt house. He dismounted and tied the horse's reins to the fence. The house looked just as small and rough as it had the last time he was here, the night he and Kate conceived their son. The sunshine lit up the shingles on the roof, the grey boards on the outside walls, and the chickens pecking the rough grass in the yard. He climbed the wooden steps to the veranda where an ugly old woman with grey hair and eyes that popped out of her face sat on a wicker seat. She wore an old straw hat and worked a pair of knitting needles in her gnarled fingers. She looked at him with a wrinkled, jowly face. Her eyes narrowed.

"Mr. Best, Katie's waiting for you inside," she said with a tilt of her chin at the door. Henry opened it. The kitchen was tiny and cramped compared to the one in his house. A black iron stove was on the right and a tall dish cabinet, clearly handmade, to the left. Kate sat at the table. She wore a grey skirt and a white shirtwaist with a dark blue kerchief tying back her hair. She frowned when he stepped through the door. On the table beside her, a cradle rested. It was sturdily constructed with a bonnet overhang and elaborate carvings on the sides. Kate's brother, the woodworking ape, must have made it. Henry saw that whatever he thought of Seth otherwise, the man was indeed skilled with his hands.

"His name's Albert," the girl said. "He was feeling poorly this morning, but Granny and me doctored him up and he's better now." Henry placed his hat on the table and looked at the baby. His son lay on his back with his head turned to the right. He wore a white cap and dress and his nose was a little runny, although his colour was fine. To Henry's astonishment, Albert was identical to a younger brother of his who had died of infantile paralysis. It was a moment before the former chairman could speak.

"Well the devil, Kate, but this is a damned handsome boy," he said at last as he sat down. Kate watched him with suspicion, but for the moment all the arrogance had vanished from Henry. He took the cradle in both his hands and rocked it gently from side to side. Albert yawned and turned his head. Drool ran down the baby's smooth chin as he looked at his father with bright blue eyes and stuck his tiny fist in his mouth. Henry was sure his son would keep those blue eyes. By the time he was grown, women would be busting down doors to be with him, just like his father.

"Soon as he's walking, I'll get him a pony," he said. "We'll go out riding together."

But the scowl on Kate's face only deepened. "Yes, you made me a lot of big promises too. What's the reason you can't get your girls a pony?"

The man sighed. "For Christ's sakes girl, don't start. Look, I know I'm a scoundrel. But in this world, only the strong survive. I am prepared to do what's right for this boy of mine. We'll wait a year or so and then I'll marry you." He leaned forward and spoke to Kate as if she were an especially pretty child. She rocked backwards and grabbed the edge of the table for support. Her mouth fell open. "Yes, I'll make an honest woman of you," Henry insisted while she stared at him in disbelief. "How does that sound? Damned tempting I'd say; you'd be a wise young lady to jump on it." Kate sat blinking. For a moment, all she could think of was how, a year ago, she would have danced with joy to hear Henry propose to her. But all she felt now was revulsion. Anger appeared on the man's face. "Well, you don't have to look like you stepped in a dog turd!"

"I wouldn't have you on a silver plate, Henry Best. I'd sooner marry a frog." Her voice rose. "You think I want to end up like Ellie?"

Henry drew back in amazement. A girl without a penny who lived in a shed was refusing him? "Listen, if you were my wife, you'd have anything you want: clothes, jewels, a big house, a fine horse and buggy. After I buy an automobile, I'll hire a driver to take you around in it. You'll be the premier's wife and you'll have all the fine ladies in Calgary to call on you. Are you going to have any of that here in this damned hut of yours?"

The disgust on Kate's face only grew. "Did fancy clothes and jewellery and darned buggies do Ellie any good?"

"Never mind Ellie!" Henry's face was red with growing indignation. He rose up and paced the length of the tiny kitchen rubbing his fists together.

Kate spoke without thinking. "Well, somebody ought to mind poor Ellie." She paused, blinking in surprise at the words that had just come out of her mouth. For a long time, she had hated Ellie Best. But ever since she had heard Lucille's graphic description of the woman on her deathbed with her arm sawed off, Kate felt only pity for her. She looked at Henry and continued. "God knows you never gave a damn about her, just like you'll never give a damn about me."

"Aw, c'mon now! You're my boy's mother and I…"

"And you'll be running around with other women the minute we're home from the church!"

At first, Henry only shrugged and chuckled. When Kate scowled, he opened his mouth to lie, saw it was hopeless, and closed it again. "And look how you've raised your girls," she continued. "You think I want a nanny bringing up my Albert? You think I want him passed around from house to house, just like them?" She paused. "When he's older I'll tell him about you; he can go make up his own mind then. But for now, I don't want you around my boy."

Henry drew back. He blinked rapidly with growing fury and took several deep breaths. In the face of his rising anger, Kate's mouth stiffened with resolution.

"Well, Little Miss High-and-Mighty thinks she's too good for me." His voice rose. "You think I'm a bad influence? How about when I tell a judge I don't want my son growing up with the town pump for a mother?" Kate cried out with indignation. "You'll be hearing from my lawyer." With that, he reached for his hat on the table, but then he cried out with surprise and jerked his hand back. "What the hell is that thing?"

Dinah had appeared. She sat on top of the crown of Henry's derby hat, flexing her legs. Henry raised his hand to knock the spider off his hat, but in a reflex Kate's arm shot out and restrained him.

"No! Don't!" For an instant, she pictured the hot water her family would be in if Dinah killed a second person. Henry, meanwhile, stared with wide eyes at the creature on his hat. *A purple spider.* Kate followed his gaze and her own eyes hardened. "That's Granny's Amazon jungle spider. Your wife came in here aiming to smother Albert to death, until Dinah bit her."

Henry shot her a horrified glance. His mouth fell open. He retreated a step with his eyes fixed on the creature, remembering how Ellie had raved about it. Dinah, meantime, took a dislike to the stranger in her house. She raised her front legs in a threat display and hissed. Henry jumped back as a droplet of venom flew onto the kitchen floor. "If you try and take Albert from me, I'll sic her on you," Kate continued. "No one will ever know. You don't believe me? Go on, take your hat."

Instead, Henry spun away with a defiant shout. "Goddamn the thing!" Without his hat, he strode out the back door.

Outside, on the veranda, the old woman barked out something as he passed her. *These crazy Pruitts can all go to hell*, he thought as he gritted his teeth and descended the stairs. His bare head felt exposed with the wind blowing on it. He heard the back door of the house open, and one of the chickens squawk and flap its wings as it scurried away. The sound of the opening door and the chicken distracted Henry. All the warning he had of Lucille's attack was a flash of grey.

What felt like a spear drove itself into his abdomen just above his groin. All of the air burst from his lungs in a rush. He groaned, clutched his wound, and dropped to the ground. Lucille fell on him with her parasol. He just managed to curl up before she landed three hard blows with it across his back. Up on the veranda, Kate squeaked and lowered the muzzle of her rifle. She had come within a hair of shooting Lucille. Then Lucille took her parasol in both hands and struck Henry across his back a final time with all her strength. "That's for Stanley Birch!" she screamed. Seth then trapped her from behind in his arms and dragged her back. Lucille struggled furiously in her husband's grasp. "You want to be premier? I'll see to it you won't get elected to sweep horse manure!"

Kate flew down the steps. As Henry lay on the ground, red-faced and gasping, she pointed her rifle in his face. "You're not taking Albert. I'll kill you if you do."

"Not if I get him first," Lucille called out.

"That's enough!" The old woman in the straw hat made her slow way down the veranda steps. "Katie, put that gun away. Now!" She turned to Henry. "You! You just sow trouble wherever you are. I want you out of this yard and away from this house. Go!"

Henry grunted and dragged himself to his feet. With his hair dishevelled, and his hands clamped over his abdomen where Lucille had stabbed him, he hobbled across the yard and untied Sultan from the fence. He mounted with difficulty and rode away, slumped over the horse's neck. Clumps of dirt flew as the horse vanished up the road.

With the man gone, Granny set her hands on her hips. Her eyes blazed and her bristly chin shook with anger as she glowered at Kate and Lucille. "Honestly, you act like a couple of wild savages, the pair of you," she declared.

"He said he's taking Albert," Kate cried as she set the butt of her rifle into the ground. She wiped her eyes. "I'll not let him."

"Then he'll have to track us down to Uncle Noah's in Vancouver," Granny said.

Meanwhile, Lucille stood in front of Seth, who had placed a hand on each of her shoulders and was rubbing them back and forth. "Don't worry, Kate," she said. "No one's taking the baby."

As soon as he arrived back at his house, Henry jumped off Sultan and hastened inside. He staggered to the telephone in the parlour and called Doctor MacLean, who promised he would come as soon as he could. The former chairman hung up the phone and climbed the stairs to the bathroom. He could feel bruises forming on his back where Lucille had beaten him with the iron shaft of her parasol, and the part of his abdomen where she had stabbed him with the point throbbed with pain. She had missed his genitals, thank Christ, but she had come horribly close — close enough for Henry to want Doctor MacLean to examine the area. He ground his teeth a moment before he took the bottle of Doctor Shoop's Restorative out of the medicine cabinet. He swigged at it, gasping at the foul taste, before he sat down on the toilet.

There the former chairman boiled with indignation. *How dare that little minx refuse me?* He remembered the disgust on Kate's face as she had done so. His rage simmered up again, but he comforted himself with the certainty that the wench would regret her sassy mouth when Henry secured custody of Albert. What judge would deny the claim of a successful businessman against an impoverished girl with a soiled reputation? As for Miss Apple Tart, as soon as he was finished with the doctor, Henry was going to get his shotgun, go back to the Pruitt house, and blow the woman's head off. The whole town could watch when he impaled her body to the ground with that damned parasol.

He shivered when he remembered the spider on his hat. Just like Ellie had raved, the thing was huge and its orange and yellow markings warned of a deadly venom. *Christ, where had it come from?* Henry wondered. He shuddered all over at the memory of what that creature had done to his wife's right hand. At that moment, a knock came from the front door. As he stood up to let in Doctor MacLean, Henry made a decision. He would phone Corporal Brock and demand he find that menace, squish it, and bring it back to him. He would not have another peaceful night until he knew that spider was dead.

Doctor MacLean, clutching his bag and wearing his white coat, followed Henry back up the stairs to his office. While they climbed, Henry told the doctor that fractious Sultan had been feeling his oats and had bucked him off — he didn't need it spread all over town that a woman had beaten him. Up in his office, he dropped his trousers, unbuttoned his union suit, and while the doctor examined him, his agitation began to subside. His gaze rested on the head of the black bear hanging on the wall across from him. He had shot that bear in the Kananaskis; his steady aim had impressed even the Indian guides. But when Doctor MacLean pulled at his scrotum, Henry looked down and frowned.

Dubiously, the physician shook his head. "Well, there's a bruise here, but that isn't what concerns me. Are you still chasing the ladies, Mr. Best?" he asked.

"You bet your ass," Henry replied.

"Do you frequent brothels?"

He blinked, frowned, and drew back. "No." But then, he remembered the mine executives' gathering in Fernie. "Well, I don't make a habit of it. Why are you asking?"

The doctor rummaged about in his bag and took out a hand mirror. He grasped Henry's penis and lifted it, showing him the ugly red sore in the shape of a skinny triangle on the underside of the organ. "See that? It's a syphilis chancre." He released Henry's organ and it dropped.

"But that's not possible!"

While the doctor put the mirror back in his bag, Henry could only stand with his eyes wide and his mouth open. The revelation struck him with the force of a shovel and he had to grasp the edge of his desk to keep from falling down. In his horror, he forgot all about Kate, Lucille, and the spider. He shook his head rapidly.

Doctor MacLean shrugged. "It certainly is possible, when a man keeps running around with bad women."

Henry buttoned up his union suit with the rapid motion of his shaking hands. *It isn't syphilis! It can't be.* "Look doctor, I'm no monk, but I only went to that brothel once. And I wore a rubber. You're wrong about this."

The doctor waved his hand with impatience. "Did you wear a rubber all the other times?" He looked at the former chairman of Dominion Coal with disgust and placed a pad of paper down on the desk in front of him. "Now, I need to know every woman you've been with so we can let her know. Every woman in the last couple of months."

Henry gawked at the physician. There had been the brothel outside Fernie, the woman on the train to Calgary, cousin Ralph's housemaid, and a few others he couldn't think of now. He growled, snatched up the pad of paper, and hurled it down to the floor in a rage.

"No! It's not syphilis!" He paled. "My girl in Fernie. Her husband'll kill her when he finds out."

Doctor MacLean looked at where the pad of paper lay. "Well, if he kills her, he'll hang for it. Now, I need those names. Sorry Mr. Best, but it's my duty as a physician to keep this from spreading. Right now, you're a menace to the public health. I'll also call Doctor Mewburn in Lethbridge. You need to start with the mercury right away…"

Henry grasped his head. *Not the mercury!* He would have to sit in a sweat room wrapped in blankets and breathe deeply of the toxic fumes from a tub in front of him. In addition to the misery from the broiling heat, his hair and teeth would fall out and drool would run in a river down his chin. If he survived the treatment, he would come out of it a doddering old man. But the only prospect worse than the mercury treatment was not taking it. He would go along for one, five, maybe even ten years, but the syphilis would rot him from the inside out, starting with his genitals. The bones in his face would swell and twist so that he looked like a monster and as the disease ate up his brain, he would lose his mind. Then, he would end up in a madhouse babbling like an infant.

Henry raised his fists and railed at the ceiling. Truly, his misfortunes were piling up like boulders in the Frank Slide. First, he had lost a thousand dollars to Lucille Pruitt, then he had lost his job, and now he had to take the mercury treatment. He was the unluckiest bastard in the world.

Chapter 19

—⁓—

Tuesday, September 1, 1903

MATTHEW BROWN'S FUNERAL took place in Stony Point the next afternoon. A dozen men gathered outside the sawmill. They wore somber black coats and trousers and black armbands around their sleeves. They talked among themselves in subdued voices; many shook their heads and spat on the ground as they discussed the circumstances in which Rupert and Mrs. Pruitt had found the body. Soon, the music of the Stony Point band came from down King Edward Avenue. Behind the musicians, a pair of black horses pulled the hearse. Luther Hartley and the fiddlers marched forward while the young man who usually played the spoons and washboard played a drum that he beat in time as the band marched. They were playing *The Internationale*. Smiles at once lit up the downcast faces of the mourners. Brown would have enjoyed the defiance.

The hearse pulled up outside the lumberyard gate. The horses lowered their heads and snorted. The pallbearers, which included Rupert, Pearson, and Seth Pruitt, carried the polished wooden coffin on their shoulders from the sawmill and loaded it into the back of the hearse. Another man placed a wreath of white flowers on top of the casket. As the hearse rolled out west of town to the cemetery, the men of Stony Point fell in behind it. The band kept playing as they walked up the dirt road. In spite of the sad occasion, the music from the band lifted everyone's spirits. The mourners walked with a swagger in their gaits as they followed the hearse inside the cemetery grounds.

Meanwhile, the women prepared the Oddfellows' Hall for the wake that would take place as soon as the party of mourners returned from the cemetery. Lucille, Granny, and some miners' wives emptied the baskets of food the women had prepared and set the plates of fried chicken, sandwiches, and cakes out on the table near the front doors of the hall. Lucille forced herself to smile as she worked. It made her uncomfortable whenever anyone talked to her as if she were some kind of heroine for finding the bodies. Strictly speaking, she supposed that if the woman were still alive she would have given Ellie Best the hundred-dollar reward her posters had promised. As it was, she had donated the reward money to the fund the union had collected for Matthew Brown's widow and children.

Lucille admired the flower arrangement that stood on the raised platform at the back of the hall. A large wreath of white lilies and forget-me-nots from the United Mine Workers of America rested on a stand. Next to it was a picture of Matthew Brown with black bunting hanging around the wooden frame. He had been a small, slightly built man with a homely face. But there was a twinkle of humour in his eyes as he stood in the picture wearing the white jersey of the Stony Point baseball team. He looked exactly like the kind of man Stanley would have had for a friend and Lucille regretted that she had never met him. She turned around on hearing Kate's voice behind her. The young woman had gone to the General Store to fetch sugar for the punch; while on her way back, she had stopped by the Post Office where there was a letter for Lucille from her sister. Lucille tucked the letter into her bodice to read later. There was a racket at the door behind her as the party of mourners returned from the cemetery.

Soon, the Oddfellows' Hall was filled with people and the roar of conversation. Men and women lined up to write their names down in the guestbook that stood on the small round table in front of the portrait of Matthew Brown. They then moved to the receiving line to offer their condolences to Gracie Brown who had arrived that morning with her brother from High River.

Lucille stood in the line next to Seth. Discreetly, she craned her neck over the heads of the people in front of her to look at Matthew Brown's widow. Mrs. Brown was a slender woman with a pale complexion and prominent eyes; she wore a black dress and a black veil pinned up over her plain hat. When she had entered the hall, she had been carrying a year-old baby girl under her arm; when the restless infant began to squirm and cry, Gracie had passed her daughter over to her brother who was also carrying her three-year old son. Lucille looked away with sorrow on her face. In addition to her own nephews, Edward and Abner, here were two more children without a father.

Eventually, she and Seth stood in front of Mrs. Brown. Next to the widow, Rupert greeted the well-wishers. Wearing a black suit, stiff collar, and a white carnation in his buttonhole, the union organizer looked strange, especially with his carefully pomaded hair. He gestured with both hands to introduce Lucille. "Ah, here's Mr. and Mrs. Pruitt. She's the lady who worked so hard to find your husband, Mrs. Brown. The man who we found with Matthew was her brother-in-law."

Gracie first looked at Lucille with curiosity. She then cried out and flung both her arms around her. Surprised, Lucille could only pat the woman on the back as Gracie spoke. "Oh ma'am, I didn't think anyone would ever find Mattie. I was in such despair — I didn't even have a body to mourn over. It was horrible, not knowing what happened to him. You took such a burden off my shoulders."

Next to his wife, Seth chewed his lips to suppress his pride. Lucille was unable to speak for a few moments. She began to realize the importance of what she had done and how much it had meant to a widow and her children.

"Yes," she said, at length. "That was how my sister felt about her husband."

"You must give me her address so I can send her some flowers," Gracie said. Lucille wrote down Lottie's address and gave it to the woman. Gracie hugged her again and turned to the next person in line.

Lucille then drifted in front of a stranger. This man greeted her with enthusiasm, shook her hand, and thanked her for the great service she had done for both Mrs. Brown and for Local 2322. He spoke with a mild British accent and had a dark complexion and a neatly trimmed beard. Lucille had noticed earlier how the coal miners had treated this man with some deference. She curtseyed to him, and she and Seth moved away.

As they walked through the crowd to the food table, Seth said, "Know who that fellow with the beard was?"

She shook her head. "I've no idea."

"That's Frank Sherman. Biggest wheel in the United Mine Workers of America. All the boys say he'll be District Chairman before the year's out."

Later, after the dinner and speeches, Lucille went outside with Seth. Her husband sat down on the log bench beside the door to the hall. He took his sack of tobacco and his clay pipe out of his coat pocket, and while he sat filling his pipe, she tore open the envelope of the letter Kate had brought her earlier. It was from Lottie, dated on the same day as that on which Lucille had sent her sister the telegram from Frank after finding Stanley's remains.

"Dear Lu," she read the letter aloud as Seth listened. "I'm so thankful. Now I know Stanley's not lying in a ditch somewhere." Lucille paused. She found her handkerchief in her purse and wiped her eye. Seth rubbed her shoulder and puffed on his pipe; the pungent smell of his tobacco met Lucille's nose. She sniffed and continued reading.

"The insurance company tripped all over itself to pay my benefit, especially after Mr. Parr started talking court action."

Lucille clutched the letter to her chest a moment and beamed. "Mr. Parr — that's our lawyer," she explained to Seth. "He was the best man at Stanley and Lottie's wedding. Do you know, I think he's been carrying a little torch for her." For a second, she wondered if her sister would ever marry again. Then she shrugged and continued reading. "Edward and Abner are both well. They don't really understand about their father yet, but they will one day, and I know that having a grave they can visit will help. For now, they miss you terribly, and they want to know when Aunt Lu's coming home."

She paused again. She and Seth would be leaving on the train for Winnipeg tomorrow. Even though their journey was for the sad occasion of Stanley's funeral, she found herself shaking with anticipation. It seemed like years since she had seen her sister and the boys.

"I expect we'll all join you and Mr. Pruitt in Vancouver later on," Lottie's letter concluded. "I'd like a place to start fresh, and I'm looking forward to meeting your new family." Lucille could only sit and smile. Soon, her family would all be together again in a new city.

Although she wanted an early start, the next day Lucille woke up later than she had intended. Seth's half of the bed was empty, and enough sunlight was coming in for her to see Dinah crawling across the white bedspread. The spider's legs rotated with mechanical precision as she laid a thread behind her. She was hungry for a mate, and had worked all night to hang all over the house a string laced with her receptive female hormones. After Dinah crawled out of sight down over the foot of the bed, Lucille rubbed her eyes and sat up with a grimace. She felt listless and her head was a lead weight on her shoulders. But she had dozens of things to do. She gritted her teeth and slid out of the bed.

She recovered from her lethargy as soon as she finished breakfast. Lucille first sat down to write some final letters of thanks to the one or two politicians who had shown a genuine concern for Stanley and the few newspaper editors who had helped her, especially Eye-Opener Bob in High River. She then sent off a quick telegram to Lottie saying that she and her husband were taking the afternoon train out of Stony Point and she expected to reach Winnipeg by Saturday at the latest. Lucille beamed while she pictured Edward and Abner hopping around for joy knowing their Aunt Lu was coming home at last.

When she returned from the telegraph office, she pulled all of her outerwear from the dresser drawers slowly, in case Dinah was sleeping in them. Lucille sorted through her skirts; only one had not survived Stony Point: the one she had used to beat out the Dominion Day fire. She then hung all of her and Seth's clothes up on the clothesline outside and brushed them vigorously.

The rest of the family was also busy. Seth packed his tools into a pair of trunks; he would ship them to Uncle Noah's in Vancouver when he and his wife returned from Winnipeg. Kate fed the chickens, changed the straw in their coops, and weeded the garden. She picked a tiny cucumber and stared at it in wonder. There was hardly a mark on it. She showed it to Granny, who *humphed* while she paused from beating a rug. Although Kate had been skeptical at the time, she and the old woman had strung threads of Dinah's webbing on the wire fence surrounding the garden. The smell of the spider's venom had kept away the raccoons and rabbits.

The neighbours and friends had heard that Lucille was going back to Winnipeg. An hour after lunch Mrs. Ruzicka, Mrs. Homeniuk, Miss Tetyana, and Lanka dropped by with a loaf of bread. Granny greeted the Galician women with enthusiasm and sat down with the guests in the parlour. Kate served them tea. Lanka was sad when she learned the Pruitts were leaving for Vancouver, but she recovered when Kate promised that she would leave her and her family the yard chickens. During the visit, Mrs. Ruzicka bounced her godson in her lap and chattered to Albert in Ukrainian while Lanka said that her father was happy to be back at work. After all the struggle at the picket line, a dues checkoff was the only concession Dominion Coal had made to the workers. Lucille gritted her teeth. She remembered the company goons beating the miners on the picket line. Clearly, the men would soon have to fight again for their rights. The struggle would go on for years. As she said goodbye to the Galicians, she muttered a prayer to herself that Mr. Ruzicka and all the other miners would be safe.

Afterwards, Mrs. Perkins and Mrs. Baxter appeared. In the pleasant summer weather, Mrs. Perkins wore a white shirtwaist and a blue skirt. Her hat had a skinny little feather sticking up out of the brim, which reminded Lucille of a mailbox with its flag up. Mrs. Baxter wore a grey bodice and skirt. Between them, the two women carried a basket full of sandwiches and cakes for Lucille and Seth to eat on their journey. Lucille took the basket with many thanks and welcomed them inside. Mrs. Perkins's eyes were twinkling and she rubbed her hands together in happy anticipation. Mrs. Baxter was grinning like a cat. Mrs. Perkins knew something no one else in town did, and as they sat down in the parlour, Kate poured them cups of tea and Granny demanded to hear the news. Mrs. Perkins lowered her voice and Lucille, Granny, and Kate leaned forward to hear.

"Has anyone heard anything of Mr. Best?" The other women looked at each other and shook their heads. After she had thumped him across his back with her iron parasol, Lucille had waited in the yard with Kate's rifle under her arm, expecting Henry to return any minute for a second round. But he had never appeared, nor had he made any more noise about taking Albert away from Kate.

"Something strange is going on," Mrs. Perkins continued. "I had Mr. Carter in the shop a while ago; he's been working at the Best house for years. This morning, he went there and he found his wages in the mailbox with a letter saying he wasn't needed anymore. He told Nellie the house was all locked up and the curtains were drawn. It looks like a haunted house now."

At these words, Lucille pictured Ellie Best's forlorn ghost wandering around the empty mansion in search of her amputated arm. Or maybe the wretch was still screaming about how she had never been able to do anything. She folded her arms a moment and shuddered.

"Even the horse is gone," Mrs. Perkins continued. "It's awful strange. Even if he'd lost his job, nothing would stop Best from parading through town with his nose in the air. He's too ornery and proud to do anything else."

"It's not like him, not like him at all," Mrs. Baxter said. "He's really taking it hard, losing his job."

Granny grinned to herself as she heard this news. She had had her revenge on Best for the way he had used Kate. Next to her, Lucille made a face.

"Well, it's a shame how that happened to such a wonderful man," she said. "I'm sure everyone will be so sympathetic and ready to help, since he was always so honest with us all, and so quick to help out other people himself. You reap what you sow, my mother always said."

Kate had begun to titter halfway through this speech, and at its conclusion she was laughing aloud. Mrs. Perkins clapped her hands. "But that's not all. We're getting a new Mountie next week," she said in a burst. "Corporal Brock got rotated to the Yukon." All of the women gasped.

"Isn't that rich," Mrs. Baxter exclaimed. "After a week, all that'll be left of him is a red coat and a hat. The mosquitoes and black flies will eat him down to skin and bones."

The laughter that came from the women in the parlour was so loud that Seth came inside to investigate. Lucille laughed hardest of all. Poor Corporal Brock! He had spent this summer between a boulder and a granite slab. Had he investigated Stanley's disappearance, he would have angered the powerful. Now, because he had failed to investigate, the powerful were furious with him because Lucille's letters had caused them so much embarrassment. She felt sorry for him for one second.

But the Pruitt family was not done with Corporal Brock. At four o'clock that afternoon, Lucille was packing her clothes away into her bags and hatboxes. Kate had gone to the livery stable to rent the mule, which would carry the bags and Granny to the train station. A few minutes later, Lucille lifted her head from her work. Kate's rapid footsteps ascended the stairs of the veranda. She burst into the kitchen, pink-faced and breathless. Albert was crying in her arms.

"Corporal Brock's coming down the road! His face could stop a clock!"

Everyone jumped. By the way Seth jammed his hat down over his head, Lucille could tell how angry he was at the Mountie's endless intrusions. Over on the kitchen counter, Dinah had taken possession of the hat she had stolen from Henry Best. The stylish brown derby was now covered in silver webbing and presently, on its crown, Dinah sat with her legs rotating while she stitched more threads. Not even Seth dared take the hat from her, but with the Mountie approaching it was imperative someone put her out of sight. Lucille rose and hurried over to hide the spider and her loot while Seth blocked the corporal's way. Her tongue poked out in concentration as she lifted the hat and slipped it inside the cupboard. Dinah, thankfully, knew she was a friend and refrained from attacking her.

Outside, with his pipe in his teeth, Seth lowered himself down on the steps of the veranda, denying the Mountie access to the house. Ribbons of smoke shimmered upward as he puffed, and he watched Corporal Brock with amusement. The Mountie clearly had been drinking. His eyes were somewhat bloodshot above the wrinkled bags, and his complexion in general was unnaturally red. He listed to one side as one of the chickens pecked around his feet in their stiff riding boots.

"It's damned neighbourly of you to come and see off my wife and me before we go to the train station," Seth observed to the corporal. "We're going to Winnipeg for her brother-in-law's funeral; you know, that man Henry Best's goons killed because Brownie told him Dominion Coal was cheating the miners."

Corporal Brock scowled. "I'm not here about that, Pruitt. I'm here about that spider in your house, the poisonous one that killed Mrs. Best. Mr. Best phoned me yesterday and said he saw it. It was a great big ugly purple thing."

"Mr. Best's been drinking too much, and so have you. If you want, you can go up to the attic and put any spider you find in a jar and take it with you when you go to the Yukon. You'll be needing a few; I understand the mosquitoes up there are grizzly bears that fly."

In exasperation, Corporal Brock grasped the brim of his hat. He was just on the point of throwing it onto the ground among the pecking chickens when the back door to the house opened. Granny Aitken came out first, followed by Lucille Pruitt, and then Kate with the baby. The homely old woman wore a black dress and the battered old straw hat, which had become familiar to Corporal Brock from his days at the picket line. In her hand she carried her favourite weapon: her walking stick with the knob at its end. She descended the stairs step by step on her arthritic feet, and looked at the Mountie with tiny old eyes that glittered with hostility.

"What do ye want in my house?" she demanded as she reached the bottom of the stairs. She brandished the stick. Corporal Brock lifted his hands and retreated several steps. Lucille, who was standing behind her, laughed to see how the old woman intimidated the policeman. Even hulking Seth did not strike terror into the Mountie like Granny did. "You've been skulking about here enough!" She shouted at the Mountie with outrage. "Ye go find whoever killed our poor Mrs. Pruitt's brother-in-law and leave us honest folk be! And if I find you've been snooping about in our house when we get back, I'll have the law after ye!" She looked at Seth, who had stood up to let her pass. "C'mon laddie, you've a train to catch." Corporal Brock threw up his hands.

"Damn the spider!" he shouted. He walked unsteadily out of the yard, through the gate of the white picket fence, and the sound of his boots crunching in the road's gravel was the last Lucille heard of him.

Granny *humphed* with satisfaction. She walked over the rough grass to sit down on the tree stump near the tall, bushy pine tree. The chickens, hoping she might give them something to eat, followed her and wandered around at her feet as she sat.

"I'll go fetch the mule," Kate said.

Less than an hour later, the family stood on the platform of the Stony Point train station. Lucille put her hand in Seth's arm and looked around. Nearby was a yellow handcart loaded high with parcels, bags of mail, and other items to be shipped on the train. A little distance down the track, a boy in blue overalls climbed the ladder of the water tower and stood ready to swing the long pipe over the engine. Beyond the water tower, a row of young birch trees were showing yellow leaves.

My gosh, Lucille thought to herself in amazement. *It's autumn already.* Here in Stony Point time had blown past her like one of those new automobiles. She thought of her mission to find Stanley Birch and the many things it had brought her. She had acquired a family: a husband whom she loved so much her stomach turned to jelly whenever she looked in his eyes, a sister in Kate, and a grandmother in Mrs. Aitken. She even had a nephew in Albert. She had stood up to defend the miners and earned their regard and that of the townspeople. The injustice she had witnessed, and the courage of the miners during their strike, had given her a new purpose in writing her book about the struggle of the working man. Last of all, and what meant the most to Lucille, was that she had found Stanley. Her dear brother-in-law, to whom she owed so much, would rest in a decent grave, and his widow and sons knew where he was.

She glanced over her shoulder at the town behind her. That cantankerous old stick, Polly Wilson, was sweeping the front step of the General Store. Lucille would miss this town so badly.

Suddenly, the blast of a train whistle sounded in the distance to the west. The train soon pulled into the station with a huffing engine and a white blast of steam. Seth picked up the picnic basket that Mrs. Perkins and Mrs. Baxter had packed. Lucille threw her arms first around Kate, who dabbed at her eyes with her handkerchief as Albert whimpered in her arms.

"Good bye, Kate. I'll be back as fast as I can." She turned to Granny and hugged the old woman.

"Ye must write to us now and send telegrams to let us know you're safe. And ye must bring back our laddie as soon as you're able," the old woman declared.

"I will, Granny."

On Seth's arm, she pulled up the hem of her skirt and climbed up the narrow stairway into the coach of the train. Granny and Kate stood together on the platform and waved, until the train gave another great blast of steam and huffed as it pulled out of Stony Point.

Acknowledgements

—∭—

My greatest thanks for your time and interest which were most important to the creation of this work:

To the staff of the Highwood Motel, Blairmore, Alberta, the Frank Slide Interpretive Centre, Frank, Alberta; the Crowsnest Pass Historical Museum, Coleman, Alberta; and that of the Stanley A. Milner Public Library, Edmonton. I also wish to thank the Writers' Guild of Alberta.

Lines from "The Late Colliery Explosion at Patricroft, Wigan," come from *Danger, Death, and Disaster in the Crowsnest Pass Mines, 1902-1928*, by Karen Lynne Buckley (University of Calgary Press, 2004).

With warmest wishes I send my regards to: the T. E. Eaton Corporation, Mr. Grant MacEwan, R. C. McLeod, J. William Kerr, Frank R. Antin, Sharon Babaran and Larry Felske, Bruce Ramsay, United Western Communications Ltd., Tony Hollahan, The Crowsnest Historical Society, Laura Johnston, Editor, Candas Dorsey.

Finally, my thanks to Inanna Publishing and especially to Luciana Ricciutelli, my editor, for all her patience and belief in this novel.

Photo: Danica Stonhouse, Shoot or Be Shot Photography.

S. Noël McKay has lived in Alberta most of her life. She attended the University of Alberta before starting a career in the transportation industry. She currently lives in Edmonton, Alberta, with her cat, Cletus. Both enjoy snowboarding. *Stony Point* is her debut novel.